A Night
as Clear as Day

A Night
as Clear as Day

R. J. ROSENBLUM

Written by today's freshest new talents and selected by New American Library, NAL Accent novels touch on subjects close to a woman's heart, from friendship to family to finding our place in the world. The Conversation Guides included in each book are intended to enrich the individual reading experience, as well as encourage us to explore these topics together—because books, and life, are meant for sharing.

Visit us online at www.penguin.com.

New American Library
Published by New American Library, a division of
Penguin Group (USA) Inc., 375 Hudson Street,
New York, New York 10014, U.S.A.
Penguin Books Ltd, 80 Strand,
London WC2R 0RL, England
Penguin Books Australia Ltd, 250 Camberwell Road,
Camberwell, Victoria 3124, Australia
Penguin Books Canada Ltd, 10 Alcorn Avenue,
Toronto, Ontario, Canada M4V 3B2
Penguin Books (NZ), cnr Airborne and Rosedale Roads,
Albany, Auckland 1310, New Zealand

Penguin Books Ltd, Registered Offices:
80 Strand, London WC2R 0RL, England

First published by New American Library,
a division of Penguin Group (USA) Inc.

First Printing, June 2004
10 9 8 7 6 5 4 3 2 1

FICTION FOR THE WAY WE LIVE

REGISTERED TRADEMARK—MARCA REGISTRADA

LIBRARY OF CONGRESS CATALOGING-IN-PUBLICATION DATA:
Rosenblum, Robert J.
    A night as clear as day / R. J. Rosenblum.
        p. cm.
    ISBN 0-451-21118-9
    1. Women veterinarians—Fiction. 2. Blind musicians—Fiction. 3. Divorced women—Fiction.
4. New Hampshire—Fiction. 5. Abused wives—Fiction. I. Title.
    PS3568.O795N54 2004
    813'.54—dc22   2003025672

Set in Bembo

Printed in the United States of America

For Sergeant P.

—and all who loved him

The darkness is no darkness with thee,
But the night is as clear as the day;
The darkness and the light to thee
Are both alike.

—*The Book of Common Prayer*

Chapter 1

It was the kind of glorious blue-sky September day that shone down on the Earth and encouraged you to believe whatever endeavor you were about to undertake was bound to go well. A new business, a new love affair, even a war, if launched today it would surely be blessed with success.

Looking at the countryside passing the bus window, Gaye Foster was filled with exactly that kind of confident optimism about the change she was making.

She had moved quickly, grabbing at the job found through an Internet ad without even waiting for a face-to-face meeting with her employers, nor a visit to the area where she would have to live. On the latter count, at least, the view from the bus assured her she hadn't been too rash. Gently rolling pastures partitioned with long walls made of piled stones, dairy farms set down in verdant shallow valleys, cows grazing or lying in the shadows of scattered copses of old trees—it was all so clean and pretty, like one of those perfect pastoral paintings by an old Dutch master. On wooded hills the foliage was already beginning to put out its autumn display of golds and reds and purples. It brought the old axiom to mind: *Just what the doctor ordered*. Gaye savored the irony: the particular doctors she had in mind would have ordered her to do anything but flee to this rural haven.

"West Greenlea!" the driver called out as the bus passed into a tunnel of shade created by huge ancient elms and maples arching over the town's broad main street. A minute later it arrived in a central square and pulled up in front of a redbrick bank building. After they'd driven north through two dozen stops, only four passengers remained from the full load that had left Philadelphia. Gaye alone rose to get off. She'd brought no luggage other than an overnight bag, so the driver didn't have to leave his seat to open the outside luggage hold. "Enjoy your visit, miss," he said cheerfully, as she approached the door to get off.

Visit? Gaye realized he'd assumed from her minimal baggage she couldn't be staying longer than a day or two. "Thanks," she said. So much the better if she was mistaken for a casual traveler rather than what she was—a kind of fugitive. A visitor was more easily forgotten, in case anyone tried to retrace her movements.

The bus pulled away, and Gaye saw that in the center of the town square was a small park with a statue, the stone figure of a soldier atop a granite plinth. This had to be "the Civil War Memorial," where she'd been told someone would meet her. She crossed over to the park. A few benches were placed at intervals, all of them empty. Indeed, there was no one to be seen anywhere up or down the street. It didn't surprise Gaye that this small New Hampshire town should be deserted on a Sunday afternoon, but it concerned her that no one waited to receive her. The bus had made an unscheduled stop en route for a passenger with motion sickness, so she had arrived late.

Gaye sat down on a bench and contemplated the statue in front of her. Chiseled into its base were the names of the twelve good men of West Greenlea who had gone off to die for the Union cause in the Civil War. She read down the list of names, and pondered that amazing period when the nation had been ripped asunder by violent passions resulting in so much death. Her thoughts veered abruptly into the loss of a life that had left her own heart so bruised, all due to passions gone wrong. Though not a death, she reflected sadly, that would ever receive a monument.

A fine-boned woman with a fair complexion and russet brown hair she had always worn short, Gaye Foster was not infrequently mistaken for being far younger than her true age of thirty-one. Even with her husband she had been asked on occasion to show proof of age before being served alcohol.

Gaye glanced again at her wristwatch. Another ten minutes gone by . . . Suppose the agreement had fallen apart somehow? Would she just be left sitting here? But the man who'd interviewed her on the phone had sounded perfectly sincere. She thought back over the two conversations they'd had, a long one after she called in response to the ad, then a briefer second one after her school records and professional references had been received. She had learned from her interviewer that he and his wife, a pair of veterinarians named Wilson and Frances Bennett, had founded their rural animal clinic thirty-eight years ago, a "mixed practice" that dealt with both domestic and farm animals. Within the past year he had been forced to give up driving—for reasons as yet unexplained—and leave all the farm calls to his wife. Now, he explained, they were finding it impossible to keep up with the demands of covering the wide area of countryside they served. They needed an associate to join them, someone willing to work long hours, since it wasn't uncommon to be called out at night.

Gaye had to confess she wasn't the ideal candidate for a practice dealing with large animals. After graduating veterinary college six years ago, she'd taken a job caring for the lab animals in the testing facility of a pharmaceutical firm that developed pet-care products. This proved to be routine work, and she had happily abandoned it after a year to move to a Philadelphia veterinary practice dealing almost exclusively with domestics—cats, dogs, parakeets, and the occasional "exotic" such as a monkey or a ferret. She'd been there since, so her experience with such animals as cows, horses, donkeys, pigs, and sheep remained academic, going back to classes at vet school.

Her interviewer wasn't deterred. "You'll do fine," he'd said, "as long as you're willing to learn, and don't have any trouble accepting a bit of advice now and then."

Gaye got the impression that the older veterinarian and his wife would have to close their practice if they didn't quickly find help, and their quickness to overlook her deficiencies suggested they'd had trouble finding anyone attracted by what they were offering. Veterinary medicine was booming these days—most vet schools had more applicants than spaces—but a farm practice wasn't where the money was. And few young, single women—a group that accounted for more than 70 percent of current DVMs—wanted to stick themselves away in a quiet rural area.

The situation suited Gaye perfectly, however. First, of course, because she needed a refuge. But, too, she was tired of dealing with the pampered pets of urban hermits and the neglected pets of people too busy to provide proper care. She wanted to be involved with animals living in a natural habitat, making their contribution to the natural community of living things. Nor did it matter that her earnings would be drastically reduced. In Philadelphia she'd worked up to an annual income of nearly $80,000. The job in West Greenlea offered a starting salary of only $32,000. But in a rural backwater that money would go far enough. She wouldn't mind giving up restaurant dinners, clothes with designer labels, or hundred-dollar haircuts. The luxuries she craved now were peace and safety.

Checking her watch, she saw another ten minutes had passed. Should she call, find out why they were late? She'd already given up her cell phone—too easy to trace—so she scanned the square, looking for a public telephone. All the nearby shops were closed. She wished now she hadn't sold her car, a means of moving quickly and independently if necessary. Yet, with a smaller paycheck in the offing, the money from selling her '98 Honda provided funds to set herself up here, and move on if the job didn't work out. She'd been told, too, that the job here included a vehicle for her use.

If there *was* a job. She'd grabbed so quickly at the offer maybe her prospective employers had become suspicious. Rather than stew about it, Gaye decided to relax herself with a walk, a brief look around. She started to reach down to bring her bag along, but there didn't seem to be anyone who'd run off with it. Maybe if the person coming to meet her arrived while she'd stepped away, the bag would mark her presence. Walking to the edge of the park she surveyed the main street branching off on either side, seeing a bank, hardware store, clothing shops, the staple businesses of any small town. The sign over one nearby storefront, Curl up and Dye, made her smile when she realized it must be the beauty salon. What looked like a more inviting direction for a walk was the road intersecting the main street. On the opposite side of the square from the bank, it headed past a church, continued between a short avenue of small brick row houses, then plunged back into the countryside, rippling away over a series of low hills. On the side of the square by the bank, the road dipped down a short steep hill from which extended a couple of other side streets, then continued through the entranceway to one of those old covered wooden bridges that still dotted rural New England. Gaye was lured in that direction by the cool darkness of the old bridge and the faint babble of the stream rushing beneath.

It took only a minute to walk down to the bridge. Adding to the quaintness of the old landmark was a faded sign preserved above the entrance:

ONE DOLLAR FINE
TO DRIVE ANY TEAM FASTER
THAN A WALK ON THIS BRIDGE

The sign confirmed Gaye's hope that she had arrived where the values and rhythms of a simpler time survived.

She became aware suddenly of a car horn blaring in short, quick blasts somewhere behind her. From the square! She spun around and ran back up the hill. Before she'd gone halfway the honks started coming in shorter bursts.

A vintage black Ford pickup, covered in dust, was pulled up next to the park. The passenger door was nearest to her, but as Gaye ran toward it she could see through the open windows to where the driver stood on the other side, reaching an arm back into the cab to press the horn. Gaye couldn't see his head, only his slim torso up to the shoulders clad in a frayed denim work shirt. She shouted to be heard over the horn as she ran up to the passenger door. "Hello! I'm here! Hello . . ."

The driver bent down to peer through the opposite window.

Gaye was surprised to find herself facing a woman. The insistent blowing of the horn had prepared her to confront a masculine temperament.

"Where the hell you been?" the woman snapped, irritated at having to wait a mere minute or two.

Gaye stared back at her. This, no doubt, was Frances Bennett, wife of the man who'd hired her over the telephone. She was somewhere in her mid to late sixties, the skin of her face seamed and burnished by plenty of time outdoors. But she was one of those lanky women whose looks adapted to age in a way that kept her stunningly attractive. A narrow face with well-defined cheekbones, the mouth and chin strong without overbalancing the other features, a thin, straight nose and large eyes of clear, pale blue, ice under an arctic sky. Her long hair—the ivory white of a former blonde—was gathered back into a ponytail by a blue-and-yellow linen kerchief, the one visible touch of feminine decoration.

Let's not start off on the wrong foot. Gaye held back her own complaint. "Sorry—I went to take a look at the covered bridge. Never saw one before," she added, a personal touch to help melt the ice.

"Well, if you're around long enough, you'll see more than your share."

The woman's *if* seemed to contain a subtle warning. Not a promising start, Gaye thought. Barely a minute spent with one of her bosses, and already she was intimidated. She started toward the park bench. "I'll get my luggage."

"I saw a little bag over there—already tossed it in back. What else you got?"

"That's all."

The woman shot her a curious glance. The suspicions were planted now, Gaye thought.

"Well, we've wasted enough time here," the woman said. "Get in." She opened the door and slid behind the wheel.

The surly greeting was so different from the friendly welcome Gaye had wishfully imagined, it was enough to shatter the optimism that had buoyed her about taking the new job. If she'd been alone, she would have probably allowed herself to cry. But she steeled herself against breaking down, and yanked open the rusty passenger door.

However badly things might turn out here, she reminded herself, she was still in a far better place than she'd been yesterday.

Chapter 2

"In case you haven't guessed," the older woman said as they drove out of town, "I'm Frankie Bennett."

In a brochure for the Bible Hill Animal Clinic Mr. Bennett had mailed her, Gaye had seen the woman vet's name given as Frances. From the look of her, hearing she used a masculine version of her name wasn't surprising.

"Guess you had to cool your heels a bit after the bus got in. Couldn't be helped. Had a call as I was leaving to meet you—a farmer had a cow cast her withers. Animal could've bled to death."

Not an apology, but it showed at least some awareness of the anxiety she'd caused. Gaye noted, too, her use of the term *cast her withers,* which few younger vets would apply to a bovine uterine prolapse. "These things happen," Gaye said amiably.

After a pause, Frankie said, "Been up this way before?"

"Never to New Hampshire. But I used to go on ski weekends in Vermont when I was a kid. And I've spent a few summer vacations in Maine."

"Weekends and vacations," Frankie said tartly. "Quite a change for a city girl to come live in a place like this full-time."

It sounded like another warning. "You think I won't like it?"

The other woman tossed her a look marked by a hint of contrition. "Not being too nice, am I?" Gaye's silence was an answer in itself. "But it's hard to rush over straight from an emergency. And, well, there are . . . other things. . . ." Frankie trailed off and hunched over the wheel, concentrating on her driving.

Whatever that meant, Gaye found her disaffection for Frankie Bennett moderated by sympathy. She remembered the extra burdens the older woman was forced to assume because of her husband's lost ability to drive. Trying for a friendlier tone, she asked, "Where's *East* Greenlea?"

"Ain't one. No just-plain Greenlea, either. Might've been once. Lots of towns up this way have died and disappeared."

Gaye worked to keep the conversation alive. "Is it far to the clinic?"

"Few miles."

"You found a nice name for it—Bible Hill."

"Just happens to be the name of the place it's located."

Gaye studied Frankie with a sidelong glance. The lack of any welcoming warmth might stem from the fabled reticence of rural New Englanders, but Gaye sensed something deeper. Throughout the hiring process on the phone, she'd dealt only with Frankie's husband. Was it possible he didn't have his wife's approval, that Frankie Bennett didn't want her here? Maybe the issue ought to be confronted here and now. . . .

But Frankie spoke first. "Looks like you don't expect to stay very long."

"Why?"

"Bringing nothing but that itty-bitty bag. Our nights are already getting cold; you'll need warm things. Where are all your clothes?"

"Oh . . . I . . . didn't want to lug a big suitcase around. The rest is being sent." She'd cover the lie in the next day or two—go off somewhere, buy a trunk and whatever wardrobe she needed, and ship it to the local post office. She'd just have to claim it herself so the Bennetts never saw the postmark.

But Frankie wasn't ready to drop it. "Could've sent your stuff ahead, so it'd be here for you."

"There was so much else to do. Turn off the gas, pay the phone bill, say all my good-byes . . ." Did the excuse sound too feeble? Of course, she hadn't said good-bye to a soul. She shifted the subject. "Had to sell my car, too. I was told you had one for me to use."

"Nope."

"But—"

"Not a car. It's a truck."

"Fine. Whatever gets me around."

After a second Frankie said, "Didn't think you'd be traveling alone, either."

"But I told your husband. I'm . . . not attached."

"That's not what I meant. I've just never heard of a vet who didn't keep an animal or two. Seems a little strange you got no pets at all."

"I did have a dog," Gaye said quickly. "Until recently."

"What happened?"

She couldn't answer at once, not while the loss, the horror that came with it, was filling her mind. Then she dropped a black screen over the vision. "He died," she said flatly.

Gaye was aware of Frankie looking at her again with those suspicious eyes, and turned to the sunny landscape for escape. She felt that a wall against easy communication with this woman had now been established. It might have been breached if she could have been honest and open—about the reason for leaving her clothes behind or what had happened with Hero. Yet Gaye had seen nothing to assure her the truth would be received by Frankie Bennett with sympathy rather than doubt.

The truck swerved suddenly onto an unpaved side road. Gaye caught a quick glimpse of a signpost at the turning, a cracked, weather-beaten board with faded dark letters on a white-painted background. She managed to read the names listed one above the other at the bottom—*Wilson Bennett, DVM* over his wife's. The road cut through a broad meadow, then began climbing a hill with an empty hay field to one side and a fenced pasture on the other where a few animals grazed—some goats and sheep, a couple of horses, and a calf. The road crested to a level plain where a group of buildings stood. At the center was a large farmhouse with a porch across the front, the kind of sprawling structure that had accumulated over generations, wings and stories added as they were needed. The once-white paint of the house was dingy and flaking, and Gaye could see where the attic roof of a rear extension had partially caved in. Clustered around the house were several outbuildings in similarly woebegone condition: an enormous barn with weathered gray siding, a garage, a long henhouse—a wire-enclosed yard in front was filled with scampering chickens—and a greenhouse with many broken panes of glass. Between the buildings were a couple of sizable gardens planted with vegetables and flowers. Amid weeds and withered blooms, patches of color and food for harvesting could still be seen, but the gardens were obviously as ill-tended as everything else on the property.

Frankie stopped the truck in front of the main house and hopped out. She went to the back, dropped the tailgate, and grabbed Gaye's small valise.

"Let me carry that," Gaye said, following. Despite its size, the bag was heavy, a laptop, running shoes, and three thick veterinarians' reference books crammed in with a small assortment of clothes.

But Frankie proceeded straight up the porch and into the house as if she hadn't heard. Dropping the valise by the door, she shouted, "She's here!"

Gaye followed slowly through the front door, as apprehensive at meeting her other employer as an orphan facing her last chance for adoption.

The entrance hall was much less gloomy than she'd expected based on the exterior of the house. Golden afternoon sunlight flowed in from windows in rooms off to both sides, as well as through a door at the rear of the hall that led to a kitchen. Every wall Gaye could see was hung with blocks of photographs and colorful paintings in all sizes and styles, some like the work of children, others impressively professional. All pictured an animal or two, household pets as well as all kinds of farm animals. On the ones close to her, Gaye saw cards slipped into the corner of a frame, or inscriptions written on the canvas saying "Thank you" or similar sentiments.

Numerous other touches added to the impression of a home that had been comfortably occupied by one family over a long period. Through a wide portal to one side lay an immense living room, its floor covered by frayed Persian carpets, and an array of sagging, well-worn furniture arranged around a fireplace. The pungent smell of wood smoke hung in the air; not from recent fires, Gaye thought, but a residue of all that had seeped over the years into every fiber of the house. As she looked into the living room, a mound of tawny fur in front of the cold fireplace twitched—a dog she recognized as a golden retriever.

"Miss Foster! Welcome!" The greeting pulled Gaye's attention back to the hallway. A motorized wheelchair was speeding toward her from the rear, a man sitting in it with his hand outstretched, a broad smile on his face. Will Bennett's admission that he could no longer drive a car might have prepared her, yet on the phone his voice alone had conveyed such energy that this first sight of him took her aback. The closer he came, the more his appearance contradicted the plain fact that he was disabled. A handsome man, broad across the chest and shoulders, with a full head of dark gray hair, a trim mustache, and lively brown eyes, he reminded Gaye of matinee idols she'd seen on television in old black-and-white films . . . most of all the older Clark Gable.

The wheelchair stopped in front of her. A gray cat that had scampered along with it started walking around Gaye, rubbing its fur against her leg. But Gaye was focused on Will Bennett as he stood slowly from the chair. He was a few inches over six feet, tall enough so that when he reached full height she found herself tilted back, looking up.

He disarmed her with a light laugh. "Nothing like a pretty girl to get me up on my feet." As their hands clasped, Gaye felt how lax his fingers were, even the minimal grip achieved with effort. After the handshake he sank back into the chair and pushed a lever to maneuver it backward. "Well, come in and let's get acquainted," he said. "Or would you like to settle in first?"

Settle in? Living arrangements had never been discussed; now Gaye realized the job might also come with a room on the large property. "I wasn't expecting to live here," she said.

Bennett talked over his shoulder as he drove the chair toward the rear of the house. "We've got plenty of space. There's an apartment over the garage for you—three rooms, kitchen, TV, washer and dryer. Did I forget to mention that? I'm sure you'll find it—"

"I've got to have my own place," Gaye broke in, more strident than she'd intended. But she was almost desperate for privacy. "Somewhere separate."

He stopped to look at her. Then, without a trace of resistance, he said, "It was only to help cut your expenses. But, sure, whatever you want." He continued into the kitchen.

The room was equipped with ancient appliances, its center filled by a round oak table encircled by eight unmatched chairs. The kitchen had the same aura of comfortable neglect as the rest of the house. A long bank of windows over the sink and stove looked out on one of the tangled gardens. Will stopped his chair at a row of under-counter cabinets, and opened one. "Coffee or tea?" he said, reaching in for a pot.

"Whatever you're having." Gaye turned around to indicate that her answer included Frankie, who had fallen silent since Will appeared. Gaye found her standing in the doorway, still eyeing her sharply.

Will seemed to perceive the tension in their locked gazes. "Well, I vote for tea," he said quickly. Taking a kettle from the cabinet, he wheeled himself toward the sink.

Frankie charged forward. "I'll make it. You sit with her." She snatched the kettle from her husband's lap.

Will rolled up to the table and motioned Gaye to join him. "So you see why we need you," he said. "I can still take care of the animals that people bring here, but so much of our business involves going out to the farms."

"Where's the actual clinic?" she asked.

"Out behind the house. I'll give you a tour later."

"What kind of office hours do you keep?"

"I did explain to you that we're pretty much on call?"

"Yes. But what's the basic schedule?"

Frankie laid cups and saucers on the table with a clatter. "A schedule would be dandy," she said, moving off to the refrigerator. "Ten-to-five weekdays like the rest of the world, even throw in a

Saturday morning. But Will's always kept an open door. Doesn't give a hoot when they show up."

He gave Gaye a smile, an apology for his wife's crankiness. "Animals can't tell time," he remarked.

"They're not the ones who pay us, either. Though the way he lets the bills slide"—Frankie looked at Gaye as she poured cream into a pitcher—"you'd think he's waiting for our four-legged patients to write the checks."

Gaye smiled at the remark's wry edge, though she perceived the sharp undertone. The dynamic between the Bennetts was clear enough, the common friction between opposites who attract.

The teakettle let out its whistle like a referee calling time, and Frankie busied herself finishing the tea. Finally Gaye felt it was reasonable to ask Will, "What's the cause of your disability?"

"Amyotrophic lateral sclerosis," he replied evenly.

"Lou Gehrig's disease," she murmured despite her shock, supplying the term laymen had given the affliction since it had ended the playing days of the legendary Yankee first baseman.

"Sounds almost friendly that way," Will said. "Something you're lucky enough to share with a great sports hero."

There were few diseases less "friendly" in the way they attacked the human body, Gaye reflected. From some random point in the nervous system the cells began to die, inexplicably, incurably, spreading out through the whole network of ganglia, until the motors of life, large and small, were all besieged, overwhelmed. It could start with the most innocuous symptom, an odd patch of numbness on the skin, and from there the disease marched outward, sometimes slowly, sometimes rapidly, leading inevitably to loss of the ability to move the limbs, to swallow, to speak, to breathe on one's own. Often it took away the ability to see or hear.

"But it's not too bad yet," Will continued when he saw Gaye's dismay. "I still have the use of these, pretty much, thank God." He held up his hands. "And I haven't lost a bit of what's in the old noodle." One hand tapped his head.

That could yet prove the cruelest part, she thought. Even into its later stages, the disease often left the mind intact, able to contem-

plate day by day the growing helplessness of the body turning inex-
orably into a lifeless husk. To avoid going on staring sadly, she forced
herself to speak. "How long have you known?"

"Over a year." He sounded positive, as if grateful for so much
time. ALS was as unpredictable as its sources were unknown. The
English physicist Stephen Hawking had lived with it for forty
years—even though he was reduced to total immobility. There were
cases where death came in not much longer than the period Will
had already mentioned.

Frankie came to the table and banged down a metal tray loaded
with spoons, sugar bowl, cream pitcher, and a crockery teapot. The
spoons jangled. "So there it is," she said flatly, as if merely referring
to the tea and not Will's fate. She looked bleakly at Gaye. "And so
here *you* are."

However unwelcoming Frankie seemed, Gaye realized now she
ought not to take her unpleasantness personally. What Frankie could
never welcome was the disease, the intruder that had broken into
her life to pillage the treasure of golden years she might have otherwise enjoyed with her husband. She must, Gaye realized, resent her
presence simply for objectifying all that had been lost . . . and all
there was yet to lose.

Once tea was poured, cream and sugar doled out, conversation,
too, was shared in warm little portions. Small talk about Philadelphia, where Gaye acknowledged she'd grown up, and where Will
and Frankie had met while both attended the renowned vet school
at U. Penn. Asked about the origins of her desire to be a veterinarian, Gaye obliged by recounting the special interest in animals she'd
discovered when she'd been given a pet rabbit at the age of five. The
Bennetts told her how they'd decided after receiving their degrees
to found their practice here, a choice made because Frankie's people were from this area, so she knew property was affordable for a
young couple starting out.

After second cups of tea, Will took Gaye to see the clinic. To facilitate his access, a wooden ramp had been built from the kitchen door
down to a concrete path. Ten yards away along the path lay a one-story
shed, windowless on this side, but with a door at the midpoint. This was

"the back way in," Will explained. He opened the door and flipped on a light switch. They entered a storage room filled with everything from animal feed, bandages, disinfectants, and syringes, to paper towels and cleaning products. The next room into which they passed was lined with cages of various sizes where animals could be kept for observation and recovery after surgery, or boarded for owners who had to be away.

"The boarding is rare, though," Will said. "It's not like the city, where people are always leaving pets while they fly off on holiday."

Only one of the cages at floor level was occupied. Curled up inside Gaye saw a medium-size black-and-white dog with a bandage wrapped around his head to cover one eye. As she approached, the dog sprang up and shoved its nose through the grating. She tickled the muzzle.

"This is Cookie," Will said. "He's a working dog—herds sheep for a lady over in the next county."

That confirmed her guess that Cookie was an Australian Border collie. It was an amazing breed; she had seen films of Border collies shepherding flocks with as many as a thousand sheep across mountain-sides in New Zealand, commanded by nothing more than whistles or calls of different pitch made by the owner. "What happened to Cookie?" she asked.

"Owner brought him in yesterday with his eye swollen shut; thought it was just a bug bite at first. The animal wasn't acting sick, went right on doing his job, but when it didn't look any better after a week, in he came. All I saw when I checked the eye was a round black hump in the corner, looked like nothing so much as a big tick sitting on the surface. I sedated Cookie so I could take it off. When I put the tweezers on it and started to pull . . . it just kept coming. What the poor fella actually had in there was a twig about the length of a tenpenny nail. Must've been chasing some of the flock through bushes or low trees, and this thing plunged straight on in."

"And he never gave any hint of distress?"

Will shook his head. "He'll be going home tomorrow."

"How's the eye?"

"Vision seems okay. A downright miracle—but not the first I've seen."

He and Gaye lingered by the cage, silently contemplating the dog's valor. In humans it would be called heroism, and lauded as an uncommon virtue. But in dogs this selfless determination to disregard pain or danger to perform their tasks was practically taken for granted. Of course, that was because they were lower than humans in the animal order, assumed to be dumber, less sensitive. But Gaye believed it was because of something truly nobler in their character. It had been true of her dog, certainly. Wasn't it to save her that he had let himself be murdered?

"Show me the rest," she said quickly, turning from the cage. She didn't want to think about Hero.

When Will switched on the overhead lights in the next space, Gaye saw she was in the heart of the clinic, with separate areas furnished to provide an examining room, a laboratory, and a surgery. The laboratory consisted of a small alcove with a microscope, a blood analyzer, a computer, and a couple of other diagnostic aids lined up along a counter. A padded table standing at one end of the large space demarked the examining room. At the opposite end was the surgery—a stainless-steel operating table, a couple of large sinks, and the apparatus of tubes and tanks required for anesthesia. Beside the sinks was another metal surface grooved with deep channels for sluicing fluids to a drain—for postmortem procedures. Fitted in here and there were a refrigerator for keeping medicines, a few small tables on casters, chairs, and adjustable-height metal stools. Occupying one corner, along with a foldaway screen of thin lead shielding tacked over hinged boards, was an X-ray machine. By its bulk, Gaye thought the machine might be as much as fifty years old.

Will saw her eyeing the relic. "Got that free from the local hospital when they upgraded a few years back."

It was all a discouraging sight to Gaye. In Philadelphia, she'd worked with diagnostic instruments that were state-of-the-art and made for veterinary work. There were four separate examining rooms, two fully equipped operating rooms, a staff that included certified technicians to assist the four DVMs, not to mention a receptionist and the man who did all the cleaning up. Gaye had come to disdain such opulence and up-to-the-minute technology, aware it was intended as much for show as medical excellence, a way of justifying exorbitant fees even for such simple procedures as a toenail paring for a poodle. But looking now at the other end of the spectrum, this facility so spartan and sadly old-fashioned, she felt wistful for the top-of-the-line place she'd left.

"It's not what you're used to, I suppose," Will said, correctly interpreting her silence. "But remember, Gaye, beauty may be only skin-deep—even when it comes to a veterinary practice."

She was both embarrassed and impressed that he'd read her thoughts so exactly. He was already rolling away to a pair of swinging double doors across the room. He pushed one open and pointed through it. "Out there is the waiting area, dispensary, and the reception desk."

She took a quick glance without venturing through the door. Like the rest it looked utilitarian, indecorous. "So you *do* have a receptionist?"

"Lori Michaels, a local girl. She's been with us for years—fills in all the gaps around here."

At least she wasn't going to be doing the sweeping up herself, Gaye mused.

She made one more brief circuit around the central room. Charts provided by pharmaceutical manufacturers tacked to the walls. Glass-fronted cabinets stocked with more supplies. In the lab alcove was a chalkboard with notes scribbled across it: reminders to restock certain items, a record of the most recent time Cookie had been fed and what he had eaten.

They were back in the house in half an hour. Frankie had disappeared from the kitchen.

"If you won't be using the apartment," Will said, "why not stay in a room upstairs—just till you find what you want? Though if you prefer, there are a couple of motels not too far away."

"I'd be happy to stay here. Dr. Bennett, please don't think I'm completely antisocial because I turned down your apartment. I just need—"

"You don't have to explain," he said. "It's completely understandable."

She gave him a grateful smile. But knowing how far from completely understanding he had to be, she was tempted for a moment to tell more. Even in her brief time with Will Bennett, she had seen he was a perceptive and sympathetic man. After weeks of facing her ordeal alone, she longed for a confessor, an ally, a friend. But she stifled the urge to confide. Whatever her first impression, this man was a stranger. She mustn't forget that what had brought her here was misperceiving the true nature of men she had known far longer.

Gaye retrieved her overnight case from near the door. Unable to climb the stairs, Will told her which room on the second floor would be hers. She ought to be comfortable there, he said; it had been his daughter's. "I don't know where Frankie's gone," he added. "But she'll be back to make dinner. We'll eat around seven."

She paused before starting up. "Would you mind if I skip dinner? I'll probably just get into bed."

"Suit yourself. You're not feeling ill, I hope."

"No. Just tired. Very tired."

He nodded sympathetically. "Traveling can wear you out."

Not merely traveling, she thought as she continued her climb. Running. Running for her life.

Chapter 3

The rabbit provided a convenient answer to a common question, but of course there was more to why and how Gaye Foster had chosen to become a vet.

She had lived the first few years of her life on Philadelphia's suburban Main Line, on an estate large enough to allow for keeping not only dogs, cats, and a rabbit, but the horses her mother rode daily. The money for such extravagance, a fortune made in local banking, was from her mother's side of the family; though as time went on her father earned enough to support a lifestyle no less privileged. A medical student at the time of his marriage, once Owen Foster began practicing his specialty of cardiac surgery, his brilliance was soon recognized. With a growing reputation as one of those surgeons who had the special healing gift known to peers as "the hands," Foster was earning $25,000 for each of his heart operations while still in his thirties. When he declared a need to live in the city, closer to the hospitals, it couldn't be denied.

Gaye's mother remained attached to her animals, however. She began staying over at the estate, spending nights away from her husband with increasing frequency—until she never left the country. Gaye was eight years old when her parents' arrangement began, too young to analyze the nuances. She revered her mother, a beautiful woman accomplished enough at the equine sport of dressage to have been an alternate on two Olympic teams. But Gaye also experienced her as being quiet and self-contained, at times remote. So she did not think it remarkable to live in the city with her father, and visit her mother at the estate only on occasional weekends. Even though her father, a typical successful surgeon, was dedicated to his work and rarely had time for her.

As she grew older, Gaye found the weekend visits to her mother becoming more emotionally draining. Her mother vacillated un predictably between welcoming the visits and retreating to her bedroom to avoid her daughter entirely. Gaye's attempts to break through these moods could bring on hysterical tirades in which her mother chastised her as disloyal for living with her father. Gaye began to regard stays at the estate with such trepidation that, prior to a visit two weeks before her high school graduation, she had actually stopped in a church to pray it would go well. Throughout her school years, only her father had attended her performances in school plays, witnessed her achievements at sports and the bestowing of special awards. For her graduation, she had wanted—needed—her mother to be present.

She was relieved, therefore, to be greeted by her mother this time with warmth and affection. They went for an afternoon ride on the horses together, and that evening sat by the fireside and talked—the sort of catching up with each other they hadn't done for years. Her mother seemed—no words summed it up better—a new woman. Gaye was emboldened to remark on the transformation, and ask the cause.

"I've reached a decision," her mother replied, "and it makes things that have always troubled me seem very small, and everything else seem very easy."

And what was the decision?

"I simply want to do what will make you and your father happy."

It was the perfect prelude for Gaye to bring out the printed invitation issued by the school. Her mother received it gratefully, and hugged Gaye in a way that left no doubt she would be pleased to attend the graduation. But Gaye was made happier still when her mother said she had a special gift to mark the occasion, something to provide a lasting reminder of how much her mother loved her. At this point a maid brought in a puppy on a leash.

Throughout her years of living in the city, Gaye had longed for a dog of her own, and her father had always denied the wish. But she had a lasting memory of those early years when she'd romped with the animals at the estate, and the comfort their company provided during her mother's sulks. She'd had a particular fondness for a handsome German shepherd her mother owned. The puppy she was given now was of that breed, and receiving it at this moment repaired the bond to her mother that had become so frayed during the years apart: The dog embodied recognition of who she was, of what she cared about, of the part of her that came from her mother. The name that sprang to mind as soon as Gaye saw the male puppy symbolized its importance in her life: Hero.

For all the significance initially attached to the gift, it was magnified a thousandfold by what happened two days later. Returning home from her graduation rehearsal, Gaye was met at the door by her father. He steered her to a chair in their living room, then reported the accident that had happened that morning. Her mother had been thrown from a horse and died of a broken neck. Because of his own tolerance as a physician, it seemed not to occur to him that such a graphic description might add to the shock for his daughter—which was sufficient to put Gaye into a near-catatonic state of grief. Except to attend the funeral, she remained in bed for days and ate almost nothing. She did not attend her own graduation.

Throughout this period and the summer that followed, it was the companionship of the dog that sustained her. While she was in the depths of her grief, Hero would curl up beside her on the bed, leaving only when taken for a walk by a housemaid. He seemed to be almost supernaturally attuned to her moods. Even when she was up and about, the dog stayed close to her. From the first, the leash was unnecessary. Again and again she would think back to the sentiment her mother had expressed in presenting her with the gift—that it was to be a lasting reminder of how much her mother loved her. There were times Gaye thought the animal was, in some way, a medium for her mother's spirit. Weren't there, in fact, venerated Eastern religions that believed in reincarnation, the passage of souls through animal and human forms, even interchangeably?

When it came time to leave for college, Gaye learned that Wellesley, where she had been accepted, permitted no dogs in the dorms except those serving as guides for blind students. So she enrolled instead at a community college near home. Later, learning that off-campus living was allowed at the University of Pennsylvania, she transferred. Arriving at the point where course selection could be linked to career choice, she first considered premed: as the daughter of a surgeon, she had witnessed the nobility in healing people. But then the bond she had with Hero, and the remembered love for animals that had been her mother's, made her decide she'd be happier in veterinary medicine.

Her father wasn't pleased. Being a vet was "only playing at being a doctor," he said. If she had a desire to heal and save lives, why not follow in his footsteps? In the end he yielded to her choice, but she was left feeling it would be wise to escape from his sphere of influence. Instead of remaining at Penn, she applied to Cornell University's College of Veterinary Medicine in Ithaca, New York. It was widely considered the top vet school; acceptance there was an achievement in itself. Veterinary medicine was becoming an extremely popular career choice for young women, and there were multiple applicants for every place at institutions offering the degree of DVM—despite the fact that it was notoriously more difficult to achieve than a standard medical degree. To treat people required knowing only human anatomy and pathology. To be a vet you had to be familiar with the distinct anatomical differences and separate diseases of many species and subspecies.

At Cornell, Gaye was permitted to live in a dormitory with her dog. She formed friendships, but concentrated on her studies to the extent that none were close. Men were easily attracted to her gamine prettiness and often asked her out, but she encouraged no lasting relationship. She accepted that the tendency toward self-containment was another trait she shared with her mother.

After receiving her degree, Gaye accepted a job with a manufacturer of pet pharmaceuticals based in North Carolina. Geared to research, the position paid substantially more than starting salaries for first-year associates in regular practice, but Gaye soon realized she wanted the satisfaction of hands-on work at healing. She missed, too, the greater variety of life in a large urban center—and also thought she'd be happier again living close to her father, all that was left of her family. Through the Cornell placement service, she learned of the opening at the domestic practice in Philadelphia, where she spent the next five years.

Owen Foster was busier than ever, operating several times a week, and now heading the department of cardiology at one of the largest city hospitals. But he made an effort to be more attentive to his daughter than in the early years—influenced largely by the woman who had become his steady companion. A therapist for children with learning disabilities named Nancy Kassar, she liked Gaye and had a keen understanding of the emotional consequences of the younger woman's upbringing and her mother's death. Responding to Nancy's urgings to show more parental concern, Owen Foster augmented his daughter's income so she could afford a good apartment near his own, and he gave her a car. And he confessed his wish to see her develop a more fulfilling personal life.

"I'm worried by seeing how much time you spend alone," Owen told his daughter one day over a lunch together. "You have to overcome this attraction to solitude."

Hearing it put that way, Gaye understood that what truly worried him was seeing this aspect of her mother's psyche. "I'm not *attracted* to being alone," she countered. "I just don't happen to know too many people I enjoy spending time with."

While she was irked by his meddling, Gaye couldn't dismiss her father's comments as unreasonable. She was twenty-six when she came back to Philadelphia, and she'd never had a real boyfriend. At vet school she had made a cold-blooded decision after her first year—somewhat on the order of giving herself an assignment in basic biology—that she ought to experience sex. After a few evenings out with the most attractive of the men who pursued her, she went to bed with him. She'd enjoyed it well enough to continue sleeping with him for several weeks, but she'd never felt any true emotional attachment. When he spoke of wanting a steadier commitment, she'd stopped seeing him. After that, there were a couple of other men she'd "tried out," but the experiences were unfulfilling. By the time her father began lobbying her to get out more, she was through with casual lovers for the sake of experience or letting off sexual steam. If she were going to be with a man, it had to be one who tapped into emotions she'd never been able to release before, someone who could cure her of the feeling that perhaps she was meant to be alone.

"You ought to know better than anyone," she said to her father the next time he brought up her social life, "that being with the wrong person ends with making you feel even more alone than being by yourself."

"But you can't meet the *right* person if you don't try. If you had a job at my hospital, you'd have scads of young doctors hovering around—charming, good-looking guys, a lot of them. As it is, you meet more animals than people."

"Animals are owned by people. I meet plenty."

"Not the right kind, Gaye. The animals you see are family pets, kept by married people and kids. How many single men have a pet? The ones who do . . . seems to me they're usually a little . . . weird."

"Seems that way to you only because you're not an animal lover."

"Don't tell me a pet doesn't become an object of affection for whoever owns it—and that affection can go too far. I hear these old women on the street talking to their poodles as if they were their *children.* You get a guy who loves his dog *that* much, he's not someone you want to spend your life with."

"So is there a guy who'd want to spend his life with me? Considering how much I love Hero?" she asked in a tone of bemusement, not as a challenge.

"Want the truth, my dear? However much you love that dog, make sure it never becomes a replacement for the greater love you should have in your life—for someone you can talk to, share your problems with, have a family with. Some people do get the balance wrong and go overboard."

Gaye heard it as a reference to her mother, and was moved to defend her. "Mom wasn't happy with you, Dad—just as lots of women aren't happy with the men they marry. But not because she loved anyone or any*thing* else too much."

Still, his campaign to match her up continued—but the next time he didn't talk in the abstract. There was a young surgeon he was mentoring in the cardiology department, he said, as fine a doctor—and as fine a person—as he'd ever encountered. Smart, skilled, attractive, this was a young man, said Owen Foster, he would be damn proud to have as a son. "Though I'll settle for son-in-law," he quipped, doing his best to keep the blatant sales pitch in a light vein.

On this occasion they were having a Chinese supper, and Nancy was along. "Owen, look at the pressure you're putting on your daughter!" she said. "Practically telling the poor girl, even before she meets this man, that it's an arranged marriage. Gaye, I wouldn't blame you for taking a pass."

"I'm only trying to give her a sense of how terrific the guy is," Foster said. "Look, Gaye, I know I've been bugging you about getting out more, but this is the first time I've dared to suggest actually fixing you up on a blind date."

True. "Okay," she said with a show of forbearance. "Suppose I agree to meet this protégé of yours. Can we make a deal? I'll go this once, and then you'll lay off. Stop judging the way I live and making me feel like a misfit, stop suggesting candidates for husbands even if they're gorgeous and have a better shot at being famous heart surgeons than DeBakey and Christian Barnard and you all put together."

Owen Foster laughed lightly before he said, "It's a deal."

Which was how she came to meet the man she'd married.

In the phone call Brian Leahy made after her father passed along her number, they agreed on lunch at a simple luncheonette around the corner from the hospital. Neither of them wanted an evening out with all the dressing up, the commitment to spend hours together even after the probable realization that there was no chemistry.

But that Wednesday Gaye had walked away from lunch humming. The deal had worked out, all right. No more being harangued by Daddy . . . because she was pretty damn sure he was going to get exactly the son-in-law he wanted. Brian Leahy seemed to be everything her father had said, and more: charming, smart, good-looking. And he hadn't just brought a boring rose to give her at lunch; he'd walked in with a paper bag, inside which she found a ham bone. A present for her "famous" dog, he said, because he thought she ought to know he had his priorities straight. And of all the good things she'd noticed about him, the best was that, from every indication, he was genuinely interested in her. All in all, Gaye felt that in Brian Leahy she had found a perfect dreamboat.

On that lovely afternoon she hadn't an inkling that her dreamboat was going to sail her into a perfect nightmare.

Chapter 4

Gaye started work. After two days of searching for a place of her own, she was still at the Bennetts', so at nine o'clock she left the main house to walk over to the clinic. It was a fine morning, cold but sunny, and she paused when she stepped outside to marvel at the clear sapphire sky and breathe the brisk, clean air deep into her lungs. The job might be second-rate, but there were benefits.

Frankie had set off earlier to do a round of vaccinations at two dairy farms, but Will was at his desk in the small office carved out of one corner of the big central area. From there he could view the rest of the space through a glass partition, and he called out a "Good morning" when he saw Gaye enter. She went to the door of his cubicle and he told her the first appointment was booked for nine-thirty. In the meantime, he said, "Make yourself at home."

As she started away, he called out, "And you don't have to wear that uniform here. . . ." It was a reference to the long white doctor's coat she had on over her regular clothes—a leftover habit from Philadelphia, where the animal hospital felt it assured clients they were in good hands. After mulling it over for a second, Gaye left the coat on. She liked the badge of professionalism.

She had brought along her reference books and a satchel containing her stethoscope and a few other personal instruments, and now she toured the main area looking for a place to set up a workspace. At one side of the refrigerator she found a small shelf where several boxes of bandages and rolls of paper towels were piled up. It was merely a yard wide before it ended at a wall, but by storing the supplies along the floor beneath, she created a niche big enough to lay out her things and leave a surface at a good height for writing if she perched on a stool. Quite a change from Philly, where she'd had her own phone, a computer link to the main database, and two extra chairs so she could talk privately with clients.

It struck her now that she'd yet to see a computer. Glancing over at the Bennetts' office, Gaye scanned the scene beyond the glass partition. Piled up everywhere were old veterinary journals, manufacturers' drug samples, and other odds and ends—but no computer. Yet there had to be one. The advantages of a computer for running any kind of medical practice couldn't have been ignored. Gaye went out through the double doors to the reception area. When she'd taken a peek the other evening, she hadn't seen much beyond an area with a row of chairs lined up, a picture window looking out on a paved parking strip, and a reception counter at one side. By the sunlight flooding through the window, the place looked less bleak. There were pictures of animals and charts related to their care on the wall, a kiddie-size table and chairs in a corner where children could wait, a shelf of books and magazines. Next to the door was the chest-high reception counter. Gaye looked behind it. On a desk area were a phone, an electric typewriter, and all the usual stationery supplies. Across an aisle from the desk were several metal file cabinets, a coffeemaker atop one of them.

She heard the door open behind her and turned. A stocky young woman with long untamed dark hair and a round freckled face was coming in from the parking lot. She wore a brown shapeless sweater over jeans, and cowboy-style boots that raised her height to an inch more than Gaye's.

"Hey," she greeted Gaye, her dark eyes lighting up, "you must be the new doc. I'm Lori." She unhooked a sacklike purse from her shoulder and heaved it onto the reception counter. Before Gaye had a chance to say anything, the young woman opened her arms as if to embrace the waiting area. "Well," she said, "whattaya think of Bible Hill?"

So this was Lori Michaels, the all-around helper Will had mentioned. Gaye liked her on sight, her own sagging spirit given an instant transfusion by the energy of the local girl. But she couldn't pretend to be thrilled with her new place of employment. "It's quite a change for me," she said.

Lori picked up on her tone. "Oh, right—come from the city, didn'tcha? I've heard there's animal hospitals down there five stories high—walk in and you're not sure if maybe you went in the wrong door and you're where the people belong." She looked around and laughed. "Well, we don't want anyone thinkin' they're at the wrong place. You come to Bible Hill, right away you know this place is for the birds, and goin' to the dogs."

Gaye wasn't sure how to react. Was the remark made with good-natured affection, or real criticism veiled by humor?

Lori saw her uncertainty. "Don't mind me, Gaye. I've been wearin' the ball and chain here a few years, so I've earned the right to take some shots at the old dump. Truth is, I love it, and the Bennetts—such great people. What they do . . . it's amazing. You'll see."

"I hope. But they seem so . . . I mean the clinic seems behind the times. There's not even a computer."

"What difference does that make?" Lori said, truly puzzled.

"Makes it easier to track patient records, look up medications, cross-reference common symptoms by species or breed or geography to help with your epidemiology, simplify billing, speed up the—"

"It all gets done," Lori broke in. "As for speed, I move fast enough."

"It's the ease and convenience. The quicker simple tasks get done, the more time you've got for other things."

Lori moved around behind the counter. "But the slower they get done," she said, "the fewer mistakes there are."

It was on Gaye's lips to say computers produced more error-free work than people, but argument was futile. From the look of things, the idea that simpler and older was better was the governing principle at the Bible Hill Animal Clinic.

Lori filled the silence. "Anyway, it's not like we're so jammed up we don't have enough time. Dr. Will . . . you see, he can't handle near as much as he used to. Speeding things up might only make things more difficult for him."

Gaye gave up her lobbying. "What's on the schedule for this morning?"

Lori pulled a sheet of paper from a cubby under the counter with lines of her penciled scrawl. After scanning it, she gave a summary. They all sounded like routine matters: a dog scheduled to receive a heartworm shot, a cat with an intestinal blockage probably caused by an unregurgitated hairball, a young goat with an infection where a new horn was forming. What impressed Gaye as she listened to the summary was Lori's obvious familiarity with the animals involved and their owners. As she described each case, she included some little detail of past history. The cat with the blockage was unusually old and had been in with the problem before; the goat was one of many kept by a woman who "makes the best goddamn cheese, and treats those little critters better'n most folks treat their kids—I mean *real* kids, not the goat kind."

Will appeared, pushing one of the double doors half-open with his chair. He said, "Good morning" to Lori and asked if she'd made the coffee yet, then motioned Gaye to join him inside. He stopped his chair by the table in the examining area. "Our first visit this morning is for—"

"Heartworm shot," Gaye put in.

"Yes." Will looked pleased by her initiative. "I'd like you to take care of it."

"Just the shot, or you want me to take the patient by myself?"

"I'll observe, but you handle everything."

A test. Fair enough. She'd been hired on the basis of credentials and a long-distance interview. No way to know if she was truly any good until she did the job under observation.

Lori came in to say the coffee was almost ready, and she had just seen Geronimo arrive in the parking lot. Will told her to send the dog right in.

Moments later a gigantic heap of white fur bounded into the main area. Gaye identified the dog at once as a Great Pyrenees. An ancient breed dating back to the centuries before Christ—its fossil remains had been found in archeological digs—it had been used through the medieval period by peasants to guard their flocks from wolves and bears. The appeal of its size and snowy fur had eventually made it a favorite of aristocrats, and it was the official dog of the French royal court in pre-Revolutionary times. Gaye had tended several in Philadelphia, where it was a popular pet in families with the affluence to keep and feed such a large animal. But along with its size it had the inbred instinct to function as an excellent guardian for livestock, a purpose it might be serving here in farm country.

Daunting as it was to see a 120-pound snowball hurtling toward her, Gaye stood her ground. Entering behind the dog was a burly, bearded man in a windbreaker and overalls. He whistled through his teeth, and the dog pulled up short. The man apologized to Gaye for any fright the dog had caused, but she assured him she wasn't bothered. Then Will introduced Gaye to the owner, a sheep farmer named Gus Dowd.

"Dr. Foster is going to be doing the things I can't do anymore," Will told Dowd, who nodded sympathetically.

It moved Gaye to hear Will refer candidly to his growing infirmity. She realized now that being assigned to give the injection wasn't merely a test. Controlling a frisky animal of this size would be hard for a man in a wheelchair.

Gaye's first priority was always to put the patient at ease. No less than for humans, visits to the doctor produced anxiety, even fear, in animals; they sensed that in this environment of strange sights and strange smells, serious things could happen. Gaye's custom in reassuring dogs was to get down on her haunches or sit cross-legged on the floor, so she could interact at their level. When she did it now, the big shaggy white dog stared back at her a moment as if puzzled—as did the owner. She was aware, though, of a small approving smile from Will Bennett.

Thereafter the dog responded well to her. Though he was scheduled for only a shot, she was able to start with a quick general exam, checking the ears for mites and fungus, making sure that toenails and dewclaws weren't growing so long as to curl into the flesh. Then she held the dog's chin and looked into his eyes.

"Reading his mind?" the owner asked.

"No, Mr. Dowd, I'm looking at his eyebrows. Have you checked them lately?"

Dowd shot a perplexed look at Will, to which the older man re turned a small nod that signaled he also wanted the answer. Dowd turned back to Gaye. "His eyebrows, miss?" He smirked. "No, I do confess I haven't looked."

"You should. They're starting to curl downward. See . . . ?" Gaye waited until Dowd had bent down to inspect them at her level. "As they keep growing, they could curl into the eye and cause an irrita-tion. It's not unusual with this breed. These need to be clipped."

Dowd looked to Will again. "You never said anything about Geronimo's eyebrows."

"Could be our new staff member knows more than I do."

"I doubt that," Dowd said, "though maybe more about plucking eyebrows."

"Not plucking," Gaye said curtly. "Clipping. I'll show you." She asked Will where to find small scissors.

Instead of telling her, he rolled to a cabinet, took a pair with fine points from a drawer, and brought them to Gaye. She then demon-strated the clipping for Dowd, instructing him in the amount to clip, to be very careful of the scissor points, and to continue monthly checks to be sure the eyebrows were never curling into the eye.

After she gave the antiheartworm shot and the dog left with his owner, Will gave a very complimentary assessment of Gaye's perform-ance. With one exception: "Your advice about the eyebrows was good, but you made it plain you were annoyed by the way he took it."

"I don't mind if he asks you to confirm my advice—you've been his vet for years. But when he mentioned 'plucking' the eyebrows, I got his message. Women do that, not men. He was belittling my ad-vice because I'm 'the girl.' "

"Maybe you're being too sensitive."

Was she? Maybe she was too sensitive about everything. Her nerve ends had been raw for months.

When she gave him no more than a shrug, Will said, "There's a lot that needs changing around here, Gaye, and maybe a lot you can teach us. But give it a little more time than overnight, and try to laugh off some of the things that get your dander up."

Because of how gently he'd done it, Gaye felt chastened by Will for being humorless. He might not be so quick to criticize, she thought, if he knew what had stolen away her ability to forgive an insensitive remark. But there wasn't time to dwell on it. Lori reappeared to say that Mrs. Rankin was waiting with Ginger.

"Ask her to come in," Will said. "And don't forget my coffee!"

Before leaving, Lori asked if Gaye wanted coffee, too.

"Cream, no sugar," Gaye said, and thanked her.

"A little more advice," Will said when Lori had gone. "Take the sugar—always. Her coffee's completely undrinkable without it."

She looked at him, astonished. "But you seemed so impatient to get it!"

"Second morning she came into work—years ago—Lori brought in a coffeemaker, and she's been starting the day by making me coffee ever since. It's her gift." Will's little smiling shrug explained the rest. He simply couldn't bring himself to prick the balloon of pride Lori took in her daily gesture.

As the cat was brought in, Will told Gaye he would take this case himself, but she should stand by to help out if needed.

Mrs. Rankin was an elderly widow who was devoted to her female calico, and distressed by the serious blockage, obvious in the way the cat's abdomen had become distended. "Hasn't had a real good poop for days," she told Will.

He instructed her to put the cat on the examining table, but remain to stroke it and pacify it. It would be best, he said, if the cat would lie on its side. He let the owner caress the cat for a minute until the animal obligingly lapsed into a reclining position. Then Will rolled his chair up closer to the table and, holding his hands very slightly above the reclining cat but not touching it, he began to move them back and forth through the air in a slow undulation that conformed exactly to the outline of the cat's abdomen.

"What are you doing?" Gaye asked.

"Ray-keys," said Mrs. Rankin, "like he always does."

"What?" Gaye said.

"Reiki," Will said. "Old healing technique from Japan by way of Tibet."

"For cats?"

"For any living thing."

Gaye watched another few moments. "Do you mind explaining how those hand movements help?"

"This is a preliminary stage. I'm trying to sense where there's a change—call it a dead spot—in the field of energy around Ginger, the chakra, it's called, so I can deal with the proper acupoint—" He broke off and gave Gaye a shy smile. "I sound like a crackpot, don't I? Suppose I just give you a book about it later."

The rest of the session she observed in silence. After moving his hands over the cat, Will put them together, the fingers steepled, and held them like that above one place on the cat's stomach. After several minutes he moved back from the table.

"Think that'll do the trick?" the old woman said.

"We'll see. . . ."

The woman swept the cat up into her arms.

"Hold on, Ellie." Will rolled his chair to a tall, polished wooden chest divided into many small square drawers, each one labeled on the front. Gaye could see he wanted something from a drawer on one of the top tiers, because he stood from the chair and started to raise one arm. But then he dropped weakly back into the chair. He turned to her.

"Legs aren't doing it for me today. Would you come over here, Gaye, and open that drawer?" He pointed to one at the uppermost right corner.

As she came to the chest, Gaye was able to read several of the labels in front of her, unfamiliar words inked in a neat script: *Hyocyamus Niger, Hypericum, Performatum, Hamamelis Virg.* As she was seven or eight inches shorter than Will, she couldn't read the label on the drawer he'd indicated, but Gaye supposed it also held some medicinal substance she'd never heard of. To obtain the remedy, she had to reach up over the edge of the open drawer and blindly pinch two fingers around one of many small glass vials she could feel. When she brought her hand down, she saw the vial contained a brown powder.

Will gave it to Mrs. Rankin, and told her to brew a tea from it that should be added to milk or cream or whatever tempted Ginger.

"Nothing's tempted her lately."

"Try fish broth," Will suggested. "Add catnip if necessary."

As soon as Mrs. Rankin had taken Ginger away, Gaye asked Will about the substances in the chest.

"They're homeopathic remedies," Will said.

"You practice homeopathy on animals, too?" Gaye didn't reject the idea that substances harvested directly from nature had medicinal properties, but her own experience in research inclined her to believe that even those worked best when refined for use in prepared pharmaceuticals. She was influenced as well by exposure to her father's work, where modern lifesaving medicine made possible by the development of new surgical techniques and antibiotics accomplished so much. She'd also often heard her father lump together homeopathy, crystal cures, massage therapy, and acupuncture as "all that New Age crap."

"Homeopathic medicine works on all living things," Will answered. "Same as reiki." Reading the skepticism in her expression, he added, "Assuming you believe it works at all."

"So what did you give Ginger to clear the blockage?"

"Clear it? I couldn't. Poor cat has an inoperable tumor. I've told Ellie Rankin, but she chooses to forget it. Everything I did today was to ease the cat's discomfort, improve her appetite, and if I'm really lucky shrink the tumor mass. Ginger is all Ellie has for family. As long as the cat's not suffering she needs to keep her, and I want to help her do that."

The learning process went on through the morning. When Will spayed another cat that was brought in, she saw him use acupuncture along with conventional anesthetic as part of the surgery. He explained that it allowed him to administer a lighter dose of the chemical, which made the surgery safer and the recovery quicker.

The goat brought in for treatment of an infection was also given something from Will's chest of homeopathic remedies. Antibiotics could be the best cure for certain infections, he admitted to Gaye, but he preferred to avoid their use whenever possible because applying them too liberally helped to create resistant strains of virus and bacteria.

"You have to remember that whatever new strains may get started in animals will work their way up to humans through the food chain. The healthier we keep that goat, the healthier we keep ourselves. He makes cheese people eat."

In fact, Gaye saw that Will accepted a few pounds of the cheese—more than he or Frankie could possibly use—from the goat's owner as payment for the visit.

By the time the morning's work ended, she had seen and heard enough to understand that the circumstances which had forced her to uproot herself completely from one life and flee to another had provided her with a rare and valuable opportunity to enhance her knowledge and skill. It wasn't enough to say that Will Bennett was no ordinary veterinarian, nor that he was simply gifted or good at what he did. He had an approach to dealing with animals that seemed unique and phenomenal.

It was indeed sufficient to make Gaye wonder if fate didn't play a part in bringing her to Bible Hill. For whatever pain and suffering she had endured before coming, she saw the possibility now that it might be more than balanced by the chance to become as good as Will Bennett at doing the work she loved.

Chapter 5

The afternoon's appointments were all farm visits Frankie would handle by herself, so Will told Gaye to take the rest of the day to continue her hunt for somewhere to live. It had become obvious to him that a place of her own was essential. Even in Gaye's few minor interactions with Frankie, the tension persisted.

With Will, there was a different problem that confirmed her feeling that some distance from work was essential. She had already developed a soft spot, and as her respect and affection for him grew, she knew it would become more difficult to be a close witness to his decline and death.

Over the preceding two days, Gaye had been busy. She opened an account with the local bank and drove to a shopping mall in Littleton to fulfill her ruse by buying clothes and shipping them to herself. She had also checked the sparse collection of rentals advertised in the two regional weekly newspapers, even those that required her to travel as far as thirty miles from West Greenlea. All she'd seen were dark basements and airless attics in other people's homes, abandoned farmhouses she hadn't the time or money to make livable, and a dilapidated house-trailer next to a lumber mill where the buzz saw started at six a.m. every weekday.

The truck set aside for her use was a battered red '87 Dodge with a worn-through driver's seat, exhausted shocks, and an engine that produced dark, oily exhaust. After she'd spent two days driving the country roads, her back ached from the constant unabsorbed jolts, and she felt guilty about polluting the clean country air she'd breathed so gratefully this morning. Rather than travel far afield today, Gaye thought she'd seek out a bulletin board in West Green-lea that carried local notices, or try directly canvassing the natives.

As she arrived in town, she spotted Curl up and Dye on Main Street, and it made her smile again. Then it struck her: what better place to make inquiries? Women traded all kinds of local gossip in beauty parlors; it just might include who had space to rent. She pulled the truck to the curb outside the storefront.

The salon had two chairs, only one of which was occupied by a customer faceup in a sink getting a rinse from the shop's owner, a cheerful middle-aged bottle blonde. Gaye introduced herself as a new vet coming to work at the local animal clinic, and explained her quest for a place to live. Somewhere with just a little charm, if possible, but essentially just clean, quiet, and habitable without putting more into it than a coat of paint. Did the ladies know of anything?

"Gonna work at Bible Hill, eh?" the owner said when Gaye finished her pitch. "About time the Bennetts got some help. Terrible what's happened to Will; such a good man. That Frankie can be a pill, I don't mind saying, but underneath she's salt of the earth, too. Wouldn't take my guys anywhere but Bible Hill." She flicked a nod at two cats lying on a padded bench in the window. "I'm Flo Campbell, by the way. So let's see: What can we do to fix you up?" She leaned over the customer with her head in the sink. "Millie, you know of anyplace for—what's your name again, hon?"

"Gaye Foster."

Flo repeated her question. "You know anywhere Gaye could move in?"

The customer pulled upright, her lank brown hair dripping around a broad, homely face. "Got that place I fixed up for Jodie right under my own shop."

The hairdresser shied back. "Really? Jodie's gone for good?"

" 'Fraid so," The dripping woman focused on Gaye. "My daughter's been at massage school over in Burlington, and two years she's been saying she's coming back to set up here. But now . . ." Water flew off her head as she shook it. "There's a guy, and I think she's saving all her massages for him."

Gaye didn't need to see the place: a would-be massage parlor beneath another shop wasn't going to fill the bill. But she wanted to be polite. "Maybe you should wait a little longer. You fixed this place up especially for her."

But the woman was already out of the chair, wrapping a towel around her wet hair, bundling herself into a coat, and telling Flo she'd be back for the finishing touches. In a minute Gaye was being marched down Main Street. Along the way the woman introduced herself as Millie Howell and followed up with a constant patter. She was an exceptionally tall, hefty woman who moved at a fast clip and talked faster, her face animated by lively expressions that overcame her homeliness and made her very appealing. "It's exactly what you asked for, hon. Move-in condition, touch of charm, not just four walls. All new kitchen—no dishwasher, but who needs a dishwasher—just roll up your sleeves, for pity's sake! You can use the linens and dishes I bought for my girl. Nice patterns."

They had turned a corner to walk down a hill. At the bottom, where the side street ended, Gaye saw a stream running past—the one that ran beneath the covered bridge, she guessed. They turned again onto a street running parallel above the stream, both sides lined with vintage two-story wooden buildings separated by wide alleys.

Millie unlocked the door of a ground-level shop on the down-hill side of the street. "I'm taking you in this way so you can see the shop, too," she said, "give you an idea of what you'll have overhead. But you've got a separate entrance in the alley around the side." She went to a wall and flipped on a few light switches.

Suddenly Gaye was surrounded by small bright-eyed faces staring back from every side, on chairs, tables, long shelves, propped up at the base of walls, in corners. *Dolls!* The ceiling lights caught their glass eyes in ways that gave them an animated sparkle, and spotlighted several dressed in clothes of particular grandeur—a red velvet evening gown, a lace bridal dress. Amidst the figures were dollhouses ranging from small and simple to amazingly elaborate, with two and three floors of furnished rooms. The switches Millie had thrown also activated tiny perfect fixtures within them—chandeliers, bedside lamps, wall sconces lining stairways.

Gaye let out a reflexive laugh of delight. It seemed comically unreal to come across this fantasy tucked away in a small town—and as the special domain of this oversize woman. Was Millie Howell a bit crazy? What sense did it make to devote herself to this esoteric business in a town that probably had one-tenth as many people as she had dolls. "You *sell* this stuff?" Gaye asked.

"Yes'm—but not straight out of the shop, if you're worried about overhead traffic. I'm not here at night either; my house is across town. I keep this place just as a showroom, and every so often people come through. But most of the business is mail-order." She moved to a table, grabbed a booklet off a stack, and thrust it into Gaye's hands. "My catalog," she said proudly.

The cover had picture of a beautifully dressed doll, and the address and Web site for a business called Happy Dollydays. Gaye riffled the pages: pictures of dolls and their clothes, houses, and miniature items from furniture right down to tiny rolling pins. Millie Howell was crazy like a fox, Gaye realized. It didn't improve her expectations, however, as Millie opened a side door at the midpoint of the shop, revealing a narrow, dimly lit flight of stairs. The apartment under the shop was another dim basement, no doubt.

"Of course, I'll keep this locked," Millie said, preceding Gaye down the stairs. "You won't have to worry about anyone coming in from above."

Gaye was already preparing her polite refusal when Millie opened the door at the bottom of the stairs. Gaye stepped through—and so much light flooded into her eyes that it was a few seconds before she could make out anything but an open space ending at a wall of light. As her vision adjusted, she saw that the end of the space was a wall of glass windowpanes from floor to ceiling. The late-afternoon sun poured in upon a combination living and dining room furnished with flowered fabrics on comfortable furniture, a sofa with needlepoint pillows, brass fire tools by a fireplace, an oval hooked rug on the floor, and a dark oak table on which silver candlesticks stood. It looked like nothing so much as a room from a dollhouse made large. Gaye remembered dreaming as a little girl of living in such a cozy home. Her relief at finding it, mingled with the nostalgia of all those childhood dreams, was so great that tears sprang to her eyes, and she moved quickly to start touring the apartment so the landlady wouldn't notice.

The kitchen was around the corner from where the stairs entered the living room, everything new, as she'd been told, a slate floor, butcher-block counter.

The windowed wall looked out on an incline of grass and bushes that ran down to the stream. Since the building stood on a hillside, its lower floor was totally open to the light. The rear of the apartment was actually an enclosed porch separated from the living room by three sets of French doors that stood open now but could be closed against colder weather. At the side of the porch a door led out to a patio perched above the grassy slope. Gaye noticed some split logs stacked beside the patio, wood to feed the fire on the cold evenings ahead.

At the front end of the apartment, past the kitchen, doorways off the living room led to a bedroom and bath, each with a window looking out to different sides of the apartment. The bedroom, too, was furnished in the best dollhouse style: flowered wallpaper, lace curtains, chintz apron around a vanity. A bit too "girlie," perhaps—Gaye could see why the daughter might not want to move in—and yet she loved it for herself. As a temporary place, anyway.

Gaye went back to Millie, who waited in the living room. "This was going to be a massage parlor?" she said, incredulous.

"Who said *that*? Jodie might have done the odd massage here, but she was going to do out calls—bring the table around, y'know. Though I never thought there'd be enough business in the area to make it worth her while."

Gaye drifted off to look at the stream again; she was already imagining herself reading a book on the sunlit porch on a Sunday, listening to the relaxing babble of the rushing stream at night. . . .

"Of course, you can move in your own furniture," Millie said.

As with her clothes, in the hasty getaway Gaye had left behind every stick of furniture she owned. But she wouldn't have changed the apartment. "I love it the way it is," she said.

They left by the separate entrance from the kitchen into an alley, and climbed a steep flight of wooden steps that led up to the street. On the walk back to the beauty parlor they completed the agreement. The monthly rent was $450. That included the electricity, but not the phone. No deposit necessary. Gaye could just pay a couple of months in advance, and move in tonight if she wanted. One more night at the Bennetts' would make a more gracious leave-taking, Gaye thought; she told Millie she'd come the next day after work to leave a check and pick up the keys, and move in at the same time.

And the lease? Millie stopped outside Curl up and Dye and looked Gaye in the eye. "Let's say you'll just stay as long as you're happy."

Perhaps she was forgoing a lease because she thought her daughter might yet return and need the place, Gaye thought. Or was it because she detected the vibrations of uncertainty coming from her tenant? In any case, that was how they left it: Gaye would stay as long as she was "happy." Of course, she took the meaning of the word only in the loosest colloquial sense. It had been so long since she had been truly happy that she didn't hope for more than to be simply satisfied and unafraid.

She returned the next evening to Millie's showroom to pick up keys to the apartment and write a check on her newly opened account. As she was leaving, Millie handed her a paper bag.

"What's this?" Gaye said.

"Look inside."

The bag contained a loaf of bread and a sandwich baggie holding a few spoonfuls of salt.

"A little tradition we have when someone moves into a new home," Millie said.

Gaye was touched by the welcoming gesture—the sort of old-fashioned neighborliness she'd hoped to encounter when choosing a haven.

But later, after she'd done all the initial moving in, she thought back to the sentiment expressed by the tradition and wondered if it was even appropriate. Was this truly her new home? Or only a stopping point until circumstances forced her to move on? How soon would that be? She couldn't believe she would really be left in peace. Tonight, alone for the first time since she'd fled, she felt the fear creeping through her again.

To recapture the lovely imaginings of safety and serenity, she built a fire in the fireplace and tried to settle in front of it with a book. But the awful images kept intruding into her thoughts. His face contorted by rage . . . smears of blood covering the city sidewalk . . .

Desperate to clear it all from her mind, she went out back to look at the night sky and listen to the whispering rush of the stream. It ought to remind her of the distance she'd put between herself and the threat. But as she stood in the dark, looking across to the far side of the flowing water, where trees grew along the bank—a thick stand of trees in which anything or anyone might hide—her agitation only increased. He could be lurking there. Gaye peered out into the blackness beyond the reach of light from her windows. Like a child imagining monsters in every shadow of even the most inaccessible place, the threat seemed almost real. Of course he *wasn't* there. But that didn't calm her fears. If ever he were to learn where she was, wouldn't he come?

The insistent barking of a dog broke into her thoughts. For a second she took that, too, for part of her grim reverie. But it went on and she realized it was coming from a neighboring house not too far away, a dog out for his evening ramble, reacting perhaps to a fox or a squirrel.

Odd. The sound of that bark . . . Those who didn't own dogs might not realize it, but the animals could have voices as distinct as people's. And this barking in the night was so reminiscent of Hero's. It comforted her somehow. If she could imagine monsters, then why not a protective spirit to keep them at bay?

Gaye turned back and went into the apartment. She locked the patio door and returned to the easy chair in front of the fireplace.

The logs were still glowing, sending out an enveloping warmth. She nestled into the chair and conjured a picture of the dog lying on the hearth—the way things had been for a while, the way it was always *supposed* to be.

She drifted off at last to the memory of a time when she'd been happy.

Chapter 6

Her wedding day. She couldn't have been happier then.

There had been no letdown after that first meeting. After each date with Brian Leahy a bouquet would arrive with a card from him blessing his luck that she cared for him. Six months to the day from their lunch came the evening at Le Bec-Fin, when he'd arranged for an engagement ring to be brought atop the dessert she'd ordered. He'd gotten down on one knee to make an old-fashioned proposal—right there, with every customer and waiter in the place applauding her acceptance. Yes, Brian was a bit of a show-off, which could be jarring for someone of Gaye's quiet nature, but she accepted that as a small price to pay in the inevitable attraction of opposites. As the child of a surgeon, she was well aware that the appreciation of the crowd was commonly sought by men who aspired to be the best in a profession where admirers could be so grateful they might even be called worshipers. To be a great heart surgeon, daring to tamper with the most essential organ of life, required the same ego that bred exhibitionists.

No small part of Gaye's happiness on her wedding day was knowing how well she had served her father by giving him this "son" who reflected his own talents and ambitions in so many ways. Owen Foster had ended his toast at the wedding dinner by announcing that his new son-in-law would henceforth be his partner in his cardiology practice.

The honeymoon was another of his gifts. Anywhere they wanted, Foster said. Gaye deferred to Brian on the choice, and he picked Italy: the timeless antiquity of Rome, followed by the brilliant religious art of Florence, then the Byzantine decadence of that most unique floating city, Venice. He called it a "cocktail" of life's mysteries and possibilities.

If she wasn't quite as happy on the honeymoon it was only because her dog had to be left in a kennel. The smooth, effortless sail they had taken from first love into the beginning of marriage continued undisturbed . . . until Venice. There, in that unreal place, a maze of streets made of water as much as stone, during an afternoon stroll they had stumbled onto a shop in one of its alleyways that sold masks, the kind worn in the Venetian *carnevales* still held on certain holidays—devilish hybrids of beast and bird. Gaye regarded the masks as grotesque, but Brian had bought two—one more birdlike, the other leonine—saying he'd use them to decorate his office or home study.

Later, at their hotel by the Grand Canal, he put on the more beastlike of the two as if playfully. Then, still wearing it as he undressed, he asked Gaye to don the other. Wouldn't it be exciting to make love this way? he said. To pretend they were not themselves but different people—or even animals? At first she made light of the idea. Why should she pretend to be anyone or any*thing* but herself? She was thrilled to be herself, his wife, and to know he—no one else but he—was hers.

But he teased her for being prudish, then sulked when Gaye refused even to try the mask "just to see what it feels like." When she declared the whole idea out of the question, he dressed again and stalked out of the room. It was the first show of temper she'd ever seen from him, their first serious fight.

And for what? If he wanted to experiment with sex, wasn't that for her pleasure, too? While he was gone, Gaye lay down naked on the bed, turned out the light, and put on the birdlike mask. For hours she waited like that, awake in the room lit only by the reflected play of light from the canal. She did not cover herself or leave the bed. As a form of penance she did not want him to find her any way but *this*, ready and willing to oblige what, after all, seemed a playful nuptial favor.

At last the door opened, and his shadowy figure slipped into the room. He saw her, and without a word he undressed and put on the other mask. Then, still without a word, he took her, and it went on that way through the night. She obliged him, giving herself in new ways, and couldn't deny being excited by the experience. Yet that excitement included an element of uneasiness; she did not want to repeat the experience.

In the morning she was relieved to wake and find him asleep beside her, unmasked, as was she. His first words on waking were "I love you." To her relief, he said not a word about their night games, as if no less embarrassed by the aberration. And the rest of the honeymoon was as plainly wonderful as the first part.

Back home again, they settled into the comfortable town house Brian had bought before they'd married, and their married life continued the idyll. Then, during a home-cooked dinner one night, he told her a bypass he'd performed that day had been particularly stressful. The patient had died on the table, then had been revived by the surgical team. The bottle of wine they'd drunk wasn't enough to relax him completely, he said. He needed sex—and not their ordinary lovemaking.

"Where did you get those?" she asked when he showed her the handcuffs.

"Downtown—one of those places that sells all kinds of stuff to make it more fun."

It wasn't her idea of fun, she said.

"Whatever word you use," he said, "you don't have to make it sound weird. Lots of people enjoy it, or there wouldn't be shops with shelves full of this stuff. They sell to all kinds of people, lawyers, doctors . . . sex therapists."

She was caught again between wondering if it was fair, denying him something relatively harmless he needed from her; or whether he was pushing the boundaries beyond what she had a right to refuse. "You never mentioned liking this kind of thing," she said.

"I've never wanted to experiment with anyone else. Don't you see, it's something to share with the only person in the world I trust completely?"

She yielded then. But this time she didn't like the experience at all. Playing games of dominance and submission, being shackled and unable to resist, was fine for couples where both consented freely. But it wasn't her idea of pleasurable sex, Gaye told him. Nor did she like being pressured with the implication that to refuse meant she was any less loving.

There were no apologies, but he listened without argument, and another period passed during which they were basically compatible. Except there was a change in the way he treated her. At first it was barely noticeable, perhaps a mention of his disappointment after she'd done the grocery shopping at her failure to remember he preferred one brand of breakfast cereal over another. Then, gradually, his comments became harsher. The flowers she'd arranged in the living room were "too gaudy," or made him feel like he'd "walked into a funeral parlor." The dress she was wearing to dinner with friends was an "ugly" color; he wouldn't go out unless she changed. What Gaye minded most, however, was the way he began to pick on Hero, and her affection for the dog. "Sometimes I think it's freaky the way you care for that animal," he'd say. "Not natural, somehow. . . ."

Was it the strain of his work that made him speak so insensitively? Gaye made excuses for him in her own mind. There were still evenings he'd arrive home bringing an unexpected gift, or take her out for an evening as romantic and carefree as before they'd married. She did what she could to accommodate him.

Until the argument reared up again in the bedroom. He'd brought home more things from a sex shop: leather halters with chains attached, clips and vises to be attached to the most sensitive parts of the body. Things designed to enforce restraint, and even induce pain.

"Darling," she said after he had laid out his display on the bed, "you need help."

"Do I, or do *you*? Why won't you at least try? How can you reject something when you don't really know how it would feel?"

If she did not draw the line here and now, then what would

come after? How soon would it be before she had to face that they were incompatible? What she agreed to do was exactly what he asked: try, on the condition that he would stop if and whenever she asked. Which was very soon after they began. Except that he *didn't* stop. Heedless of her pleading and crying, he continued. This, exactly this, was part of what she should enjoy, he said. The pain, the humiliation, were elements in the surrender of will, the expression of unconditional love.

At one point, aroused by her cries, Hero had run up the stairs into the bedroom. Her husband's first reaction was to make the profane suggestion of including the animal; but then he'd locked the dog out of the room.

It was dawn before he put away all the paraphernalia and left to go to the hospital. There were two difficult operations scheduled for the day, he said. Second only to her father, he had become a star cardiac surgeon. Being linked together in practice was working to build both their reputations.

Gaye called in sick to her own job. She remained in bed all day, immobilized less by her pains than by confusion and shock, comforted only by the dog beside her. What was the right next step to take when you discovered the person to whom you were married was not the person to whom you'd said "I do" at the altar? She was desperate for support and advice to steer her in a hopeful direction, but the embarrassment of admitting her humiliation restrained her as surely as any of the hateful contraptions she'd worn the night before. She doubted her father would take her side against Brian—and she simply couldn't bear the embarrassment of confiding in him. The only other person Gaye could think of consulting was her father's companion. Nancy had been an ally in the past . . . but they had never shared these kinds of intimate secrets.

Throughout the day Gaye remained frozen by indecision. She bolted to her feet at last only because she'd heard her husband returning home, his footsteps on the stairs. The dog stood beside her, growling, teeth bared.

Her husband came no farther than the threshold before stopping. He wanted to apologize properly, he said, beg her forgiveness, but he wouldn't come any nearer if she would be frightened. Gaye hesitated, and then, as he admitted to being ashamed of causing her any hurt, forcing her to do things against her own wishes, he began to weep. Finally she opened her arms to him. He promised to do whatever was necessary to get his impulses under control. Then he sealed the promise by presenting her with a velvet covered box he'd kept concealed under his suit jacket—inside, a stunning diamond bracelet.

How foolish and weak of her, she would think later, that all it had taken to be won over was the glint of a few tears and the sparkle of a string of diamonds. Within another month the promises were broken. They'd argued because she'd picked up his clothes from the cleaner, and a jacket was returned with a button missing. What kind of idiot was she, he railed, to accept the item without noticing the flaw, demanding repair? Gaye's attempt to placate him by offering to take it back was refused; he couldn't expect it to be done right unless he did it himself!

She rebuffed him that night when he came to bed wanting her, and he exploded in instant fury. No shouts or insulting remarks, though. He simply overcame her struggle to hold him off. She could only wonder as he forced himself into her whether it could be called rape when it was done by your husband. It was a long time before he was finished; then he put on his robe and went downstairs to make himself a sandwich.

This time she was the one who walked out. As she left the house, the dog at her heels, she saw him at the kitchen table, blithely immersed in reading the day's newspaper while he ate.

The doorman at her father's apartment building told her Dr. Foster wasn't at home, so Gaye sat in the lobby and waited. When her father arrived late from a meeting at the hospital, he was astonished to see her. He took her upstairs and listened patiently through all that poured out. Which wasn't quite the complete story. Some things she was too embarrassed to tell; others too ashamed to admit.

"You've had a hard time, haven't you?" he said sympathetically when she was through. "I'll talk to him."

"Talk to him?" she echoed, numb with disbelief.

"What do you want me to do, Gaye? Go over to your house right now and throw him out? It's *his* house, too. Good Lord, he's . . . my partner, a brilliant doctor who's never done anything personally or professionally—at least not in my experience—but behave correctly, as a perfect gentleman, and—"

"So you don't believe me?"

"I didn't say that. But this is a complicated matter. I owe it to him to hear his side. Not just to determine what's true or false, but for the sake of saving *your* happiness. You married this man because you love him. Is that over and done with? Suppose this could be . . . straightened out?" She didn't have an answer, not yet. "So then what do you want?" her father asked. "Why did you come to me?"

"Because I thought you'd help," she answered plaintively.

"And that's what I want to do. To help you *both*. I care about you both. That's why I'll start by talking to him."

She stayed with her father another week, during which he acted as go-between, bringing back reports of Brian's heartfelt regret and willingness to undergo therapy, carrying forth her terms for returning home. In every way he encouraged the reconciliation.

And there was a tranquil period after she went back. There were arguments, but none more serious than exist in most marriages. Of course, she worried even if it was over some petty matter that it might go too far, as in the past. But Brian seemed to have himself under control. He was seeing a therapist, which evidently made the difference. He continued to function brilliantly in his work, sought after no less than her father. Over several months Gaye's fears of a recurrence receded. Brian suggested the idea of having a child, and he thought a Caribbean holiday might offer a chance to unwind as well as serve as a romantic getaway that might ensure conception. It sounded wonderful, Gaye conceded . . . but she didn't want to put Hero into a kennel. It hadn't been an issue when they went on their honeymoon, but that was more than two years ago. The dog was almost eleven now—getting old for his breed—and she didn't want to leave him in the care of strangers.

It was a flashpoint for Brian. As he saw it, she was making a choice between him and "that goddamn fucking dog." From that point on he was practically a declared enemy of the animal, never willing to share any part of caring for Hero, at night always locking him out of the bedroom. His insensitivity to Gaye escalated, too. The next time they had sex, there was an element of the physical domination that intruded in the past. He held her down, proceeded without preliminaries. When she objected, he acted as though he hadn't heard.

Afterward she lay awake through the whole night, uncertain of what to do. Could she go back to her father?

She went instead to her father's companion, Nancy. Perhaps it was what she ought to have done in the first place, confide in another woman. This one was a therapist, after all, skilled at listening by training, and prepared to empathize. After listening to the story, Nancy declared her willingness to do whatever she could to help. She promised to speak to Gaye's father the next time they were together.

Gaye waited in suspense the next evening. Brian had called to say he'd be home late because her father had asked him to dine with him; there were things they needed to discuss. She guessed the invitation—with a couple of scotches to start, some wine at the meal—was intended to induce an atmosphere in which her father could be stern with Brian, but without rupturing their personal and professional relationship.

She was in the shower, washing her hair before getting into bed, when her husband returned and came striding straight into the bathroom. He yanked open the shower door, gripped her by the arm, and dragged her out of the stall, naked and dripping. "You pathetic bitch," he seethed, shaking her. "Always running to Daddy, trying to pull me down, wreck my career! You really think he'd toss me overboard because you don't like to get fucked? Don't you dare ever do that again!"

As she stared at his face, disfigured by fury and contempt, she thought for one second he might even lose control and beat her. But then he just pushed her roughly back into the shower, where she crumpled onto the floor and stayed for an hour, the water beating down on her like she was a lost dog in the rain.

She should have left that night for good—easy enough to say—but she could only feel crushed, terrified, hopeless. The echo of all those times her mother had screamed at her, accusing her of disloyalty, kept running through her brain. Maybe she had been disloyal again; this humiliation was what she deserved. She went on for more than a week in that state, operating in a veritably schizophrenic drift. She went off to her job each day and performed capably, no one aware of what she was suffering in her private life. Each evening she returned home and fell back into a childlike inability to take charge of her life. She ought to leave, she knew, ought to seek help—yet she couldn't. All she was able to do was mutely endure his behavior of the moment—displays of affection interspersed with cruelties, demands in the bedroom that became even more debasing, practically torturous.

Then one Sunday morning the fog cleared. He had been called away early to the hospital by the sudden availability of a heart for a transplant candidate. While he operated, Gaye faced hours of being alone. She wasn't a religious person, but when she heard the sound of bells wafting very faintly on the morning air from a church some distance away, it prompted her to seek a solution in prayer. Like a small child at bedtime, she knelt by her bed and simply asked for help.

Whether it was a message from a divine source or simply a private admission of despair that cracked through her inertia, she couldn't say. But as soon as she rose from her knees, the old homily was in her mind: *God helps those who help themselves.* She packed two suitcases, then sat at the kitchen table composing a long letter to him. She wrote of good memories, regrets, sympathy for the extraordinary stresses in his work, and of retaining still the slim hope that somehow he might get control of his demons. But she didn't offer any hope of reconciliation. Looking back, she was no longer sure she had truly loved him—or if the emotion that had thrust them together was only the desperate wish not to disappoint her father. How else could she have given herself to a man so wrong for the needs of her own heart and soul, been so blind to his true nature? She ended the letter by telling him she didn't know yet where she would be living—it wasn't always easy to find a good sublet where a dog was allowed. Her workplace would have to be their contact point.

The first call to the animal hospital came from her father, again the intermediary. Her response was that she needed some time away, and Brian should take time as well to consider his options. But if there was to be any hope, she said, he would have to speak for himself. Before hanging up, her father appealed for her to be discreet. Brian's work was valuable, he explained, and shouldn't be "compromised."

She moved from a hotel to a sublet apartment, and there was a month during which he made no contact. Then one day she emerged from work to find him waiting outside. He asked her to get in his car and go with him for a nice dinner somewhere so they could talk. Only at that moment did she discover the revolution that had occurred in their relationship: She was afraid to be alone with him, afraid of the unpredictable impulses that might be sparked by something she said or did. So she made excuses—she had plans for the evening; he'd have to call in advance if he wanted to see her.

It was enough to cause the very eruption she feared. She was still his wife, he said, she had no right to refuse him! Then he tried to force her into the car. She broke away, ran back into the animal hospital, and stayed there, reassured by the presence of coworkers, until she was sure he had gone.

One veterinary technician who had witnessed Gaye's anxiety at leaving work over the next few weeks—never departing alone, always seeking someone to walk her to her car—suggested she ought to consult a lawyer, and get a restraining order, to keep her threatening spouse at bay.

Mindful of her father's caution to act with discretion, Gaye was reluctant to put anything on the public record. Then one night, when, as she always did, she took Hero out to accompany her as she jogged, Brian pulled his car up beside her in the street. He drove slowly alongside, urging her to come out with him for a drink after she brought the dog back home. She told him she'd leave the dog, then come back out to the car. But that was only a stratagem to get home again safely.

When she didn't return to him, he rang her doorbell. She talked to him through the intercom: she'd be willing to see him, but during the day, in a public place. It didn't satisfy him. He kept trying to cajole her into coming out—or letting him in. That very persistence began to seem threatening. "Go home, Brian," she told him. "Please. We'll talk tomorrow."

"Why not now? Nothing's going to change. Don't you understand?" he said, as if it was meant to be charming. "You're never going to get away from me. Never ever. I love you too much to ever let you go."

Why should it terrify her so to hear this, words that if said in another context, by another person—by the man she could recall loving so much on her wedding day—would have been a welcome pledge? Tonight they constituted a threat. She would have called the police . . . except that his voice stopped coming through the intercom, and when she looked out her window she saw that his car was no longer in front of the apartment building.

The next morning Gaye called the woman lawyer recommended by her friend at the animal hospital. She discussed filing for divorce—and getting a restraining order. In regard to the latter, she was advised to act moderately. Her husband's words did not represent an actual threat. Beyond some unpleasant grabbing and pushing in previous encounters, had he done her any real harm? To take steps that could damage the public reputation of a doctor esteemed for his valuable work was a serious matter. To act on no more than what Gaye described ran the risk of predisposing a judge against her, making her appear hysterical and vindictive, her husband the wounded party.

Gaye instructed the lawyer simply to notify Brian by letter that she would be filing for divorce, and all further contact should be through the lawyer's office. The letter mentioned that a restraining order would be sought only if he harassed Gaye further at her home or place of work.

Since the night he'd accosted her while she was jogging, Gaye had taken Hero out for his exercise as soon as she returned from work, while the streets were more populated. But a night came when she let it wait until after she'd returned from dinner with a friend from vet school who was visiting town. In recent weeks there had been no sign of Brian; it seemed the lawyer's letter had done its job. She had walked a couple of blocks and turned a corner to go back when the car came screeching to a stop alongside. Brian was already getting out when she turned, and she had only to see his face to know he was in a volcanic rage.

He waved a piece of paper in one hand as he charged toward her, ranting, "What the fuck is this? You're going to set the law onto me? For what?"

The dog was on a leash, but he sprang forward to defend her so forcefully that the strap yanked free from Gaye's hand. "Hero, no—stay!" she shouted, and the dog instantly planted himself, though he kept growling, his teeth bared menacingly. Brian kept his distance.

"I want a divorce, that's all," she said. "I haven't done anything else. But you're out of control, Brian, and—"

"Out of control?" The words inflamed him further. "How the hell could I do my work if I didn't have the most *perfect* control? I just don't like being threatened with this legal bullshit!"

The dog tilted forward, as if he might break from his stance. Gaye took a couple of steps forward and bent down to pick up the leash.

"I'm not worried about your damn dog," Brian said. "Let him bite me—that'll be the end of him."

"Brian, please," she appealed, "leave us alone."

" 'Us,' you say! Not even 'me.' It's you and that fucking dog—like you're more married to him than me. If you weren't so crazy about that dog maybe things would be different."

"What's wrong with you?" Gaye pleaded. "Why keep this up? If all you want to do is hurt me, it's better for both of us if—"

"Don't tell me what's better," he screamed even louder. "Just try to look at it my way!"

His way? It dawned on her that he wasn't merely enraged. Where she was concerned, he had lost his hold on reality. "There's no point in talking any more," she said, backing away. She had to pull Hero with her because he continued straining at the leash, staying between her and the threat.

Brian watched them go without speaking, but from the expression on his face it was clear the rage was still mushrooming up within him. Never taking her eyes from him, Gaye kept edging backward until there was a gap of thirty yards. Then, glancing over her shoulder, she turned and started to jog. The dog trotted along, and she dropped the leash so they could both move more freely. She had almost reached the corner to begin circling back to her apartment building when she glanced over her shoulder once more and was relieved to see her husband getting into his car. Giving up. She turned the corner, and had jogged halfway along the next block when the squeal of tires pierced her ears. With another backward look she saw the car wheeling around the corner, roaring toward her. It was a one-way street, the direction opposite to the car's, but it was late and there was no traffic, nothing to keep it from bearing down. Gaye broke into a panicked run. If she could get to the next corner, there was a busier two-way street—

She could hear the engine roaring closer. Shooting another glance backward she saw that he'd driven half up onto the sidewalk, and the car was going too fast to outrun.

A split-second decision. She stopped, whirled around, and glared defiantly into the headlights. Let him get out, rant some more, exhaust his anger. Hero would protect her.

The moment she turned, he applied the brakes. The car skidded to a stop no more than a couple of feet away. As if the dog understood exactly what was happening, what he needed to do, he ran to the driver's side and got up on his hind legs to paw relentlessly at the window while he barked ferociously, keeping the threat at bay.

The car faced her, unmoving, headlights blinding her. But her husband didn't try to get out. Gaye's heart pounded from the exertion of her run and the terror of realizing how close she was to death: If he gave in to the impulse to thrust his foot down on the accelerator . . .

The stalemate went on for a minute . . . two. She stood in the headlights trying to catch her breath. The car confronted her, motor idling, her husband a faceless shadow behind the glare. The dog's claws scratched at the window glass, and his fierce barking continued ceaselessly.

Then from a window somewhere along the street a man shouted roughly, "Can't you make that damn dog shut up?"

That ended the crisis, she thought. People were at their windows, witnesses; nothing would happen now. "C'mon, Hero," she called, "let's go!" She started away. The dog stopped barking, but he didn't move from the car. "C'mon, boy, we're going home."

At last he trotted slowly after her. She clapped her hands, which usually made the dog move faster, but this time he seemed oddly reluctant to leave. After prancing forward a few yards, he'd halt and look back at the car until Gaye summoned him again. The car continued to idle where it had stopped.

Finally she was able to continue ahead with the dog at her side. They were almost at the corner when she realized Hero had stopped once more. She turned—and what she saw made her heart stop. The car was careening toward her again, squirreling back and forth across the curb, but coming on, coming at her. And the dog was standing squarely in the path, barking as if he thought his ferocious protest might by itself be enough of a barrier to save her.

"Hero!" She shrieked the dog's name with every ounce of breath she could put behind it. But he didn't move—while the car sped nearer. Impelled by the idea that she could pull him out of the deadly path, she started forward—then, horrified, she saw the animal actually spring toward the car as if believing the thrust of his body against the onrushing mass might stop it. Before Gaye had gone two steps it was too late. The car thudded into the animal, tossing him into the air and off to the side. The car swerved off the sidewalk, back into the street.

For an instant she remained wide-eyed with horror and disbelief, paralyzed. Then, as she watched the car speed off, a single word ripped from her throat: "Murderer!"

The taillights disappeared around the corner, and she ran to the dog.

No life was left in the mangled heap of blood-soaked fur. Gaye was still on her knees crying when a police car came, called by someone in a building on the street. The caller left no name; no one seemed to think it was worth tracking down. A dog had been hit by a car. No big deal.

That night, after bringing Hero's body to the animal hospital and preparing him to go to the pet crematory in the morning, Gaye moved from her sublet to a motel on the outskirts of Philadelphia. In the morning she called the partners who operated the animal hospital to explain that a family emergency required her to leave work immediately. She also instructed her lawyer to continue divorce proceedings, but not to go forward with the restraining order. It wouldn't stop Brian from coming again, she knew—she'd read enough stories in the tabloids of women stabbed or shot to death by husbands under court orders to stay away. He was the sort of man who made his own rules.

What she had to do from this day forth was to stay clear of him until she could find a place to start over.

Chapter 7

Gaye was settling into a satisfying routine at Bible Hill. She could feel her veterinary skills being refined and expanded by working alongside both of the Bennetts. From her first day on the job she'd been allowed to take on a full schedule of treating the domestic animals with which she had experience. By the third week she was accompanying Frankie on farm calls, being tutored by her in diagnosing and treating the ailments of farm animals. She began to participate in routine procedures she'd studied in vet school, like animal vaccination and calving. The older woman remained irascible in their interactions—which might have been unbearable if Gaye hadn't wisely insisted on living apart from the Bennetts. Yet Gaye soon realized that Frankie Bennett, like her husband, was an exceptional vet from whom there was much to learn. If she was—as Flo Campbell had said—a bit of a pill, it was a pill worth swallowing. The stresses put upon her by Will's illness were probably more to blame for her being ill-tempered than any character flaw.

Even over a few weeks, Will's condition had noticeably declined. The day he had welcomed Gaye to Bible Hill was the last time she saw him capable of rising to his feet. He still had reasonable use of his hands, and retained his optimism . . . yet it could only be weeks before his dexterity suffered to the extent that he would be forced to give up performing any surgery.

Watching his deterioration was not the only thing that made this job more demanding than her previous position. As Gaye had learned on arriving, the Bennetts expected her to be on call around the clock. By the end of October, when she began fully sharing the load of farm calls, she found herself being summoned away late at night—even awakened in the predawn hours—two or three times each week to deliver a colt or calf, or just to make a house call on an elderly lady upset because her cat had licked up some dish powder. She took it in stride, though.

Away from work, she was finding a way of life that helped to heal her battered spirit. Her initial bouts of nerves at living alone had subsided. She loved the place she'd found, enjoyed rediscovering solitary pleasures she had known before surrendering herself to marriage. To sit by a log fire while the night wind blew hard outside and relax into reading a bestseller, or watch a rented movie on the VCR, or try some new recipe from a Sunday supplement (even if it was too much to eat alone), were delicious experiences. The business Millie Howell ran overhead was unobtrusive, as was the landlady herself. Millie had stopped by a few times to make sure Gaye had enough heat and hot water, and had slipped in a few nonlandlady questions—was Gaye making friends in town?—gently indicating a readiness to lend a more welcoming hand if ever it was wanted. But Millie also took the hints that Gaye was content with her solitude.

Gaye also enjoyed exploring the quiet rural surroundings. She went on long contemplative walks over the road that passed through the covered bridge, then meandered past plowed fields and forested hills. She would be reminded then of how sweet it had been to have Hero trotting along with her on their walks, scampering after any old stick she plucked off the ground for a game of fetch. At times she could forget he wasn't there: A breeze rustling a pile of dead leaves at the roadside would cause her to turn, fully expecting to see him snuffling along behind her. This, and other small occurrences, could revive that same curious belief—or was it wishful longing?—that his protective spirit still hovered around her. Several times she had awakened in the small hours of the night because of a noise, or a need for the toilet, or for no reason; and when she got out of bed to go to the bathroom, or get a drink, or assure herself the doors and windows were secure, she would find herself taking a high step over that place at the foot of her bed where he had always slept, as if he were lying there in the dark. A Pavlovian response, sure, conditioned by all the years of taking that high step in the dark. When she turned the lights on there was nothing. And yet . . . with the lights off, there was that ever-so-faint static prickle on the skin of her legs as they passed over that place where his fur would be. Conditioning, imagination, there were all sorts of rational ways to explain it. But what Gaye liked to believe was that a good soul, whether human, dog, or butterfly, didn't disappear into nothingness. The belief allowed her to relinquish some of the anger and bitterness she felt toward her husband. Those feelings, the hatred they engendered—and the fear— would only keep her tied to him. She needed to be free.

With each passing day she did feel more liberated, surer of the choice she had made to cut loose. Though she knew she still needed to be careful. If Brian were to learn where she'd gone, she felt certain he would follow. *Never ever.* The echo of that pledge of warped love was still in her ears.

Nor was she more inclined to communicate with her father. Their last contact had been the morning after that awful night when the dog had been killed. Still hysterical, she'd phoned to tell him what Brian had done.

"Calm down, kiddo," he'd said. "I know how much you loved that dog, and it's terrible to lose him. But I'm sure Brian couldn't have done such a thing deliberately. He's a man who's dedicated to saving lives, not a cold-blooded—"

She'd hung up right then, convinced there was no hope. If he'd known where she was, he would tell Brian, convinced it was a way of helping them toward the reconciliation *he* wanted. Never mind her own wishes.

So she continued to practice the same meticulous precautions begun with her flight from Philadelphia, when she'd told no one she was leaving or where she was going. To this day even the lawyer handling the divorce didn't know exactly where she was. Gaye maintained contact with her by e-mail and weekly phone calls, but still hadn't provided an address. She would be safe, Gaye felt, only as long as she guarded her secrets.

★   ★   ★

In this corner of New Hampshire, the state line followed the Connecticut River—which was the stream that flowed beneath the covered bridge and past the meadow at the rear of Gaye's apartment. Being near the line, the Bible Hill Animal Clinic served the needs of many farmers on the Vermont side. One morning, after delivering a calf at a Vermont farm, Gaye drove to the nearest town. On the phone with her lawyer the day before, she'd been told there were papers for the divorce requiring her signature; she needed a mailing address to receive them. While she had used the West Greenlea post office to receive the trunk of new clothes she'd shipped to herself, for *these* documents—which others would see—she wanted to camouflage her whereabouts.

The town in Vermont to which she drove was Bartlett Mills. Of similar size to West Greenlea, it had a more prosperous aspect, with larger homes, and stores that included a florist, a couple of upscale clothing boutiques, and a gourmet food and wine shop. As its name indicated, it had once been a center for milling the wool produced on sheep farms in the area; but then Southern competition and centralization of the fabric industries had closed the mills. The town had suffered a long period of decline until twenty years ago, when development of a ski resort not far away spurred revival. Bartlett Mills was now an affluent community that included local professionals and people from elsewhere who kept second homes near the winter skiing and for summer getaways.

The town's post office was a small white building about the size of a one-car garage at one end of the street. Inside, Gaye found the space taken up by a front counter with a large sorting area behind it, and an alcove to one side with a wall of keyed boxes. Less conventional was the music of a Gregorian chant that issued from a stereo on a shelf in the sorting area, and the smell of incense in the air. Most unusual was the lone attendant who met Gaye at the counter, a woman wearing a brightly colored floor-length gown, with a string of colored ceramic beads the size of quails' eggs around her neck. Her long hair hung loose around her shoulders, rippling down almost to her waist, and was the color of pumpkins—obviously from dye. The wrinkled parchmentlike skin of her face and hands indicated her age to be somewhere on the shady side of seventy. "What can I do for you, dear?" she said.

"I need to sign up for a box."

The colorful postmistress slapped an application form and a pen down on the counter. "Haven't seen you around town before, have I?" she asked, as Gaye began filling out her name atop the form.

"No." Gaye stared down at the next blank requiring an address. "I don't have a permanent address," she said. "I've been staying at . . . bed-and-breakfasts in the area."

"More than one. . . ." the postmistress remarked with a coy edge.

Gaye felt the hapless guilt of a child caught in a lie. She would have backed out the door, except that she had visions of the woman immediately phoning every other post office in the area with warnings to "be on the lookout for . . ."

"Listen, dear," the woman broke into Gaye's guilty silence, "read ahead on that form; you'll see two pieces of ID are required, and one should establish a local residence—like a utility bill in your name. Without that I can't give you what you need." The blue eyes she fixed on Gaye were clear and bright despite her age. Gaye felt she could intuit her secrets—had guessed, at the least, that her "need" involved subterfuge.

"Look, I'm not a spy or a terrorist," Gaye said. "All I want is a place to collect my mail without . . . complications."

"I understand. But there are post office regulations, and it'll be my job to carry 'em out till the day they carry *me* out."

In a government office where incense burned as plain chants filled the air, and the official in charge was gotten up like a benign sorceress, it seemed faintly absurd to be lectured on regulations. But there was no use arguing. Gaye crumpled up the application form and started out. The voice from behind stopped her.

"I've an idea for you, dearie. . . ." Gaye looked back and the woman went on. "When you leave, walk up the street to the left and you'll see a general store. Fella who owns it, Bunker Chatsworth, he takes in FedEx, UPS—all the stuff I'm not allowed to accept. He'll probably accept your mail for you, too." With a wink the woman added, "And you won't even have to fill out a form."

The recognition of her furtiveness embarrassed Gaye. "Thank you," she said quietly. "I'll try that."

The general store wasn't hard to spot. Lined up across its open porch were barrels and boxes overflowing with a miscellany of tools and brooms, candles and lacquered pinecones, wax fruit and peppermint sticks, cheap plastic toys like water pistols and red firemen's hats for children. Gaye climbed the wooden steps and entered the old-fashioned emporium. An array of another thousand disparate items was distributed along several aisles reaching back into a murky limbo. In a cleared patch at the front, a couple of rocking chairs flanked a potbellied stove radiating warmth. A brown-and-white spaniel—a springer, Gaye thought—was sprawled by the stove, and one of the chairs was occupied by a man sucking on a corncob pipe. He wore khaki pants, a candy-striped shirt, and suspenders, and had an old panama hat tilted back on his head, spikes of its unraveling straw poking out at odd angles.

"Mr. Chatsworth, I was sent over by—"

The man yanked the pipe from his mouth. "Bunky's gone to the back," he said, shooting a thumb over his shoulder. "I'm just passin' the time. Plant yourself. He'll just be a minute." He gestured to the empty rocker and stuck the the pipe back between his lips.

"Think I'll just look around," Gaye said.

She wandered along an aisle with bins of cheese graters, bicycle pumps, and packages of paper plates and cups, until a figure emerged from the rear. He was rangier than the man in the rocker, but dressed almost identically except without a hat. His narrow face might have seemed stern, except the cowlick of straight iron-gray hair that fell across his forehead gave him a boyish quality.

Gaye approached him. "Mr. Chatsworth?"

He came around to walk up the same aisle. "Who wants to know?"

"I'm Dr. Foster." The professional title might earn some extra consideration. "I was told you might accept mail for me here."

He came closer. "Expecting a lot of mail or a little?"

"Not much, but I'll be staying in the area for a while."

There were plenty more questions he might have asked—like why she wasn't using the post office—but he operated with traditional New England reticence. After another moment of inspection, he said, "Sure, I'll do that. Come over here and put your name down for me."

He led her to a desk in the middle of the jumble, atop which sat an old chrome-plated cash register side by side with an electronic credit-card reader. Chatsworth pulled an invoice pad and pencil from a drawer and pushed them across the desk. Gaye wrote down the maiden name she'd been using, then put a slash after it and added *Leahy*. "That's my married name," she explained. "Mail might be addressed with one or the other."

He tore her writing from the pad, turned to a large corkboard at one side of the desk, and tacked the paper to it with a pushpin. Gaye noticed similar name slips pinned up along with mail. "I'll stop in every few days," she said.

"Any day but Sunday . . ." He tore another sheet from an invoice pad and gave it to her. "Mailing address is on there."

"This is very kind of you, Mr. Chatsworth."

"Nothin' to it. And call me Bunky or I won't know who you're talkin' to."

She said good-bye and started up the aisle, then grabbed a cheese grater and went back to pay.

"Service is free," he said, guessing rightly that the purchase was a dividend of her gratitude. "Don't have to buy some fool thing every time you come in."

"I can really use a cheese grater," she said.

He cocked an eyebrow and smiled, before ringing up $3.89 on the old cash register.

Her routine began including trips to Bartlett Mills at least once a week. She'd pick up mail forwarded via her lawyer, along with any legal papers, then stay to prepare her replies so they could be mailed off with the Vermont postmark. Letters from the lawyer reported that contacts with Brian had been amiable; he expressed regret for

Gaye's determination to proceed with a quick divorce, but promised to cooperate. He had even made reference to having done "something unforgivable" for which he was feeling terribly guilty. Her father had called the lawyer, too, expressing the wish to hear from his daughter, asking that it be relayed to her; but he was said to understand her wish for "a cooling-off period."

Yet even if the need for caution had abated, Gaye wouldn't have changed her mail arrangements. Going to the Mills, as local people called it, was a welcome part of her routine. The taciturn general-store owner, and the eccentric postmistress whom she saw when sending off replies, were people with whom she felt it was easier to share a few minutes of small talk or even reveal some minor personal truth because they existed in another orbit than where she worked or lived. She began opening her mail in the general store rather than walking outside first. And, when preparing things to mail back, she'd sit in one of the rocking chairs and warm herself by the stove. Bunky Chatsworth never pried, but Gaye stopped monitoring every word or expression to conceal her problems. After opening the first bill from her lawyer, she let out an involuntary gasp at the amount— so she told him why, and that the bill was to a lawyer handling her divorce. When she noticed the spaniel in the store pawing at his ears more than normal, Gaye discovered he had mites, and invited Bunky to bring the dog to Bible Hill for a free checkup, revealing at last exactly the kind of doctor she was.

The postmistress was a different matter. Though no less well-meaning she was unabashedly eager to learn everything she could about Gaye or anyone else who walked into her domain. If Gaye brought in envelopes to weigh for postage, the address would be noticed and used in an effort to elicit information. "Attorneys-at-law, eh?" the woman remarked, when Gaye was sending off documents. "Does that explain why you're hiding away up here? On the lam from a subpeenie?"

"No, I am not on the lam," Gaye countered with mock indignation. By now the old woman's snooping struck her as more amusing than annoying. It would have been cause for alarm if it were less brazen and out in the open.

"Just hard to figure why a pretty girl like you sticks herself away all by her lonesome. I mean, if you're not a moll for Bugsy somebody, or in a witness perfection program 'cause you're one of them Sopranos."

Nosy as she was, Dot Callan ran her little piece of the U.S. government in a way that gave Gaye a lift whenever she walked in, as it did for most of her customers. There was, for example, her regular opera contest. She would put one of her Maria Callas recordings on her stereo, and post office visitors would be invited to hit Maria's highest notes along with the diva. Anyone who managed it received a free first-class stamp.

But Dot's main pastime was ferreting out information, and she used means other than straight interrogation to get the job done—like the tarot cards with which she idly amused herself whenever the counter was quiet. Whoever walked in would be offered a "reading," which of course involved having a few questions answered. Then, too, there were her cordialities.

"Thanksgiving's coming up," she said when Gaye made a mail run in mid-November. "Got some special holiday stamps. Where you plannin' to be, by the way?"

Gaye wasn't even ready with a lie. She had totally forgotten about the holiday. "I haven't decided yet."

"No place to go? Why not come over to my place? It'll be just me and my boy. I'll bet you and him would get along a treat."

So Dot was looking to match up her son. Given the old lady's age, her "boy" must be no youngster, and his single status didn't augur well for his attributes. Even if she were ready to look for a new relationship, meeting the son of this eccentric old woman certainly wouldn't be the place to start. "Thanks very much, Dot," she said. "I appreciate the invitation. But like most folks at Thanksgiving, I'll be going home."

Her *new* home, but it provided a polite excuse.

The first big snow hit in the middle of the week before Thanksgiving, a steady daylong fall that left the countryside sparkling white. Gaye had a few appointments on Thursday morning, including a surgery to spay a cat, but the afternoon was clear. She caught up with a little paperwork, but then Will told her to take the rest of the day off.

"Much too nice a day to stay cooped up here," he said.

"Suppose I take you out for a drive?" she offered. She didn't mind driving the truck now: She'd found a good mechanic in town who gave her a valve job and new shocks for under three hundred dollars. "The hills are so beautiful."

"No, I'm a little tired. Gonna stay with Frankie and take it easy." More and more that was his answer when there was nothing to keep him at the clinic.

The sun was shining when Gaye left work, the snow-covered hills sparkling brilliantly under a china-blue sky, and she was seized by an urge to use the special day to do something active. She thought then of Diamond Valley, the ski resort not far from Bartlett Mills.

She hadn't skied in more than twenty years. Gaye couldn't mark the last time exactly, except she knew it wasn't too long after her parents had split up. There had been several ski holidays prior to that time, holiday weeks spent in Colorado or Utah—her father loved the sport. After the separation he had taken Gaye away to Vermont by himself, driving home the point that "things don't have to change just because you're no longer with Mommy."

Of course, things *were* different. Perhaps that was why she hadn't wanted to go skiing since that time. Today, though, without the need to show off anything to her father, she thought she might enjoy it again.

Diamond Valley wasn't as big as some of other popular Vermont ski centers, but it had a good range of slopes from the steep black diamond runs to the gentler nursery hills good for learning. Arriving on a weekday, and before the school holiday, Gaye was pleased to see the lifts fairly empty; there would be little waiting. She left her heavy parka in the truck, then went to one of the ski shops at the base of the mountain to rent equipment and to complete her outfit—she was already wearing a wool sweater—with a pair of ski pants.

At the hutch where they sold lift tickets, she hesitated when offered the special discount for a series of lessons with a five-day ticket. She'd been a good skier as a child, and was curious to see how much might come back by itself. But she was loath to commit herself to five days before she knew if even one would be fun. She bought a ticket just for the afternoon, and took the short lift up to the top of the nursery slope to fool around on her own

After nearly an hour of flopping over, struggling back to her feet, laboriously clashing her skis to "herringbone" back to where she could again glide down a few feet before taking another tumble, it was plain the skill she'd had twenty-odd years ago wasn't going to return by magic. Still, she wasn't ready to seek instruction. Right now she was simultaneously sweating from her effort and chilled by the cold, bones and muscles aching from the bruising and twisting of trying to move around on these damn barrel staves that made each foot feel twelve feet long. Her fondness for skiing might never return, she thought. Gaye released her bindings and shouldered the skis so she could move more easily across the snow on her way back to the shops.

Her path took her past the loading area for chairlifts that gave access to the more demanding trails, and she kept her eye on the hillsides in case she had to dodge out of the way of hotdoggers who came swooping down, racing for the chairs to take them back to the top. That was how she happened to spot the two men descending at high speed, zigzagging across a steep slope in perfect unison, movements so closely matched, they seemed almost to be manacled together. They were on a path that would intersect with hers if she kept walking, so she stopped and waited for them to go past. As they zoomed nearer, Gaye saw they were indeed joined—after a fashion. The man in front was holding one of his poles straight out behind him, and the man following—staying slightly to one side—had a grip on the ring near the tip of the pole. Gaye noticed, too, that unlike the man in the lead, the second man wasn't wearing ski goggles; dark lenses covered his eyes, but in ordinary eyeglass frames, and so dark they appeared opaque. It struck Gaye now that the reason the second man was holding on to the pole, staying so close, could be that he was blind. It wasn't because he needed any help to ski. He was beautifully balanced, matching his path and his speed to the man leading him in a way that might be possible only by someone who didn't rely on sight at all, but could fine-tune his movement according to an acute sensitivity to the sound of the snow being cut by the skier in front, or the feel of the contours of the mountainside rushing beneath his own skis.

Gaye watched admiringly as the two men pulled up together in a spray of snow just by the lift. "Another run?" she heard the man in front ebulliently shout to the other.

"Hey," the blind man called back, "I'll stay till it gets dark!"

The self-deprecating humor was clearly deliberate, because the first man laughed and gave the other a playful push before they climbed together into the next free chair and rode away up the mountain.

And you're going home? Gaye chided herself. *You've got the good luck to be able to enjoy this day on this mountain with all your senses, and you're giving up after one measly hour?* She stepped into her bindings again. Damned if she'd even allow herself a lesson until she'd pushed herself to the limit.

Trudging back to the nursery slope, Gaye wondered how many other times in her life she might have given up too soon. In her marriage? No, she'd really tried, but she couldn't have gone on with that another day. With her mother, then? Had she tried hard enough to understand the torments of a woman abandoned, unable to hold on to her only child? Maybe there was no general lesson to be learned, except that there had been a time in the past when she'd loved to ski, and she'd been good at it, and no matter what had happened in her life to sour her on it, it was time to let go of blame and regret, and let herself recapture the pleasure.

Whipped along by that goal, she was skiing again by the end of the day. Aching like hell, yes, but at some point the "muscle memory" had kicked in, and she was gliding down an intermediate slope without a fall, not racing, but turning smoothly, keeping her balance. The cool wind on her face felt good, and what felt even better was to have found her groove by an exercise of will, a refusal to give up. She'd had enough for today . . . but she'd come back.

She was walking away from the ski shop after turning in her rental when she spotted the blind man waiting in the area where skiers could catch a shuttle bus or be picked up by a ride. She had an impulse to run over and thank him for the part he'd played in her turnaround, but a station wagon pulled up to the curb, driven by his friend. The blind man opened the door, and a gorgeous gold-and-black German shepherd dog jumped out of the passenger seat. The size and coloring were so similar to Hero's that Gaye was momentarily startled, as if by the materialization of a ghost. The blind man stooped and embraced the dog—his guide dog, of course, left to sleep in the car while his master skied. Gaye hung back, watching. How she missed having that kind of affection, the selfless protective devotion! Except to seek it too quickly in a replacement seemed to belittle the love she had felt for the animal she'd lost. No less than with people, there had to be a period of mourning, of coming to terms with loss.

After greeting his guide dog, the blind man opened the rear door of the station wagon for the animal to jump in, then got into the front seat. Because he'd inspired her, and because the dog looked so much like her own, Gaye was drawn even more to speak to him. But before she could move a step, the car drove off.

She smiled off the small disappointment and headed for her own car. She'd surely be coming back to Diamond Valley on days off throughout the winter, working to improve. Sooner or later she might bump into the blind man and have a chance to thank him.

Chapter 8

On the Friday before Thanksgiving week, Will told Gaye to take the Wednesday off so she could enjoy a long holiday weekend in Philadelphia. She hadn't said a word about going there; she guessed his assumption arose from the mention of her ties to the city over tea the day she'd arrived, coupled with the fact that it was a traditional time for families to gather. In fact, in her two months at the clinic, Gaye had yet to reveal anything of her personal problems. She thanked Will, but explained she would be at work as usual through the weekend.

The Thanksgiving holiday had never really been a good time for her. For as long as Gaye could remember, its emphasis on jolly family celebrations of abundance and good fortune had contrasted starkly with what she experienced: her mother absent, the meal made by a maid or eaten in a restaurant, her father always called away to a hospital—and later Brian, the only child of a widowed mother, similarly busy. Gaye had never sat down to a Thanksgiving dinner that matched the festive image depicted in TV commercials. She preferred to be alone and eat what she pleased than to submit to one more charade of festive tradition.

But hearing she wouldn't be with family, Will insisted she observe the holiday with him and Frankie. "We're setting a place, saving the drumstick for you, and that's that. Don't let us down."

She had to relent. "All right, thanks. But make mine white meat."

The dinner proved to be precisely the sort of strained, melancholy gathering she'd anticipated. With Frankie out of sorts from all the work of having prepared far too much food for just the three of them, Gaye herself a refugee from domestic disaster, and Will in the throes of a wasting disease, they made a sad group. Will's plight was particularly hard to watch at a feast table, as Gaye could see the developing symptoms of dysphagia—difficulty in swallowing—which he tried to hide by cutting the tiniest morsels of solid food, and shielding his winces by rubbing his face with a hand or his napkin. The poignancy was only heightened by Frankie's reminiscences of past Thanksgivings, when there would be as many as two dozen at her table, including friends from the area and the Bennett children.

Family being a natural topic of conversation on this holiday, the Bennetts shared details about their two children, an older daughter and a son, and the reasons they were absent. The daughter had gone to Harvard Law School, which led to a position as a corporate attorney attached to the Paris office of a large American firm; there she had married a Frenchman and was pregnant now with their third child. The Bennetts spoke with pride about the life their daughter had made, traveling so far from "this little corner of New Hampshire."

They had less to say about their son. He was on the West Coast, not married. He'd gone out there years ago because he was interested in computers, and that was where high-tech companies were turning people with computer knowledge into millionaires. "But it hasn't worked out for him," Frankie concluded. Her generally dour tone made it sound like the boy's life was already over.

"There's time yet," Will put in, always ready to add a brighter note to his wife's pessimism.

After receiving some insight from the Bennetts into their family, Gaye felt she ought to reciprocate with at least a few details about her own. She tried to oblige without giving too much away, explaining that she hadn't gone home because she knew her father was busy, and dredging up a few marginally pleasant memories of past holidays, like the time her father had been able to schedule a consultation in New York so that she could see the huge parade Macy's sponsored on Thanksgiving Day. But after two hours of dodging the Bennetts' efforts to probe her life, there could be no doubt she was deliberately working to preserve anonymity. By the time Frankie brought out her homemade pecan pie, accompanied even by the most harmless questions—"Did you always have pumpkin pie at your Thanksgivings? Do you like pecan?"—Will already felt obligated to protect Gaye from interrogation. "Just cut her a piece," he told Frankie. "She doesn't have to eat it if she doesn't like it."

"Pecan's fine," Gaye said. Self-conscious now about all her evasiveness, she added, "I think I ought to tell you both that I'm not actually in touch with my family at all. My mother died many years ago, and my dad . . . well, he has a very successful medical practice with a man I had to . . . to separate from. The two of them get along just fine, but I'm here because I had to get away from . . . from everything that *was*—and I've been here long enough now to know it was the right thing to do. You've been very good to me, both of you, and I'm content here. So please don't be offended if I keep to myself. It's very painful for me to talk about the way things have been. I just want to look ahead, not back." She left it there and picked up her fork.

That pretty much killed conversation over coffee and dessert. Gaye declined a second cup of coffee, thanked them for a wonderful meal, and excused herself. Will went with her to the door, and she told him she'd be in the office tomorrow morning as usual.

"There's nothing booked for tomorrow," he said. "Lori has the day off, so there's no reason for you to come in if you'd also like—"

"I'll be there," she repeated. "I have some follow-up lab tests I can do, and I'm interested in having a look at that crow."

Veterinary centers around the country were cooperating with the Centers for Disease Control in a program to track the epidemiological status of West Nile virus. Since a common indicator of its presence was its effect on birds—which could die from eating insects that carried the disease—local farmers had been notified to bring any dead birds they came across to local vets. The carcasses were frozen for collection by the CDC, or qualified veterinarians might examine the animals to see if some cause other than West Nile was responsible for the death. The freezer at Bible Hill presently contained the carcass of a crow turned in three days ago that Gaye wanted to investigate.

Will remained by the door as she went out. "Gaye," he called as she opened the door to the truck, "you mean it, I hope. You really are happy here?"

Content, she'd said, not *happy.* But she nodded.

"Good. Because having you . . . well, I don't think we could've done better . . . and I know Frankie can be a little off-putting at times."

"Frankie's a wonderful woman. She's got a lot to deal with."

"Yes, she does. I just wasn't sure if it's because of her . . . that you don't seem completely comfortable with us. You know, it can help to have people to talk to—especially when you've been through a hard time."

She was moved by his concern, and a wave of compassionate caring swept over her as she looked at him. Ravaged and humbled by a cruel disease, yet he was worried about *her.* Maybe it was because of the holiday—its link to family—and the lost connections they were both feeling today, but at that moment a bond was formed in which they accepted each other as partially replacing the missing piece.

Gaye came back to the door. Standing by his wheelchair, she grasped his hand. "One of these days, Dr. Will, I may very well have a lot of things I'll need to get off my chest. This isn't the day. But whenever it comes, I know there couldn't be a better guy to talk to." She bent down and kissed him on the cheek. "And please tell Frankie I'll take her pecan pie over pumpkin any old day."

Friday at the clinic was dead quiet. Will came in early, and Gaye made coffee for both of them—"So this is what it's supposed to taste like," he said when she gave him his cup—then they went to work separately. He pushed some papers around on his desk, while she ran blood screens on some animals that had been brought in before Thursday, as well as routine tests on a dairy herd Frankie was monitoring for hypocalcemia, the condition also known as milk fever or "sad cow syndrome" that was often a cause of diminished milk production. At noon, Will said he was going to have lunch with Frankie, then take a nap. Gaye didn't expect him to return.

She had looked forward to this opportunity to work by herself, and balance the everyday demands of the job with a task related more to research. Earlier that morning she had moved the carcass of the dead crow from the freezer to thaw in the surgical area. While it was still in the frozen state, she had excised some tissue samples and returned them to the freezer to use later for preparing slides of possibly infected tissue for microscopic examination. Now she put on a sterile gown, preparing for the dissection. On her way to the surgical area, she turned on a radio that sat on a shelf, and twiddled the dial until she found a local station broadcasting classical music. A piece that sounded like Mozart was playing: good dissection music. She reached into a box of sterile latex gloves on another shelf, found it empty, and went looking for a new box. Grumbling in annoyance, she searched everywhere until finally one unopened box turned up in the storage room. Obviously Lori wasn't keeping track of their surgical supplies, a result of the decline in the number of procedures Will had been performing.

Wearing a fresh pair of gloves, Gaye went to the stainless-steel sink, where the crow was thawing. As she reached to pick up the carcass and transport it to the operating table, the telephone in the examining area rang. Gaye hesitated through a second ring. Lori was off; she'd have to answer herself—but to pick up the receiver she'd have to strip off the sterile gloves . . . then she might be called upon to drive off twenty-odd miles . . . whereas if she didn't answer, she could go on with the activity she'd planned.

A third ring.

Then she recalled that an extension also rang in the Bennett house; they'd pick it up, and Frankie would then take the mission upon herself. Gaye hurriedly stripped off the gloves and grabbed up the phone—in time to hear Frankie answering on the extension: "Animal clinic . . ."

"It's all right, Frankie," Gaye put in quickly. "I'll take it."

"You don't have to," Frankie said.

"Please leave it to me."

A man's voice chimed in, "As long as I can have at least one of you, I'll be satisfied."

Gaye heard the click as Frankie hung up her extension. "This is Dr. Foster," she said. "How can I help?"

"I was wondering if I could bring my dog in today."

"Is he a regular patient here?" Not a requirement, but if there was a record it could be helpful.

"No, I use a vet over here in Vermont, but they're closed for the holiday. I live in Bartlett Mills, and Bunky Chatsworth told me to try you."

"I see. What's wrong with the animal?"

"That's what I'd pay you to tell me. I could bring him right away."

"So it's an emergency?"

"That depends. . . ."

Curious answer. "On what?"

"Whether you judge by the dog's need or mine. I'm not sure it's anything serious, but I'm worried. Maybe I shouldn't be, but . . . the sooner I could have him looked at, the better I'd feel."

He was speaking quietly, in a firm voice, but from what he'd said and the mention of Bunky, Gaye presumed he was one of those elderly codgers who liked to come into the store and sit around the stove, the dog his only regular companion. The man's request was the kind that either of the Bennetts would oblige without hesitation, and the questions would be answered simply by an examination. "Okay," she said, "bring him in."

"Thanks. I should be there in half an hour." He hung up.

It was clear from the relief she heard in his voice exactly how much he loved his pet.

Half an hour didn't give her time to dissect the crow. She returned the carcass to a plastic bag and stowed it in the refrigerator. Then she killed some time neatening and reorganizing shelves of surgical supplies, and taking notes on items that ought to be restocked.

When fifty minutes had passed, and the calm background of Mozart had given way to the thunder of a Beethoven symphony,

Gaye's annoyance began to rise. Half an hour was easily enough time to drive from Bartlett Mills. Maybe the codger had changed his mind, or decided he didn't need to worry. . . .

Her ear picked up the faint sound of a car door slamming in the parking lot. She got up from her niche, where she'd been making notes, and went out to the reception area. Through the window she saw a taxi stopped outside, a tall man and his dog standing beside it. Dressed in a waist-length ski jacket over jeans, the man was facing away as he talked to the taxi driver, who was also out of the cab. The man said something that made the driver laugh, then turned around to walk into the clinic. Now Gaye saw his dark glasses: it was the blind skier she'd seen at Diamond Valley! And the dog was his guide, the handsome German shepherd. Today the animal was strapped into the leather harness with its rigid U-shaped handle, which the blind man grasped, arm extended, as he followed the dog's lead. Gaye watched as the dog came to the door of the clinic and halted until the blind man opened the door; then the dog led him inside.

"Hello . . ." the blind man said after the door closed behind him. He cocked his head as if listening intently.

Gaye wondered if he knew she was already there. As she looked at him, she couldn't help feeling what a shame it was he was blind. The dark glasses didn't hide the fact that he was quite attractive: tall and lean, brown hair just long and curly enough to give him a raffish look, and touched faintly with gray along the sides. All in all, she thought, he had the sort of movie-star good looks that could have taken him anywhere, if he weren't limited by—

"Hello," he said again, more assertively, as if certain he wasn't alone.

"Uh . . . hi, I'm here," she answered, waking herself from a stare. "I'm Dr. Foster. You're the man who called from Bartlett Mills?"

"Right. Sorry we're late. I had trouble getting a taxi. More people in the area than usual—for the long weekend."

"If I'd known you . . ." She censored herself quickly from referring to his disability. "We make house calls, you know."

"I don't mind getting out. Nice to see what's happening in the outside world."

Gaye was slow to respond; his colloquial use of the word *see* emerged so casually, without a hint of irony, yet it rocked her a little. He'd slipped off his ski jacket now, revealing a checked red-and-black lumberjack shirt beneath, and he held the jacket out in front of him. "Is there a place to hang this?"

"Oh . . . sure." She took the jacket and put it on a coat pole. "Well, let's have a look at your dog," she said. "Our examining area's in back—this way. . . ." As she edged toward the double doors, she noted that the dog moved quickly to stand close to the blind man's side. Feeling the guide against his leg, the man grabbed on to the stiff handle of the harness, and they followed Gaye together.

"What's his name?" she asked. "It *is* a he, right?"

"Last time I checked. His name's Rud."

She addressed herself to the dog. "Okay, Red, let's see what you weigh. C'mon over here. . . ." She moved toward the scale platform inset into the floor.

The man had let go of the dog's harness, but the animal didn't move a muscle.

"He'll only answer to his name," the man said. "It's *Rud*, not Red."

"Rud," Gaye repeated.

"Short for Rudyard, as in Kipling."

"Aha. So you like Kipling?"

"I don't know. I've never kippled."

The most ancient joke, but Gaye couldn't help laughing.

The blind man broke from his deadpan delivery and laughed with her. "Sorry," he said, "couldn't resist. Rud, do what the doctor tells you."

At once the dog walked from his master's side to stand on the scale by the door. It was amazing enough that he went calmly, Gaye thought—often animals fought getting on the scale simply because the shiny metal platform was an unfamiliar surface. But this one had retained what she'd asked, and gone to the scale as if he understood exactly what was expected of him.

"He's very smart," Gaye observed as she plucked a pen and paper from her niche and made a note of the dog's weight.

"Got to be when you're in charge of a lug like me."

Gaye turned to him and smiled—then felt a small pang of regret as she was freshly reminded that he couldn't see the smile and know she'd enjoyed his modest remark. "How old is Rud?" she asked, to add to her notes.

"Six."

His weight was in the ideal range. "Okay, tell me what the problem is. At a glance, Rud seems fine. Eyes bright, coat gleaming, nice and trim, and he responds quickly. What's got you worried?"

"Something's wrong with him."

"Yes, I understand. But what? Tell me how you know."

The man paused, his brow furrowed like a student in a classroom, uncertain of his answer. "He's not moving the way he usually does, for one thing. And, well, I just feel him telling me that . . . something's wrong." He tossed up his hands, overcome by the futility of explaining. "Look, what I have with Rud isn't the ordinary kind of connection most people have with their pets. You have to understand, he's part of me. That's the way it has to be. There are times he seems to know what I need before I say it, where I'll move before I go. And it works the other way. I feel things from him that go beyond what he'd reveal in the ordinary way by the sounds he makes, or loss of appetite, or any of that."

Gaye had only treated one guide dog in the past, a black Labrador brought to the hospital in Philadelphia. In that case it had been clear the animal was being mistreated. She had discovered then that it was no less rare for some blind owners to abuse the animals on which they depended than it could be for men to abuse their wives. Though obviously that wasn't true here. This relationship of man and dog seemed to be exactly what one hoped and imagined in a situation of such dependency.

"You say he's moving differently. Can you be more specific about that?"

"It's subtle . . . and not a persistent thing. It comes and goes. Like a limp that lasts for one step—then it's gone. I thought he might have cut his foot on something. But I've checked. No sign of anything wrong."

Gaye moved to the examining table. She pulled a wide sheet of sterile paper from the broad roll at one end, and smoothed it over the padded surface. "All right. Let's get Rud up here so I can get a closer look. Mind if I take the harness off first?"

"I'll do it." The man leaned over to the dog, still close beside him. Gaye noticed that his hands went straight to the buckles without fumbling, as if the eyes behind those dark glasses could see.

When the harness was off, she patted the table. "Up here, Rud, let's go."

The dog turned a quizzical look to the blind man—who seemed to know the dog was waiting for assurance. He nodded and the dog bounded up. The surface of the table was slightly more than two and a half feet off the floor, and Gaye saw that the dog managed it in one effortless motion.

She started with the routine things first, stethoscopic exam of the respiratory system, palpating the chest and abdominal area. As she worked she kept up a soothing patter. "That's good, Rud. . . . Just take it easy, boy. . . ."

"Would you mind letting me know what you're doing," the blind man said after a minute, "so I can picture it?"

"Sure. I've just checked his heart and lungs. Everything's fine there." She took an otoscope with a penlight from the pocket of her coat. "Now I'm looking into his eyes . . . the ears . . . also fine. Next, the legs . . ." She felt the bones of each, ran her hands along the tendons, peered at the footpads and the spaces between, and told the man what she was doing at each stage. "No sign of anything yet. What I'm going to do now is try to manipulate the legs a little, see if any movement causes pain."

"So you're going to hurt him?"

"I'll be gentle. I'll just grasp each leg and make it work a little. You may hear him protest, because dogs don't like to have someone moving their legs for them."

"Who does?" the man said.

Gaye pushed the dog over on his side, grasped one foreleg and started to pull it out to full extension, and the dog instantly barked at her and yanked the leg out of her grasp. "Hey, give me a chance,

Rud," she said. "This is for you." She reached for the leg again, and the dog retracted his paw and gave a low growl. Gaye turned to the man. "Would you do this for me? Hold the leg and extend it, then move it side to side, extend the muscles a little. Repeat the motion five or six times. We'll see if he gives any indication of undue pain, more resistance in one case than another."

The man cooperated, manipulating the foreleg and hind leg on one side. The dog made no protest. "Didn't bother him at all," the man said.

"Roll him onto his other side. We'll do the other legs."

Foreleg first, no complaint.

Then the hind leg. This time, too, Gaye observed no resistance. But after the man had waggled the leg a couple of times, he said, "It's this one. He doesn't want me to know . . . he's trying to act as if it doesn't bother him. But I feel a hitch, the faintest little tug . . . like he wishes I'd let go, only he won't fight it."

Gaye's gaze switched between the man and the dog. Could their communication truly be so finely tuned? Could the dog suppress the natural reflex to whimper or yelp in order to oblige such a sophisticated impulse as a desire not to *worry* his master? She could scarcely believe it.

"I wouldn't be too concerned about Rud," she said. "If the pain he feels is so small he can mask it easily and, as you say, it's intermittent, then it can't be too serious."

"Or he doesn't want me to *know* how serious it is."

Gaye couldn't blame him for stubbornly crediting the dog with such humanlike consideration. After all, in a real sense his life was entrusted to the care of the animal as much as vice versa. She avoided debating the merits of his belief. "I can only give you my opinion. If there was anything more than a minor pain, he'd let you know."

"What do you think is causing it?"

"A touch of arthritis, most likely, the earliest phase of the kind of joint degeneration that's very common from years of use. He's young, but this breed is prone to that. Another possibility is a joint mouse."

"Joint mouse," he repeated. "What's that?"

"A small chip of bone inside a joint—might be in the pelvic area, at the hip or the leg joint. With certain motions, sporadically, this chip could float into a position that causes pain. Assuming it's very minor pain, the chip would also be extremely small—enough so it could even break up or dissolve. And if it didn't, it could be treated with surgical removal."

"Well, if that's what Rud needs—"

"I'm not saying he *does*. To the contrary, my best medical advice is that you probably have nothing to worry about. I could give you some mild anti-inflammatory, but I'm not even sure that's necessary. He didn't give the least sign of being in pain—at least, not that I could see."

The blind man nodded, and rubbed his hand over his chin thoughtfully.

"How would you know whether it's arthritis or this mouse problem?"

"Joint mouse," she said. "Do an X-ray. But I was thinking I could save you the expense. The kind of agility Rud exhibited when he jumped up on this table would be hard to manage for a dog with any kind of joint problem."

"How much is an X-ray?"

"We charge seventy-five dollars. Add that to the cost of the visit, and your cab here and back, you're spending a couple of hundred— and I really don't think it's necessary. I understand how important Rud is to you, and I'll certainly do the X-ray now, if you want. But I'd recommend waiting at least a couple of weeks. If you see any progression of this problem, something more to worry you than this . . . vague sense something's wrong, then of course it can be done."

The blind man had remained by the table, where the dog lay on his side. He put out his hand and stroked the animal for a few seconds, silently communing with him. Then he turned to Gaye. Even knowing there were sightless eyes behind those dark glasses, she had the feeling he was looking at her as he spoke. "You think I'm worried over nothing, don't you? That I'm being . . . a little neurotic."

"Absolutely not. Caring as much as you do is natural, and so is worrying when you care that much. What might be less natural is to go on worrying when there doesn't seem to be anything much to worry about. Coming here makes sense. What also makes sense is a little bit of wait-and-see. Sorry, I mean—"

"That's okay." He smiled and gave an accepting nod. "Okay, Doc, I'll go along with your advice. Let's give it a little time. Rud?" He had only to say the name and start moving away before the dog hopped to his feet and leaped from the table to the floor.

Gaye watched, and again there wasn't the least indication of any problem in movement. She picked up the harness she'd put aside and handed it to the blind man so he could put it back on the dog; then they walked out to the reception area.

"Thanks for seeing me today," he said. "I'll pay you now. Cash okay?"

Gaye told him the visit and basic examination was sixty-five dollars. He pulled a wallet from his pocket, reached inside it, and almost instantly pulled out three twenties and five ones, which he held out until she took them.

She couldn't help asking. "How do you know what you're giving me?"

"Easy." He held the leather wallet out in front of him and opened it so she could see the contents. There were several inner pockets, each holding bills of different denomination.

"Clever," she said.

He slipped the wallet back into his pocket. "Simple. What would be clever is if I could teach Rud to pay the bills." She laughed. "My coat?" he said.

She pulled it off the pole and handed it to him. He put it on, and the dog led him to the door. They went out to the waiting taxi. Then it struck her that she'd never even asked his name, only the dog's. "Who are you?" she called out quickly. "I mean . . . I need your name for the medical record."

He'd opened the taxi door and already put the dog inside. "Toby," he called, turning to face her again. "Toby Callan."

Callan? Could this be Dot's son? Hardly the misfit loner she'd imagined. But the disability might explain why he was still single. . . . No, that wasn't enough to account for it. Not with a man like this. Not only was he instantly attractive, but easygoing, amusing, athletic . . . and he had a soft spot for animals. Toby Callan would surely look like a catch to anyone who had eyes.

As she closed the door and watched the taxi drive away, Gaye gave a regretful shake of her head. Too bad she'd refused that invitation from the eccentric postmistress of Bartlett Mills. It could have been the one Thanksgiving dinner in her whole life where she had a good time.

Or would it have mattered to Toby Callan whether she was there or not? He hadn't shown the least spark of interest in her beyond what she could do for his dog. He had asked for her to give him a visual description of each step in her treatment, and of where things were—but he'd shown more interest in how to find the coatrack than whether she was young or old, fat or thin.

Gaye added her notes on the visit to a card with the patient's name and the name of the owner, and left them with the cash she'd been paid at the reception desk, where Lori would find them for filing and depositing on Monday.

Then she went to pull the dead crow out of the refrigerator. Why the hell should she care, she mused as she prepared for the dissection, if this man wanted to know what she looked like? Maybe what lay behind the fact that Toby Callan was unmarried was simply that he didn't want to be otherwise.

And the way things were, she didn't feel one damn bit different.

Chapter 9

Dear Lord, help me! She wanted to scream it out, but she was made mute by terror. One moment she was sitting in the dollhouse, all the rooms starkly empty except for the one where she sat in its lone chair facing a cold, empty fireplace—and in the next moment she'd known: He was out there. Now all she could do was stand and stare into the dark forest.

Until, out of nowhere, the dog went darting into the trees—not her dog: the blind man's! And she went chasing after it. Then suddenly she was looking down at the animal's body lying in mounds of dead leaves, ripped open so she could see the beating heart, until she became aware of the shadow racing up behind her, then ramming into her with such brutal impact that it sent her hurtling upward into—

Gaye arched up off the bed, her body stiff with fright as her eyes snapped open. Gasping as if she'd just run a mile, she stared into the darkness of the bedroom. Her hand groped for the bedside lamp, found the switch. The light fixed her at last in reality. Flowered wallpaper and chintz, the warmth of blankets and the down comforter her landlady had supplied. But a feeling of safety didn't return with the light. She wrapped herself in the comforter and went to the window that looked out at the stream, the woods beyond. A three-quarter moon bathed the tumbling water and snow-covered ground in bluish light. All quiet. Her pulse began to slow.

Back in bed, she nestled into the covers, mourning Hero again. She passed then into reflecting on the blind man, the extraordinary bond he had with his guide dog. How much harder it would be for him to bear the inevitable loss of his animal—which served, after all, as his eyes? The guide was six years old, she remembered; given a shepherd's average life span, he would die in seven or eight years more at the most. Judging Callan to be in his early forties, she suspected he must've suffered the loss of one or two such dogs already—maybe more, depending on how long he'd been blind. (Was it from birth?) The death of his dogs must always be heart-wrenching. Who knew better than she?

Gaye could understand why he'd been so worried at any sign of a decline. And it relieved her to feel that his worry was needless. She'd given a good diagnosis—a touch of arthritis. If it did get any worse she'd put the dog on glucosamine. Though it wouldn't be hers to prescribe, she realized; Callan would go back to his regular vet.

Her mind stopped turning as drowsiness overcame her again.

Saturday morning she took her customary trip to Bartlett Mills to collect her mail. At the general store, Gaye greeted the man who sat in one of the rockers at the front—she'd seen him here often and still didn't know his name—and he nodded in reply. She went to the desk where Bunky was rolling up coins for a bank deposit. Seeing her, he unpinned her mail from the corkboard and handed it over.

"Thanks for the business you sent me," she said.

"What business would that be?"

"Mr. Callan."

That earned a nod.

Gaye stood by the desk to shuffle through the forwarded mail. Overdue bill for the credit card she'd cut up, health insurance bill, solicitation from Cornell for alumni contributions . . . and an envelope with the return address of the office for Pennsylvania First Cardiology Associates, sent to her abandoned sublet. The mere sight of that one upset her. She pushed it all into the pocket of her parka unread.

"Nice fella."

Chatsworth's voice drew her attention, though she'd lost his thread.

He saw her blank look. "Toby Callan."

"Oh, yes—very nice." It was an opening to satisfy her curiosity about Callan, but she was loath to take it. In Bunky's domain, the New England disaffection for prying was the rule. "Nice dog, too," she said.

"Poor Toby was in a twist about that animal."

"It was nothing to worry about."

"That's good," Bunky said.

Gaye went to the front of the store and sat in the unoccupied rocker. She opened the one piece of personal mail—a typed letter with another slip of folded paper clipped to the top:

Dear Gaye,

Your attorney says she's in contact with you but still refuses to confirm to me that she knows where you are. I hope you get this. Brian and I both regret deeply that you feel it necessary to shut us out of your life. I can tell you that the degree of your husband's remorse and worry has been so great that I advised him to take a break from his duties. It's a loss not to have him operating—he's needed; but he has agreed until he can get rested and return fresh.

If you do receive this, I urge you to call me. Not knowing what you're doing, I have no idea whether what I've sent along may be useful, but I don't like to think you could be in need and I hadn't done everything possible to help.

It was signed, *Daddy*—printed on a word processor like the rest.

Gaye unclipped the folded slip of paper. As she had guessed, it was a check payable to her. The amount surprised her, however: $10,000. She realized at once that the only place she could transact it was her new bank in West Greenlea—and the canceled check would reveal her whereabouts. Maybe that was his motive for sending it. Gaye tore up the check and the letter, and shoved the fragments into the potbellied stove.

Her neighbor in the other rocking chair went on sucking passively on his corncob pipe, but from the glance he gave her, Gaye guessed he'd followed the action play by play.

On her way out of the store she grabbed one of the Vermont regional newspapers from a rack. The weekend stretched ahead of her, and she wasn't sure how to fill it. Maybe a movie tonight at one of the malls. Life on this side of the state line seemed slightly livelier than on the other, and she felt lonelier suddenly than she had for weeks. The effect of the letter, she guessed, tugging at the strands she had cut, forcing her to reaffirm the choice of isolation.

Outside, she paused before getting into her car, her gaze turned toward the post office. No rule against prying there. Why not turn the tables on the nosy postmistress, pump Dot Callan for the info on her son? And *then* what? The letter just received, its reference to her husband's remorse—and to his hiatus from work—raised new concerns in Gaye. Suppose he used the hiatus to try locating her?

Maybe that awful dream was prophetic.

Alone and lonely as she felt, Gaye decided that exploring a new friendship with a man was pointless, perhaps even unfair, until the dangers and disarray from which she'd fled had been fully dealt with and eliminated.

She ended up staying in over the weekend, putting up a couple of extra shelves, dipping into books and magazines without finishing anything, nibbling meals while standing at the open refrigerator. And sleeping, the kind of long, leaden daytime naps that Gaye knew derived more from depression than fatigue. When she riffled quickly through the local papers in the evening, no diversion looked appealing. Love stories and action mayhem at the movies, roadhouse bars with three-dollar-a-drink happy hours. On Sunday morning Gaye called Frankie at home to let her know that if any farm calls came in to please pass them to her, but the day remained quiet.

So she was happy to get back to work on Monday, thankful

for the full schedule of appointments Lori gave her when she walked in.

In the afternoon there were two cats to be spayed, and shortly before the first of the surgeries Will called Gaye into his office to tell her she would be responsible for both, assisted by Lori.

"Fact is," he said, "I've kept going longer than I should have. If I'd gone on, you'd have been right to turn me in to the board."

"Oh, Will, everything I've seen you do has been—"

"Never mind," he broke in, and waved off any further reassurances. "I got away with it, thank God, but I won't be doing any more cutting. It'll be just you and Frankie—and she leaves all the small-animal stuff to me. You have my full confidence, Gaye."

"Thanks." It was approaching time to prepare. She started out, then paused. "I'd like you to stay with me, though, and do the acupuncture where you think it would help. I need to begin seriously studying with you, Will, so I can do it myself. And I'd like to learn the homeopathic remedies. Would you teach me?"

"Sure. All you've got time for, anyway."

It struck her only after she'd left him that his proviso was the gentlest reminder that it wasn't really *her* time that was the limiting factor.

During the two surgeries Will performed acupuncture as an aid to the anesthesia, but perhaps because of his earlier candor, Gaye detected for the first time that he seemed less deft in inserting the fine wire needles at the proper acupoints. Not so much as to affect the surgeries, yet it made Gaye all the more impatient to understand and begin practicing the techniques herself.

She was still finishing up paperwork for the procedures when Will wheeled himself through the main room on his way to the back door. "Stop in at the house on your way home, and I'll give you a few books to start you off on the acupuncture and what-not."

As she did her paperwork after he'd gone, Gaye reminded herself that a visit to the house would also be an opportunity to suggest the purchase of a computer for the clinic. For the hundredth time since coming to Bible Hill, she grumbled as she prepared things for a card file that it was pure stubborn foolishness not to have switched over to more convenient technology for record keeping. Her exasperation had reached the point that she was ready to spend her own money and set up the new data filing system herself. Assuming, of course, that they did intend to keep the clinic open. Hard to be sure what Frankie would do after Will was gone . . .

As she did on all winter afternoons, when the darkness came early, Lori left work at four-thirty. Before closing up herself, Gaye looked in at the second of the spayed cats, which was spending the night in a recovery cage. She replenished the water and left some food. Then she went to the farmhouse.

The kitchen was dark, the house quiet. Maybe Will had gone for a nap, after all. Gaye went forward to the living room and saw him slumped in his wheelchair beside a fire of quietly crackling logs, Nutmeg—the golden retriever, more commonly called just Nutty—sprawled at his feet. A single lamp burned on an end table nearby, but there was no book in Will's lap, and his eyes were in shadow. Gaye couldn't tell if he was dozing, so she stepped forward carefully.

"No need to creep around," he said.

"You looked asleep."

"Dreaming, that's all—but wide-awake."

"Is Frankie around?" Gaye asked. She didn't think the computer should be advocated without including Frankie in the conversation—even if she might be harder to reason with than Will.

"Gone to get groceries, I think. But she got those down for me before she went." He waved to a stack of books on the lamp table. Gaye went over to look at them. From the titles on the spines she could see the selection mixed texts on the history and practical basis of traditional Eastern medicine with studies of Confucian philosophy and Zen beliefs. "Your homework," he explained.

"Great. I'll get started right away. Anything I can do for you before I go—get you some tea, maybe?"

"Just sit with me a minute. Something I want to ask you."

She felt a bit apprehensive as she took the wing chair opposite. Maybe it was the dark, quiet house, or the absence of Frankie, but his need to keep her carried emanations of something weightier than she was prepared for.

"I saw in the case log that you took a patient yourself on Friday."

"Yes, a man from Bartlett Mills. That's all right, isn't it? He phoned, very worried about his dog, and—"

"It's fine. But in the record you wrote down the owner's name as Callan, and just the initial T. Would that be Tobias?"

"He gave his name as Toby."

"Yes, that's how he's known."

"So you know him?"

"Very well. Both professionally and personally."

"Personally? In what way?" Gaye relaxed into her chair. Here was an opening to satisfy her curiosity she felt less self-conscious about seizing.

"Back in the days I could get around," Will replied, "Frankie and I used to go at least once a month to see him perform."

"What kind of performance?"

"Toby's a piano player, a very good one. Sings, too. He's been entertaining in the piano bar over at the BHI since . . . must be twenty years or more. You ought to get over there, Gaye. He does all those great old songs—you know, the Astaire stuff and what-all. Does 'em every bit as well as Fred, if y'ask me."

"What's the BHI?"

"Local lingo for the Blue Hill Inn. Nicest place in this neck of the woods. Just a few miles the other side of that ski resort." Will gestured in the general direction of the state line.

"Diamond Valley?"

"Right." Will fell silent, his head bobbing a little, seemingly keeping time to some tune in his head he could remember hearing.

But what was his purpose in bringing up the blind man? He couldn't know she was so intrigued with him, Gaye thought. "It was a standard examination," she prompted. "I charged the regular fee. I told him I didn't see any need for special—"

"It's not about any of that. I was just surprised to learn he came in."

"I told you, he was worried. And his regular vet was away."

Will nodded thoughtfully.

She pried a little harder. "Why would you be surprised, Will?"

For a long moment he remained silent, his head sunk down on his chest. "For many years we took care of one of his dogs. Then he stopped and went somewhere else. I guess . . . it was too difficult. . . ."

"Coming from the Mills, you mean?"

"No. The associations, the reminder." He raised his head to look at her. "See, I was the one—well, of course, because we'd always taken care of the animal—when the time came, I put his dog to sleep. Amazing animal, he was. Let's see now, what was his name? Tenny, that was it . . . actually the name was Tennyson, named for the poet, because there was some line about a dog in one of his poems that Toby liked. Well, that dog was with Toby fourteen years, most of it on the job. But the guides get old, and when they're not so sharp anymore you need a new one. Of course, Toby kept Tenny even after he got his new guide. And then, eventually, it was just time . . . so he brought the dog here. And I . . ." Will faltered and cleared his throat. "Well, as you know, it's part of the job. But in all my years, I don't think it's ever been harder. Toby held that dog in his arms while I put him down, and afterward . . . I left them, and he stayed for hours. And every time I'd look in on him, he was just sitting there, holding the dog." Will shook his head as if trying to throw off the memory, a little like a dog shaking off rain. "Up to that day, he'd been coming here, bringing the new dog, too . . . also named for a poet, if I remember rightly."

"Rud?"

"Yeah, that's it. For Rudyard Kipling—'cause he wrote that nice dog poem." They were both silent a moment. Will might have been reciting the poem in his head. Gaye's knowledge of Kipling started and ended with *The Jungle Book.* "Anyway," Will resumed, "from that day Toby didn't come here again—until you saw him." Will gave another shake of his head.

"He couldn't have blamed you," Gaye said. "You were only doing what had to be done."

"Sure, that's right," Will agreed. "But I guess just coming across our threshold would be a reminder for Toby of something that was so hard for him. Or maybe he just found a vet closer to where he lives. One way or the other, it was just easier. . . ." Will let out a slow sigh.

Euthanizing an animal—especially someone's beloved pet (and how much harder if it was their "partner" in living)—was the thing all veterinarians found hardest about their work. Arguably, it accounted for the fact that clinical depression was a common problem among vets. After any day in which she had to euthanize an animal, a melancholy always settled over Gaye. She guessed that, even in recalling the experience, Will was stricken by that same feeling.

Before she left, Gaye hoped she could lift Will's mood. "It's always a kindness," she said. "You have to remember that, Will—and I'm not saying I don't have to remind myself, too. Because it's hard to be the one responsible for taking away a life that's meant so much to someone. Just never forget that it's because of the love we do it: to spare an animal the pain, all the indignities. And we don't kill the love, do we? That goes on."

Will nodded. "I know that, Gaye. A kindness, that's just what it is. A very great kindness." He gave her a smile, as if perceiving she needed to see it.

She smiled back. In that moment of connection, it occurred to Gaye that in relating this whole episode he might have meant to tell her, too, that the kindness was one he wished someday to receive himself. For a second the weight of the realization seemed to become almost palpable, pinning her to her chair. She felt herself gazing at Will with a longing to spare him the indignities that were inevitable in his situation. She wondered if anything could be said about it, if she should explore his feelings on the matter.

And then she bolted up from her chair, forcing herself to throw off the weight, the very thought. "I should be going. You sure there's nothing I can get for you before I leave?"

"No, my dear, I'm fine. And Frankie'll be home soon."

She picked up the books he'd set out for her, then moved near his chair. It felt uncomfortable to be standing over him, and, with the books in her lap, she eased down into a crouch to look into his face. "I'll start on these tonight. Do you think maybe we could tell

Lori to arrange appointments so there's a free hour each day for a kind of . . . master class? I could get so much from you, Will."

"There's a lot we could get from each other," he said.

Outside, sitting in the truck before starting the engine, his last words echoed. What did he think he could get from her? How much kindness did he expect?

Chapter 10

The Blue Hill Inn was one of those sprawling white-pillared survivors from a time before vacations and holidays for Americans meant flying off to somewhere halfway around the world. In those ancient days, you didn't escape from America on a holiday; you went looking for more of it, and found it here in its most genteel form. When it was built in 1903, there had been 180 rooms in two three-story wings branching off a grand marble-pillared lobby. Along the whole front ran a porch where people sat in rocking chairs reading or just looking at the new arrivals, and along the back was a stone terrace that overlooked a lake and the eight hundred bucolic acres beyond. It had been a place that attracted its clientele simply by offering a place to rest, be pampered, take long walks, play a game of horseshoes, and breathe clean mountain air.

But in the age of jet travel the formula had lost its appeal, and starting in the mid-fifties, the inn had declined into a run-down ramshackle white elephant. Then, twenty-five years ago, the property had been bought by a Boston developer. The grounds were improved with tennis courts, a golf course, and an outdoor swimming pool to match the restored indoor "nautatorium." The rooms and baths had been modernized, and the old lobby, with its vast dining room and a dozen salons for playing cards and writing letters, had been reconfigured to create several restaurants—one of which was lauded in every travel guide for serving some of the best French food in the Northeast—and two separate bars. One bar was reserved for those who sought only extended conversation over multiple drinks. The other, called "The Inglenook," was a cozy warren of dark corners and candlelit tables, spaced around a baby grand piano and a very small dance floor.

Toby Callan was only the third piano player who'd ever worked at The Inglenook. The first two had each been booked for several weeks at the time the renovated hotel reopened in the spring of 1981. Toby, too, had been hired initially for only six weeks. But he had immediately added to the transient clientele with a following among local residents, who started coming regularly. Seeing the advantage of steady year-round customers, the management had tried Toby out for two more months, then a year contract . . . and then no contract at all, just an understanding. Toby had been playing long enough now at The Inglenook that there were couples who'd fallen in love at its candlelit tables whose children—unmarried college students with a taste for something besides disco—were now patrons. In the early days there had been no dance floor, only a piano with stools around it where people could sit and sing along, and the tables. But Toby performed the kind of songs in the kind of way that could inspire couples to launch into an impromptu whirl across the carpet, and when the carpet had started to wear through, someone got the idea of replacing it with a more durable patch of polished oak.

On this first Thursday in December, however, the little dance floor was empty, and not quite half the room's thirty-odd tables and banquettes were occupied. All the same, not a bad turnout for a weeknight just after the Thanksgiving crowd had left.

Gaye left her coat at a check room across the lobby, and paused at the bar's entrance so her eyes could adjust to the room's darkness while she chose a place to sit. In a spotlit area up front Callan sat at the baby grand, just beginning to accompany himself in a ballad. Rud was faintly visible lying in a shadow behind the piano bench. Gaye stood listening as he sang the first lines of a lyric: "I see your face before me/Haunting my every dream. . . ."

She recognized it as a song on an old Sinatra LP she'd had in college. Gaye had always had a fondness for this kind of music—saloon songs and show tunes. It was the music she could recall hearing as a child, wafting through those enormous rooms at her mother's estate.

She chose a table on a fringe of the room. Listening to nostalgic love songs alone in a bar made her self-conscious, glad for the cover of darkness. Though she'd been eager to hear Callan perform since her conversation with Will, anticipating this unease had made her put off coming. But after being at loose ends for half the week, she'd given in to the urge. Pathetic as she might look sitting alone in a bar, at least she didn't have to worry that her appearance here would be regarded by Callan as the act of a desperate woman chasing after him. He never had to know she was here.

Which made it crazy, she realized now, that she'd been so attentive to the dress she'd worn, doing her makeup, worrying at all about how she *looked*. If she cared at all about what he thought, it would have been more meaningful to dab on some perfume. But that was an attractant she'd given up wearing after leaving Brian.

The last note of his song died away. There were no applause, but a gray-haired woman sitting with a man at a table near the piano said conversationally, "Nobody does it better, Toby. . . ."

"Okay," he said, immediately playing a little introductory riff, "for all you Carly Simon fans . . ."

The woman laughed. "That's not a request, baby! I mean nobody does it better than you. I loved the way you sang that last one." She sounded slightly in her cups.

"Well, thanks, Lucy," he said. "What would you like to hear?"

"My favorite—you know . . . what's it called?" The woman started to sing in a hoarse voice, off pitch. "Lovely, lovely, never change. . . ."

" 'The Way You Look Tonight,' " Toby said, getting it despite her poor rendition. His hands landed on the piano keys in a mellow introductory chord, and he went into it in a nice, easy, lilting rhythm. The woman nodded and smiled, and her hand went across the table to link with her companion's.

Gaye was immediately a fan. He sang in a strong baritone, a little husky and rough on some of the notes, but very distinctive. His touch on the piano was jazzy rather than lush, with dexterous little fills and inventive tuneful improvisations between verses. But more than anything else, it was the way he got into the lyric that held her and his audience. The people at the tables were listening, not gabbing away, as most people did in a bar like this.

A waitress materialized out of the dark and asked Gaye for her order. "Probably shouldn't have anything stronger than a beer," she said, thinking out loud, "I'm driving. . . ."

The waitress cocked her head. "You're of age, right?"

Gaye laughed. "Wow—is it that dark, or do you need glasses? Never mind, just bring me a ginger ale."

"Okay, hon, but there's a minimum." She pointed to a little card on the table. "We have snacks, too. You can use it up that way. The nachos are good."

"Just a soda'll be fine."

The waitress left, and Gaye took a closer look at the card: the minimum was fifteen dollars. She focused on Callan again, not unimpressed. He wasn't earning at the big-city level, maybe, but he was obviously appreciated as more than a run-of-the-mill saloon pianist.

He did a few more songs, stringing together a mix of ballads and catchy finger-snappers, some requested from different tables around the room. The longer he played, the more Gaye loved listening to him. Watching him, too, was part of the pleasure. He looked so happy when he was doing a bright up-tempo song like "You Make Me Feel So Young," smiling at the words. He looked so genuinely fulfilled as he delivered on a request that must surely be done to death around here, "Moonlight in Vermont."

She wasn't sure how long she'd been sitting there when he announced he'd be taking a break after the next tune—and then launched into a bouncy version of "Jeepers Creepers": "Jeepers creepers, where'd you get those peepers?/Jeepers creepers, where'd you get those eyes?"

It hit her suddenly that in most of the songs he'd been singing— probably the largest part of the repertoire of thousands of such songs—being able to see was virtually equated with being able to feel, to love. What was the line that had gone by minutes ago in "You Make Me Feel So Young" without her realizing it then? "And ev'ry time I see you grin, I'm such a happy individual. . . ."

Suddenly his blindness—which his joy in performing made her forget—seemed to her all the more cruel for all the inescapable reminders of what he couldn't experience that he must have sung thousands of times. The words of one song after another cascaded through her mind: *Blue moon, I saw you standing alone . . . I only have eyes for you . . . I'll see you in my dreams . . .* And yet there was no sign he held anything back in performing; he gave himself fully to perpetuating the romantic idea that love was so much about what could be *seen*. It struck her as very brave to be able to do that; she felt a hopeless longing to be able to rub a magic lamp and ask a genie to let him see.

". . . where did you get those eyes!" he finished on an exuberant high note. Everyone in the room applauded, and a few of the customers—obviously from the regular winter crowd, which would have once included the Bennetts—called out invitations for Callan to join them for a drink. He declined with polite excuses—"Wanta get to a TV and find out what's happening to the Celtics." Some of the people he answered by name, identifying them by voice alone as he had the woman Lucy. "I'll be back in a while," he concluded, and stood up from the piano. Rud immediately sprang to his feet, too. The dog came around to the piano bench, where he could make himself known by pressing against the blind man's legs, and Callan grasped the rigid harness by which Rud would lead him. They moved together toward an alcove close to the piano that led backstage, and Gaye had an instant of wondering if she should make her presence known before he was gone. But his refusals to others made her decide against it.

Gaye noticed now that the dog had halted and was looking around, as if he might head off in a new direction. Callan was obviously surprised. "What's wrong, Rud?" she could hear him say from across the room. "To my dressing room—c'mon, this way . . ." But the dog headed toward the audience. Callan gave a sharp tug on the harness, pulling him back to the course he wanted. "No, this way," he said.

The dog pulled up short again, then continued in the direction he wanted to go, marching forward so forcefully that Callan was visibly pulled off balance before yielding to follow. "What is it, boy? What's gotten into you?"

Gaye could only watch as it became clear that the guide dog was threading a path through the tables to where she sat. The animal stopped right in front of her. He kept his eyes level, staring straight ahead at her knees as though deliberately— even guiltily—avoiding eye contact with her.

Callan knew the dimensions of the room well enough to realize he'd been led to stand near one of the fringe tables. His expression behind the dark glasses was plainly perplexed and annoyed. "I hope you're not someone tempting the dog with food," he said. "That's bad for him—and for me. He's got to know I'm the source of his—"

"I didn't do anything," Gaye said. "He came over here on his own."

At the sound of her voice, Callan cocked his head. "I know you. . . ."

"Yes—Dr. Foster. I saw Rud at the Bible Hill Clinic last week."

"Ah. So that explains it. . . ."

"You mean *this*? I can't imagine he recognized me."

"Picked up a scent. . . ."

"I'm not wearing perfume."

"A trace of something he remembers from the clinic—a germicide, alcohol?"

Faintly indignant, she said, "I do wash at the end of the day, Mr. Callan."

He smiled. "Well, then, I guess it's just your very own smell he likes."

The suggestion stirred up her self-consciousness again. "How's Rud been?" she asked, putting things back on a professional basis.

"I was thinking of calling you, as a matter of fact."

"You're still worried?"

"Yes. But I won't take up your time with it while you're having a night out. I'll—"

"It's all right," she said. "Nothing else is taking up my time."

His eyebrows went up. What she'd said, Gaye realized, gave away that she was alone. "So," he said, "you came by yourself?"

"Dr. Bennett told me you perform the kind of music I like."

"Not disappointed, I hope."

"Anything but."

There was a momentary silence before he asked, "May I sit down?"

"Certainly. I'm sorry—I should have . . ."

He groped for the back of a chair, found it, and seated himself. The dog settled next to the table. "Sure you don't mind being consulted away from the office?" he asked.

"I don't mind giving advice, in general. But, ethically, if the dog has been in the regular care of another vet, I really shouldn't give—"

"Rud walked over to you. Can't he consult any vet he wants?"

"I don't think he was using his nose to make a decision about his medical care."

"Don't be so sure."

She couldn't tell if he said it lightly, or if he was truly suggesting, as he had in her office, that the animal's intelligence was enough to actually be aware of his own health.

The waitress had seen Toby sit down, and she returned to the table. Resting a hand on his shoulder, she let him know she was there before speaking. "Anything I can get you, Toby?"

"No, thanks, Kim. But I'll buy the doctor a drink."

Gaye shook her head. "Thanks, but I've still got most of this one."

"Anyway," Toby said to the waitress, "don't hit her for the minimum. She's my guest."

Gaye started to object, but he shushed her.

"Right," the waitress said. "Hey, Tob, would you do 'Yesterday' for me next set?"

"You got it."

The waitress lingered an extra second or two, her hand still on Callan's shoulder. It was enough to make Gaye examine her, and wonder if there could be something between her and Toby. She was in her late thirties, and her blond hair was carelessly combed, but she was still quite attractive—with no rings on either hand. Working late nights in an atmosphere permeated by liquor and love songs, it seemed likely she had linked up with Toby at one time or another.

"So tell me about Rud," Gaye said when the waitress left.

"There's still this little hitch in his walk I feel sometimes."

"It's only been a week."

"Yes, but it's worse. Not much, but I do notice it."

"Then I suppose you should have the X-ray done."

"I'll bring him in."

"Look, I've just moved into the area, Mr. Callan, and—"

"Toby."

"Toby," she agreed, and went on: "It's important for me to observe the protocols. Being new around here, I don't want to do anything that gives the impression I'm stealing patients away from any other—"

"But if it's what Rud wants . . ." He saw her start to react, and hurried on. "I'm serious. I think he's drawn to you."

"You can't really believe he's choosing his own doctor."

"Maybe that." Toby leaned a bit closer over the table, and smiled faintly before adding, "Or maybe, because he's my best friend in the world, he thinks you're someone I should get to know better."

Before Gaye had a chance to offer any reply, he stood. "I think my break has lasted long enough," he said. "Anything I can play for you?"

"I like it all."

"First one'll be for you, though. C'mon, Rud, let's go tickle the ivories."

As she watched them walk back to the piano, Gaye was seized by a strange mix of warring emotions, crosscurrents of longing and dread. Maybe it came from being in such a dark and shadowy place, but she felt simultaneously that the unseen hand of destiny had placed her exactly where she was meant to be, where the wounds and fears she had suffered might be healed by friendship with this man, and at the same time that some harmful, negative force was swirling around her, even binding them together. Perhaps it was because of the dog, his resemblance to Hero, the horror of her own pet's loss casting a shadow over what was otherwise a lovely encounter.

In a moment the disquiet passed. She was simply tired, she decided, her emotional reserves still depleted. As soon as he'd sung that first song, Gaye thought, she'd call it a night.

Callan seated himself at the piano, and turned his head in her direction. Then he played a jazzy, gently upbeat introduction and started to sing: "I've got the world on a string. . . ."

Wherever that worrisome cloud over her soul had come from, it was blown away as soon as he started. She closed her eyes—joining him in blindness—and let her mind sail into the images painted by the words.

"Life is a wonderful thing, long as I hold the string . . ."

It occurred to her that, in a way, he did have to keep hold of a string to make his way through life. But if he was aware of the metaphor, it was a tether for which he was obviously very grateful; there seemed to be some extra gusto in the way he belted out this song.

Or was it, perhaps, because this one wasn't tied at all to seeing real, earthly visions?

She was swept up in his song completely, and when he came to the final lines of the lyrics, they came back to her suddenly, and she sang along.

"What a world . . . what a life . . . I'm in love."

There was no bill to pay, the waitress reminded her. She was his guest.

Driving home, the Vermont moon lighting the road, she couldn't stop singing that final song. Perhaps she didn't really have the world on a string, but just for the moment, she felt that she did.

Chapter 11

Gaye hoped he'd follow up quickly. It troubled her that she might have given a faulty assessment of the dog's condition. Callan's complaint of a barely noticeable irregularity in the animal's movement was so vague and insubstantial, she'd been inclined to write it off as suspect—a kind of hypochondria projected onto the animal by a master so dependent on its well-being.

But Gaye was no longer inclined to regard Toby Callan as prone to any form of self-deception. He impressed her as being attuned to his dog's behavior in ways that went beyond any ordinary interaction between pet and owner.

She recognized, too, that his dog's intelligence was beyond the norm. Not that she believed Rud could choose the doctor he wanted to handle his case—thinking back to Callan's joke still made her smile. But it no longer seemed too far-fetched that the animal might mask his condition in order to go on performing crucial tasks he was trained to do, a dedication to duty akin to the willingness of athletes to play through pain.

But when she didn't hear from him by midafternoon on Friday, Gaye presumed Callan had succumbed to the same aversion that had kept him away from the clinic since the death of his previous guide. Just as Lori was leaving for the day, she grabbed up a last phone call at the reception desk, then popped into the examining room to ask if Gaye would be willing to take a walk-in ready to come in the next half hour. Both Will and Frankie had already left.

"What kind of problem?" Gaye asked.

"Mr. Callan—says you saw his dog a week ago . . ."

"Put the call through on the extension as you're leaving," Gaye asked Lori. She picked up the phone in the examining room. After exchanging hellos, she said, "I'd be happy to look at Rud, but it's late now—"

"I know. Sorry I didn't call earlier, but my mother twisted her ankle slightly in the snow, so Rud and I had to do her shopping."

She noted the way he referred to them as a team—one that could function as a caregiver to a disabled old woman. "I'll see Rud anytime," she assured him. "But we should do the X-ray, which I'd then develop and evaluate. If it can wait 'till morning, we could take as much time as necessary."

"I suppose overnight isn't going to make a difference."

"Unless you see any sign he's in pain—"

"No. Tomorrow's fine."

"I can meet up with you in the morning over at the Mills. I'm there Saturday mornings to pick up my mail, and I'd like to save you those taxi fares."

There was a pause. She supposed he was processing why she crossed the state line for her mail. Then she heard him laughing. "So *you're* the one," he said. "Mom was telling me I should track down some mysterious lady who tried to rent a P.O. box. Said you were cute, and she'd sent you up to the general store." He laughed again. "So maybe that's the answer. . . ."

"Answer to what?"

"It was sight, not smell, that made Rud head for your table last night."

"Is that supposed to be a compliment, Mr. Callan?" she asked wryly. "That dogs find me attractive?"

"He knows what's good for me, that's all."

It felt suddenly like they were going too quickly. "Be at the general store tomorrow at eleven," she said crisply.

"See you there," he replied.

Toby Callan had quite a line, Gaye thought after cradling the phone. It was dawning on her, in fact, that his way with the ladies had probably been finely honed with a great deal of experience. With that glib tongue, a dog as a handy conversation piece, and his beguiling way with a love song, he could well be a world-class Casanova.

She'd better watch her step, Gaye told herself. She had to find her own way through life's obstacle course without a guide.

A morning kaffeeklatsch was in progress when she arrived at the store. Toby was there, occupying one of the rocking chairs, Rud stretched out at his feet. The other rocker was occupied by a silver-haired man wearing an expensive-looking leather jacket with dark flannel slacks, looking like what the locals might call a "city slicker" with a second home in the area. Bunky and the other habitué whom Gaye had seen several times before were also sitting around the stove, on stools.

". . . damned if I'd give them my business," the habitué was saying as Gaye entered. "Havin' a fancy clothes boutique is one thing. But you let one of them places in here and it's the beginning of the end. Next thing you know the whole street's lit up with pink neon signs and chain stores end to end."

She closed the door behind her, and Rud lifted his head to look at her.

"Oh, c'mon now, Fred," Toby said. "Coffee, that's all they sell."

"At two bucks a cup!" Bunky put in, adding to his friend's condemnation.

"We don't need their damn coffee." He left his stool. "Mornin', Gaye . . . I'll fetch your mail." He walked back to his corkboard.

Now Toby rose to his feet and faced the door. "Hello, Gaye."

"Good morning, Toby."

The other two men looked at them, and Gaye felt self-conscious again.

Then the man in the leather jacket stood. "Hi. I'm Norm Stephenson." He stepped forward, his hand extended to Gaye.

By performing the amenity of introducing himself, he confirmed his more cosmopolitan roots. At the general store people met, talked, and exchanged gossip without trading names. Gaye had only just learned by listening to Toby that the man she'd seen here many times—who'd never introduced himself—was named Fred. As she shook Stephenson's hand and gave her own name, Gaye noticed that the hair that went with his gray eyes must have turned prematurely; in every other physical aspect he seemed about the same age as she was.

"So, tell me, Toby," Gaye said, "what's this big summit meeting about?"

"That old devil progress," Toby replied. "Do we bar the door or let it in?"

"If that's your fool idea of progress," Fred grumbled. "Havin' one of them franchise outfits sellin' coffee flavored with blueberries or horse dung or what-all."

"The coffee's good," Stephenson said. "Don't knock horse dung if you haven't tried it."

Toby laughed, and even Fred leaked a grudging smile.

Bunky returned with a handful of envelopes and passed them to Gaye. "One's certified," he remarked. "Dot brought it in and asked if I was willing to sign for it, bein' I'm custodian of mail at this address. Hope I did right."

"That's fine, Bunky, thanks." Flipping through the mail, she saw the certified tag was on something from her lawyer. "Ready to go, Toby?"

"I'll get my coat." He took a few measured steps to a counter over which he'd thrown his windbreaker, scarf, and gloves. While putting them on, he needled Fred about how nice Main Street was going to look when they started putting up the skyscrapers. Then he turned to the door and raised his arm slightly from his side; the dog moved just enough so the harness slid right under Toby's hand.

Leaving with him, Gaye's self-consciousness went up a notch. To let the others know it was strictly business, she gave the dog a pat and said, "Okay, Rud, let's go get you that X-ray."

By the truck, after he'd prodded the dog into the passenger seat, Toby said, "Thanks for giving us a ride. I hope you're not regretting it now."

She acted shocked. "Why would I?"

"I don't know . . . except you sounded anxious about what people might make out of you and me going off together."

She was flustered by how easily he'd nailed it. Relying only on what he could hear, the mere shading of an inflection, he must pick up lots of information that went unheard by others. "Small towns," she said cryptically. "You know—the way people talk."

There was a taut silence as they started out. The dog sat up on the seat between them, looking out at the road with no less focus than if he were driving. Reminded of the many times she'd driven like this with Hero, Gaye hooked her arm over the dog's back and ran her hand over his fur.

"Toby," she said finally. "I wouldn't want you to think I'm anything but happy for us to be friends. But things have happened in my life that . . . well, I guess they've left me feeling I need to be careful about . . . what I do. That certified letter Bunky gave me—it's probably legal papers related to a divorce I'm seeking. And being in the middle of that . . . well, I suppose I just feel I need to be careful about . . . people getting the wrong impression."

"Sure. Makes sense," he said evenly.

They fell back into silence. It was a magnificent day, the sky clear blue, sunlight sparkling on the snow-covered landscape. In the quiet, Gaye was acutely aware of having this beauty to appreciate, while all he had was darkness.

On an impulse, she asked, "Shall I tell you what I'm seeing?"

"I'd like that."

"Where we are now, the road winds between low hills. Often when I drive past here I see black-and-white cows grazing all over the hillsides, but today the ground is covered with snow, the fields empty and white except for a few gray dots where stones poke through, casting little shadows. The sun's shining, and it makes the snow look like someone sprayed diamonds all over it. In the sky there are a few clouds, long white strands, pulled by the wind like wisps of cotton, and overall it's that gorgeous shade of pure translucent blue I think you only see . . ." She had been running on thoughtlessly, she realized.

"Go on," he urged when she stopped. "This is something I never get from Rud."

It was a brave joke, but she couldn't laugh. "You see only on a winter day, I was going to say." She hesitated, then dared to reveal the thought that had blocked her words. "All my talk of colors . . . I didn't know if that made any sense."

"Yes, of course. I remember colors. I even remember that blue—that special winter-sky blue."

"So you haven't always been blind?"

"I was fourteen before I started losing my sight."

He seemed open to answering all her questions. "What caused it?"

"The condition is called retinitis pigmentosa." He went on to explain that it was hereditary—though it might skip generations—and incurable, a progressive degeneration of that sensitive layer of the eye that translated to the optic nerve the light and color received through the lens. His awareness of it had started with faint grayish blotches at the center of his vision, barely noticeable at first. By the time he realized they weren't just shadows and his mother got him to a specialist in Boston, he'd probably had the condition for two or three years.

"The diagnosis was tough to take when I first got it," he said. "I was told that in a few more years I wouldn't be able to tell an apple from a football, and there was nothing anyone in the world could do about it. But when you're a kid, you really don't think in terms of what's five or ten years down the line. A week later I could still catch a pass. Even two years later I was still playing right field on the high school baseball team."

His world grew progressively darker, though, the shadows reaching to the edges of his field of vision—and one day he got beaned by a fly ball, which let three runs score. He gave up athletics, but managed to finish high school still maneuvering on his own.

"In college," he concluded, "that's when I needed my first guide dog."

Gaye did some math. Rud was six, Will had said the previous dog lived to be fourteen, and Toby had been nineteen or twenty when he got his first. She put him in his mid-forties, which left a gap of at least five years in the equation. So Rud must be his third guide, and he'd already gone through losing two. She could understand how wrenching the experience must be. These animals were hardly separate entities; without them, he couldn't live as he wished.

"I saw you skiing," she said abruptly. "I was at Diamond Valley, and I saw you coming down the mountain with a friend and it just bowled me over. How beautifully you moved, Toby, that was part of it. But the main thing was that you were doing it. Later, at the end of the day, I saw when you met up with Rud. He looks very much like a dog I had till just a couple of months ago. . . ." That was *it*, she realized—why she had launched this confession. "That dog was very important to me, and losing him hit me very hard—still does. And seeing Rud, I felt . . . connected somehow. . . ."

"To Rud or to me?" he asked.

"Both of you. But that's not why I'm telling you this. I want you to know that the kind of bond you have with him is something I know about and understand. And the feelings you have about Bible Hill, the reason you didn't come back for so long, I can sympathize with that."

When she finished, he didn't answer right away, just nodded. At last he said, "I always liked Will. I hope he understood, too."

"I think he did."

There was a longer pause. "So you like to ski?" he said finally.

She guessed he wanted to move on to a happier topic. "I did once. I'm pretty bad at it now. So bad I was ready to give up that day—till I saw you."

"You know that guy you just met back at Bunky's—Norm Stephenson? His dad built Diamond Valley. It belongs to Norm now. Hell of a nice guy. That was him skiing with me that day."

The mention struck Gaye as an odd detour in their conversation. She suspected Toby might have mentioned it to gauge her interest in Stephenson.

"I didn't recognize him," she said. "But I never looked at the other guy."

Toby smiled. "Well, if you haven't given it up, suppose I take you skiing sometime?"

"I'd steer you straight into a tree."

"Don't worry; I'll lead."

She wondered how he could. But Toby struck her as a man who didn't make idle boasts. It would be interesting to see how he managed it.

They didn't speak for a while, but it was an easy silence now. "Tell me what you're seeing," he said then.

"We've just starting going down a long hill toward the river."

"Heading for the old covered bridge?"

"That's right. We'll cross it in a minute."

"Is it still painted red?"

"The paint's pretty well faded, but yes."

"Don't go too fast," he said, "or you could get fined a dollar."

She laughed. Behind his eyes, she knew now, he saw it all.

Chapter 12

The clinic was quiet and empty when they arrived. Lori didn't work Saturdays, and Gaye guessed the Bennetts were having their lunch. Perhaps it was best Toby didn't run into them; she didn't know what kind of emotions might be stirred up by a meeting with Toby.

She led him to the corner of the examining area where the old X-ray machine stood partitioned off by plywood panels that had been covered on the side nearest the machine with wafers of lead. Unlike the more modern apparatus designed especially for veterinary use, this relic from a local hospital emitted a higher level of radiation, and was clumsier to operate. The area to be X-rayed had to be held tight against a black plate under which the film had been inserted, while the wide-mouthed ray gun was positioned to aim directly down upon it. Though a human patient could be instructed to lie still and keep any particular body part pressed tight to the plate, animals had to be firmly held. One person was required to position and restrain the animal, while another operated the machine. As for the extra dose of radiation, Gaye didn't know exactly how much higher it was, only that the amount was significant. If you were anywhere near the machine while it was in use, you were advised to wear a lead-sheathed smock and mask. There was also a lead screen with a small plate-glass window for the operator to step behind while the machine was activated.

After explaining all this to Toby, Gaye started to escort him behind the screen, intending him to control the switch that activated the machine while she attended to positioning and holding the dog.

Toby held back. "I should be with Rud. He'll be calmer for me."

"I don't want you exposed to the radiation," she said.

"Why not? I'll be easier to find if I glow in the dark."

"Toby, this isn't a joke. It's better if—"

"Look, if it's all right for you to stay out here, so can I."

She helped him into the smock and mask, as she described what she needed. "From what you've described so far, there's no way to pinpoint where the problem originates. So I'm going to do a survey radiograph—a full-body X-ray—then I'll also do a couple limited to his hindquarters, two on each side, since hips are a common problem area in shepherds. You need to make Rud lie perfectly still, first on one side, then the other."

She went behind the screen and set the dial to time the first exposure. Through the window she saw that the dog was playing dead, stone still, although he wasn't being held. "If he'll stay like that," she called to Toby, "you can come back here with me."

"He'll move if I leave him," Toby said. "Go ahead; it's all right."

Gaye pressed the button to take the picture.

Between each X ray, she had to insert a new film cartridge under the dog, but the series proceeded quickly. Once Toby set Rud in a position, told him to remain that way, and soothed him with a few caresses, the dog obeyed—as long as Toby stayed nearby. If he moved too far away, the dog sat up.

Between pictures they said very little. But at one point Toby spoke about Will. "I heard he hasn't been well," he said. "I was sorry to hear that."

"It's truly a shame," Gaye said. "He's a very special man, gifted at what he does, and he's near the point when he won't be able to work anymore."

She was ready to take the next X-ray, and no more was said.

The series was done in fifteen minutes. Gaye gathered the X-ray plates under her arm. "Let me put these in the darkroom; then I'll take you home."

Toby removed the smock and mask by himself and handed them to her. "Aren't you going to tell me what they show?"

She put the items on a hook behind the machine. "Developing them takes half an hour; then I'll want to study them. Reading X-rays is a little like seeing at night. You have to look at them awhile to be sure of what's there in front of you. Rather than keep you hanging around through all that, I'll drive you back and call you later with the results."

She considered whether to bring him over to the farmhouse, where he could have the company of the Bennetts, but wasn't sure they'd want to be disturbed or that Toby felt comfortable about re-connecting with Will. She decided he could find his own way to their door if he wanted to try.

She watched him get into his coat and buckle Rud into the harness. "Where will you be walking?" she asked.

"Wherever Rud wants to go."

She knew the snow in the fields was deep. "He's likely to stay along the roads, isn't he?"

"I hope so. I didn't wear boots." The dog started for the door.

"Toby, I can rush this a little, and you could wait here if you want."

He turned around and smiled, then let go of the harness and came back toward her a few steps. For a moment he hesitated, his head cocked as if he were trying to pick up some very faint sound from her direction. Then he said, "There's not much of a future for us, Dr. Foster, if you're the kind of person who's going to worry every time you're left alone."

It's not me I'm worried about, she almost blurted out. But of course he knew that. "Okay, I get it. See you in an hour."

The darkroom was actually a closet in the rear storage area fitted out with a red bulb in the light fixture, and water was brought in through a hose. Gaye mixed the chemicals—developing bath, fixer, and rinse—extracted the film from the five plates, and began the process-ing. Enveloped in the dim red light while she worked, all the distinc-tion of colors eliminated and solid objects reduced to black lumps, she found his blindness stayed on her mind. He handled it with such grace and humor. Didn't he ever resent it? she wondered. Grieve for the loss of his sight? Wasn't the loss of sight an increment in the loss of life?

The drift of Gaye's thoughts revived her concern for Toby—out there sauntering along the roads where cars went speeding by. Would drivers seeing a man strolling with a dog in the country assume he was sightless? She feared for him. And, in the depth of that fear, she perceived the level of feeling that went beyond merely humane concern for a disabled man. *There's not much of a future for us. . . .* The prospect of a future with him intrigued her. Since the trouble with Brian escalated, she hadn't thought of the future, of anything past an ending to a mistaken marriage—to her fear. Now she saw the first glimmer of a life that might come after.

The images were emerging on the film, outlines of bone and tissue. Gaye moved the films through the fixative, swirled them through the water, and clipped them into the drying rack. Then, through the closet door, she heard someone come into the storage room through the back entrance. She left the films to dry and stepped out of the closet. A trail of shoeprints, damp from snow, went across the cement floor to the examining room.

Frankie was there, just removing her coat. She gave a start when she saw Gaye. "Where'd you come from?"

"I was in the darkroom, developing X-rays."

Frankie went to the black satchel she'd put down on the lab counter. She pulled a handful of glass vials from the bag. "Gonna do some tests on blood samples from those sick pigs out at Beckendorf's farm. Want to be sure we're not lookin' at an outbreak of enzootic pneumonia. If you're not tied up anymore, and you'd like to help . . ."

Gaye was always anxious not to displease Frankie. "Be glad to, as soon as I'm done. I have to look at the X-rays first; the owner'll be back soon for a consult." She wasn't sure what made her think it was wise to withhold Toby's name.

"What's the case?"

"A dog—shepherd with some occasional irregularity in his gait."

"Who's the owner?"

She had to answer. "Toby Callan."

Frankie nodded again, and went about separating the blood from her vials, preparing some samples to go through the blood analyzer, others to be put on slides for microscopic examination. Gaye started back to the darkroom, relieved the name had produced no fallout.

Frankie spoke out suddenly. "Stopped comin' to us, y'know. After Will put his last dog to sleep." Gaye faced her again. Frankie went on without looking up from her work. "Never called, not a word. We don't mind folks goin' elsewhere; that's anybody's right. But happening that way made Will feel so bad, like he was to blame or something." Frankie shook her head. "Not right," she muttered, and switched on the blood analyzer.

"It's not a matter of right or wrong," Gaye said. "You must realize that. There were feelings involved that Toby couldn't control. He probably couldn't face walking in here again. It evoked something too painful."

"Came back now, though," Frankie observed sourly.

"Six years have gone by. And he needed us."

At last Frankie looked over at Gaye. "Or it could be he heard our new associate's a pretty young woman." Gaye shrugged off the suggestion with rolled eyes and a toss of her head, but Frankie continued: "Think he's not up to it, young lady? Mr. Callan's well known in these parts—blind as he may be—for havin' what they call an eye for the ladies. Made a hit with more than his piano playing, too, I can tell you. Enid Telcher's daughter, up the road in—"

Gaye cut her off. "I don't want to hear gossip, Frankie."

"Up to you," Frankie replied, with the blameless air of a sentry who had only tried to head off an ambush.

Gaye felt compelled to defend her disinterest. "He's a very attractive man; I can see that. I'm sure all sorts of stories about him have been passed around. That's what people do in places like this."

"That's what people do everywhere," Frankie said. "And wouldn't you guess some of the stories, in some of the places, have got to be true?"

The X-rays would be dry. Eager to escape the exchange, Gaye turned away to return to the darkroom. Then she paused. "Frankie, he's very worried about his dog. I hope you won't pick a fight with him when he comes in."

"It's your case," was all she said.

"Good. Thanks."

The films were ready for viewing. Gaye brought them to the examining room and clipped then to the light panel on a wall behind the X-ray machine. While Frankie continued to concentrate on her work in the lab area on the far side of the room, Gaye reviewed the pictures of the dog's anatomy. She saw nothing at all that looked worrisome, no bone spurs or chips that might affect a joint, no whitish blobs around tissue that might be tumor mass, no obviously torn muscle or fraying cartilage. She knew, however, that in this mazelike monochromatic image of the inner body—complex systems all compressed into this flat, transparent sheet—an anomaly could hide as easily as a new planet hiding at the edge of a galaxy. Seeing no problem certainly didn't prove that no problem existed; only that, if there was anything wrong, it couldn't be seen with an X-ray.

Assuming, of course, that she wasn't missing something. Gaye called across the room, "Frankie, would you mind having a look at these?"

Without a word, Frankie lifted her eye from a microscope and came to stand in front of the light panel. "Any idea what we're lookin' for?" she said as she started scanning the films.

"Something that's affecting mobility, but not to any major degree. Mr. Callan"—Gaye was careful not to use his first name—"hasn't been able to pinpoint an affected area, foot, leg, hip. The way he talks about it, he seems to be sensing the dog's pain more than noticing any actual physical result."

Frankie went on looking at the films, but her eyebrows went up in a signal of skepticism at Gaye's observation.

"Naturally his relationship to the animal is remarkably close," Gaye added. "He'd have a very acute sensitivity to variations in movement."

"Well, these sure look clean as a whistle," Frankie said. She turned from the panel. "Course, if I had it in mind to meet a pretty woman who works at a veterinary clinic . . ."

This time Gaye couldn't even take Frankie seriously. She let out a laugh, and then let out her feelings. "Frankie, you are one tough nut to crack. You've made up your mind that Toby's a skirt-chaser, so that's that. Poor guy won't ever get the benefit of the doubt."

Frankie laid a hand on Gaye's shoulder. It was the first time she'd made such a gesture, obviously meant to console that she had some sincere words to impart. "Here's a couple of differences with livin' in a big city. Out here there's a lot of space between people, and you can't always get close to the ones you want. There's lots of trees, too, but pretty women ain't growin' on 'em. So don't assume I'm sayin' something so awful about Toby Callan if he's got a mind to shrink the space a little between himself and a good-lookin' girl to warm a winter's night."

Gaye still shook it off with a laugh. "Toby's not the kind of man who'd play games like this because . . . he wants sex."

Frankie snorted, "Is there another kind of man? My Lord, girl, haven't you learned a thing from bein' so close to animals?" She went back to the microscope.

Gaye gave the X-rays another ten minutes of scrutiny. She'd had a second opinion now: not a sign of anything wrong. She glanced at the clock; Toby would be returning any minute. Should she discount his worries because of another woman's cynicism? She walked over to Frankie. "I'm going to proceed on the basis that something *is* wrong—"

"Your case, I told you."

"But I'd like your opinion. Let's say there *is* something, and the X-ray didn't pick it up. What would you advise?" Normally Gaye would have felt confident enough to plan treatment on her own. But the possibility that she had been too quick on Toby's first visit to discount his concerns made her eager for support.

Whatever Frankie's doubts, she appreciated being consulted and took a moment to consider it. "Movement affected without mechanical defect," she mused aloud. "Points to likely brain or spinal involvement."

That confirmed Gaye's conclusion.

"You'd need a CT scan of the brain if it's a lesion or deep

tumor. Have to go elsewhere for that, and wherever its done it'll cost a fair bit."

"I'm sure Toby wouldn't think about the expense."

"Even so, before you go that route I'd do a spinal-fluid evaluation. Cheaper and easier—we can do it here. You'd be looking for any trace of blood leakage or neoplastic cells."

Neoplastic cells were markers for the presence of cancer. Nicer to think Toby's complaint might just be a maneuver, Gaye thought. But Frankie's advice was exactly along the lines she had been considering herself, which made her feel more confident about undertaking the procedure.

She heard someone come into the reception area—Toby returning. "Thanks for your help, Frankie."

"That's what I'm here for," Frankie said.

Like most of her terse replies, this one seemed to have a little bite to it. It brought an awareness to Gaye that for all the weeks she'd been at the clinic, this was the first time she had sought Frankie's counsel. When she'd asked for help on their farm calls, that was as a student needing a teacher. This was Gaye functioning as a colleague, showing respect for the wisdom and experience of an elder. Gaye had done that consistently with Will, but not until now with Frankie. Maybe it could be the first step in bridging the gap between them.

Toby and Rud came through the doors to the examining room. "Ready for us?" he said brightly.

Gaye went to receive him. "Yes, I've had a good look at the X-rays."

His head turned sharply toward the lab area. Evidently while Gaye was approaching, he'd detected sounds from a different direction. "Frankie's here," Gaye explained.

Toby faced the bench. "Frankie!" he exclaimed warmly. "How are you?"

Gaye gave Frankie an anxious glance.

"Not too bad, Toby," Frankie said. "Will's the one who's not so good these days."

"I know. I'm very sorry." Toby hesitated, and Frankie looked back to her work. "I've missed seeing you over at the inn. Maybe you could bring Will some evening. We'll cheer him up."

"Hard for him to get around," Frankie said.

"It could be managed, though," Gaye put in. She wanted the rift that had developed to be healed.

"Maybe," Frankie said, but with a finality that discouraged any further attempts at persuasion.

Gaye moved toward the light panels. "Come over here, Toby. We'll review the X-rays."

He followed her voice. "Is it bad?" he asked.

"Not in the least. I don't see a thing in any of these to worry about. Going by these alone, Rud's in fine shape." Toby nodded, but he didn't look relieved. "You don't look like I just gave you good news," Gaye observed.

"We've just had a good long walk. Something's affecting him. I can feel it. It's even more noticeable today."

"Tell me what you noticed. Let's try to pin this down."

"He was a little slower, for one thing. Not much—no one would notice it but me. At times I got the impression he was . . ." He paused again, groping for the best way to convey what was, again, only a subjective, indefinite idea—an impression. "He was moving kind of gingerly, as if his feet hurt."

"The roads are salted in the winter, Toby, and the footpads are sensitive. Maybe—"

"I know how he walks when the salt bothers him," Toby erupted. "I know the goddamn difference. This is something more serious!"

Gaye glanced over to the lab bench, hoping Frankie hadn't missed the outburst. This wasn't a man who was faking distress.

Frankie stayed bent over the microscope.

"But listen, Gaye," he resumed, moderating to a milder tone. "If your judgment is that he's okay, then—"

"I didn't say that, Toby," she cut in quickly. She suspected he'd been on the verge of politely ending the visit—after which he would have gone straight to consult someone else. "Whatever I say is only because I don't want you worrying unnecessarily. But I promise you, as long as you have the feeling that something's bothering Rud, I'll keep working to find it."

"All right," he said quickly. "So what's next?"

She parroted what Frankie had suggested: testing to determine whether there was brain or spinal involvement; the spinal tap and examination of the fluid would be the logical first step. "We could do the tap right now," she told him. Frankie would be available to assist.

"A tap involves putting a needle in, right?"

"We make it painless."

He pondered it a second. "Let's wait on it just a little. I think Rud's seen enough of doctors for one day."

She didn't press him to make the appointment. She wasn't sure the delay was really because he still intended to return to Rud's usual vet.

Toby said a nice good-bye to Frankie, and Gaye left the clinic with him and Rud to drive them back to the Mills.

They were both subdued on the ride. Her attempt at conversation died quickly. He repeated his hope that Will and Frankie would make it over to the inn, though he predicted it wasn't likely. "She's pretty mad at me, I guess."

"No, she's not," Gaye countered automatically.

"Yes, she is," he said quietly. "And she's right to be."

Before Gaye could bring up anything else, he asked her to turn on the radio, and she obliged. At his request, she tuned to a local station that played country-and-western music. That preempted conversation for the rest of the journey.

Perhaps it was just his preoccupation with the unresolved questions about the dog that had caused the mood to change. But Gaye thought it might be due to his feeling disappointed in her—because she had failed to make a diagnosis and provide the sure cure that would dispel his worry . . . or because he'd gotten the idea that she doubted him. Maybe Frankie's cynical notions had insidiously taken root, colored her responses in ways that he could detect. His radar was all the more sensitive for operating without sight.

Whatever the cause, the connection she'd felt deepening had been oddly weakened, maybe even broken.

Just as they rounded a bend where the houses of Bartlett Mills came into view, he said, "Drop me off at the store again. I've got some shopping to do."

How had he known when they were so near the town? Feeling the truck take the curve, she supposed. "I'll wait and bring you home."

"No, thanks. Rud and I can walk."

Was he declaring his self-reliance? Or had he seen enough of her for one day? She didn't press it; her instinct for dealing with Toby was gone.

As soon as she stopped outside the store, he said some polite words about how much he appreciated being driven to and from the clinic, and reached to open the door.

She couldn't let him go without trying to clear the air. "Toby, let me help you."

"Rud's the one who needs help," he said.

"I know, I know. That's what I meant." Then she added, "But I do, too. The courage you have—the first time I saw you I knew it was something I needed. That's why I want to . . . keep our connection. We will, won't we?"

"I can't see why not," he said evenly.

She let him go.

She was miles away before she realized that, for him, the words promised nothing.

Chapter 13

G aye guessed the certified mail was legal papers relating to the divorce, and had put the envelope aside until a time when she was certain her lawyer would be available for advice. Before leaving for work on Monday, she opened it. Inside were copies of briefs pertaining to a cross-motion Brian had filed citing her for abandonment. She put in the call immediately.

Her lawyer was a woman in her mid-fifties named Helen Barash who had been recommended by a divorced nurse at the Philadelphia animal hospital. Twice divorced herself, the attorney was dedicated to obtaining the fairest possible terms for her clients. She was smart and humorless, but a relentless advocate whose one quirky dash of character color was ownership of a motorcycle that she rode on weekends with a group of other graying women bikers called the Silver Rockets.

"In a legal context," she told Gaye over the phone, "abandonment means to leave without cause."

"Without?" Gaye objected. "But you know—"

"You had plenty of cause—yes, *we* know that. Furthermore, a claim of abandonment isn't applicable until an absence of one year has transpired."

"So it's nonsense. I've been gone only—"

The lawyer broke in again. "Your husband will try to date the charge from the first time you left him—if after returning you denied him your . . . marital favors. There's something called constructive abandonment that exists even if you're in the home, but not sexually available."

"Is this the Middle Ages?" Gaye cried out. "What he wanted from me was a hell of a lot more than—how did you put it?—marital favors."

"Gaye, right now this isn't about what's true or false. It's legal strategy. If your husband can make the case that you left for selfish reasons while he was being a good and caring provider, you may forfeit claim to material benefits you left behind—alimony, share of joint property—on top of which he'd have cause to make substantial claims against you. These could include property you acquired in the marriage, as well as damages for his mental pain and suffering, and lost income because he had to curtail operating after you left. In his position that alone could amount to a great deal of money."

"I want to be free," Gaye declared. "I don't give a damn about money."

"Sweetie, you're not free if you're saddled with debt. Either we fight this abandonment charge, or the courts may let your husband call the tune. There's even a potential for him to delay the divorce indefinitely by saying he's willing to take you back whenever you come to your senses."

"I came to my senses when I left."

"Again, that has to be proven."

"So how do we do that?"

"Bottom line? You come here and speak up for yourself in court."

The mere suggestion of being near Brian caused a knot to form in Gaye's stomach. "I'm not ready to do that," she said.

"It doesn't have to be right away. I can put up a pretty strong paper wall for now. But if you *never* show up to defend yourself, it's going to look like you're guilty of what he says."

"Does it matter that I don't feel safe when I'm anywhere near him?"

"It will matter," the lawyer said, "when a judge sees with his own eyes how frightened you are."

No matter for how long it might be postponed, even the

prospect of having to go back cast a cloud over Gaye as she went about the ordinary business of her days. The more immediate cause of her sadness, however, was the way things had been left with Toby Callan. As the week passed and he didn't call to pursue a diagnosis for Rud, she was sure he must have sought further advice elsewhere. Which didn't feel merely like losing a patient, but already losing a new friend. She had no idea what she might have done differently, yet Gaye blamed herself for not handling the case well. Perhaps the underlying cause was those small-minded doubts Frankie had planted.

Nagged by the belief that she'd lost Callan's respect, and with Brian's legal maneuvers weighing on her mind, Gaye felt her bright little dream of having a future being extinguished. The idea of escaping into this whole new life struck her suddenly as futile. She was an alien here; sooner or later she'd have to go back where she belonged.

As if to drive home the lesson, she returned to her apartment from work on a frigid Wednesday evening to discover a pipe had burst in the kitchen, causing a flood. When she telephoned Millie, a machine answered with a message that she had taken some of the dolls on holiday for a few days—her way of announcing she was on a pre-Christmas business trip. Gaye located a local plumber willing to come at night and repair the pipe, but the coziness of her nesting place was compromised, rugs ruined, and the place suffused with dampness.

The week only got worse. Will had started dedicating at least an hour each day to instructing her in the veterinary application of homeopathic remedies and the technique of reiki, but after Monday he begged off the next two days because he felt too tired. Then on Thursday, during the hour when he always went back to the farmhouse to have lunch, Frankie came running into the clinic through the rear, crying and begging for help: Will was unable to breathe, choking. She had already phoned for an ambulance, but she was terrified he would suffocate to death before help arrived.

Gaye dashed over to the farmhouse, Lori right behind her. They found Will slumped in his wheelchair, gasping, but able to breathe again. After a few minutes he had recovered enough to be able to speak and account for the episode. In the midst of eating, he'd been unable to swallow his food. Seized by panic, he couldn't recover the reflex. But then his throat had cleared enough somehow that he could draw breath, which eased his panic, and then—as he put it— he had "remembered" how to swallow again.

When the ambulance came, Will rebelled against being carted away. He was checked over thoroughly by an intern, who still advised going to the hospital, but had to relent when Frankie joined Will in refusing to consent to a hospital admission. Over the intern's shoulder, Gaye saw him note on his report that it was a domestic choking incident resolved without treatment.

She understood, however, that Will's dysphagia had reached the critical point. He could no longer be certain of summoning the basic reflex that would allow him to safely ingest solid foods; liquids, too, would be problematic if not lethal. By force of will, by enduring pain, he might manage—at times. But the absolute confidence that he would never fail himself was gone, and the ability itself would be increasingly unreliable. He would eventually have an intravenous diet. The breathing reflex would soon diminish and fail, too, and he would need to wear an apparatus to flex his diaphragm.

That evening Gaye felt at her lowest since the night she had seen Hero run down before her eyes. She made herself tea, toasted a couple of slices of bread, and spread them with butter and raspberry jam, but left most of it untouched. She sought warmth by building a fire, but made no effort to keep it going. She couldn't pretend that the despair would be so easily chased away by nursery foods or a flame. Until tonight she had always felt there was something to refuel her hopes: the fresh air of a new place, the possibility to be trained in techniques that might make her a special practitioner of her profession, the encounter with a man who inspired her and stirred romantic yearnings. But all that potential had vanished. Measured against such inconstancy, how much more unbearable was the haunting loss of her dog. A dog, only a dog! But a mind and a heart that had always been devoted to her, never wavering, ever available with comfort and companionship.

Gaye wished she could shake off this despondency. Would it cheer her up if she drove over to the inn and listened to Toby play? Or would she only feel worse if he acted as distant as when they had last been together?

The risk seemed too great. She went to bed and lay sleepless in the dark for a long time until fatigue overwhelmed her.

When she came awake suddenly this time, it wasn't running from a dream. Her fragile sleep had been shattered by a noise: Someone was in the room with her. Lying frozen with fear, she listened to the sounds around her. Breathing—the faint inhale and exhale of respiration—from a corner of the bedroom. Or was it just the sigh of wind through a crack in the windows at the end of the apartment? Should she turn on the lamp . . . or was she safer in the darkness?

Slowly Gaye lifted her head from the pillow so she could look toward the corner from which the sound emanated. Something, yes, crouching there. She could definitely hear it breathing. Then it moved, the faintest twitch, but she caught a glint of light—*two* faint pinpoints—reflected rays bouncing from outside the room into the mirror on the wall across from the bed . . . then she caught the eyes of . . . of whatever crouched in the corner. Those two pinpoints seemed to be aimed at her. Two eyes, black as the night, except for those beams of trapped moonlight.

"Hero?" she said softly.

What impelled her to speak the name, she had no idea. But when it was said, she knew it was right. At that moment she realized she must be in a dream after all. Even so, even if it was unreal, she wanted to see him, to call him to her. She reached out, groped for the bedside lamp, found the switch.

The corner was empty except for the small vacuum cleaner she'd left there after cleaning silt left on the rugs from the flood. No dream, but the plain tableau of reality. Those faint glints of light must have come from the machine's black plastic casing.

Must have . . .

Why not a ghost? Did an animal not have a soul as much as a person, a spirit that might survive?

Gaye switched off the light, hurrying back into the darkness, hoping to recover what had fled. Lying back, she whispered the name, trying to summon him back. An illusion, maybe, but oh, such a sweet one.

Yet as she lay blanketed in the blackness, the experience of a minute ago replayed fully in her mind; the sensations she had felt stirred in her nerves. He had been here! Her desperate need for solace had somehow conjured his spirit. Or so she chose to believe. Like the Native Americans, who invested animals with spirits, or Buddhists, whose concept of reincarnation held that souls migrated through animals as they ascended through successive rebirths to attain humanity.

So she was not alone. Wholly comforted by that belief, Gaye fell back into a dreamless, untroubled sleep.

Will felt well enough the next day to spend an hour giving further instruction in the practices and principles of reiki. The underlying philosophy, which Gaye had learned from her reading, was that the body of any living thing was permeated by a life-force energy that was constantly interchanged with the unlimited energy of the universe. The word itself, *reiki*, conveyed this idea: in the Japanese language, *rei* meant spirit, and *ki* meant the life-force energy. In the unhealthy body of any living thing, this vital energy was believed to be lacking, blocked. The accomplished reiki practitioner was trained to sense where such blockages existed—as Gaye had seen Will do— and, by certain manipulations of the hands, open channels to the universal energy so as to begin the healing process, or at least to accelerate it. The lesson today consisted of demonstrating some of the specific hand positions that were prescribed for channeling energy to different parts of the body.

In all their tutoring sessions, Will was careful to let Gaye know that he advocated neither reiki nor homeopathy as an all-out substitute for conventional veterinary medicine, only as aids that expanded the repertoire of available healing methods. "Sometimes they work. Sometimes they don't," he said. "Just like everything else we've got in the bag. But the more you carry, the better your chances of finding something that does the trick."

Will's matter-of-fact presentation of such arcane phenomena as universal life-force energy being channeled into the body encouraged Gaye to think that she might gain some insight from him about her experience of last night.

After the tutoring session, she asked, "Will, do you believe in ghosts?"

He was wheeling himself back toward his office, but now he spun on a dime to face her. "There's a humdinger from out of the blue." He edged toward her, his eyes studying her face. "You seen a ghost around here?"

"I don't know. Could be nothing but wishful thinking."

She described her experience in detail from the moment of waking up, hearing the faint respirations, seeing the eyes glinting at her in the dark, chasing the phantom with the light, then returning to the darkness, still unable to shake the belief that it had truly been there, the only thing in the world that loved her unquestioningly.

"So," Will said when she finished, "not just a ghost . . . but a ghost *dog*. But why ask what I believe?" he said after a moment. "He didn't come to me. I've never had any ghost come to me, for that matter—on two legs, four legs, wings, or whatever. Though that doesn't prove there's no such thing. All it proves for sure"—he wheeled himself up closer, as if to share a secret—"is I never lost anyone yet who loved me enough to come back for a little visit."

He spun back the other way again, and rolled off into his office.

When she drove to the Mills to get her mail the next morning, she was feeling a hundred percent better about everything. Silly as it was to believe she had the spirit of her dead pet hovering around her, it was a fact that the turnaround in her dark mood coincided with that moment in the dead of night when she felt his spirit was with her. If there was hope in her heart again, why question what had put it there?

As she parked in front of the general store, she saw Toby sitting outside, halfway down the front steps, his elbows on his knees, chin propped in his hands. Beside him was Rud, sitting erect on his haunches. Together they had the aspect of being on guard.

As soon as Gaye got out of the truck, she could hear the sound of talk and laughter coming from within the store. It seemed odd that Toby wasn't participating in the morning kaffeeklatsch. "What are you two doing out here?" she said as she came to the steps.

"Waiting for you," he said. As he stood up, his hand felt the Braille face on his wristwatch. "Been here two hours already, just in case you came early."

"What's the problem?" Her eyes went to the dog, who was also on his feet now, nuzzling her hand.

"This time I am," Toby said. "Sometimes I can be a terribly thickheaded, bad-tempered, ungrateful jerk. I've been feeling rotten about it all week—the way I behaved after that visit to your office last Saturday. It wasn't fair, Gaye, taking it out on you. But when you started talking about the possibility of something being seriously wrong with him . . ." Toby's hand reached out to touch the dog. "I couldn't deal with it. All I could do was . . . go away."

"I appreciate your telling me this, Toby. I was afraid I'd mishandled the case."

"You couldn't have handled it better—*all* the problems."

"Thanks. Anyway, I hope the report on Rud came out well."

"There's been no report. I haven't followed up."

"But . . . this past week . . ."

"I told you, I wasn't dealing with it well. I should have called you, but I was embarrassed about the way I'd acted. That's not the only reason, though. Rud needs to be tested; I know that. But I . . . I don't want to hear the bad news."

"Toby, that kind of fear is what keeps lots of people from getting treatment that saves lives. It's no different for Rud. Chances are it's a minor problem, but even if it weren't—"

He broke in. "It's nothing minor, Gaye. That much I know."

"Toby, he's practically asymptomatic. There's no reason to be so pessimistic."

"Only one: I know him."

No point in arguing further. Toby's stubbornness seemed to confirm the diagnosis she had made earlier—of Toby—that he was afflicted by a form of hypochondria, a fear of illness projected onto the dog. The cure was simply to prove his fears baseless. "Then let's not waste any more time. We'll do the spinal, and if that doesn't give us some answers we'll go for a full-body scan. If I can't find a co-operative vet with the equipment, we can arrange it with a conventional hospital. Whatever may be going on with Rud, let's make him better." Toby gave a slow, somber nod. "I'm sure it'll be all right, Toby. But let's not wait any longer."

"Does it have to be today?"

"No. It's not a complicated procedure, but I should have someone to assist me, so let's plan on Monday. Come to the clinic at ten. We'll do the tap and have the results by afternoon."

His expression brightened at last. "That works out fine, 'cause I was thinking I might use today to make good on that offer of mine." She looked at him questioningly. "To take you skiing," he said. "Are you free this afternoon?"

Free. There were resonances in that lovely word that reminded her of all the ways in which she was not. Available, though—that she was.

Yet how would he do it? Expert as he was, could a sightless man deliver on his claim to steer her safely down an icy slope? *Well,* she thought, *let's see him try.* She linked her arm through Toby's. "I'd like nothing better, sir, than to go skiing with you."

"Great! Shall we take my car or yours?"

"Well, mine's right here—" Only then did she get the joke. "You're awful," she said.

Meaning, of course, anything but . . .

Chapter 14

At Diamond Valley, Toby had a friend who owned a place that sold and rented equipment. The owner was not only happy to allow a good discount, but to look after Rud while Toby was on the mountain. Toby advised Gaye on every aspect of choosing the best equipment, and insisted on paying for the rental. Because she hadn't dressed for the mountain that morning, the shop owner permitted her to take good ski pants and a stylish jacket from the shop's assortment of new clothing. "Buy it if you like it," he said. "Or I can just put the stuff back on the rack when you're done."

In the good-natured kidding that went on between Toby and his friend, Gaye caught a hint or two that she was far from the first date Toby had brought into the shop for outfitting.

They went next to a central lodge, where he kept his own equipment and clothes in a locker rented for the season. After suiting up they went out to a nursery slope, where Toby planned to give her what he called a "driving lesson" —training her in the techniques that allowed him to lead when they went down the mountain. As they rode a lift to the top of the short slope, he described the method. It required, first, that they be linked together, though not so close as to hamper their maneuverability. To make the link he took one of her ski poles and one of his, and tied the handles together with the leather straps that usually slipped over the wrist. This created a flexible double-length linkage, with the tip of each pole at

either end. As they skied, they would each grip one end by the "bas-
ket," the round metal ring at the tip of each pole.

"You'll stay to one side and behind me by the length of the
link," Toby explained. "I'll lead, but you steer—our path will depend
on which way you want me to go. You can tell me which way to
turn, and how sharp the turn should be, by using a clock face for
our reference. Ten o'clock would be a fairly sharp left, eleven
o'clock less, but you just have to say 'ten' or 'eleven.' "

"So one and two would be to the right," she offered.

"Exactly. Shout out the number to make sure I hear, and I'll respond right away. You can use half hours, too, up to two-thirty, and
tell me to go faster or slower, but remember speed is partly determined by the degree of turn. So if you tell me to slow down, I may
take a sharper turn. Here's the most important thing: whatever turn
you tell me to take, take the same turn by yourself—don't wait for
me to pull you into it. Got it?"

"Right. We're only linked so I can steer you, not for you to
pull me."

"Check. And while we're under way, tell me what's coming up
in front of us. Steer us away from other skiers or any other obstruc-
tions. Think you can handle all of that?"

"I'll try."

"Last thing: 'nine' or 'three' means full stop. If you lose your hold
on the link, shout it out right away. I'll stop and you can catch up.
Otherwise, stop me only in an emergency, because if we're linked it
could end in a pileup."

"Roger, Captain."

They got off the lift, took hold of the link as he instructed, and
started their first run. The nursery slope was wide open, and gentle
enough so that it was impossible to go too fast. After a couple of
runs from top to bottom, Gaye felt confident she could keep them
comfortably out of trouble. She kept up a constant report on what
she saw ahead, providing occasional bits of detail to paint as full a
picture as possible for Toby. At times she even painted in colors, re-
membering that he could see them in his mind: "Ten-thirty . . . tod-
dler in a green snowsuit just took a fall about forty feet ahead . . .

lady in blue doing a slow herringbone . . . better go to one-thirty. . . ."

Gaye got a kick out of being the pilot, and took pride in believing she did a good job of it. She could feel her skill at the sport improving, too. In part it came from reviving those pathways in mind and muscle established in her youth, when she'd been a good skier, and from starting to trust those reflexes more. But there was something else: Toby skied so effortlessly that just being near him, having her movements linked to his, elevated her own ability.

After a third run down the nursery slope, she was eager to try something harder. "Let's go for more, Captain. How about an intermediate slope?"

"Sure you're up to it?"

"Raring to go."

"Okay. Follow me, and just make sure I don't run anyone over."

At the bottom of the mountain where all the different lifts converged, he knew his way without needing much guidance. He was able to lead the way toward the lift for an intermediate run, and all she had to do was direct him so he could maneuver through the more crowded areas without any collisions.

As they sat side by side on the chairlift, riding up the mountain, he said, "Tell me the view."

She felt remiss in having to be asked. "Oh, sure. I was just assuming you already knew what it was."

"It's never the same. It changes . . . according to who tells me about it. That's one of the advantages sometimes of seeing the world through somebody else's eyes. It's never the same."

Gaye took a moment to gather in the sight: She wanted to give him the best view he'd ever had. "It's very bright today," she began, "one of those days when the air seems especially clean and clear, and the lines and colors are sharp and pure. The trees are all like Christmas trees, lines of them on each side of the snowfields, deep green, each one throwing a shadow on the clean white snow, the line of shadows sort of like . . . like a saw blade. People are racing down below us, a hundred moving dots against the white sparkling snow, all the colors of their clothes looking as if . . . handfuls of confetti were fluttering over a field of diamonds. Up at the top, the wind is blowing, lifting little gusts of snow off the ridges, leaving very faint white trails against a sky the vivid blue of . . . bluebells or cornflowers. Those little wisps of snow are almost like the condensation of our breath in the air, as if the mountain itself is breathing. It's . . ." She ran out of ideas. "It's just beautiful, Toby." She looked at him, wishing she could have done better.

"Thanks," he said. He turned to her. "And you've got beautiful eyes."

They hit the intermediate slope, a long, winding trail down the mountain. With each run she became more confident and daring, letting him go faster, trusting his skills and her own. The exhilaration of speeding along with the wind in her face was heightened by the joy of sharing it with him, making it possible for him, and the accomplishment of recovering sufficient skill to keep up rather than dragging him back. Halfway down their third run, as they came to a wide-open piece of the piste with no other skiers visible ahead for a couple of hundred yards, she shouted out, "Twelve, Toby!"

She started her own turn, but corrected quickly when he didn't respond at once. "That's straight down the fall line, Gaye," he shouted back over his shoulder.

"Twelve, damn it! Who's driving?"

"You'd better be damn sure," he warned.

"You'd better listen this time, or we'll crash. . . . Twelve goddamn *noon!*"

And simultaneously they headed straight down, until she saw a group of skiers ahead, and slowed their descent with a quick "one-thirty."

When they came to a stop at the bottom, he said, "You're a madwoman." Then he leaned in close. "And the best driver I've ever had."

"It's easy . . . when you're driving such good equipment." She wanted now to try for more, and suggested they go to a steeper run.

"A black diamond? Oh no, not yet."

"Please. I can handle it."

"I'll bet you can. But let's leave it for next time, okay?"

Hearing there would be a next time was enough of a thrill.

They took two more fast runs down the intermediate slope before Toby suggested they turn in the rental.

"I'm not tired," she said.

"I don't like to leave Rud for much longer than a couple of hours. C'mon, the mountain'll be here next time we're ready."

When they got to the store, Rud was reclining in a corner. But as soon as they walked in he jumped to his feet and ran to Toby. Observing the quickness of the dog's responses, the obvious acuity of his senses, Gaye doubted again that there could be anything seriously bothering him.

She turned in the skis and boots, but decided to buy the clothes she had used. When Toby's friend began writing up a bill, she could see the prices were half what had been on the tags. "I don't want you losing money on me," she told him.

"Toby and I have a pact," he said as he added up the bill. "I give his ladies a deal. He comps me at the inn and sings the right songs to put my dates in the mood."

There it was again, a reminder that she was only one in a long line.

Toby caught it, too. "Damn it, George. You make it sound like I'm in here every week with somebody new."

The friend looked up with an embarrassed wince. "Hey, I didn't mean . . . Just, you know, well, there have been—" He broke off with an apologetic shrug and went back to finishing the transaction.

In the truck on the way back to the Mills, the dog curled up on the seat between them, she said, "Thank you, Toby. That was the best day I've had for a long time."

"Me, too."

She glanced over at him, searching his expression to gauge the depth of his sentiment. Behind his opaque dark glasses, his features were unreadable. But how could it be as special for him as it was for her?

She took a risk. "Tell me something: are we out on a date, or did you just . . . take me skiing?"

He turned to her, smiling slightly. "What makes you ask that?"

"When your friend mentioned other women, you sounded concerned about what I'd think."

"I am, yes. I don't want you getting the idea that I'm a playboy who's just putting another notch on my belt."

"You've had a lot of women, though, haven't you?"

He took a few seconds to answer, obviously going through the reasons she'd asked, and how best to answer. "Over time, sure. I can't deny I like women. And you know, they come through the hotel, they have a couple of drinks in a dark bar and hear a sentimental song, and imagine they're in love. And this"—he flipped a hand up toward his glasses, indicating his blindness—"it touches them, I guess. They want to be nice to me."

"It's more than that—you *know* it's more than that."

"Sometimes. Not usually."

She took the risk farther. "It's a lot more than that with me."

"I already knew that," he said quietly.

They were silent for a while. Then he put out his hand, reaching across Rud toward her. She lifted a hand from the wheel and touched his, and their fingers played lightly, testing the first tentative sensations of intimacy. Just that much excited her more than any touch she could remember.

Oddly, it frightened her, too, and suddenly she drew back. He turned to her, surprised.

"I'm not sure what I can give you, Toby," she said.

"What have I asked for? Just be with me. I don't want more than that."

"The problem is I'm still—"

"Married," he put in. "That's no secret."

Was that the word she was about to say? Married? Or might she have said, "still frightened?"

He went on. "But it's over, isn't it?"

"I want it to be," she said. "I'm afraid of doing anything that might stop that from happening as soon as possible."

"And you think being with me is taking a chance?"

How much could she tell him? What would he think of her if he knew she had entered into marriage with someone who terrified her now? Didn't that make her seem foolish, her judgment faulty? How would his opinion of her be affected by her choice to

live virtually in hiding—or if he learned that she was defending herself against the charge of "abandoning" her husband? Would he want
to be "the other man" in a relationship with a woman whose
husband—if he knew where she was—might stalk her to this refuge,
release his violent impulses against anyone he regarded as a rival?

Or were her fears overblown, the leftover terror of a nightmare
that was over?

At last she replied: "I like being with you, Toby. But you should
know right up front that . . . my marriage has left me a little scared
and unsure of myself. More than a little, to be honest. I don't feel
ready yet to trust my own feelings, or anyone else's. I want to spend
time with you. But I need to go slowly, very slowly. Baby steps, that's
really all I can take."

He nodded. "So how about this: We'll cross that bridge the same
way we came down the mountain. You tell me where to go and how
fast. Sound okay?"

"That sounds," she said, "just right."

They linked hands again, and were quiet until they were approaching the Mills. As before, Toby's knowledge of the turns in the
road attuned him to the moment when the first houses came in
sight.

"I'd like you to have dinner this evening at my house," he said.
"But is that too big a step—bringing you home to meet Mother?"

She laughed. "With *your* mother especially, that would be much
too big—if I hadn't already met her."

Chapter 15

She followed his directions to a street running up a hill on the far edge of town. Spaced along the street were two dozen small houses, basic one-story Cape Cod style, all with front yards, all backing toward pine-forested hillsides. As she drove up the street Gaye saw indications that this must be the poorer section of the town, an area where workers in the now-vanished woolen mills to which the town owed its name must have once resided. At least half the houses were long past due for repainting. In the backyard of a house at the bottom of the street several broken-down old cars were being left to rust.

The Callan house was at the top of the hill, where the street stopped at a dead end. Another small Cape, it was distinctly better tended than its neighbors, with a fairly fresh paint job of pale yellow siding and forest-green trim for the windows and door. A winding path of intermingled blue and red slate had been laid from the street to the front door; a large copper weather vane atop the chimney was in the shape of an Arabian oil lamp—the sort from which a genie appeared when rubbed. And the mailbox was topped by one of those gadgets of painted wood that moved when wind turned a bladed wheel: in this one a tail-coated conductor waved his arms up and down to conduct a painted orchestra.

As they went up the path, Toby said, "I'm not the decorator."

Inside, lights were on against the dark winter evening, but the house was quiet. Toby paused in the small entrance hall and listened for a moment. "Mom must be doing a reading," he said, and bent to unbuckle Rud's harness.

"Reading? Of what?"

"She does the tarot. Didn't you know?"

Freed from the harness, Rud ran from the small entrance hall into a living room at the right and stretched out on the floor.

"I've seen her fooling around with those cards at the post office."

"On government property it would be fooling around," Toby said. "Around here she takes it seriously. There are people who come now and then and pay to get her advice. There's a little room at the back just for the purpose—the 'reading room,' she calls it."

Gaye wondered how much Toby himself subscribed to occult practices, but stifled any remark that would question his beliefs or seem critical of Dot's.

He led the way to the kitchen. Driving across town he'd asked to stop at a food market so he could buy the makings for dinner, and offered to get whatever Gaye felt like eating. "You decide," she'd told him. "The way I've been taking care of myself lately, anything cooked by somebody else will taste great to me." Happy to be surprised, she'd let him go into the market by himself with Rud, and didn't know what he'd bought.

Carrying two bags of food and wine, Toby proceeded to the kitchen with sure steps, taking a turn off a short corridor when necessary, knowing exactly when to stop and deposit the bags on an island counter. He started to remove packages, cans, and bottles, leaving some on the counter, and crossing the kitchen to put others in cabinets and the fridge.

"What can I help with?" Gaye asked.

"Not a thing. I want to show off. But would you like a glass of wine while you watch?"

"I'll wait for dinner."

The plan was to eat early, since Toby still had to work this evening. The inn usually liked him to start at seven o'clock, but they gave him some leeway, and he'd said it would be all right to go in as late as eight. Gaye sat down at the round kitchen table by a corner window as Toby cooked. Moving around effortlessly, he put things away or set them on counters for preparation, got out pots, pans, and utensils, laid them out where he wanted them. He went right to a peg where a white linen apron was hanging, put it on, and tied the strings behind his back. Even functioning within dimensions he knew well, even knowing where everything was kept, and being able to count steps and measure his movements in one direction or another, the sense memory that allowed him to maneuver so quickly and confidently amazed Gaye no less than seeing a blindfolded magician perform an escape stunt. A few times she saw him reach out and his hand arrive slightly off the target he was seeking, yet his adjustments were quick, and he was never so wide of the mark that he seemed to be groping in the dark.

He was no less adept when it came to preparing the food. Only once, when he pulled a large-bladed kitchen knife from a woodblock holder and started rapidly chopping up some celery to throw into a pot, did she half rise from her chair, prepared to intervene if there was a mishap. But of course he managed the task easily; in fact, he chopped at the *rat-a-tat* rate of an expert chef—much faster than she could have done.

The main dish he was cooking, he said, would be coq au vin, to be accompanied by wild rice, asparagus, and what he called "a simple salad."

"But when Mom comes in," he added, "I've got to tell her it's plain chicken in the pot, or she'll accuse me of putting on airs."

While he prepared the meal, Toby responded to questions of Gaye's prompted naturally by being in his home. How long had he lived here? What had brought them originally to Bartlett Mills? Her mild probing led eventually to hearing a fairly full biographical account.

The house had belonged originally to his grandfather, Tobias Deerfield, a worker in one of the small woolen mills that had lined the Vermont side of the Connecticut River in the early part of the century. When the mills began failing in the twenties, he had set up a garage in the town and had made his living selling gasoline and fixing cars. His only child, a daughter, was Toby's mother. Uninterested in her father's trade, Dot had gone off to Boston, taken a secretarial course, worked a few years in an office, then, after her father died, returned to Bartlett Mills to be with her mother. They had gotten money to live on from selling the garage, and Dot had augmented that with a job at the local bakery. The baker's son was Billy Callan, Toby's father.

"At the time my mother went to Boston, Billy was only fourteen years old," Toby said. "But the way I've heard it from Mom, he had a crush on her from the first time he saw her in the bakery buying a loaf of bread. When she came back to town, he was twenty. He went to work on her and never let up till she said yes."

Dot had been twenty-seven, her husband just twenty-two, when they married, but according to Toby it had been a good marriage. Before their first anniversary, she was pregnant with their first and only child.

"Right after they found out she was expecting me, my father was called up for the army," Toby explained. "They still had the draft then, but he didn't mind; it seemed like a good thing for him. The GI Bill would pay for further education, and there was no fighting anywhere; he didn't expect to be in danger. After his couple of months in training, he was sent to Korea. The war had ended a few years before, but there were still occasional skirmishes along what they call the DMZ, the line between North and South Korea, the odd bullet flying back and forth." Up to this point he'd been chatting easily, adding to the story without hesitation as he answered Gaye's questions. Now he paused, his head drooped, and he became very still.

Gaye didn't have to ask what came next.

"He was out riding in a jeep, part of a routine patrol," Toby continued finally, and went on breaking off the root ends of some asparagus. "Winter of 'fifty-seven. I was born early in 'fifty-eight. Never saw him—even when I *could* see."

Gaye listened in stunned silence as Toby finished off the family history. To provide for Dot and her child, and in recognition of the sacrifice of the only one of the town's citizens to die in military service since World War II, the local selectmen had arranged for Dot to take over the post office job as soon as the postmaster at that time retired. She'd held the job now for forty-three years. "When she says they'll have to carry her out," he concluded, "she means it."

He arranged the asparagus to steam and moved on to mixing some oil and lemon juice and vinegar for salad dressing.

"Sad story, huh?" he said, when Gaye remained silent. Obviously his bravado was meant to dispel the sadness, take them both out of it.

She confessed her thoughts. "I was wondering if never knowing your father at all could be easier than having him for a while, then losing him. That's what happened to me with my mother. My parents divorced when I was young, and I didn't see her very much after that. Then she died when I was in high school."

"I'd say that's harder," Toby replied. "You can't really lose what you never had. What about your father? Is he alive?"

"Yes." She paused, reflecting on the irony. She felt sorry for Toby, for the loss of never knowing his father. She'd grown up with hers, and she had no desire to see him. "We're not speaking these days," she said quietly.

Toby turned his face to Gaye, and seemed about to ask the cause of the rift, but they were both distracted by the noise of Dot loudly chatting with someone as she emerged from behind a closed door and took her client to the front door. "The reading's ended," Toby said.

Dot could be heard calling a good-bye to her departing visitor. "Don't worry, dear. You're in the waning moon. . . . See you next week."

A moment later she came bustling into the kitchen. As usual, she was dressed flamboyantly, tonight in an orange kaftan with wide yellow stripes. Seeing Toby, she began, "Poor Lydie Fenster, worried about her—" She stopped short when she noticed Gaye at the table. "What's this? Our local fugitive from justice hiding out under my roof?"

"Dot, I told you I'm not—"

"Oh, tut, can't I pull your leg a little? I'm delighted to see you, dear. Goodness, took long enough to get you here. Told you weeks ago you ought to meet my boy." She stepped over to the stove, took the lid off a pot, and bent over for a sniff. "Smells to me like you two got off on the right foot: he wants to impress you with his cooking." She slapped the lid down again. "What is that, anyway?" she asked Toby.

"Chicken in the pot."

"How soon can we eat? You know how hungry I get after a long, hard reading, and this was a doozie."

"Food's ready," Toby said as he finished tossing the salad. "Set the table. I'll give Rud his dinner. Then we can sit down." As he removed his apron, Gaye noticed he hadn't spilled a drop on it.

"C'mon, you," Dot snapped at Gaye as she started pulling dishes and silverware from drawers, "give me a hand with this."

Gaye pitched in at once. She didn't mind Dot's bossy style; she took it for being treated like one of the family—with a kind of warm irreverence she'd never experienced from her own mother or father.

It wasn't just Toby's cooking that Gaye enjoyed when they sat down—mouthwatering as it was—but the atmosphere prevailing at the Callans' table. As Dot gossiped shamelessly about all the characters who'd passed through the post office that day, and Toby told about his day on the mountain, the fun he'd had skiing with Gaye—and praised her prowess—she realized it was probably the first time she'd shared a home-cooked meal with other people in years (or had she ever?) where there were no underlying tensions to spoil her appetite. With her mother or father or Brian, even at the Bennetts', it was never simply a time to relax, savor the food, let troubles fade away amid the glow of good companionship. But here with Toby and his mother, hearing the way they joked or lightly scolded each other for their foibles, she had a glimpse of the basic human pleasure that was possible with good, gentle people who truly cared about each other. Whatever sorrows and hardship this mother and son had endured, it had bonded them in mutual respect as well as love. This, Gaye thought, was how life *could* be in a family.

The meal was concluded with a store-bought lemon sherbet that Toby took from the freezer, and spiked with a splash of raspberry liqueur. He offered coffee, but when Dot expressed a preference for mint tea, Gaye seconded the choice. Toby got up from the table to put on the teakettle.

Alone at the table with Dot, Gaye grabbed quickly at a topic for sociable conversation. "So, this card thing I've seen at the post office is more than a hobby?"

"Oh, a lot more. It's how I help people—my ministry, you might say."

"I always thought it was just a kind of fortune-telling."

"Don't know what could be more helpful than telling people what they've got in store for 'em."

Dot's faintly defensive tone suggested it might be wise to switch to another subject. Gaye didn't believe the future could be predicted with cards or tea leaves or crystal balls, but she didn't want to find herself debunking Dot's beliefs in front of Toby. "I see what you mean," she said mildly. "I can think of a lot of times it would have helped me to know things in advance. Thanksgiving dinner with you, for one. If I'd known how Toby cooked—"

Dot bypassed the detour into small talk. "I'll do a reading for you," she broke in. "Right now."

"No, thanks."

"You just said it would help you to know things in advance."

"Well, yes, but that's if you can *really* know."

"Think I can't read the cards?"

The talk was going just where she hadn't wanted it to go. "No, I'm sure you can. But . . . you said it's tiring for you, and . . ." She cast a glance at Toby, who was cleaning up while he waited for the water to boil. If only he could see her expression, pleading for his help. "We're all so relaxed now."

"Best time for it."

She called for help. "Toby, your mom wants to give me a tarot reading."

"On the house!" Dot shouted out.

"Grab it," Toby said. "That's a gift worth at least ten bucks."

"Twenty-five," Dot countered. "I'm not going to give her a quickie. I'll do a nice ten-card Celtic cross spread." She patted Gaye's hand. "You'll like this, dear. Tell you everything you need to know."

Toby reaffirmed his assurance with a nod and wink. "You don't want to miss this, Gaye. Listen, I've got to get to the inn. You stay, get your reading from Mom, then come over and let me serenade you."

She wanted to go with him, but refusing now would be too complicated.

After Toby left for the inn, Dot brought Gaye to her "reading room," a small square chamber at a rear corner, probably intended at one time for nothing more than storage. Dot had fixed it up with scarlet velveteen draped from the ceiling as in a pasha's tent. On a ledge around the edges of the room, half a dozen candlelit lanterns of Middle Eastern design gently lit the surroundings. There was barely room for more than the room's only furniture, a card table covered with more of the red velveteen, and the two chairs facing across the table. On the table was one more glass-shaded lantern and a deck of cards.

Dot lit the candles in all the lanterns, turned off the ceiling light, and seated herself opposite Gaye. She picked up the cards, then leaned across the table as if to impart a secret. "I suppose you think this is a bunch of nonsense," she said.

"No, I wouldn't exactly call it—"

"Doesn't matter. What works, works, whether you think it's nonsense or not. You want to think it's just crazy old Dot fooling around, that's not going to hurt the reading. What'll hurt is if you ignore what I say and forget it. So pay attention and try to remember, because it may do you some good."

Gaye nodded. The sincerity in the older woman's tone was undeniable; she *meant* to do something important and valuable—whether she could or not.

Dot thrust the deck into Gaye's hands. "Give these a shuffle, much as you want, and hand 'em back."

Gaye obeyed, holding on to the cards long enough to assure Dot her involvement wasn't perfunctory. As the cards were mixed, Dot embarked on a little lecture about the history of the tarot—the first decks appearing in Europe in the Middle Ages from murky unknown origins, the tarot's use for divination developing only from the nineteenth century onward. When Gaye handed the cards back,

Dot rattled on with an explanation of the deck itself, tossing off unfamiliar words and facts so quickly Gaye couldn't make much sense out of what she was hearing. The deck was divided into two sections, or what Dot called "a major and a minor arcana" of twenty-two and fifty-six cards respectively. She explained the minor had four suits, which were wands, cups, swords, and pentacles. Though difficult for Gaye to absorb, Dot's knowledge of the complexities was impressive in itself.

While she talked, Dot had been peeling cards off the deck and laying them down on the table in the design she called the Celtic cross. What took shape in front of Gaye was a group of ten cards with the first two laid one over the other at the center, the next four around it as if at the four points of a compass, and a final four placed end to end in a line at one side. On each card there were colorful pictures of figures, or objects, or castles, and all had a caption relating to the picture. The Hermit, The Fool, The Tower, The Moon, Justice, Chariot, and The Hierophant were some of the captions Gaye saw in front of her. The cards weren't completely unfamiliar; not only had she seen Dot fiddling with them at the post office, but there had been a girl at vet college who had often given playful tarot readings for others in the dorm who had questions about their love lives.

Having completed the design, Dot put aside the rest of the deck and spent a long time studying what she had laid down. As her eyes roamed from one picture to the next, she made little noises like groans of regret or moans of approval. At times she muttered softly, not speaking to Gaye, but commenting to herself on what she saw. "Mmm . . . too bad . . . ah, better . . . yes, a good moon . . . but there, that looks difficult. . . ."

In spite of her skepticism, Gaye's anxiety rose as she sat through this performance. "Well?" she prompted, working to sound bemused. "Will I live?"

Dot raised her eyes and regarded Gaye gravely. "You've had a terribly hard time, haven't you? You've suffered, been subjected to brutal unkindness, and faced great danger."

Gaye stared back at the older woman. Of course, this much might

have been merely guesses, surmised from what was plainly known—
that she was escaping from *something*—yet the statement had been
delivered with confidence. More than that, Dot's words carried a
tremulous note of empathy, as if the older woman truly sensed the
degree of harm, even what had caused it. A mix of revived hurt and
anger and shame struck Gaye mute.

"This spread—the Celtic cross, as it's called—can tell us many
things," Dot went on. "About your past, and influences from the past
that may still be blocking you; about your present situation, and the
good and bad elements in it; and your state of mind, how others see
you, as well as what the future may bring—depending on how you
meet the challenges of all the factors at work."

Gaye was captivated now. In the flickering glow of lamplight,
under the tentlike canopy, she could almost believe she had been
transported to the cave of some ancient oracle. Even if she hadn't
surrendered to the notion that the random display of some fanci-
fully decorated cards could divine the entire plan of her life, she was
moved by the evident commitment of Toby's mother to provide the
gift of insight with the prospect of help and healing.

As she interpreted one card after another, according to its place
in the design, Dot certainly came close enough to describing the
past and present situations that Gaye had to respect her intuition.
Talking about a card called the Tower, she said that it revealed Gaye
had endured a time of imprisonment, where she had been subjected
to nothing less than a form of torture. As part of this imprisonment,
she had been a victim of falsehoods, deluding herself or being led to
illusions that left her shattered when she realized their falsity. Yet,
too, there was a positive side to the appearance of the Tower in her
reading: it promised release, and an opportunity to rebuild on firmer
ground without false illusions.

When Dot expounded upon the meaning of the Moon card, and
the Hermit, and the Hanged Man, which had all appeared in the assortment of cards she referred to as "the spread," it all seemed relevant to Gaye. The weak tendencies in her behavior had to be
replaced with strength, she was told, so she could give herself to her
work, to life, even to love, with the trust and total commitment that

had been stolen from her in the past. There was someone now who deserved such a commitment from her. . . .

At this point Gaye's objectivity kicked in again. It sounded like Dot was simply electioneering for her son. It could be that everything she'd said was only to put Gaye in the right frame of mind to be receptive to Toby.

Though, on the other hand, Dot surely knew by now that Toby was no wallflower who needed his mother's help to get a date.

By now the reading had lasted at least half an hour. Gaye was ready for it to be over. She shifted restlessly in her chair, and Dot got the message.

"We're almost done, dear," she said. "There's just the matter of what lies before you to be told. I've left it for last because . . . it's the most worrying part of all I see here." She leaned closer over the cards, her hands prodding them, moving them slightly as if she wished they could be rearranged. "Something evil is lurking out there," she resumed, looking away vaguely toward one of the curtained windows.

"Where exactly?" Gaye challenged her.

She faced Gaye again. "In the world, in your future. But you have the advantage now. Knowing this, you can be ready for it. The cards tell me you can defeat it, as long as you stay on your guard."

"Defeat it how? What is it?" Gaye was more annoyed than frightened. Fine if Dot amused herself by pretending to tell fortunes, but she'd gone too far if she thought it permissible to give these dire warnings.

"I can't tell more, my dear. I don't see everything. But taken together with the rest—this indication from the Hanged Man that you may find new love if you will only trust yourself to believe in it—I could take a guess that your hope may be connected somehow"—she hesitated again, and her gaze fixed firmly on Gaye's, as if to affirm the absolute sincerity of her prescription—"to my son."

For a second Gaye looked at Dot wide-eyed, amazed by the blatant exposure of her matchmaking. The whole reading, the resort to the tarot, was suddenly revealed, after all, as little more than a joke.

Gaye couldn't keep herself from breaking into laughter. "Oh, Dot," she gasped, recovering, "really . . . you don't have to go through all this for Toby. He's doing fine on his own."

Dot shook her head. "You don't understand, dear girl. This is deadly serious. There are indications of . . . of a life, or perhaps lives, that may be lost. What I see here. . ." Her hand waved vaguely over the cards on the table. "If I were going to be selfish, I'd warn my son to stay clear of all this. But I can see a bond is forming, and he may be what saves you."

Gaye's amusement had reverted to irritation, yet she kept a rein on her temper, certain Toby would be turned against her if she were inconsiderate of his mother. This episode had to be kept in perspective; fortune-telling was virtually a hobby for a woman with a clutch of eccentricities. Whatever portents of doom appeared to Dot in the arrangement of small cardboard illustrations, however seriously she took it, the prediction was only a product of her quirky imagination.

Gaye pushed her chair back from the table. "Well, if your warning is what saves me, it's hardly enough just to say thank-you. But I do . . . appreciate it."

Still seated, Dot kept gazing at her with a look of earnest concern. "Take heed of what I say."

"Yes. Yes, of course. And you can tell Toby, too, that it would be good if he keeps an eye on me—well, you know what I mean."

"Yes, I do. And I will."

Gaye edged toward the door of the room. "So are we done?"

"Yes, dear. You go along. I'm going to stay here a while. I need to look at the cards a bit more. . . ."

When she left, Gaye didn't drive over to the inn. Toby would ask to hear the results of the reading, she was sure, and talking about it would be too awkward. She didn't want to be critical of his mother; nor did she feel she could report to him that she had been urged to believe her safety, perhaps her very life, depended on staying close to him. Either she'd have to dismiss Dot as a kook, or else she might appear to be hysterical or grasping, conniving to trap him.

Let him hear the news of her dire future straight from the original source, she thought. Let him decide for himself if it was nonsense—or if he liked the idea of being the white knight upon whom her life depended.

Chapter 16

Gaye lifted her eye from the microscope, and looked blankly at the wall in front of the lab counter, mentally practicing the report she'd have to give Toby. The spinal fluid clearly revealed the presence of neoplastic cells, the irregular cellular material that constituted a marker for cancer in any animal. Factoring in Toby's previous descriptions of the problem with the dog's movement, and X-rays that showed bone and musculature in the limbs free of irregularities, Gaye strongly suspected the cancer was impinging upon the spinal column. An osteosarcoma, or bone tumor, involving the vertebrae was one possibility. In the larger-breed dogs like shepherds it wasn't common. Yet that, too, should have been detectable on the regular survey radiograph that had been done previously. Gaye had just studied the X-rays again, and still saw nothing. More likely there was an undifferentiated carcinoma, a variety of tumor mass that wouldn't show on an ordinary X-ray, since it might not produce any visible decrease in joint space or misalignment of the vertebrae. Rather it could form within the spinal canal and begin to put pressure on the spinal cord, thus causing pain, or some interference with neural impulses, either of which would account for the "hitch" in Rud's movement that Toby had detected.

Considering all her previous assurance to Toby that his worries were probably baseless, it was going to be hard to face him with such discouraging possibilities. Still, Gaye was resolved to present him with a realistic picture. She'd already sugarcoated things too much, her judgment affected by simply wishing for the best, and believing that his own fears, based on the vague evidence he'd reported, were overblown.

But more than the bleak medical picture made it difficult to face Toby. There were also unresolved tensions in their personal situation. Since he'd left to go to the inn after the Saturday-evening dinner, they hadn't talked until he'd arrived for this morning's appointment. After Dot's reading, and her failure to show up at the inn, she'd expected a call from him—surely he would have asked Dot about it. But there had been no call. A few times yesterday she'd contemplated picking up the phone herself, then decided it was his place to call.

When they met at the clinic this morning, he had seemed reserved with her. "I missed you Saturday night," was all he'd said.

"Sorry. After what your mother told me, I felt like going home instead."

He didn't follow that up with any questions. From then on it had been all about the dog. Unless he initiated it, she didn't feel comfortable departing from her professional role.

Now, while this odd gap in their communication still existed, she had to go and tell him that his dog—as much a partner in life as any human could be—could be terminally ill.

Gaye picked up the phone and pressed the button that rang the intercom at the reception desk. "Lori, is Mr. Callan out there?" When Rud recovered from the anesthesia, Toby had taken him for another walk while she continued her lab analysis. That was nearly two hours ago; she expected he'd be back by now.

"Yes, he's sitting right here," the receptionist said.

"Has he been there long?"

"About an hour."

Gaye thought for a second. "I'll come out," she said.

She went to the coatrack, put on her parka, ski cap, and boots, and went to the reception room.

"Okay, Toby," she said, forcing the brightness. "I've got the results." He rose from his chair, and Rud stood with him. "Listen, I've been bent over doing the lab stuff for hours. Would you mind if we get some fresh air while we talk? I know you were just out, but—"

"Fine with me."

Gaye felt some of her burden relieved. Away from the clinic, she felt the bonds of strict professionalism would be loosened.

Toby knew by now where coats hung in the reception room, and got his own. Then he picked up Rud's harness from the floor by the rack and buckled it on. As they reached the door to go out, he turned to the reception desk. "Would you call a taxi for me now?" he asked Lori. "Tell 'em to come in half an hour."

Leaving the clinic, they headed down the long, sloping road that led up to the Bennett property from the public highway. It was another clear, sunny day, but the thermometer had gone down a few degrees since the weekend, and the cold was stinging if you walked toward the wind. In this direction, though, the wind was at their backs.

Gaye looked toward a line of clouds on the horizon. Delaying the hard part, she said, "Weather report said there's a big snowstorm on the way. Have you heard anything about it?"

"So," he said, ignoring the question, "is it that bad?"

"Bad as what?" she said.

"Bad enough that you don't come straight out and say, 'All clear.' Bad enough that you need to get some fresh air, and talk about a snowstorm instead. Bad enough"—he stopped and turned to her—"that Rud's going to die."

No sugarcoating, she reminded herself. "I don't know how bad it is, Toby; that's the truth. The sample I've just examined did contain evidence of cancer. That presents us with three questions. Where exactly is the cancer? How far advanced is it? And is it a kind that may be responsive to treatment, or something aggressive and resistant?" She paused so he could respond.

He pondered it for a couple of seconds. "Any guesses?" he asked quietly, and began to stroll forward again.

More clouds had gathered, and one had drifted across the sun. The darkening of the day made the prospects seem bleaker. "I wouldn't leave anything to guesswork," Gaye said. "Particularly not mine," she added guiltily, "considering the advice I've given you up to now."

"You told me whatever you were able to see."

"But you knew better, and I didn't listen."

"I had the advantage of *not* seeing. Just feeling."

She glanced at him, and once more felt the emotional tug of a desire to understand what had caused the gap that had opened between them. "Anyway, we're one step closer to knowing how to treat Rud. Since the survey radiograph didn't show where the problem is, we need to do a CAT scan."

"Will a CAT scan work for a dog?"

He meant to lighten the moment, she knew, but she kept to her resolve not to let the facts get lost. "That's computer-assisted tomography—which gives us a full cross-section of the body, and can register organic material and see into spaces X-rays won't show. We aren't equipped to do it at the clinic, but I can set it up . . . or maybe your other vet—"

"Set it up, Gaye." He gave her a reassuring smile. "Don't forget, Rud picked you for his doctor."

They had reached the bottom of the hill. They stopped at the turn to the two-lane highway, and stood silently for a long moment. She thought Toby was already grieving for his dog.

"These things can be curable," she said.

"Let's hope. But the feeling I get from Rud is that he's not expecting to be around for too much longer."

"How, Toby?" she demanded. "How can he possibly be telling you that? Really!" However much she respected his instinct, she was irritated by having to go forward in any healing process hampered by his defeatist attitude.

"You want specifics?" he answered calmly. "He's already pushing me to get his replacement."

"How?"

"He takes longer. . . ."

"What does that mean?"

"He's always been right there when I need him. Instantly. He could even anticipate my movements. Now he'll let me wait a bit before he's there, just a little. It's all very subtle, Gaye, nothing that would be noticed by anyone but me. But it's his way of saying to me, 'You need somebody else.' "

"Or . . . he doesn't have the same energy."

Toby shook his head. "No. This is different."

His mother's eccentricity must have been passed along somehow—and maybe this was it. How different was a belief that the future could be foretold from believing animals possessed this humanlike degree of sensitivity? Yet, true or not, it was what Toby believed—and, as a sentimental notion of his bond with Rud, was worthy of being preserved. The best way to argue against the belief was simply to cure the dog. She turned up the hill again. "C'mon," she said, "I'll drive you home."

"I've ordered a taxi."

Why did it feel now as if he were rejecting her favors?

The wind swept down against them as they walked back up to the clinic. With the raw cold knifing into the exposed skin of her face and the discouragement she felt, the sense that he was retreating from her was even harder to bear. She had to know what had caused the breach since Saturday. "Toby," she blurted, "about what your—"

"Listen, Gaye—" He started to speak at exactly the same moment.

He pulled up on Rud's harness, and they turned to each other.

"You first," she said. A medical question, maybe.

"My mother told me what was in the cards for you. I thought that probably had something to do with . . . well, scaring you off would be one way to put it. Am I close?"

"Ballpark," she agreed.

"The part I couldn't guess was whether what scared you was being mixed up with folks you'd decided were a little nuts, or the pressure she was putting on you . . . about me."

"Why didn't you just call and ask me?"

He took a breath and let the exhaled vapor trail slowly into the air. "Look, it's hard enough to ask even now. It wouldn't be if you could have just laughed it off, and come to the inn, and . . . we picked up right where we left off. You didn't. Now I don't know how to argue against any fears you have—about me, or my mom's reading—without maybe making things worse."

"It's always better to talk," she said.

"Is it? I think it depends on what people say."

The cold was chilling them both. They started moving uphill again.

"What could you say that would make things worse?" Gaye asked.

"How about this: Loony as my mother may seem to some people, I trust what she told you. If you think she's playing games with you, then you'd assume I'm guilty of the same thing."

They walked in silence while Gaye mulled over his answer. "What makes you believe she's really got this ability to tell the future?" she asked at last.

"For one thing, her predictions generally come to pass. Oh, I know, the language she uses can be ambiguous sometimes; the way people interpret it is what may give it validity. But ask the local people who visit her—not the post office customers she kids around with, but the ones who trust her. She gives them good advice."

"Advice is different from telling the future."

"Another thing," he went on quickly, "Mom's very careful with what she tells people. For her to go as far out on a limb as she did with you—to worry anyone with the threat of danger or harm—that's taking a huge responsibility. It's a risk she'd happily avoid, if she didn't care so much to help you."

"She hardly knows me," Gaye said. "Why should she care more about helping me than any—"

He didn't wait for the rest. "Because she knows you matter to me."

Didn't that bring the whole discussion back to a mother's matchmaking? Gaye wondered.

"And one more thing," Toby said.

But Gaye didn't want to hear more. She could understand why he would have been reluctant to get into defending Dot's tarot reading. Listening to more of his defenses, she thought, would probably just add to her confusion and irritation. He was right: It didn't make things any better.

"Toby," she put in, "I'm glad you spoke to me about this. More than that, I'm happy to hear that . . . I matter to you. Your mother put me on the spot with that reading because she told me to lean on you. Did you know that?"

"She said I could help you."

"Only that?" Gaye let out a short, dry laugh. "She practically said I needed you to save my life. Anyway, that made it hard. . . ."

"It shouldn't have," he said. His hands came up from his sides, found her arms, and gripped them. "It's okay if you need me. I need you, too—for him." He nodded to Rud.

From the way he was holding her, she anticipated being pulled into a kiss, and she wanted it. But he turned away suddenly, his acute hearing having picked up the sound of the taxi turning up the hill. He released her and stepped back. "I'll see you soon, huh? You'll set up that scan thing?"

"Sure. Soon as possible." She was deflated by the abruptness of his departure.

The taxi pulled into the parking lot and Rud started pulling Toby toward it. "Want to hear me sing tonight?" he called over his shoulder. "Make up for what you missed?"

Her mood lifted. "I'd love that."

"Come around nine."

The taxi driver seemed to know Toby. He'd hopped out to open the door for him. Toby put the dog in first, then stopped before following. "I don't expect you to save him," he said to Gaye. "Just make it easier."

Damn! she thought as she watched the taxi go down the hill. He could place his faith so easily in the future predicted by an arrangement of cards . . . and then dismiss all the hope connected to her skill and training.

It made her mad all over again.

Chapter 17

Unfortunately, Toby's worst fears were justified.

The scan done the following week at the animal hospital in Montpelier, the nearest vet facility with CT equipment, revealed an intramedullary tumor impinging on the spinal cord. In the opinion of an oncological specialist who reviewed the results—and was obviously far more experienced in interpreting the images than Gaye—it was an astrocytoma affixed to the cord and wrapping around it, making it inoperable. Surgical invasion would certainly cause critical paralysis, probably death. Radiation bombardment couldn't be completely ruled out, but prospects for positive results were minimal at best. Even if the cancer were cured, such treatment would cause almost certain paralysis. The recommended therapy was thus limited to painkilling drugs, administered according to need as the cancer progressed. This would allow Rud to go on for as long as possible performing his function at the side of his master.

Gaye sat with Toby as he heard the prognosis—consistent with his expectations. He took the news stoically, and asked only one question: "How much time do we have?"

A few months, give or take, was the way the oncologist put it. Such a cancer didn't always follow a set schedule of growth. It might progress slowly, or suddenly have a spurt. In any event, it would reach a critical point in its attack on the spinal cord once nerve function was radically affected; then, even after the dog had been enjoying mobility and seeming relatively well, the decline would accelerate, limb function cease, organs soon begin to fail.

On the first part of their long drive back to the Mills, Toby showed no inclination to talk. Gaye had commiserated with him when they emerged from the consultation, and didn't want to encourage any false hopes now. Leaving him to his thoughts, she tuned the radio to a classical music station.

During the week it had taken to arrange the scan, they had spent a lot of time together. Every day after work she'd gone to the inn to hear him play. He'd arrange to have dinner for both of them brought to the bar from the restaurant, and they would be together during his breaks. On Saturday they went skiing again. This time, at the end of the day, there had been a few thrilling runs down a more advanced black diamond trail. On one, while racing along at a good clip, they'd taken a frightening spill and both had gone tumbling over several times before coming to a stop. Their safety bindings had released, however, and they came up laughing, neither sustaining more than a minor bruise or two. Gaye had not only insisted on finishing the run on the same trail, but going right back to the top again. Toby balked, but she ignored him.

"Damn it, Toby," she railed, "if you want to go and sit on your ass, all right. But then I'll take another run alone." She started for the lift, and he glided after her, bumping heedlessly into other skiers, and shouting with mock alarm, "Stop, thief! Somebody stop that woman!"

"Not very nice, calling me a thief," she said after they hooked up again.

"Aren't you?" he said. "You've robbed me of my senses and stolen my heart."

They did another fast run down the expert trail without mishap.

Then, on his Sunday off, he'd suggested they drive down to Hanover to tour Dartmouth College. There was a fine-art museum on the campus, Toby said, with a good collection of both modern and Old Master paintings.

Her turn to resist. "That can't be any fun for you—me looking at paintings."

"Listen," he said sharply. "I don't ever want you to stop look-ing at the world because I'm blind. The more you look, the more *I'll* see."

At the museum she described the paintings for him. She found that the exercise enhanced her own appreciation of the art. In fact, the more she wanted him to see, the more she saw for herself.

Yet, with all the time they'd spent together, she had avoided going back to his house or inviting him home with her. The prospect of encountering Dot again, being subjected to more of the woman's badgering and warnings, made Gaye apprehensive. And bringing Toby to her own place for an intimate domestic evening was bound to encourage the notion that she was ready to go to bed with him. Not that she hadn't felt the desire; there had been times at the bar, listening to him sing some haunting love classic like "Body and Soul," when she was overtaken by the sort of unbridled hunger to be with him that seemed akin to the hysteria of teenage girls swooning over a rock idol. But her passions were at war with her scruples. She wasn't willing to commit adultery. No matter that the infidelity would be to a husband she no longer loved; in fact, the marriage from which she was escaping had been corrupted by sex—specifically, sex in which the moral responsibility between partners was violated. If she were to compromise morality for the sake of her own pleasure, Gaye feared it might poison the potential for some-thing finer with Toby.

She did wonder, though, if she were being *too* careful, rationaliz-ing only because the experiences she'd had with Brian had spoiled her for being with any other man, wary of simply being used, of being desired without being loved.

"He lived up here, you know. . . ."

They'd been on the road an hour, and a Bach flute piece was playing on the radio. Gaye's mind had been carried off by the music into a debate with herself about whether to risk inviting him home tonight. "Sorry . . . what'd you say?" She reached to turn off the radio. Her hand accidentally brushed over his as he stroked the dog, who was sleeping between them on the broad front seat. Even that tiny touch aroused her.

"I was thinking about Kipling," Toby explained.

"Does that mean you're ready to kipple?"

She was grateful for the smile she got out of him. Obviously it was the connection to Rud that had started this train of thought. Maybe it was a way into sharing his sorrow.

"Most people don't know he lived in Vermont for a while," Toby said. "Near Brattleboro."

"Really? Hard to picture Kipling on skis. India, the land of Gunga Din, burning-hot places like that, that's what he wrote about."

"He built a house here in the 1890s, called it Naulakha. Lived there three years, then had a big fight with his alcoholic brother-in-law and went back to England."

"Naulakha," Gaye echoed. "What's that come from?"

"It's a Hindu word meaning 'precious jewel.' "

She glanced over at him. The relevance to his feelings about Rud was plain. "But that's not why you gave Rud his name, is it? Will said it had something to do with one of Kipling's poems."

" 'The Power of the Dog.' Know it?"

"All I know is a line or two from that other famous one." She intoned one of its climactic lines: " 'If you can keep your head, while all about you are losing theirs—' "

" '—then you'll be a man, my son,' " Toby finished.

"Maybe that's what turned me off Kipling. I didn't want to be a man."

He smiled. A moment later he began to recite:

There is sorrow enough in the natural way
From men and women to fill our day;
But when we are certain of sorrow in store,
Why do we always arrange for more?
Brothers and sisters, I bid you beware
Of giving your heart to a dog to tear.

It could have been a song lyric, the way he delivered it, giving just the right weight to every word, pausing here or hurrying a lit-

tle there, conveying the rhythm but in a way that made it fresh, and
muted what might have seemed a hackneyed singsong.

> *Buy a pup and your money will buy*
> *Love unflinching that cannot lie—*
> *Perfect passion and worship fed*
> *By a kick in the ribs or a pat on the head.*
> *Nevertheless it is hardly fair*
> *To risk your heart for a dog to tear.*

> *When the fourteen years that Nature permits*
> *Are closing in asthma or tumors or fits,*
> *And the vet's unspoken prescription runs*
> *To lethal chambers or loaded guns,*
> *Then you will find—it's your own affair*
> *But—you've given your heart to a dog to tear.*

Halfway through the verse, when he mentioned the cruel duty
of the vet, she felt the first sting of tears forming in her eyes and put
her foot to the brake. Now she pulled the truck over quickly to stop
at the side of the two-lane road. Cheap sentimentality, some would
call it. But here and now it was the truth for both of them, and her
eyes were too misted to drive.

Without a break in his rhythm, Toby continued:

> *When the body that lived at your single will*
> *With its whimper of welcome is stilled (how still!)*
> *When the spirit that answered your every mood*
> *Is gone—wherever it goes—for good,*
> *You still discover how much you care*
> *And will give your heart to a dog to tear.*

> *We've sorrow enough in the natural way*
> *When it comes to burying Christian clay.*
> *Our loves are not given, but only lent,*
> *At compound interest of cent per cent.*

Though it is not always the case, I believe,
That the longer we've kept 'em, the more do we grieve;
For when debts are payable, right or wrong,
A short time loan is as bad as a long—
So why in Heaven (before we are there)
Should we give our hearts to a dog to tear?

Finished, he turned to the window on his side, pushed his dark glasses up on his forehead, and began wiping a hand over his eyes. Gaye sniffled away her own tears.

"Damn it," he said with a self-conscious chuckle. "Gets me every time."

She reached over to caress his face with the back of her hand. Only the dog lying between them kept her from throwing her arms around him and pulling him into an embrace.

"I'm so sorry about Rud, Toby. I know how hard it is."

" 'The fourteen years which Nature permits,' " he repeated from the poem. "Tenny got that, my last dog. First time I came across that poem was right after he died. But this poor guy . . ." He petted Rud, who had pulled himself up, and was glancing back and forth from one to the other, curious about all the tears and sniffling. "You agree, though, don't you?" Toby asked Gaye. "The best—the only thing—is to let him go on this way as long as possible. Because if I thought anything, anything at all could be done . . ."

"It would cripple him," she said quietly. "Worse, it would take away his reason for living. What he lives for, what he loves to do, is to help you. You know that's true."

Toby fitted the dark glasses over his eyes again, and nodded several times, making sure it had sunk in. Then his hand went to his wrist, fingertips grazing over the Braille watch. "Hey, we'd better get back on the road," he said. "I've got to play tonight."

For the rest of the drive they talked. About everything—almost. Her growing-up years, and his. Her hopeless teenage crushes, and all the young hearts he hadn't meant to break. Their likes and dislikes in books, movie stars, baseball teams, even politicians. The enjoyment of their work. And, of course, their dogs. The one part of her life Gaye avoided mentioning was her marriage, and anything connected to it—so, while she talked fondly about Hero, she said nothing about the way he'd died.

Toby's stories involved not only Rud, but his two previous dogs. It became clear from what he said about them that his tolerance for a belief in Dot's supernatural ability to foretell the future extended to a spiritual acceptance of an afterlife. Hard as it was to lose any of his dogs, he said, he believed that, in some way, each one continued to transmit something of his spirit—his heart, as Toby spoke of it—to the next.

The assertion reminded Gaye of when Hero had seemed to appear before her in the dead of night. "You're telling me they're in a . . . a dog heaven somewhere?" she said.

"Heaven? I don't know what you'd call it. But I know it's not just for dogs, either. It's for all of us . . . anyone who's lived a good life. It's said that our pets wait for us on the other side."

"A nice idea, anyway. I'd like to think I'd see Hero again."

"I'm expecting to be with all my guides," Toby said. "That's my idea of heaven—a place where I'll be able to sit down at a banquet with all my dogs, raise a glass, and thank them. And be able to see what they all look like."

Gaye smiled, and lost herself for a second in his sweet fantasy. "What about ghosts, Toby? If they survive, has one of them ever come—"

"They wouldn't," he broke in quickly. "Don't you know the theory of why ghosts come back to haunt us? They're unquiet spirits, Gaye, lives that ended in too much sadness or violence or in some way that left things . . . unfinished. They can't pass over in that state, so they come looking for completion, peace. I didn't like losing any of my guides, but they knew they were loved, and they died peacefully. They were all ready to go."

By those rules, Gaye thought, she certainly could have had a visitation. But she hated to think that the ghost she'd seen was looking for completion. After the gruesome, vindictive death her dog had suffered, she couldn't imagine what could be done to blot out the horror and give him peace. It was easier, much easier, for her to relinquish the illusion of a heavenly paradise for all living things. She said nothing, however, that would rob Toby of his comforting vision.

Her silence spoke to him, however. "You asked me why I think Mother's predictions deserve to be taken seriously," he said. "But you lost patience before I told you the best one."

And one more thing . . . She remembered him saying that, and cutting him off.

"My apologies," she said. "Will you tell me now?"

"I think I mentioned there was a time she went to Boston," he began. "She was young, and she lived in a rooming house with other single girls. The woman who owned the place did the tarot—that's where Mom learned it. Back then she didn't take it seriously. It was something to fool around with, a parlor game. When she came back home she continued fooling around with the cards, using them for herself sometimes to . . . well, you know, ask the kind of things any young person asks when they're wondering what's ahead in life. The way I've heard it from Mom, it was the cards that told her she should take the job at Callan's bakery . . . and that she should marry my father, young as he was. That much doesn't sound so unusual, I know. She might have made the same choices no matter what the cards said, right?" He paused. It seemed he really wanted to hear an answer.

"Sure. She was the one interpreting the cards; she made them tell her what she wanted to hear."

"Fair enough. But then what do you make of the times the cards tell you things you don't want to hear?" He didn't want an answer from her this time. "I told you about my father—how he died. But it might have been different, if he'd believed. Because Dot saw that in the cards, saw what was going to happen to him."

Gaye glanced from the road to look at Toby. His mouth was set in a grim line, and his brow was etched by the contraction of pain.

"Soon as she found out she was going to have a baby," he went on, "she did a reading. Maybe she still wasn't thinking of it as more than a parlor game, wondering if it would be a boy or a girl, or grow up to be president. But the way the cards came up, it wasn't about any of that. I've heard her tell what happened maybe a dozen times in my life, and she still trembles and cries every time. The reading . . . the way the cards came up . . . what she saw was that my dad would never see the child she'd just learned she was going to have. When she tells it, she mentions the cards—this one and that, how they told her what they did—that part doesn't mean anything to me. But the content . . . the prediction they gave her was that her young husband, the father of her unborn child, was going to be killed somewhere very far away, by a Chinese bandit! Those are the words Mom remembers using—'a Chinese bandit.' Well, of course Billy Callan laughed. At that point, you see, he worked in his father's bakery; he hadn't been drafted, hadn't thought he'd be leaving the Mills and getting anywhere near bandits, Chinese or otherwise. Even after he went into the army, it didn't worry him. A Chinese bandit? An idea from a fairy tale, from his wife's crazy imagination."Toby took a breath. "But after his training he was sent to guard the DMZ in Korea. And even though the war was over, the Chinese who'd once fought with the Koreans still had some soldiers hanging around. No one knows for sure whether Chinese soldiers were involved in the little skirmish in which my father was killed. They weren't supposed to be there, though, according to the agreement that ended the war. So if they were, in a way they were bandits."

Gaye pondered Toby's little piece of family mythology for the next half mile of road. At last she said, "Of course, this is the way you've heard Dot tell it. How many times did you say, a dozen? Maybe each time it got dressed up a little more, the way stories do."

A wry smile touched Toby's lips. "Right," he said, "it could all be made up after the fact. Except for one thing. She's got a stack of letters inches thick that she wrote to my father while he was in training, every one of them begging him not to go, reminding him over and over he'd die if he did, mentioning this 'Chinese bandit' who would kill him. Many of those were written while he was still in training, long before he was ordered to Korea. The later ones get more hysterical. There's a few, too, she wrote to his army commanders, begging them not to send him out of the country. You could ask to see them."

Gaye glanced at Toby again. No, she didn't need to see the letters. She didn't doubt what he was telling her.

Her own prediction from Dot came to mind then. She tried dredging up the exact words from memory. *Something evil is lurking . . . indications of a life lost . . .* At the time she'd taken it as a threat against her. But it struck Gaye now that the life in the balance, and the danger that threatened it, could refer to the cancer that would kill Toby's dog. Still, a prediction coming true. Though not so hard to foretell. Hadn't Toby known it without resorting to fortune-telling cards?

"Whether or not she can tell the future," Gaye said, "your mother's an amazing woman, Toby. Losing her husband the way she did, doing such a great job raising you alone, that's impressive enough."

He turned to her. "I haven't convinced you, have I?"

"It doesn't matter. Because I'm taking your mom's advice, anyway. She told me I'd be safer if I kept you around, and I'm going to try."

"Good," he said. "You won't have to try too hard."

They were silent for a while. She took one hand from the wheel and laid it over the one he had resting on Rud. Ahead, she saw some landmarks indicating they weren't far from the Mills.

She realized then that she didn't want to wait any longer. "How about I cook for you tonight?" she said. "Over at my place."

"Sounds great. But I'm working."

Disappointed, she was silent.

"So come to the inn," he said. "When I'm done, we can have a late supper at your place. How's that?"

Which meant she'd be bringing him home late. No question, then, that the invitation involved more than a meal—no cards needed to interpret that future. "You like lamb chops?" she said. "I've got some nice ones I can pull from the freezer."

"That's my idea of the perfect meal," he said. "Lamb chops and wine."

Without the ability to see, relying on his other senses and honing them all to compensate for the lack of sight, it was fair to assume that Toby Callan's touch would have developed a sensitivity that exceeded the average man's. Even so, Gaye had never imagined she could be touched in a way that made her feel so beautiful, so valuable, as she felt when Toby made love to her. Nothing in her experience, in all the times she'd been with her husband—the man who should have known her body better than any other—had prepared her to discover that sex could be this satisfying celebration of shared joy. With Brian, from the first time she'd gone to bed with him, a part of her had always been held back—merely from shyness, at first. But later it became a need to defend a vital element within herself from being violated. In the end, she was withholding so much that while Brian took her, in some sense she wasn't even there.

Gaye's fear of committing the sin of adultery with Toby vanished after she had lain with him for no more than a few minutes. Being with him made her realize that this was the first time in her life a man had truly made love to her. What infidelity could there be when now was her first time?

Though he had never probed her with questions about her past sexual experience, Toby seemed to understand from her reluctance to discuss her marriage that it was a painful area of her past. And the very way he touched her conveyed that he was aware of her fragility, knew that she needed to be handled not only with care, but with caution. Even before they'd gone to bed, he'd displayed this intuitive concern. Before leaving the inn to return to Gaye's place, he'd asked the bartender at The Inglenook to provide him with a good bottle of red from the inn's wine cellar. As a friend of Toby's, the bartender had supplied one of the finest vintage burgundies— more than a hundred-dollar bottle, at the restaurant price. Later, as they drank the wine with their meal beside the fire in Gaye's living room, Toby detected that while he was just finishing his first glass, Gaye was already pouring her third.

"Are you trying to get drunk?" he asked before she'd set the bottle down.

"No," she replied, instantly defensive. "What makes you think that?"

He picked up his own glass, sniffed at the aroma, then took a sip and rolled it on his tongue. "With wine this good, I should think you'd want to savor it a bit more, take your time finishing it."

A sassy defensive reply hung on Gaye's lips, razzing him for playing the know-it-all wine expert, the connoisseur with the refined palate. Except that he'd pegged it perfectly. She was counting on the alcohol to smooth away her apprehension, make her more receptive. They were going to sleep together tonight, and she didn't want to disappoint him.

"I guess I have been gulping it down a little too fast," she admitted.

"Take it slowly," he advised her. Then he added, "Float but don't sink. You'll enjoy it more."

He wasn't just talking about the wine, she knew, but maximizing all her perceptions. *Float but don't sink.*

Now, as they lay entwined in her bed, his prescription replayed in her mind. He kept her floating in some miraculous bubble of sensations that all seemed new, always floating higher, never sinking to a place where the full reality might have been dulled by intoxication, the pleasure corrupted—as it had been with her husband—by doubt, shame, fear, and regret.

Clinging hard to him as she climaxed, shuddering in a deluge of thrills, she wished the delicious explosion she felt could somehow fuse them together, anneal hearts and souls so they would remain a part of each other, inseparable.

As the bubble floated down and dissolved, she sighed. "Oh, my God, Toby. I never knew it could be like that. . . ."

"Takes two to tangle," he said, kissing the knob of her shoulder as he eased away.

Even that sent a tremor through her. "Now what can I do for you?" she asked.

He chuckled. "You've done it, darling. What makes you think there's got to be more?"

She shrugged. "I just feel so . . . grateful, I want you to know . . . anything you want . . . anything." Was that true? She had never said that to Brian, never could have. And what if Toby's demands were as demeaning?

"Let's just do what comes naturally," he said. "Right now I couldn't want more than this."

Lying in the crook of his arm, Gaye raised her eyes to his face and then swept her gaze down slowly over his chin and neck, his chest and stomach, and the part of him that had been inside her. He had a wonderful body, she thought, surprisingly lean and muscular for someone who did sedentary work in a smoky saloon until late at night, and he was as handsome as a movie star.

A soft whisper escaped her lips. "I wish you could see me, too." Thoughtless, she realized, as soon as it was said. A futile wish, no less for him.

"I do, Gaye. I see you this way. . . ." His hand glided slowly down her arm and formed a warm shell around one of her breasts for a moment. Then his fingers trailed down the cleft of her bosom and the flat of his hand circled slowly over her stomach. "I love the way you look."

"And what about my face, Toby? What do you see?" She remembered him saying Dot had told him she was cute, and perhaps by now the description had been refined, Dot filling in the details as on Wanted posters pinned to the post office bulletin board—color of hair, complexion, height, weight. But what image had formed in his mind from the bare facts?

"What would you like me to see?" he responded.

"*Me*. I want to be sure you see me—as I am. Not someone else."

She expected him to put his hands to her face and feel her features—a technique for limning faces she'd seen used by the blind in films. But he simply said, "Give me a picture."

Now she was stumped. *I'm cute, I'm pretty.* Speaking about herself that way wouldn't come off well. *My nose is small. I've always thought my eyes are too far apart.* How the hell did you describe your own looks? *I'm thirty-one and they still card me.* Maybe it was better to leave his own invention untouched.

"I'll make it easy," he said. "Give me a reference point—a face I'd remember from when I could see. One or two, whoever you want."

That went back—what had he said?—a little more than twenty years. Whose face had been in all the newspapers when she was twelve? "Jimmy Carter's wife, remember her? I've been told I look a little like her." Just once, in fact—by one of her high school teachers when Gaye had her hair done in a not very successful permanent before a prom—but it was a modest approximation.

"Fit for a president," Toby said, "I can live with that. But is that the best you can do? There're a lot of people in the world . . . and I'd love to think I'd seen you sometime, somewhere."

There was, too, the actress she'd been compared with—dozens of times, for that matter, a resemblance so close it was often remarked on when her celebrity look-alike was alive and more prominent. Gaye hesitated to mention it, however; a movie star—it would sound boastful, even if the resemblance was undeniable.

"C'mon, help me out," Toby coaxed. "There's a whole reference library to choose from. Eleanor Roosevelt? Joe DiMaggio?"

She laughed. At last she said, "Ever see Audrey Hepburn?"

"No."

"Really? She was very popular when—"

"I mean no, you couldn't . . . Audrey Hepburn?"

"Well, yeah, sort of . . . more or less . . . so I'm told."

He smiled. "I saw her in a movie called . . . I don't know; I forget the name . . . but in this one she played a blind woman being threatened by a couple of murderous dope dealers. I was nine years old—I couldn't have imagined then I'd ever be blind—but seeing her in that . . . I had the biggest crush on Audrey Hepburn from that day on. Then there was *Breakfast at Tiffany's* . . . and that one with Fred Astaire, with the song, 'Funny Face.' " Toby tilted his head down as if to look at her. "Audrey Hepburn? Imagine that."

"But not exactly, you know. Like that . . . sort of. Only . . . me."

At last his hand came up and his fingers played lightly over her features for a minute or two. "Yeah," he said, and then again with more delight, "yeah . . . I see you." Then he laughed, and kissed her. "Imagine that," he said again when he eased away. "My very own 'funny face.' "

Chapter 18

This, at last, was happiness. To wake every day being glad of where you were, what you would do, whom you would meet, the way each day would begin and end. To move through the world feeling protected and cherished by one person in particular, someone who seemed kinder and braver and sweeter than anyone else you'd ever known. To be truly loved and truly love in return.

Once it had seemed so unattainable, this sense of well-being. Having found it, Gaye could hardly remember why she had once felt so hopeless. Being happy was easy . . . once you were.

Christmas came, and then the New Year, times that through most of Gaye's past life had, like Thanksgiving, always seemed artificially cheerful, days when others could unite to celebrate and appreciate gifts and count their blessings, but when she could feel nothing more than an unrequited wish to join in the holiday spirit. Now, at last, the wish was granted.

Since the night she and Toby had first made love they had been a couple. In the evenings after work she would go to the inn to listen to him play, and sit with him during his breaks. The exceptions were when she was called out after the clinic's regular hours to a farm or to attend to some pet emergency. Such occasions were becoming more frequent as Will's condition deteriorated and Frankie was required to stay close to him, leaving Gaye to take over almost all the night calls.

Even then, however, she would try to meet up with Toby by the time he was finished. Most nights they went back to her place. Then at dawn she would drive him to the Mills so he could be with his mother when she woke, have breakfast with her, and do whatever shopping was needed—as he always had. They talked of living together, but Toby didn't want to leave Dot on her own. For her part, Gaye wasn't ready to surrender so quickly the newfound satisfaction of ruling over her own domain. Not that Dot ever made Gaye feel anything but welcome when she visited, though she still linked her delight in the relationship that had developed with her son to her own prognostications. She never ceased sneaking in the occasional reminder that there was a threat lurking in Gaye's future, and that her security depended on staying close to Toby. Her Christmas gift to Gaye had been a beautifully illustrated deck of tarot cards. "Learn to read these for yourself and you'll see," she'd said. "Without my boy, you'd be in big trouble."

As the days passed and Gaye became used to her happiness, she regarded Dot's warnings as nothing more than a quirky extension of the maternal wish to see her son settled into a stable relationship, at least before she passed on. Dot had seen women come and go in her son's life for a long time; she was hauling in her occult "hobby" as insurance against having him someday wind up all alone.

While promises of forever were never spoken aloud between them, Gaye felt secure in believing that her future was with Toby. He was aware of her quest for a divorce, though he didn't pry into the situation beyond what she was willing to share. (Gaye assumed, though, that Dot observed and reported on the amount of legal papers that she sent off from the Mills post office to her lawyer's office—traffic that was getting heavier as motions and cross-motions were filed fighting Brian's accusations of abandonment.) In spite of her growing intimacy with Toby, the details of her marriage, the events that had marked its decline, the brutalities that had sent her fleeing from it, were things she never wanted to talk about. Recalling them would only give them a relevance she was desperate to forget. One night she woke from a hideous dream in which she saw Hero run down again—but not instantly killed, his mangled body dragging toward her, leaving a swath of black blood on the ground.

When she woke crying, Toby beside her, he comforted her . . . but even then she did not speak about the dream, or the cause.

"Just a nightmare," she said. His enfolding warmth was all she needed to soothe away the awful vision.

But finding happiness did not mean every potential cause for sadness or worry was erased. Along with the ongoing unpleasantness generated by her divorce, there was the even more disheartening situation with Rud. The prancing step of a robustly healthy dog had diminished to a staid walk, with an occasional pronounced lameness in one hind leg. He was noticeably eager to lie down when he could, and slower to rise when needed.

Still, the deterioration was significantly slower than anticipated. Painkillers were required—he let it be known with whimpers and howls when they were needed—but so far only in moderate doses. The instruction Will had given her in reiki and homeopathy, supplemented by her study of the disciplines, allowed Gaye to apply them in Rud's treatment, and she was sure they accounted for slowing the progress of the cancer. No less important was the animal's spirit. As with people, the will to live, the determination to go on functioning in work that was important and satisfying seemed to bolster the body's natural defenses. Rud's determination not to desert Toby was surely helping to hold the disease at bay.

Nevertheless, the need for another guide was clearly inevitable. Toby continued to delay making any arrangements, however. Gaye had warned him that with a cancer of this kind, a stage of rapid decline might come on suddenly, and he might lose Rud before he could be replaced. But in Toby's view that very problem might be precipitated by Rud sensing—*knowing* was Toby's word—he was no longer needed.

"He'll tell me when the time is right," Toby said. "It's up to him."

As she observed Toby's sensitivity in dealing with Rud's illness, Gaye was determined to be no less cooperative and compassionate in reacting to the battle she saw Will fighting daily with his affliction. He still came into the clinic regularly, and Lori was still making appointments for him to see patients. But his ability to function had eroded to the point that there was little he could do these days beyond providing guidance and advice. While Rud's disease was progressing slowly, Will's had begun to attack critical areas of his central nervous system, and his deterioration was accelerating. No longer able to swallow, he received nutrients now through a tube in his abdomen, and a suction tube was positioned in his throat to keep him from drowning on his own saliva. Breathing was assisted by a device strapped across his diaphragm. His larynx was not yet paralyzed, but the breathing apparatus limited him to speaking in short bursts. Involvement of the upper body had also robbed him of fine motor control in his arms and hands. He could raise his arms slightly, but was unable to grasp anything with his fingers. The motorized wheelchair operated by a joystick allowed him to retain mobility.

So he arrived each morning at the clinic and kept to his routine. As always, he went first to his office and spent a while looking through the mail or the veterinary journals that had been laid out for him on his desk. He insisted on a mug of Lori's coffee being brought to him as always; he couldn't drink it, but the aroma, he said, made him feel "at home." Then he would see animals. In his working with patients, his judgment and experience remained invaluable in making diagnoses, suggesting procedures, or prescribing remedies. But in all his cases now, any examination or surgery had to be done by Frankie or Gaye, who assisted Will, as well as attending to their own cases.

Though he retained the ability to see, hear, smell, and speak, all of these faculties were already affected to some degree, and it was understood they would eventually be lost. Amazingly, in the face of this brutal fate, Will retained his grace and humor. As much as Gaye had admired him once for the unique professional skills he brought to healing sick creatures, she was inspired by the strength and courage he displayed every minute of every day in dealing with his incapacity to heal himself. Feeling her own father was lost to her, Gaye gave that special allegiance of the mind and heart to Will. There was nothing she would not do for him.

Gaye made no attempt to hide this affection, and Frankie took note of it. Late one afternoon, long after Will had left the clinic to return to the farmhouse and the last patient of the day had been seen, she and Gaye were alone in the lab together doing blood cultures. As Frankie stared at a readout unreeling from the blood analyzer, she said abruptly, "Bet you'd like to hear what Will told me last night."

Gaye looked up from a microscope. "What?"

"Says he feels closer to you than to his own daughter."

Gaye was not displeased by the revelation, yet puzzled by the time and place Frankie had chosen to deliver it. She knew already that the Bennetts' daughter lived in Paris, was married there, and had taken up the law rather than anything related to her parents' occupation. "That's nice to hear," Gaye responded. After a moment she added, "I feel very close to him, too."

Frankie gave an affirming grunt and went back to her work for a second. Then she stopped again. "Hell of a thing, isn't it—how sometimes families get put together the wrong way? I mean, here you are, a chip off the old block, while Carol, our own daughter, she never took to this work at all, didn't much like living up here, couldn't even wait to get away. She's made her life in a whole 'nother country. Now she's planning to visit, but it's only 'cause she knows she won't be able to see or talk to her father much longer."

So it was hearing from their daughter that had prompted this conversation. "Well, it's good that she's coming. They'll have some time together while he still can."

Frankie nodded curtly and busied herself for another few minutes with some bloodwork.

Gaye sensed something else remained unsaid by Frankie, a reason for commenting on the particular closeness she had seen Gaye developing with Will. Was it jealousy? Beneath her tough, crusty demeanor, Frankie was surely miserable and scared—as revealed the day of Will's emergency—but she was clearly determined to stay on an even keel most of the time. As she faced the incremental losses, her husband being stolen away from her piece by piece, her way of coping was to shut down her feelings. So perhaps she resented the emotional bond she saw growing between Gaye and her husband, felt it was at her expense.

Hoping to get at the crux of the matter, Gaye kept the conversation going. "Is Carol bringing her family?"

"Nope. For her, it's business as much as anything else. She'll only be here two or three days. Then she'll go on to Washington for some conference."

"Sounds like she does important work—even if it's not what we love to do."

A sound came from Frankie, a truncated laugh. "Think I love doin' this?"

"Don't you?" Gaye was shocked.

Frankie leaned away from the lab counter and turned a dour gaze on Gaye. "Walkin' around in cow dung and horse shit, stickin' my hands inside the guts of big beasts, worryin' about the little problems of cats and dogs, puttin' 'em to death when their time comes . . . you think that's why I took up this work? 'Cause my love for animals is so almighty great and profound?"

Gaye shook her head, dumbfounded. "Why else would you?"

Frankie replied as if to another question. "I was in med school when I met him. I wanted to be a country doctor, take care of the folks who live out here. That was *my* dream. But then he came along." She waggled her head in the general direction of where Will had gone. Her eyes took on a distant look. "Head over heels, I was. So damn lovesick, I wanted to be around him every which way. Switchin' to veterinary meds, followin' along with *his* dream—opening this place—that all made sense when it was to be with him. I didn't make the choice for love of animals, no, ma'am. Just for the love of him." Frankie looked down thoughtfully. "Kind of a joke the way life works out. Any day now I'll be stuck with *his* dream—and he won't be here."

As dryly as she delivered it, the poignancy of the confession moved Gaye. This was as honest and open as Frankie had ever been with her. But Gaye still felt something more than exposing the disappointment of a lifetime lay behind her candor. Perhaps it was a way of hinting that when Will was gone the clinic would close, and Gaye should prepare to seek work elsewhere. She didn't push for more, though. Frankie's equilibrium seemed so delicately balanced at the moment.

They went back to their separate tasks, and worked in silence for a long time. Then Gaye became aware of a change in the quality of the silence. When she checked Frankie with a glance, she saw the older woman standing at the lab counter, unmoving, staring rigidly ahead at the wall in front of her.

"Are you okay?" Gaye asked.

Frankie answered without moving. "That shepherd you're treating," she said. "You know what the end's got to be, don't you?"

"Toby's dog, you mean?"

Frankie nodded. "He's dying, right?"

Gaye was slow to answer. "Yes. Spinal cancer."

"So you'll have to put him down, won't you?"

"When the time comes," Gaye said with a reluctant nod.

"And what tells you when it's that time?"

Gaye thought she understood now what was on the older woman's mind, and it chilled her to think about it, to be talking about it even obliquely. Even so, she was curious to see where an answer to the question would lead. "When the animal is suffering too much," Gaye said, "and when Toby's ready."

"Right," Frankie said quietly, as if noting it for herself, "the animal can't tell you when, so it's really up to the owner. The owner gives you permission." There was a stool at the counter a step away from where she was standing, and Frankie moved so she could slump down onto it. Then she lifted her eyes and focused a hard gaze on Gaye. "There's a real good chance, you know, that Will's gonna be locked in. Totally."

"Locked in?" Gaye repeated. What she guessed Frankie meant to say was "shut in," unable to come to the clinic or go anywhere else.

Frankie perceived her confusion. "What I'm talking about is what's called 'locked-in syndrome.' The state of existence where a person retains their consciousness, their awareness of being alive, but all the rest is gone. Everything. They can't see, can't hear, can't speak, can't taste or move. There's nothing left but a mind locked inside a useless body, a mind that knows it's part of a living thing but has no way to take part in the life around it, no way to share what it thinks, feels, regrets, believes, hopes—if it has any hope. . . ." Frankie's gaze was still aimed at Gaye, her eyes burning as though daring her to offer any relief from the hellish prognosis.

"You don't know that's where it's going," Gaye said firmly. "His disease isn't predictable. There are people who've been given death sentences, from this and other things, who live on for years."

"Not the way they *want* to live. Not the way *he* wants."

It seemed clear now to Gaye. Frankie was flirting with the idea of assisting Will in suicide—"when the time comes"—or going even further, if Will was incapable of sharing in the act. She had called up the special bond of affection Will felt toward Gaye as a prelude to seeking support.

"How do you know what he wants?" Gaye asked tentatively.

"He's told me," Frankie said. "He wants me to help him die."

Gaye's heart began to race. She didn't want to be part of this, didn't like even knowing about it. "Frankie, I . . . this isn't—"

"I won't do it, though," Frankie interrupted, continuing on her own track. "I've told him. Made it clear. It's one thing with the animals, soulless creatures that need to be put down when they can't move anymore. But a man . . . a thinking person . . . and someone I've . . . whose been . . ." She trailed off, shaking her head as she stared down at the floor.

Gaye looked at Frankie, slumped on the stool in front of her, her lean, sinewy frame suddenly appearing withered and frail. As unapproachable as the older woman had always seemed before, Gaye was moved now to offer comfort, and she took a step, intending to put an arm around her shoulder. But even as she reached out, Frankie's head snapped up, the defiant look back in her eyes. Gaye drew back instantly.

"So he'll come to you next. Dollars to doughnuts he will. He knows you care for him, and he'll make the same appeal he made to me. But don't you fall for it! You hear me? Tell him there's no way."

Gaye stared at Frankie, speechless. How wrong she'd been, her guess at Frankie's intentions the very opposite of the fact.

Frankie's hand shot out and vised onto her arms. "Swear to me!" Frankie demanded. "Swear you won't do it if he asks." The intensity of her emotion carried to the fingertips digging painfully through the sleeves of Gaye's sweater.

In the heat of the moment, the answer came without thought. "But we do it for them"—Gaye gazed vaguely around her, to all the absent creatures who'd received their mercy here, all the ones to come—"we save them the misery, respect their dignity. Don't we owe him as much?"

Frankie ignored the question. "Listen to me, girl: I'm not asking you, I'm *telling* you." She pulled herself up to her feet, and her grip tightened fiercely. "How ever much you care for him, it's not *your* decision to make. You hear? So you give me your oath."

Oddly, the will to refuse bound Gaye's tongue. A minute ago she'd been alarmed at the prospect of being enlisted in Will's euthanasia; now she had difficulty accepting the relief of this decent promise. She seized on a thought to save her from an oath she couldn't keep. "He hasn't ever said a word about it to me," Gaye replied. "He won't, I'm sure, not if you—"

"Never mind promises," Frankie broke in. "Just be aware it's murder—that's how I see it." She released her grip on Gaye and thrust her away. "If you go against me that goes against the *law*, too, and I'll see that you pay for it. I'll have you charged with murder. That's *my* oath, Gaye—never mind yours."

Frankie's pale blue eyes rested for another moment on Gaye, glacially cold. Then she muttered, "I'll go see to Will," and walked out of the examining room.

Gaye saw that Frankie's lab tests lay uncompleted on the lab counter. Automatically she labeled the blood samples carefully according to the records spread out with them, and stored everything away along with the readouts from the analyzer. Then she tried to go on with her own work. But it was impossible to handle even the most routine tasks. Her hands were trembling too much to tune the fine calibrations on the instruments or handle the glass tubes and slides. The echo of Frankie's warnings kept replaying in her mind, and along with them she kept wondering if the older woman was right—that Will indeed might beg her help—and how she would answer if he did. How did you justify giving the comfort of death to an animal when it could no longer serve its function, but deny the greater mercy of saving a thinking human from the living death of being condemned to a dark, numb silence, locked in with the mental screams no one would ever hear or answer? Was the quality of suffering more bearable in man than beast?

Gaye put away her own work and closed up the clinic. Stepping out into the cold darkness, she looked toward the Bennett farm-house. Yellow light glowed in the windows of the living room and kitchen along the ground floor; a skein of wood smoke trailed across the rising moon, and its pungent aroma perfumed the night air. She stood for a moment, acutely aware of every message being received from her senses: the sweet, sharp, smoky odor in her nostrils, the faint dampness in the cold pricking at her skin—the tiniest hint of snow on the way, the undulating moan of the wind as it traveled across the valley. She knew she couldn't bear to live removed from all of it. How much harder would it be for Will, who had loved living here for so much longer?

But for now, thank God, there was no choice to make. Behind those glowing windows he could still feel the warmth, see the fire-light.

Gaye ran to her truck, suddenly eager to be with Toby, to capture every sight and sound and smell and taste he brought to her. A sea of sorrows all around, and she knew the tide was rising, closing in. But with him, she could still retreat to an island of happiness.

Chapter 19

Frankie's threat was based on such unyielding certainty of how Will would seek relief that Gaye found herself increasingly anxious at the prospect of being alone with him. The place in her affections Will had come to occupy in the absence of having a father who was similarly empathic made her believe that, if he did ask, she would find it impossible to refuse him. Gaye recognized Frankie's right as Will's lifelong partner to make choices he might rationally decide for himself. Yet, trained in her profession to ease the suffering of any animal beyond cure, she could not imagine denying the same mercy to a man who foresaw a hopeless future of increasing torment.

She began keeping her contact with Will to a minimum. She arranged her schedule to take farm calls in the morning—staying clear of the clinic at the time Will still came for an hour or two—and clustered appointments with other patients in the afternoon. As Will's strength waned and it became harder for him to instruct her in reiki or homeopathic remedies, their tutoring sessions had already diminished to a minimum. But he had hoped to continue whenever possible, and he would leave messages for Gaye with Lori that she could visit him at the farmhouse. Cowardly as she knew it was, Gaye kept loading herself up with other tasks as an excuse not to go.

Since her first day at Bible Hill she'd thought a computer was needed to track patient histories, prescribe treatments, and simplify billing; now she spent a sizable amount of her own money on a good mail-order desktop and the Avimark program used by most up-to-date vets—not only to benefit the clinic, but because she knew training Lori in its use and transferring years of conventional records provided a good reason to bury herself in work whenever it was needed. Initially Frankie was cross with Gaye for instituting such a radical change in clinic business without consulting her. But when she saw the advantages—and heard about them from Lori, a quick convert to the conveniences—she stopped protesting. She never praised Gaye, though, or said a word of thanks.

While Gaye managed to avoid facing the essential issue with Will, the longer it went on, the more ashamed she was. His disease was isolating him from life, from those he loved; she ought to be reaching out rather than adding to the isolation. Meanwhile her sympathies were also engaged by what Toby was facing. After a period of stability, Rud had begun to display the more serious effects of his condition. He had a persistent limp, and let it be known with increasing frequency that he needed painkillers.

On a sunny Saturday at the end of February, Toby proposed a change from the regular trips to the ski resort he and Gaye had made every weekend past. When they were leaving the general store after Gaye picked up her mail, he said, "I've got some old snowshoes back at the house. How about today we go for a hike?"

Gaye endorsed the idea at once. She had never been on snowshoes—and there might not be another chance this winter. Already there were small patches of bare ground on the hills where the snow had blown away.

The house was quiet, Dot still on duty at the post office until noon. Seeing the snowshoes already propped up by the door, Gay realized some advance planning had gone into Toby's spur-of-the-moment notion. That there might be a purpose beyond mere recreation seemed even more likely when he suggested Rud stay behind at the house. The only time Gaye had known Toby to separate himself from Rud were those few hours when they were skiing.

"Don't you think he'd like a walk in the snow?" she asked.

"Let's give him a rest," Toby said. "I can trust you to make sure I don't get lost."

The hike Toby outlined would take them up through the woods behind his house to an open ridge, the highest point close to town. They sat on the back doorstep to put on the snowshoes, frames of solid wood steam-bent into shapes much like tennis rackets, each one crosshatched with strips of tough, tanned leather. Toby demonstrated—by feel—the crude method of affixing them to her boots, wrapping several sturdier thongs of leather around the boots and her ankles and knotting them tightly.

"Where'd you get these things?" Gaye asked. They looked to her like heirlooms.

"My dad made them when he was courting my mom. She says he learned how from some of the Indians who still lived around here in those days."

"They've stayed in pretty good shape," she observed.

"I take care of them," he said as he tied on his own. "Oil the leather, revarnish the wood. And I use them only once or twice a year—it's kind of a ritual. These are the only things I have that I know he had his hands on. It's a way of communing with him, having him near when . . . when I need him."

Gaye was moved by knowing how important these objects were to Toby, and by realizing he had chosen to include her in his ritual. She wondered what exactly made him feel the need for this special communion today. The answer would emerge, no doubt, during their time together.

They started up through the woods. Toby had told her just to keep moving upward and they would get to the open ridge. He'd given her a length of rope about five yards long to tie around her waist, the other end tied around his. It was long enough so they could move freely, but not so long as to tangle as they threaded through the trees. At first Gaye stumbled along awkwardly on the large, flat things attached to her feet, Toby laughing at her good-natured complaints. Finally he explained that she shouldn't be walking, but gliding along, barely lifting her feet. After that they moved easily, and Gaye was able to take in the small wonders in a part of the countryside little trafficked by people. She saw the earliest signs of spring's renewal pushing slim bare black stems up through the snow, and the fresh tracks of small animal paws and deer hooves leaving trails across the white. She reported it all to Toby, who answered with stories of his boyhood when he'd seen all these things for himself.

"Look, there's a fox!" Gaye shouted once, so overcome with excitement she didn't choose her words.

"Which way?" he said.

"Left, two o'clock. He's red with a white throat; he just gave us that foxy look, wondering what the hell we're doing here."

Finally they broke into the open. The sun was high and full, bouncing off a curved snow-covered slope that led up to a long ridge. Under her ski jacket now, Gaye was sweating with the effort of the climb. Soon they had risen above the treetops, and when she looked back, she could see the town below them, and beyond that the black line of narrow river that divided Vermont from New Hampshire snaking away for miles, and then the vista of valley and mountain stretching away to the horizon. A breathtaking view, the best she'd had.

She stopped to take it in, and Toby caught up to her. She slipped her arm through his and pulled him close. It was becoming a reflex now to give words to what she saw when they were together, and she began to describe it.

"That's okay," he said. "I remember it perfectly, just the way it was in every season. I stored it up when I knew I'd lose it. We're here because I wanted *you* to see it."

She clung to him tighter, and scanned the countryside, imagining what that exercise had been like for him, painting things into his memory forever. When Gaye glanced at Toby she saw he had a smile on his face, enjoying the view.

"I've always come here alone—except for Rud," he said at last. "I'd talk to my dad, ask him what to do if I had a big decision to make or a problem to solve, complain about anything that was bugging me."

"If you want to talk to him now, I can walk ahead."

"I don't need that," he said. Then he turned to her. "I can talk to you."

"Anytime," she said, her voice catching.

"It's about Rud. It's time to start making plans for when . . ." He substituted a wince of pain for the words. "That's why I left him behind. I suppose you'll think it's crazy, but I didn't even want him to hear."

"No, not crazy, Toby. Nobody knows how much animals understand. Often enough it seems they can read minds."

"Anyway, I need to go and do the training with a new guide. While I'm away, Rud will need to be cared for, and I don't think Dot's really up to it."

She broke in. "Toby, if you're asking me to look after Rud, of course."

"To live with him, though. I don't want him in the kennel."

"I'll treat him like my own."

Toby took a deep breath. "Okay. That's a relief."

"Did you think I wouldn't? Toby, I should be insulted. He's part of you, and by now you ought to know—"

"Sorry, Gaye," he said, truly contrite. "I've had some bad training, I guess. I've never been with a woman before who wasn't jealous of Rud."

"You're kidding!"

"Not in the least. Same with the other dogs. Haven't you ever wondered why I'm still single?" It was a rhetorical question; his tone said he was sure she had. "There was always something about my closeness to the guides—depending more on a dog for my life, my safety moment to moment, than on anyone else—that they couldn't get past."

Gaye shook her head in disbelief. "Makes me think you just have bad taste in women," she said lightly.

He smiled. "Somehow they always got around to asking me what I'd do if it ever came to choosing between saving them or saving the dog. Damned if I know why they put it that way—it's not like we ever planned to sail on the *Titanic*—but every one of 'em worried about it."

"I don't even have to ask," she said. "I think I know."

"And that's why I'd probably save you."

"Probably," she repeated with a twist.

He shrugged. "Best I can do," he said.

"Good enough." She pulled herself up and kissed him.

The sky was clouding up a little, the wind getting brisker. They moved on to keep warm, going farther along the ridge, stopping at a couple of vantage points—where Toby told her how he remembered the view, describing almost exactly the details Gaye saw laid out below them.

At last they headed back down. On the way, she inquired about the training he planned to undertake, where he would go, how long he would stay, and whether a new dog was already waiting for him.

He'd be going to the Seeing Eye Institute, he said, the place that had provided all his dogs. He'd contacted the institute already, and there would be a dog for him when he arrived. He would train with the dog for three weeks, along with a group of other blind men and women.

As he answered her questions, Gaye realized that for all her knowledge and training, she'd maintained a few misconceptions about guide dogs. For one, she'd always thought the term *seeing eye dog* was generic for any such animal. Toby corrected her. It was a mistake many people made, but the term *Seeing Eye* was actually copyrighted by the institute, which had been established decades before any similar facility in the United States to supply dogs specially trained to escort the blind. The way it came into existence was a story he clearly enjoyed telling as he spun it out during most of their descent from the ridge.

During the First World War, the German army had made some use of dogs to retrieve troops that had been blinded on the battlefields, many by mustard gas. The dogs would be sent out onto the battlefields, and sightless soldiers who encountered them could grab on to their fur and the dog would return to its base. After the war, a wealthy American woman who was living in Switzerland heard about the rescues, and realized that the idea might be developed further. Dogs trained to live and work permanently with just one master might provide the means to steer the blind away from whatever obstacles and hazards might lie in their path. The first dogs she trained were adopted by Europeans, and then an article about her work was published in America in the most widely circulated magazine of the time, the *Saturday Evening Post*. A young lawyer from Tennessee named Morris Frank was told about the article, and wrote to the woman in Switzerland; he had lost his sight early in life, he told her, and asked if she would train a dog for him. In her reply, she agreed and explained his request could be obliged only if he would travel to Switzerland to undergo training with the dog.

"These days," Toby said, "a blind person traveling alone may not seem like a big deal. But back in the twenties you didn't get around much if you couldn't see. Unless you could afford to have someone staying by your side, you sat at home and that was it. When Morris Frank was arranging his trip to Europe to get his dog, the steamship company told him they wouldn't allow him aboard unless he agreed to be sent as freight—they actually called him a 'package.' They gave him a cabin to sleep in, but he had to agree to be locked in most of the time, let out only for brief periods when a steward would take him for a meal, or give him a walk on the deck."

It was a different story when Frank returned, however. He came with a dog named Buddy, trained so well that the lawyer was not only allowed to move freely around the ship bringing him to New York, but was able to demonstrate to a crowd of reporters on the dock—who challenged Frank to the demonstration—that he could guide his blind master across a street teeming with two-way traffic.

"The street along the piers didn't have many traffic lights," Toby said, "and the cars went so fast it was one of the most dangerous crossings in New York. But Buddy did so well taking his boss through those cars that the reporters were afraid to follow. Two guys who wanted to interview Frank as soon as he got to the other side actually hailed a cab to bring them around." Toby laughed. "Lucky for me, I guess. If Buddy hadn't been the dog he was, the whole Seeing Eye movement could have folded right there. But after that, everybody wanted to meet Frank and Buddy, and he was able to start the Seeing Eye foundation."

With the demonstrated success of the first Seeing Eye dog, and the financial support it generated, the foundation was able to estab-

lish a policy of giving dogs to the blind and sponsoring their training with only a nominal fee. To this day, Toby told Gaye, he would
receive his new guide dog and spend three weeks at the Seeing Eye's
headquarters at the same cost he had been charged twenty years
ago—an amount little more than when the institute opened its doors
in 1929: just a few hundred dollars. The same would be true for first-
time trainees, who would have to spend an extra week.

By the time Toby had finished his complimentary history of the
Seeing Eye dogs, he and Gaye had arrived in his backyard. As they
sat down on the doorstep to untie their snowshoes, Gaye said, "It
sounds like an amazing place, Toby. I'd be interested in having a look
at it myself."

"No problem. In fact, I'll need you to take me when I go for my
course, because Rud can't stay there with me. I have to give all my
time to the new dog."

"Fine. When are you going?"

"End of next week."

"So I'll have the weekend to go and come back. Where is it?"

"New Jersey—a place called Morristown. About an hour outside
New York."

Gaye was suddenly preoccupied, realizing from the geography
he'd supplied that the journey she'd be taking with him would head
her back toward the place from which she'd fled. Yes, only the general direction—she'd still be pretty far from Philadelphia—and yet,
no matter how far she'd be, a shiver passed through her at the idea
of narrowing the safe distance she'd won between herself and the
peril Brian represented. *You're never going to get away from me. Never
ever.* Going closer to wherever he was seemed to be taking a risk.

"So?" Toby's radar had picked up something from her silence. "Is
there a problem, Gaye? I know there's no Disneyland between here
and there, but we can still have fun on the way."

How did she explain this attack of nerves? It wasn't rational. It
would be best for her, probably, not to let the fear limit her options.
She wanted to be with Toby, see the place that was so important to
him. And hadn't she just told him she had a right to be insulted if
he didn't know he could rely on her?

"Of course it'll be fun," she said. "A weekend jaunt."

"Right." He collected the snowshoes under his arm. "C'mon, I'll make cocoa to warm us up." He opened the door that led into the kitchen. Rud was waiting just inside, on his feet, tail wagging, looking perfectly well.

Gaye couldn't help thinking that the dog knew exactly why he'd been left behind.

Chapter 20

As the week passed, Gaye grew steadily more anxious about leaving the haven she'd made for herself. There was no question of changing her mind, however. She was always aware it made no real sense to be so troubled about getting within even fifty or a hundred miles of the people and places from which she'd run. What made it a hard step to take nevertheless was simply that it was the first time she'd be doing it, journeying forth from where she finally felt safe and loved. But Gaye understood, too, that the end result of clinging unreasonably to whatever limited territory you defined for yourself as safe was to become a recluse, one of those people afraid to go anywhere beyond their own four walls. She knew from her lawyer that sooner or later it would be necessary to confront Brian in court. Measured against that ordeal, what she was required to do now wasn't difficult at all. No matter how nervous it made her, it was probably useful in preparing her for more demanding challenges to come.

But more than just her past history put Gaye on edge when she contemplated driving off with Toby. All the cautionary advice Dot had given her from a tarot reading still nagged at her from time to time. One phrase more than any other stuck in her memory: *indications of a life or lives that may be lost*. In the past few weeks, one circumstance after another had brought it to mind, made it seem prescient. It could relate to Rud's life . . . or Will's . . . or both. Dot had also said things that made it sound like her own life might be at stake. At the time Gaye had shrugged it off. Since then her resilience had been worn down by other worries. Now, whenever she recalled Dot's words, some of those vivid pictures on the tarot cards would begin to float up in front of her mind's eye—devils, a hanged man— and she would question whether the greatest foolishness would be to ignore such definite forewarnings.

Of course, she could take comfort from the part of Dot's reading that said Toby would be her protector. *He may be what saves you.* Not completely reassuring—there was that "may be"—but it weighed on the side of staying by his side, rather than sending him off without her. In any case, she was going to take Rud off his hands . . . and he couldn't make the first part of the journey without Rud.

On Friday, just after noon, he called her at the clinic. "Hey, funny face," he said, "all set to go?" He often used the nickname since their Audrey Hepburn conversation.

They'd agreed she would collect him and Rud in front of Bunky's store at two o'clock.

"I may be a little late," she said. "I had a farm emergency this morning, so I didn't pack yet. There's still a cat to spay, and a litter of puppies coming in for their distemper shots. Then I'll have to go home and throw some stuff in a bag before coming for you."

"That's fine. Oh, I can save you some time: Don't bother filling the truck with gas. I've been worried about how that heap of yours would stand up to a long trip, so we'll use my car."

"What are you talking about?"

Maybe he hadn't heard her. "See you at Bunky's" was all he said before he hung up.

She smiled as she set the phone down. This was going to be interesting.

Neither Frankie nor Will had appeared in the clinic either yesterday or today. Their daughter, Carol, had arrived Wednesday evening from Paris—by way of New York—and they were devoting their time to her. Gaye had enjoyed working by herself, and as she attended efficiently to the rest of the day's patients, there were moments when the uncertainty about the fate of the facility intruded into her thoughts. She didn't like to think that Frankie would close it down after Will was gone. So would it be possible, perhaps, to buy the clinic and run it on her own?

Or might she be content just to settle down with Toby, and give up veterinary practice?

At a few minutes after two, after she had seen her last patient, Gaye went to the reception desk. "I'll tidy up inside, then be on my way," she said to Lori. "I don't think Will or Frankie is coming in, so you can go early, too."

"Are you sure? There are still some bills I could get out." Lori enjoyed using the new computer.

"They'll keep till Monday. Have a nice weekend."

"Thanks." As Lori went for her coat, she paused and lowered her voice conspiratorially. "You and Toby aren't eloping, are you?"

Gaye let out a stunned laugh. "What gave you *that* idea?"

Lori shrugged. "I know you and he are . . . together . . . and it's just so rare that you take a trip anywhere."

"Well, we're a long way from eloping," Gaye said.

Lori gave a chagrined nod, and they said good-bye.

As she put the examining room in order before leaving, Gaye mused on Lori's gaffe. It was a measure of how secretive she'd been, Gaye realized, that even someone she'd worked with closely for several months didn't know she was married. At Thanksgiving she'd mentioned to the Bennetts that she'd left her husband—or had she even admitted she was married to the man she'd left? Either way, neither Will nor Frankie was the sort to gossip about her. It would probably do her good, Gaye thought, to start opening up a little more. At least to Toby. Traveling together would be an opportunity.

She was surprised to hear the back door open and close. Frankie, no doubt, coming over from the farmhouse. Gaye steeled herself to get bawled out for letting Lori leave early.

But it wasn't Frankie who came into the examining room. This woman had the same lanky build, the same austere beauty, but she was twenty-odd years younger than Frankie, with long pale blond hair fashionably cut. Though her jeans and blouse were correctly casual for country wear, they weren't the off-the-shelf variety, but the type that came with designer labels at ten times the price. This was obviously the Bennett daughter, outfitted in Paris. She spoke first. "Hello. I'm Carol Bennett. I've been—"

"I know," Gaye said, finding her voice. Her first reaction to the surprise visit was dismay, since she was already running late to pick up Toby.

"I hope you don't mind my popping in like this." She waited a second for some word of polite assurance, but went on quickly when Gaye said nothing. "I've just heard so much about you, I . . . I had to have a look for myself."

Gaye's being described as an object to be studied didn't warm the atmosphere, but perhaps it was deserved, Gaye thought; she hadn't greeted this stranger with any cordiality. "I wish it were a better time," she said quickly. "But I'm just trying to get away. I'm already late to—"

"To meet Toby Callan." Carol Bennett nodded knowingly. "My mother mentioned you had plans for a getaway. I'll let you go in a minute. But I won't be here when you return from your trip, and from the things I've been hearing . . . I thought you and I should have a word."

"What things have you heard?" Gaye said warily.

Carol Bennett ambled over to lean against the examining table. "Well, of course, it's my mother who does most of the talking these days. One thing she tells me is how much my dad likes you—how you're so much more like the daughter he would have—"

"Look, I haven't done anything to—"

"Please don't think I'm complaining," Carol put in. "I can't be anything but glad that there's someone here to provide that kind of comfort—who respects him, and shares a belief in the importance of the things he gave his life to. I know I've been a terrible disappointment in that way." She gave a dismissive toss of her head. "Animals. They're supposed to be easy to love, but to me all they ever meant was cat litter to clean up, and dog hair all over my clothes." She focused on Gaye again. "The other thing my mother's been talking to me about since I got here is more of a problem."

Gaye knew what would have been on Frankie's mind. She tried

to head off talking about it. "I imagine it's about your father—and Frankie's already made her feelings very clear on how she feels about . . . dealing with the situation."

"And you, how do you feel?"

Gaye remained mute. She made a couple of attempts to speak, opened her mouth—and nothing came out. How did you talk about *this*: helping a man to die? And with his daughter, no less.

The other woman cut short her struggle. "I think I can see how you feel," she said. "And it seems my mother's right. She's pretty sure that if Dad asks—"

Gaye couldn't keep silent now. "Look, we really shouldn't be talking about this. Just for a start, there have been no conversations between your father and me relating to . . . his wishes. So if you really care about him, then never mind talking to me. Talk with him, *be* with him, help him and your mother work this out." She should have stopped there, but she cared enough about Will to add one more thing. "And maybe you can find the time to do more than drop in on the way from here to there for a quick little peck on his cheek and good-bye forever."

A spark of ire flashed in Carol Bennett's eyes, but it faded and a thin, fleeting smile appeared on her lips. "Fair enough," she said mildly. "Unfortunately, as much as it might be a reasonable thing to expect, it's not so easy to rearrange my life."

Gaye's regret was instant. "Forgive me. I shouldn't have—"

Carol Bennett waved off the apology. "That's quite all right. I'm glad you care enough about him to tell me off. Truly. And one more thing." She stepped up close to Gaye and spoke very softly. "If it gets unbearable for him, I want you to know you'd have my support in doing . . . whatever he asked. More than support, in fact. I'm a lawyer. I'll see that you're protected."

Once more, as she had been when surprised by Frankie's stand, Gaye was dumbstruck. Carol Bennett kept gazing intently at her, sealing the pledge. "What would your brother say?" Gaye managed to ask.

"My brother." A curiously bitter half smile touched Carol's lips. "I don't think that matters."

The callousness shocked Gaye. "It will to him. I'm sure he'll be coming, too, and—"

"So they never told you," the other woman broke in. "Ted can't visit. He got busted for selling drugs out in Marin County—just trying to make a little extra money. Even with good behavior, he won't be able to go anywhere for another twenty-eight months."

The sad little exchange at Thanksgiving replayed in Gaye's mind, and she was struck by the irony that came with it. While she'd been keeping her secrets from the Bennetts, they'd had their own to deal with. The tragedy of this one was that Will would almost certainly die without seeing his son again.

Her business done, Carol Bennett headed out of the examining room toward the rear exit. But just before she was out of sight, she turned back to Gaye with a last-minute thought. "Oh, would you please give my regards to Toby? It's been years since we saw each other, but he was always a great favorite of mine." She left.

Gaye didn't wonder for too long what lay behind that parting shot. Carol Bennett was probably just a few years younger than Toby, she'd grown up in the area as he had, and she was quite beautiful. If he was a favorite of hers, there was a good chance it wasn't only because of his singing. Maybe, too, that had something to do with why Frankie regarded him as an insincere heartbreaker.

Chapter 21

Arriving more than an hour past the time agreed, Gaye braked to a quick stop in front of Bunky's and rushed inside the store. Toby was sitting in one of the rockers, Bunky in the other, Rud lying by the stove.

She apologized breathlessly for being so late.

"Relax," Toby said. "We've plenty of time to get where we're going." The total driving time to the Morristown headquarters of the Seeing Eye Institute would be about seven hours; they had planned to drive for only half that time, then stop over at an inn on the way that Toby had heard was charming.

"Got some mail for you, Gaye," Bunky said, pulling himself up from his chair to go to his desk.

Toby stood, too, and crooked an arm outward, inviting Gaye to step into an embrace. "So what did you think of my car?" Toby asked after they kissed.

"What car?"

"It's parked right outside. How could you miss it?"

Gaye hadn't paid attention to anything before rushing in. She went to the door and looked outside. A few parking slots away from the truck there was a silver sports convertible of some kind, not a make she recognized, but very sleek and obviously expensive. She turned back to Toby.

He was smiling and holding one hand high, dangling a set of keys.

"What have you done?" she demanded.

"I told you I don't think that old truck of yours is safe for a long trip."

"Toby, I don't know if you rented that car or bought it, but it's crazy."

"Didn't cost a red cent." He explained that he'd asked his friend Norm Stephenson to lend them a car. "I told him I was going off to train with my new dog and he wanted to help. He owns three or four cars." Toby grinned slyly. "I'm guessing he brought this one to impress you—I think Norm has a little crush. He waited around to give you the keys himself, but it got so late he had to go." He thrust the keys at her.

She hesitated. "I've never driven one of those high-powered race-car types."

"So you'll drive slowly. C'mon, let's get out of here. Leave Bunky the truck keys and he'll take care of it."

Bunky had returned with a fistful of mail, and gave her a nod. Gaye exchanged her keys for the letters, and accepted the car keys from Toby.

As soon as she was sitting behind the wheel of the sports car, she was glad she had bent her principles. She couldn't deny it was exciting to have this luxurious machine under her control. The smooth purr of the engine as soon as she switched on the ignition was a pleasant change from the grinding cough that came from the old truck.

She backed out of the space in front of the store and gunned the car up the street. In seconds they were flying over the road outside of town. Tucked into a small space behind the two bucket seats, Rud barked excitedly.

"Well, he likes it, anyway," Toby said.

Gaye followed an itinerary that Toby gave her, turning according to numbered routes he dictated. It was, he explained, a scenic route that would take them to a special place where they would spend the night before covering the rest of the distance in the morning.

The drive took them straight south along smaller roads with lit-tle traffic. Along the way Gaye thanked Toby several times for arranging to borrow the car—a limited-edition Japanese make, he'd told her, which had cost something over a hundred thousand dollars. It was fun to be at the wheel of such a machine, and a pleasure to have the music of a great stereo system in the background. Toby had brought some of his CDs along—Sinatra standards, Astaire movie sound tracks—and he sang along to some of them.

There were lively spurts of conversation, mostly on the light side—Toby's singing of some old Cole Porter songs prompted Gaye to talk a little about her first memories of hearing such music—in her mother's house—and that led to telling more about her growing up, her parents' divorce, living with her father, and the work he did that left so little time for her. But that was the extent of anything with unpleasant connotations. They were enjoying the drive as a carefree outing, and there was an unspoken pact not to spoil it with the more serious and sad matters weighing on both of them.

Their route had more or less followed the Connecticut River. As it flowed south out of New Hampshire, across Massachusetts, and into the state that shared its name, what had been little more than a stream defining the boundary between New Hampshire and Vermont widened into a significant river.

Night had fallen, and a nearly full moon was in the sky, when they drove into a small town on the wide mouth of the river.

"Where are we?" she asked. She had followed Toby's directions at every turn, knowing only that he had a plan to spend the night somewhere en route.

"The town's called Essex. There's an inn here I thought you'd like."

"Which way do I go?"

"Straight into town, drive toward the water. Look for the oldest inn around."

"How old?" She slowed the car to look carefully at the buildings they were passing. They had gone through a very small commercial district and now all she saw were dollhouse-style wooden houses surrounded by trim yards.

"This one has been in business since 1776," Toby said.

"You're kidding!" Though it struck Gaye now that everything around her seemed to date from the same period.

"And maybe that's a good thing, too," Toby said, "since this the first time we've ever spent a night together on the road."

"What do you mean?"

"Just in case you think I'm taking you for granted, I'm providing a little reminder of the Declaration of Independence."

Gaye laughed. Abruptly she stifled it and stopped the car to look at him. "Don't tell me you booked separate rooms!"

"I didn't know how you'd feel about it, since you're still—"

"I guess I didn't know either—until now." She leaned across the seat toward him. "I want my independence, all right, but not from you. With you, Mr. Callan, I want to be absolutely in"—her touch was at the same time playful and deliberately intimate—"only the most united states."

As they kissed, she realized she'd shed at last the fear and shyness that Brian's mistreatment had injected into her experience of sex. With Toby, with this man alone, she was able to flirt again, to be provocative, to invite, to trust in having his respect and tenderness.

To love.

Immediately after driving on, she saw a hanging wooden signboard of a golden eagle on a blue background looking much as it might have in Revolutionary days, except that a spotlight lit its name, The Griswold Inn.

The original building, with its low timbered ceilings and cozy public rooms with fireplaces, had been enlarged with a modern annex hidden behind it, but Toby had asked for one of the old rooms. He released the second room he'd reserved when they checked in. The inn accepted dogs in some of the rooms, so Rud was admitted with them.

As soon as they were in their room, Gaye embraced Toby. "I think you and I have some unfinished business," she said, still relishing the joyous ease she could take in their intimacy.

For the next hour, while Rud slept, they made love by lamplight. Gaye was constantly amazed by Toby's ability to elicit sensations from her that she had never experienced before. Was it only because she had walled them off from her husband's assaults, or was it because Toby's blindness had given him a unique sensitivity?

When they were finally lying quietly, she mused aloud, "You don't know how much you've done for me, Toby."

"You gave me some idea just a little while ago."

"I wasn't referring only to here and now. I mean, you've really helped put me back together again."

"Like Humpty-Dumpty?" His hands ran along her naked body. "You've never felt the least bit egg-shaped to me."

She drew herself up and leaned over him. "I'm being serious. I haven't said much about it, but my marriage . . . Well, when I came to work at the clinic, I was damaged goods."

He turned his face to hers. Sightless as his eyes were, they had kept their blue color, and there were moments when he looked at her without the shield of dark lenses that she felt he saw beyond surfaces somehow, could see into her. "Do you want to tell me about it now?" he said softly. The way he asked suggested he'd been well aware for a while that she'd been holding back, and that he'd been waiting until she was ready—would go on waiting if she wasn't.

It flowed out of her now, the whole history from the time her father had ever spoken glowingly of Brian, to the most recent defenses he'd offered on his partner's behalf. She hadn't meant to get into detail about the humiliations she'd suffered at the hands of her husband, but there were times as she lay in the half-light when the memories loomed so real, and the emotions unleashed were too strong to rein in. She howled with the rage she felt at Brian, and sobbed while she damned him for the specific ways he had abused her.

Through it all, Toby held her close against him, soothing her with caresses and gentle reassurances, never prying, yet also never shutting off the flow, ready to listen to whatever she needed to say. He seemed to understand that telling it just as she did was a necessary cleansing process.

When at last she had reached the point where she could say, "So I just ran away, left it all behind," Gaye felt almost as if she had undergone a cure in which a malignant mass of anger and fear and shame had been taken out of her, excised from her very soul.

He was silent awhile after she was done, letting the echoes of the ugliness die away completely. Then he said, "I wondered why you sounded a little reluctant the first time I suggested this trip. It's because of him, isn't it? You don't want to get anywhere near this guy again, do you?"

"I didn't." She hugged Toby tighter. "I feel safer now."

"You're right to be careful, though. What he did to your dog . . . it's unthinkable. If I'd been there and gotten my hands on him, I would've—"

"You'd have done what I did, I hope. Worried first about the suffering animal, never mind revenge."

Toby shrugged. "Maybe. But that kind of brutality . . . I can't imagine anyone being capable of being so cold-blooded."

"There are people who don't care a bit for dogs," she said stoically.

They shook their heads, both unable to conceive of such a failing of the heart.

They went down to eat in the Griswold's restaurant, a long room, almost barnlike, yet given a comfortable charm by old planked floors and a decor of ship prints and other nautical memorabilia relating to the town's history as a commercial port in Revolutionary days, and more recently a yachting center. A separate bar—called a taproom, as in olden times—was nearby, and a trio of men were playing banjos accompanied by a honky-tonk piano, their happy music enlivening the restaurant, too.

"It makes me feel I'm on a holiday," Gaye said.

"I hoped it would," Toby said. "The music is another reason I chose the place. It's Friday night, and the banjo band plays every Friday."

"How do you know so much about this place?"

"I'll give you the answer after dinner."

When they'd finished eating, he took her into the taproom for Irish coffee. By now, she'd guessed that he must have worked here years ago, before he'd found his permanent niche at the Blue Hill

Inn. After coffee, when Toby left their table to speak quietly with one of the musicians, she assumed he must be asking to sit down at the piano, perhaps to serenade her. But then the man to whom he'd spoken unhitched the strap of his banjo from around his neck and handed the instrument to Toby.

In the next second Toby was strumming away at the banjo as well as any of the others. Instantly he had the attention of the jovial crowd in the taproom, and he kept them in rapt silence as he went through a medley of folk and bluegrass melodies, with the other musicians just trying to keep up. He ended with a solo of wild plucking that drew a spontaneous cheer from the crowd. As he started to pass the banjo back to its owner, voices from every corner begged him to continue.

He held up his hands to speak. "To be honest with you, folks, I just wanted to play enough to impress this lovely lady over in the corner there . . . so if I've done that . . ." He gestured toward Gaye.

"I'm not the least bit impressed," she shouted back playfully. "You'll have to do much better!"

The crowd cheered.

Toby threw up his hands and took the banjo back again. The crowd cheered even louder. He announced that he'd play one more song. Then, quietly, facing her, he began strumming very simple chords in an easy rhythm and sang: "You are my sunshine, my only sunshine, you make me happy when skies are gray. . . ." At the end he made the crowd join in, everyone in the whole place serenading her.

She knew now what it meant to have a heart so full of pride and love it felt full to bursting.

Chapter 22

The next afternoon at two o'clock Gaye drove away with Rud, leaving Toby behind at the Seeing Eye Institute for the three-week training period. During that time he would live at the institute and have all his meals there, in company with several dozen other men and women of all ages who were also getting Seeing Eye dogs— some for the first time, others returning for a third or fourth time like Toby. The students stayed together on a campus of several acres in buildings that looked like the dorms of a fine redbrick college, and spent the days working along with special trainers to drill the dogs in all the routines that would be important to their everyday lives, from the simple tasks of managing in the home, to the more complex and dangerous business of going out for long walks into the center of a busy town, and getting on and off public transit.

Aside from doing their drills, the essential purpose of this time, Toby had explained, was for the dog to bond closely with the person he would be guiding. To facilitate this process, family members or others close to the person receiving a dog were not permitted to stay over; even visits were discouraged during the three weeks.

However, because Gaye had a special interest in the operations of the place, Toby had called ahead and arranged for her to spend an hour touring it with him before she had to leave. She had been fascinated to see that beyond its devotion to the training and use of guide dogs, the institute maintained a separate building with labs for veterinary research. Even more interesting, they had facilities for long-term genetic tracking, which, over the years, had encouraged breeding litters from those dogs that demonstrated a particular aptitude for guiding the blind.

When it finally came time to leave Toby, Gaye couldn't help being emotional. She was affected, first, by observing how reluctant Rud was to be put into the car. As this was the first time in their relationship that dog and master had ever been separated for more than a few hours, it was hard for both of them—and no easier for Gaye to witness. When the time came to go she couldn't hold back tears. There was no doubt, of course, that the separation was essential and beneficial; yet she'd come so recently to the awareness that her sense of security and well-being depended on Toby. Foolish, perhaps, that such a relatively brief parting between two adults should tear at her so much. Yet it felt to Gaye almost as if it were a farewell said before some long journey of exploration, or before troops went off to war.

Toby couldn't see the tears, but he heard her sniffling. "Hey, funny face," he cajoled gently, "what's that all about? I'll be home again in no time."

"I know. It's stupid."

He took her in his arms and kissed her. "Yeah—stupid wonderful," he said then. "Nice to know you'll miss me that much." Then he leaned close to murmur in her ear. "But you're setting a terrible example for the kid." He nodded toward the dog sitting up in the front seat of the car.

She smiled and wiped her tears away. "I love you," she said, then kissed him lightly once more and turned toward the car.

But he pulled her back. "Wait, I want to hear that again."

Only then did she realize she'd never actually said it until now. No matter what she felt, she was still so afraid to break the spell. To recover at last this small, simple reflex of the heart was a milestone. She looked at him squarely and said it again.

And he said it back.

Then they linked hands and laughed together.

And suddenly it was easy to go.

She went only as far as the center of Morristown, a busy midsize suburban community, before deciding to stop at a café she spotted on the main street. Having followed Toby's directions all the way down, she thought a look at a road map was in order before embarking on the long drive back. Also, she could look at the mail she'd picked up at Bunky's yesterday, and had left unread.

Rud had curled up in the passenger seat of the car, but as soon as she switched off the ignition, he sat up and looked at her wistfully. She might only be projecting her own feelings, but the poor guy already looked like the separation was unbearable.

For a moment she weighed whether or not to take him into the café: dogs were generally forbidden entry to places serving food by local health ordinances. But a specific exception was made for guide dogs for the blind, and given Morristown's affiliations she was sure there would be no objection to Rud. No doubt they saw the dogs often; the town served as the principal training ground for facing all the challenges of maneuvering safely on public streets, or shopping in busy stores.

"All right," she relented, motioning to Rud, "c'mon along." He started toward her, and instantly she realized her error. "No, no, wait!" She didn't want him getting out the driver's door, emerging into traffic. Toby would never forgive her if anything happened to Rud while he was in her care. She went around to open the passenger door.

As trained to do with Toby, Rud walked beside her into the café at a measured pace, keeping a gentle pressure against her leg in case a hint was needed to steer away from an obstacle. The dog was hardly given a glance as he went with her to a booth. After she sat, he settled at her feet under the table. A waitress came and held out a large white card with nothing printed on it. Then Gaye noticed the pattern of small round bumps covering the card. Accustomed to seeing dogs like Rud in the café, the waitress had obviously assumed Gaye needed one of the Braille menus the café kept handy.

She waved it off. "Just a cappuccino, thanks."

The waitress realized from Gaye's glance at the menu that she wasn't blind. "I thought that was a Seeing Eye dog," the waitress said. "But if it isn't, then it shouldn't be—"

"It is. I'm watching it for . . . for my boyfriend."

The waitress accepted the explanation and went off to fill the order.

Gaye opened the road map covering New England states and gave it a quick look. Never mind scenery; if she took throughway connections all the way she could shave a couple of hours off the trip back to her refuge and be able to sleep in her own bed tonight. She folded up the map and turned to the mail. Fanning it out, she saw at once that three of the envelopes had familiar return addresses printed on the corner. Two were from her lawyer, one business-sized, and one a larger manila envelope. The third, on heavier ivory stock, had been sent from the office of her father's medical practice. All addresses in Philadelphia.

Seeing the name of the city lying there inches from her eyes, she was reminded of how close she was—closer, at least, than she had been for several months. In an hour, not much more, she could be there.

Instantly Gaye felt her stomach tightening, her heart beating faster, her palms growing damp. It was clear suddenly that the anxiety she'd felt about taking this trip, coming this close, wasn't really the terror of being found out and pursued. The source had been her intuitive foreknowledge that she wouldn't let herself come this far only to retreat. All the more because she was certain now that her future was with Toby, there were things that had to be done to pave the way.

Any contact with her husband was still out of the question. But her father . . . she couldn't cut him out of her life forever. She longed to win back his emotional support, have him be part of her life, be accessible to the family she could begin to believe she might have. By now, surely, he must be coming to accept that it was not his role to save her marriage. Even if he wanted to keep his medical partnership with Brian intact, Gaye could not believe her father wouldn't welcome reconciliation with her.

That was her frame of mind as she grabbed up the envelope marked as coming from Owen Foster, MD. From its size and feel, it seemed to be an invitation.

Inside, however, she found only an engraved announcement: *This is to inform you that the offices of Dr. Owen Foster and Dr. Brian Leahy will be relocating as of May 1 to . . .* Nothing more, just a standard, impersonal change-of-address notice, sent out routinely to every name on the office mailing list.

Yet Gaye took it not as a slight, but as an extra goad to contact her father, to restore real communication. She started to put the card aside—and abruptly froze. Slowly she pulled the envelope back and stared at the front, the word-processed address: her name, care of General Store, Bartlett Mills, NH. It had been sent to her at Bunky's, *not* forwarded! Which meant that the location of the place where she went once or twice every week to personally collect her mail was already listed in files accessible to Brian. It might have been passed along inadvertently somehow—but more likely, she thought, it had been ferreted out by investigation.

Suddenly the innocuous change-of-address announcement took on an ominous significance. She hadn't received the card automatically as part of the general office mailing list. It could only be a subtle message from her husband that she hadn't escaped. To let her know that he was working to find her, had made some progress, was committed as ever to his declaration that she would never get away from him.

Quickly Gaye tore open the envelopes from her lawyer. The larger one contained only insignificant forwarded mail—offers for subscription renewals, a letter from a Philadelphia friend asking for news, charity solicitations. But the other was a letter detailing developments in the legal jousting over her bid for a divorce. The motions to dismiss the charge of abandonment against her had failed; after several postponements, a preliminary hearing was ordered for this coming Tuesday, at which both parties to the proceedings were expected to appear.

Gaye's lawyer had written to her, *There are a number of ways I can delay this, but if you are seen as unreasonably avoiding the court it will work against you. My advice is to come sooner rather than later.*

All of it only confirmed that it was important to make the overture to her father now. As long as he went on encouraging Brian's hopes, there was no chance for a sensible resolution. If she could win his understanding, enlist him as an ally in giving her a fresh chance at happiness, then Brian—or his own lawyer—might even arrive at the hearing reasonably resigned to ending the marriage.

"Let's go, boy!" Gaye said, rousting Rud from under the table. Her nerves had settled, and rather than any reluctance, she felt eager now to get started on the next leg of her trip. Having the dog along made the difference. He gave her confidence, if not as a protector then simply as a representative of Toby's spirit.

On the outskirts of Philadelphia, she stopped in a gas station to refill her tank and call her father from a public phone. No answer. But on a Saturday afternoon at not quite four o'clock, he might well be in surgery. He'd never taken weekends off—had sometimes done two, even three operations in a day.

She drove on into the central city, and went to a small hotel not far from his apartment building. This time she took Rud along with her, and no one challenged the dog. In a vestibule by the lobby restrooms she found a phone and tried again. There was still no answer at his apartment. At the lobby newsstand she bought a local paper, and sat reading for half an hour.

On her third try, he answered. Even his "hello" sounded harsh and impatient, and she had to overcome an urge to hang up. In the moment it took to gather courage, he repeated his hello twice, the rapid-fire demand of an always busy man.

"Daddy . . . it's me," she said at last.

There was a pause. "Gaysie . . ." he murmured in astonishment, reverting to an endearment he'd used when she was little.

That touched her, and his voice was instantly softer. She believed she could even hear a note of relief.

"Where are you?" he asked then.

She bypassed the question. "I'd like to see you."

"Yes, whenever you say."

"Now. I can be there soon."

"So you're here—in town?"

"I don't want Brian to know," she said quickly. "I just drove down here today. Promise me you won't tell him."

"He's been in bad shape, Gaye. He really needs—"

"Promise me!" she almost screamed, and a man who was just passing on his way to the restroom looked at her with alarm before disappearing.

"Sure, all right. I promise. So when will you be here?"

She was wary suddenly of meeting at his home, on his territory. She needed to be sure she would not be kept from leaving, or even restrained for one moment beyond when she needed to leave. To disguise her concern, she said, "I'm starving. Can we meet somewhere for supper?"

"Sure. I'll buy you a dinner at Vetri." He named the fine Italian restaurant that was his favorite, and near where he lived.

"I'm not dressed for such an expensive place," she protested.

"You'll be fine, I'm sure. And why shouldn't we go whole hog? This is a celebration! I can't tell you how happy I am that you're ready to see me again."

She agreed to meet him at the restaurant in half an hour.

After the call, she went into the lady's restroom with Rud and groomed herself to meet her father. He'd always been fairly strict about her appearance, criticizing her if she wore clothes he deemed too provocative, always more approving when her hair and makeup were spare rather than showy. As she studied herself in the mirror, it occurred to her for the first time in her life that it could be her father's influence that accounted for the gamine, little-girl look she'd kept for so long. Well, he'd have nothing to complain about today. She still had her short pageboy, and there was certainly nothing sexy about her gray wool skirt, white blouse, and blue cardigan. Seeing the image in front of her—checking herself to make sure she was acceptable—she realized how rare it had become to feel these insecurities. That was a gift of Toby's blindness. Did it matter much to him what she looked like? Yes, he was pleased to know she was pretty . . . but he never told her she was wearing an ugly color, or said her makeup was wrong—things Brian had picked on, too.

If beauty was in the eyes of the beholder, she mused, then how perfect that beauty could be when it was only in the mind's eye. As Toby "saw" her, she was always just right, wearing the right thing; she was Audrey Hepburn being photographed by Fred Astaire as she came down the steps of Sacre Coeur with a gown flying behind her like wings.

She went to meet her father, confident as never before that he would have to take her as she was.

*C*hapter 23

He was at a table in view of the door when she arrived. When he saw her enter he stood, and she proceeded toward the table without waiting to be greeted by a maître d'. Dominating her mixed emotions was a desire to repair the break, put all the bitterness behind them, and share her newfound happiness with all that was left of her family. She offered a hopeful smile as she approached.

But he glared back, recoiling slightly as if from an affront. "What are you doing, Gaye, coming in here like *that*?"

Only then did she become self-conscious about the dog beside her. By now she'd been in and out of a few places with Rud, and this time she hadn't even considered leaving him in the car. "It's a guide dog, Daddy—a Seeing Eye dog. He's allowed to be in here."

"A guide? You mean like for blind people?"

"That's right." They were still on their feet, arguing from opposite sides of the table. Gaye pulled out her chair and prepared to sit. "He's terrifically well behaved. He'll just lie down quietly next to me while—"

"Excuse me . . ." Gaye turned to see that the maître d' had come up behind her. "I'm most sorry, madam," he went on, "but your dog will have to leave."

"This is a Seeing Eye dog," Gaye said emphatically, "a guide for the blind. He's permitted in any public place."

"Don't give the man an argument," Owen Foster said sharply. "There's no reason for that animal to come in here."

Gaye shot a look at him. "I'm taking care of him. That's the reason."

Piqued by her resistance, her father glared more hotly.

The maître d' smiled at her politely. "I have a dog at home myself, young lady. But in the restaurant . . ." He shrugged heavily. "And I can see you do not need him to guide you."

"You told me you drove here," her father said. "Just leave the damn dog in the car."

He'd adopted that officious doctor-as-God tone she'd heard for too much of her life. Quietly but firmly she answered him: "I'd rather not. But I would like to talk to you, Dad. So we can go somewhere else. Or I can put the dog back in the car . . . and get in with him, and drive straight back out of town."

The restaurant around them had grown quiet, all other diners focused on the dispute.

"Gaye," her father said evenly, "be reasonable."

"Good God, Daddy, what's more reasonable than going someplace else for a bite to eat?"

Dr. Owen Foster looked at his daughter wordlessly for a long moment. One hand held the napkin he'd pulled from his lap, and his fingers clenched and unclenched around it, mimicking the manipulation he'd often done as a surgeon to stimulate a struggling heart. Then he tossed the napkin down on the table. "All right, let's get out of here," he growled. Striding past Gaye, he retrieved his coat from the check room.

"You and dogs" were his first words when they were outside, heading away from the restaurant along Spruce Street. As Rud walked beside Gaye on a leash, her father kept giving the dog baleful looks. "Always the problem. Here I want to treat you to a nice meal, sit down and try to work things out, and it goes to hell because of a goddamn dog."

"Does it matter where we eat? We need to talk—that's the important thing."

"But what point were you trying to make?" he rattled on. "A guide dog! What kind of nonsense is that? Were you going to pretend to be blind?"

"Of course not." She wanted to sit down before she explained, ease some of the tension away. She pointed to an ordinary coffee shop along the block. "Can we all go in there?"

"All," he echoed sourly. "Sure. What difference does it make?"

They went in, hung their coats on the hooks at the end of a booth, and sat down facing each other. Rud lay down under the table. A waiter came with menus. He said nothing about the dog.

"Just coffee," her father told the waiter at once, signaling that he'd lost his appetite and might not stay. The waiter looked to Gaye, who said she wasn't ready yet, and he left.

"Suppose I treat," she said to her father, making every effort to normalize relations. "Please. Give this a chance—we don't meet every day."

He gave her an ironic smile, then dragged the menu over for a look. Each retreated behind the large cards until the waiter came back. Both ordered plain hamburgers, and Gaye added a strawberry milk shake, a deliberate ploy to spark some nostalgia for those rare father-daughter outings of her youth.

"You still like strawberry," her father said when they were alone again.

She confessed. "Actually, I haven't had one of those since the last time you and I sat together in a coffee shop. When was that?"

He kept looking down at the table a second, then raised his eyes. "I guess not everyone's cut out for having kids," he said. "The problem is, they have 'em anyway. You got a bad deal, Gaye. I know that. I can't blame you for being . . . disappointed. Neither your mother nor I were really—"

She cut him off. "We don't have to go over all that. What's past is past. I'm here because I'd like to make a fresh start with you. I've done it already in some other important ways, begun building a good new life in another place. But you're the only family I've got in the world. It doesn't seem right to have to hide from you. I don't want to do that anymore."

"Good. I'm glad to hear that." His tone said he thought the problem was solved, simple as that.

"But I can't give it up," she said. "Not as long as you don't understand how scared I am."

"Of what, for God's sake? I'd never do anything to hurt you."

She gazed at him despairingly. "You still don't get it. You *really* don't get it." She leaned across the table. "It's Brian. He won't let me go. He's told me that. I'm afraid of what he'll do if he can't have what he wants. He killed Hero. Bad as that was . . . next time even that won't be enough."

She recognized the studied look her father was giving her now: the cold, analytical examination of a doctor making a diagnosis. How bad was the condition? Could he reason with her? She had to control herself not to scream out against it: *I'm not crazy.*

"Gaye, sweetheart," he said then, so maddeningly reasonable, "every day I work alongside Brian. I hear him talk to patients and their families, always caringly, and I see what he does to—"

She couldn't bear it. "Daddy, what you see isn't—"

"Hear me out!" he commanded sharply.

She sank back.

"I see him save lives day after day, week after week," he went on. "Can you understand why it's not poss—" He stopped himself, clearly intent on finding better words. "Why it's extremely difficult to believe that the *one* life he'd have no respect for should be yours, someone I hear him speak about all the time as the person who means more to him than anyone or anything else in the world, that he'd give the moon to have back?"

She met his probing gaze squarely. "Yes. I understand why it's difficult. But hard as it is, you have to make a choice—to believe me, or believe him."

"He loves you, Gaye. I know that."

"Do you know he's charging me with abandonment? Is that what makes you think he'd give anything to have me back? That he won't let me go without punishing me, making me pay?"

"Those are just words," her father said with a dismissive wave. "You're in court. It's . . . strategy. But if you'd only try again—"

"I can't! Listen to me, Dad, believe me. Because if you don't, I'll have to go on hiding from you, too. I'll never be able to tell you where I am, or anything else that's important in my life."

The waiter arrived with their food and set it out. They left it sitting on the table between them. The dog, excited by the scent of the cooked meat, stirred under the table, and Gaye put her hand down to settle him.

"So that's what the dog's really for," her father said at last. "To protect you. He's a *guard* dog—not a guide."

She shook her head and smiled, amused by the mistake. "No. He's exactly what I said. Not a guard—he's a Seeing Eye dog. And the man to whom he belongs can't be with him at the moment. He's at the Seeing Eye Institute taking a training course for three weeks. So I'm taking care of his dog." She started eating.

"Nice of you," Foster said tersely. But he eyed Gaye as if aware there was more to the story.

She put down her hamburger and gave it to him. "It's more than nice," she said. "The owner is someone with whom I'm . . . romantically involved."

Foster put down his own food and pushed the plate away. "A *blind* man, you mean? You're telling me that you're involved with a blind man?" The words carried the rising register of disbelief.

Which fired her determination to leave no doubt. "Maybe I shouldn't have said we're involved—that makes it sound complicated. It's much simpler than that. I'm in love with him: truly, deeply, fabulously in love. It's awfully early to say it, I suppose, but I'm planning to spend the rest of my life with him."

Now he erupted. "For heaven's sake, Gaye. You're still married! You ran off, and you've been gone for—what?—five months, and you turn up to tell me you're afraid the man you married is a . . . a psychopathic murderer, so you want to spend the rest of your life taking care of a blind man?" He tossed up his hands. "What the hell did you expect me to do? Congratulate you? Wish you happy-ever-after, and plead to be the one to throw another big wedding party?" He shook his head. "It makes no goddamn sense. You need help, dear girl. I *know* you do—even if you don't. You're not being rational. This kind of behavior—it's too much like too many things I've seen before."

"What do you mean?" Gaye demanded—though she suspected already, felt as stricken by his intimations as if a hot, sharp blade had been inserted slowly into her midsection. Even before he replied, she announced, "It's nothing to do with her."

"You think she never said similar things—that she didn't tell people she was afraid of me?"

"If she was, maybe there was a reason."

"No, Gaye. There was *no* reason. It was only in her mind. I'm not saying I was the perfect husband. But God knows she *never* had to be afraid of me."

As wildly unfair as it was to have her mother brought into the argument, it felt inevitable to Gaye. Whether they acknowledged it or not, that phantom hovered always between herself and her father. A thousand things had forever gone unsaid between them about her mother, about what had gone wrong in her parents' marriage, about how much they had loved each other or hurt each other.

Yet even the things that got hinted at were unbearable to hear. To realize that she was being branded as hysterical, her own cries for help discounted as illusory due to heredity, made Gaye feel that any détente with her father was futile. It wasn't his flawed logic or misplaced loyalties that made it impossible for him to sympathize with her, she finally understood, but the burden of his own history. She let him talk on without caring to offer a defense.

"I suppose it's part of feeling helpless," he was saying, "sick and helpless, that goes into having such sympathy for animals. The self-pity, hiding oneself away . . ."

Was he talking about her now, Gaye wondered, or her mother? Or was it both of them at once? There were parallels, she realized. But then, the unfairness applied to both. It went too far to say that they were sick or helpless or frightened without reason.

". . . and now this whole adventure of yours. Am I supposed to think you're being reasonable? You disappear to nowhere, run away from a doctor with a brilliant future because—you say—you're afraid he'll murder you, and instead you talk of spending the rest of your life taking care of some poor helpless nobody you've—"

She couldn't take it anymore. "Helpless?" she exploded. "You call this man helpless? Let me tell you something, Father. He's the one I lean on. I'm the poor, sad emotional cripple who's been stumbling around for too long, unable to find my way, letting myself be stepped on. Who's willing to sit here and listen to you run me down." She slid to the end of the booth and started gathering her things. "But you went too far this time—trying to make me believe there's something wrong with me, that there was something so wrong with my mother that I'm also—"

"Sit down, Gaye. We're not finished."

"I am. I've heard enough."

"Sit down!" he shouted, like a general certain his order could not be disobeyed.

But she was up, putting on her coat. "No, I'm not safe here—from Brian, or from the damage you do when—"

"I'm sorry, but you *need* to know this," he declared loudly, glaring at her. "It wasn't an accident!"

For one tiny fraction of time it was as if the words made no sense; they comprised some sort of spell in an occult language that could freeze all movement, stop the spinning of the Earth, turn everything to stone or ice.

And then the meaning crashed in on her. She knew why her mother had become part of the argument, part of his evidence for her irrationality. And she remembered—vividly—her mother's face at the moment she'd given the explanation for suddenly behaving so well, seeming so much like a new woman on that last evening Gaye had seen her alive: *I simply want to do what will make you and your father happy.*

She slumped back onto the end of the bench, one arm stuck in the sleeve of her coat, and looked at him, beseeching more of the truth.

"Of course I didn't tell you what she'd done," he went on. "What should I have said? It hit you hard enough as it was. But no horse *ever* threw her off. For all her . . . weaknesses, that was one thing she did superbly. It wasn't a fall."

"How?" Gaye asked, barely more than an expulsion of breath.

He hesitated a long time.

Until she asked again, "How did she do it?"

"In the barn. Fixed the rope over a beam in one of the stalls, got on her horse, and spurred it from under—"

Gaye let out a gasp and he stopped. She put her fist to her mouth and bit down on the knuckles, tasting blood. *I simply want to do what will make you and your father happy.* So was she to blame, too?

"I wouldn't have told you now," he said. "Except . . . if you walk out of here I don't know when I'll see you again. If ever. And you need to know why I'm worried about you, Gaye—why I can see that you aren't . . . thinking clearly, and need to get help or—"

She interrupted, speaking to him, but also voicing the thoughts that filled her mind: "How long have you had us mixed up together, I wonder—thinking I must be a little crazy or weak or confused because she couldn't cope with life? How long have you been so sure I'm like her that you thought whatever I wanted to do, whatever I tell you, had to be doubted?" There was a quiet authority in the way she spoke that forced her father to listen rather than object or reply. "If only I'd known the truth sooner— God, how I wish you'd told me the facts. It might have helped us both if you could have shared that with me. At the very least, I would have understood why the one and only choice in my life that you could ever trust, ever approve, was the one you made for me—Brian. And you still can't accept it was the only *bad* choice, the source of the worst unhappiness." She rose again. "I know what's right for me. I'm sorry you can't see that I do—but there's all kinds of blindness in the world." The dog was up, too, standing beside her. "Unfortunately, Daddy, with the kind you have, you can't find your way by just getting yourself one of these." She reached down and patted Rud. "Your blindness is so much worse." She started away.

"Gaye! Come back."

She kept walking. Curiously, Rud had stepped out slightly in front of her, leading her exactly as he would lead Toby. His gait was steady, she noticed, absent of any limp. Toby would have said that, for her sake, he was showing off how good he was at his job. She could believe it now.

As soon she was outside in the cool air of the night walking to the car, she questioned her own behavior. Not that she thought she'd been unfair, but perhaps a little too hotheaded.

Yet as long as her father couldn't state unequivocally that he believed her—still felt he needed to "rescue" her from the life she wanted—there would always be a risk he'd send Brian forth as a white knight.

Someday she could try again to close the rift. For now there was no doubt she had to keep the distance between them. She could only hope the distance was great enough to keep her safe from the husband who wouldn't let her go.

Chapter 24

On Monday Gaye arrived early at the clinic, eager for the distraction of work. Frankie was already in the examining room, applying salve to a tabby cat for treatment of a skin condition. The cat bristled at the sight of the dog entering with Gaye.

"Get him into the kennel," Frankie grumbled, with a nod at Rud.

"No, Frankie—that's not right for this dog. He's always with people." She had been taking Rud everywhere with her, and he was always well-behaved.

"He's upsetting my patient."

In fact, Gaye saw that the cat had already settled again. "Let's give him a chance, okay?"

Frankie gave a conspicuously dark frown, but swallowed any objection. "Thought you were coming back Tuesday night," she said, not hiding the implication that it would have been fine if Gaye had stayed away.

The original plan had been to drive back after the divorce hearing scheduled for Tuesday morning. But after the disastrous reunion with her father, Gaye had made a beeline for the car and immediately started driving north, a reflex need to escape. She was already past Hartford when she remembered the hearing—and never gave a thought to going back. Depressed and confused by her father's revelation, her mind churning with replays of so many moments in her youth when she'd mistaken the private despair in which her mother lived for rejection, she was too depleted of the necessary energy and courage to face her husband in court. Before coming to work this morning, she'd roused Helen Barash at home and informed her that she'd be absent from the proceedings after all.

"I'll come up with some excuse and try for a postponement," the lawyer said, "but it won't look good for you. We may have to negotiate on your husband's terms."

"I understand," Gaye said. "If it means paying a ransom to be freed from a bad mistake, I'll accept that."

The lawyer urged her once more to consider the difficulties of being saddled with debt, but Gaye didn't waver. The last time she'd heard this well-meant advice, Toby hadn't been a factor in her plans. Now she was eager to remove any impediments to being with him. She urged Helen to fight for the best terms, but reconfirmed that she'd sign *any* agreement that granted her a quick divorce.

She'd come away from the morning phone call with no regrets. To be free, to be able to make a life with Toby, that was all that mattered.

As Frankie continued treating the cat, Gaye looked at the appointment roster, a handwritten list of animals expected for treatment that Lori copied out daily and posted in the examining room. The schedule had been left fairly light because Gaye wasn't expected to be available.

"I can take the rest of these," she said to Frankie, "if you'd like time off with Will."

"No need," Frankie said.

"Where is he, by the way?" It was the first time Gaye had seen his office empty in the morning.

"Hospital," Frankie replied, her attention still focused on the cat.

Gaye was stunned. Not just by the news, but by Frankie's demeanor—the unspoken message that she preferred to lock Gaye out of the situation. It was surely more than ingrained New England reticence that had kept her from making any mention of Will's bad turn when Gaye returned this morning.

Gaye would have gone to Lori for more information, but the receptionist hadn't arrived for work yet. "What happened?" she asked.

"Got worse, that's all. But he'll be home in a day or two."

Despite the show Frankie made of discouraging all sympathy, Gaye had an impulse to comfort her. "If I can help in any way . . . pick him up at the hospital, or do something around the house, feel free to ask."

Frankie picked up her head to look at Gaye. "Just do your work, girl," she said. "That's help enough."

It developed into a busy day. With Gaye unexpectedly available, callers were accepted for walk-ins, and in the afternoon Frankie was able to get away for a couple of farm calls. Rud remained quiet, lying down in the space behind the X-ray shield. When it came time to close, Gaye almost forgot he was there.

When she called him to come, he didn't respond at once. At her second call, he answered with a bark, but didn't trot out to join her. She switched on the light in the X-ray alcove and looked behind the shield. Rud was resting on his haunches. She went to crouch before him, and cupped his muzzle to look into his dark eyes. "What's the matter, boy?"

He gave her a mournful look and whimpered softly.

"C'mon, pal, don't you want to go home?" The animal was in obvious distress, but she wanted to see how hard he would try to overcome it. Gaye stood, moved a few feet away, and beckoned. After a few seconds he rose up laboriously onto all fours. But he let out another little yelp, and she could see one of his hind legs quaking as he held his balance.

"Stay right there, Rud," she commanded, and went to get a painkiller from the vial in her tote bag. He was still dutifully standing when she returned. She tucked the pill under his tongue and waited until he'd swallowed it, then led him out of the alcove and offered him water from a bowl.

Watching him drink, Gaye thought back over all Toby's boasts about the dog's intelligence and spirit. Was it pure coincidence that the first time he failed totally to respond to a call was when Toby wasn't there to witness it? Rud's disease might be advancing more quickly than she or Toby had realized. Perhaps the time was closer than they wanted to believe when . . .

She didn't want to think about it. For the moment, anyway, he seemed better, with the painkiller beginning to take effect.

On the way to the car, Gaye glanced over at the farmhouse. It's black silhouette loomed against the darkening sky. She'd never before passed it on the way home without seeing a light or two burning somewhere within. Frankie must have gone straight from her farm calls to be with Will at the hospital. A chill went through Gaye at the sign of the dark house. It foreshadowed a future when there would be no need for light.

Reluctant to intrude on his training regimen, she hadn't talked to Toby since their parting. Tonight, needing the solace of hearing his voice, she called the institute at a time when she was sure dinner would be finished.

His delight at receiving her call came clearly through the phone, and the lift it gave her was instant balm for her nerves. Gaye put aside her own worries and complaints and concentrated on listening to him recount the details of training with his new dog.

"He's a winner," Toby summed up. "Lord Byron's going to be a great addition to our team."

In the past Toby would have spoken of himself and the dog as "the team." Gaye was touched by the way he'd included her. "So that's the name you picked—Lord Byron?"

"Will be—just Byron, that is—when he gets used to it. Right now he's spent his life as Arrow. Better for a pointer than a shepherd, don'tcha think?"

Gaye recalled that the poets for whom Toby renamed his guides had always written some laudatory verse about dogs. "What's the poem?" she asked.

"Something Lord Byron wrote for the tombstone of his own dog. His name was Boatswain, and he was just six years old when he died. I think they're the most beautiful words ever written to a dog, called 'Inscription on the Monument of a Newfoundland Dog.' Here are a few lines: '. . . the poor dog, in life the firmest friend, the first to welcome, foremost to defend . . . whose honest heart is still his master's own, who labours, fights, lives, breathes for him alone . . .' " A huskiness came into his voice, and he cleared his throat. "That's just part of it."

"It's beautiful." It would be, she realized, the eulogy for Rud—also just six.

"So how are you two getting along?" Toby came back, forcing the brightness back into his tone.

She decided not to burden him with any worries. "Fine. You know he's always easy to be with."

"And he's feeling okay?"

"He misses you terribly. I can see that."

"I'd guess he's pretty happy with you, too. Remember, he saw you first, and made the match." There was a pause. "Are you all set for tomorrow?"

It hit her suddenly. He assumed she was calling from Philadelphia; she'd told him at last about the hearing on Tuesday.

She couldn't lie to him. "I'm home again, Toby."

And immediately everything that had happened with her father, all the sorrows and doubts he'd forced upon her, came spilling out.

She was a wreck by the time she was finished, unable to speak without sobbing, lamenting the loss of her mother as if it had happened yesterday, confessing guilt at the lack of understanding she'd shown in her youth.

"Oh, Gaye darling, I wish you'd called me right away," Toby said. "Sounds like you could use a real shoulder to cry on, not just a telephone. I could come back. . . ."

"Toby, no!" She fought to regain her composure. "Listen, I'm a big girl, and you need to get your training done in the right way. I can handle things—and I've got Rud if I need a real furry shoulder to cry on."

"Okay. But if you need me, just holler—anytime."

She told him to count on it, then asked if he had any special instructions for feeding Rud, or arranging the kind of place he liked to sleep.

"Just make his every wish come true if you can," Toby said, plainly mindful of death creeping up. "Now can I ask a favor?"

"Anything."

"Look in on my mom, as soon as you have a chance. I know she misses me."

"Sure. Lunch hour tomorrow." She'd already called Norm Stephenson to say she'd returned early from her trip and to arrange to meet him. She'd return his car, pick up her truck, then see Dot.

"Great, thanks. And don't forget I'm here if you need me."

"I know."

"Just one more thing."

"Yes?"

"I love you, funny face."

After the call, she built a fire in the fireplace and dozed in front of it, Rud at her feet. Even without a melody, Toby's last words were like a song playing through her mind, soothing away all the hurts and cares that had been weighing her down. Being loved, truly and completely loved—and not just "owned"—made all the difference in the world.

Chapter 25

T he Mills post office was closed weekdays from noon to two o'clock, when Dot had lunch. Sometimes she stayed and fiddled with her cards, or used the time to keep up with official paperwork. But when Gaye stopped there today she saw through the glass door that all the lights were off inside.

She looked in at Bunky's, then the diner, other places Dot was known to frequent at lunch hour. Finally she drove up to the Callan house. There was no answer to the doorbell after three rings. Like West Greenlea, the Mills was still a place where it was common to leave house doors unlocked (though Gaye's custom remained the one learned in a big city; she'd even gotten permission from Millie to install an extra dead bolt on each of the doors to the apartment). As expected, Gaye found Dot's door open. She stepped over the threshold and called, "Dot?"

No response. Moving deeper into the house, Gaye called out again, not too loud in case Dot was taking a midday nap, though it was more likely she was still in town. Gaye was about to leave, then thought for the hell of it to have a look at the reading room. She went through the kitchen to the rear corner of the house. The door was closed. Hesitant to disturb her if she was in the midst of a reading, Gaye called very quietly, "Dot?"

"Come in," Dot's voice came back.

She was sitting at the card table in the center of the room. Curtains had been drawn over the windows; the only light came from a couple of candles in silver holders. The cards were laid out, but no one sat in the chair opposite her. She was wearing a dark red velvet caftan, which seemed curiously formal for a midday stop at home, even if it was to spend a while at some occult practice. Dot kept staring at the arrangement of tarot cards in front of her while Gaye stood in the doorway.

"Are you all right, Dot?"

Now she looked up at Gaye. "Of course I'm all right. It's you that's in trouble."

"Me?"

"Toby told me you'd be coming for a look-in. I thought I'd better see what's developing." She dropped her gaze again to the cards.

Gaye smiled as she advanced into the room. "Dot, it's sweet of you to care so much, but I'm okay."

"No, child, you're not." The older woman focused intently on the brightly colored pictures in front of her. "Remember, I told you to stay close to him?"

It rankled a bit to be called *child*. Gaye's tone hardened. "Toby needs to be where he is, and I need to be here. I'm not helpless without him."

Dot looked at her again. "We're all helpless when it comes to fate, my dear. It does with us what it will." The calm authority of her pronouncement stopped Gaye from protesting when Dot added, "Sit down, please."

Gaye told herself she was obeying simply to humor the elderly woman, building good relations with a possible future mother-in-law. Yet curiosity, too, drew her to hear Dot's interpretation of the cards. Toby's account of the warning Dot had given her young husband about a Chinese bandit who would someday kill him had made an impression.

When Gaye was seated, Dot waved her hand over the cards laid out on the table and explained: "What you see here is a spread of fifteen cards used by those mystical people who may have originally conceived the idea of embodying the unseen forces into these images, and using them to interpret events. It's called the Ancient Gypsy Spread, and I trust the power it has to foretell what may happen. Properly observed, it carries information about the distant past, the recent past, the influences that surround you in the present— and three possible outcomes of the future, depending on how all these separate elements converge."

The following description of Gaye's distant and recent past was certainly on the mark: Referring to cards representing the Hermit and the Tower, Dot described Gaye as someone who had been isolated and left to search for truth on her own because of two deaths, the first of which was "a violence done to oneself," the second of which was "a violence done to one being by another."

This much, Gaye realized, might easily derive from Toby's passing on what she'd told him about her mother's suicide and Hero's death. Yet she doubted Toby had done that. He had understood that she was entrusting him with confidences, matters of a very private nature that it was difficult for her to talk about.

Supposing even this much of Dot's reading was bogus, however, the crux was not in the description of events already transpired, but how they related to what was to come. Her detailed forecast, as related to the cards, struck Gaye as eerily on target in how it tied strands together.

"The cards here show an overwhelming presence of those from the suit of swords. These symbolize aggression, violence, misfortune, struggle. In the presence of other cards of the major arcana, what I see, my dear, is that you have somehow created a monumental anger, a virtual volcano overflowing with a fire that forces you to run from it. But this river of fire flows after you, threatens to engulf you. You had a chance, even recently, to dampen the flame, cool the fire, but you turned your back on it. Now, wherever you go, this river may follow and engulf you."

Gaye could interpret all this easily as the result of leaving Brian, his determination never to let her go, even the opportunity that had been offered by facing him in court to try dealing reasonably with him. Tempted now to treat the reading as a true warning, she asked, "Three possible outcomes, you said, not just one. What are they?"

Dot stared at the cards for almost a minute. "You may cool this river of fire somehow, and then travel upon it—though where you go leads to darkness. Or it will kill you."

"And the third?"

Dot lifted a bleak gaze to meet Gaye's. "This is the one it seemed to me you needed . . . a knight to help you. It's why I worry so much that he's not here. With him, you survive the danger. Without him, it's not so certain."

Sailing on the quieted river toward darkness was easy to interpret, too: returning to Brian. The second alternative hardly needed interpretation: The murderous impulses he had demonstrated by killing the dog would be carried one step further.

And the third? Assuming there was any substance at all to this gypsy fortune-telling, it still didn't tell her what she needed to know. What *exactly* did it mean that *she* would survive if Toby were with her? What about Toby? If there was truly danger—if Brian were to show up here—how could she knowingly put him in harm's way? Brave and accomplished as Toby was at dealing with his blindness, he'd never been faced with *this* kind of challenge, standing up against the raging jealousy of another man bent on having his own way.

Gaye sat quietly, her eyes sweeping across the display on the table. Cards. *Pictures!* In the cavelike candlelit ambience of this room, it was easy enough to be lulled into the romance of the occult, and fear for her safety on the basis of Dot's warning. After all, her fear had been living inside of her before this. Nor was that any secret to Dot, who had been a party to the measures she'd taken to conceal her whereabouts.

So should she let this ritual, these brightly colored pieces of pasteboard, determine her choices, lead her into acting like a helpless damsel in distress who needed to disrupt Toby's life? That would be weak, selfish, unnecessary, Gaye decided.

At the same time, she wanted to tread carefully on the feelings of Toby's mother. No doubt she regarded the reading as a service done out of love.

Dot was gazing at her, waiting for a response.

"Well, it's a very good thing you did this for me, Dot. I know now I have to be extremely careful. But I think I can handle it."

"If you—"

Gaye broke in at once. "Dot, you haven't told Toby about this, have you?"

She shook her head. "I've only just seen the cards."

"Then you have to promise me that you won't."

"But you need—"

Gaye cut her off more firmly. "I'll be okay. And he needs to be where he is. If he's going to protect me in some way, I certainly don't want him here without the help he'd need from his guide. And Rud . . . he won't be up to it anymore."

"My dear, the danger may be more imminent than you realize. I think you may be—it's a cliché, perhaps, but it relates to the reading—playing with fire."

Gaye reached across the table, her hands taking hold of Dot's. "I am sincerely grateful that you're watching out for me. But I'll be okay—and Toby really shouldn't get worked up about this. Promise me you won't do that, Dot, won't tell him anything that brings him running up here to hold my hand." Dot hesitated, and took a breath as if to object. "Promise me!" Gaye insisted. "I've got a right to run my own life."

A wounded look came into Dot's eyes. Gaye realized she'd overdone the demand, expressed it too harshly. But it was done now, and achieved its purpose. Dot wrested her hands free and sat back. "If that's what you want," she muttered.

"I'll be all right," Gaye repeated. "Forewarned is forearmed—isn't that what they say? Another cliché, but I'm sure it's true." She gestured to the array of cards. "You let me know what I'm up against. Thank you. I'll call you later," Gaye concluded, determined to smooth Dot's ruffled feelings. "We could have dinner some evening after work."

"Most evenings I'm busy. There are people who need this." She nodded to the cards.

Gaye let the dig go by, and told Dot she'd call anyway, and hoped they'd get together before Toby returned.

Outside, with the sun shining down, and the air warmed just enough to remind even New Englanders that spring was just around the corner, the spell cast by sitting in a small, dark, candlelit chamber and looking at cartoons of devils and jesters and hanged men evaporated.

Gaye knew she had to be careful, but she'd known that all along. As she drove away, she was amused rather than worried by thinking back on the time she'd just spent with Dot. She still felt safe in her refuge. In these valleys where the last patches of snow were just disappearing, it didn't seem likely a river of fire could overtake and engulf her.

Chapter 26

On Thursday just before noon an ambulance brought Will home. Between appointments to examine a preschooler's pet rabbit and give shots to a sheep farmer's Border collie, Gaye took a break to go over to the farmhouse and personally welcome Will. All the more since the complete rupture with her own father, she recognized the depth of gratitude and affection she felt toward Will Bennett for his mentoring and consistent kindness. She had sorely missed him at the clinic these past few days; his leavening temperament was a necessary buffer for her relations with Frankie, which were always more strained without Will present. Gaye was anxious to do *anything* that might cheer him up and distract him from his ever-darkening slide toward a difficult end.

Rounding the corner of the farmhouse to the front entrance, she saw him seated in his motorized wheelchair, flanked by a couple of ambulance attendants as he was lowered out of a side-panel door the ambulance on a hydraulic platform. A dome of shiny black plastic, like the carapace of an oversize black beetle, was strapped to his chest, a breathing pump to assist his now-paralyzed diaphragm in performing the mechanical function of drawing air into his lungs and expelling it. Even humbled by his helplessness, Will produced a smile as soon as he saw her approaching, not a manufactured smile, either, but one that made his eyes light.

"There she"—he paused for a sort of gulp—"is!"

It was the breathing apparatus that forced the interruption, Gaye realized. By the time she reached him, the chair was on the ground. She leaned down, encircled his shoulders with her arms, and kissed him on the cheek. With Frankie nowhere in sight, she didn't feel she had to monitor her emotions.

"Hiya, boss," she said, straightening up. "I'm so glad you're home."

"Me"—pause—"too." He hefted an arm and banged a limp hand against the breathing pump. "Damn . . . thing makes . . . hard . . . talk."

"Hey, Mr. B, don't mistreat your equipment," one of the attendants scolded. "You need that."

Frankie came rushing out of the house, a blanket in her arms that appeared to have been yanked straight off a bed. She barely acknowledged Gaye as she placed the blanket over Will, covering his hands and tucking it up under his chin so it also concealed the breathing pump. Gaye suspected that the blanket was as much to hide the evidence of Will's infirmity from her own sight as to make him comfortable.

"Don't . . . need," Will said. "Go in . . . warm."

Frankie didn't reply, but turned instead to the attendants and said, "Put him in the front room."

Will gave Gaye a little smile of surrender and a farewell toss of his head as he was wheeled off. Gaye preferred to believe that Frankie's treatment of Will wasn't unfeeling, only that her own welcome speeches and embraces had already been done, and she was dealing now with the practicalities.

Frankie remained nearby, but turned away as they both watched Will disappear into the house. Then she glanced at Gaye, as if casually, asking, "Don't you have appointments?"

Automatically, Gaye started walking briskly back around the house to the clinic. But almost at once she regretted yielding so quickly to Frankie's dismissal. Surely it was a moment to try knocking down that wall of cool reserve that had stood between them since the moment they'd met. The glint she had noticed in Frankie's eyes just now was not the icy glare of rejection, but a film of tears. Her Yankee grit and pride might prevent her from admitting the need for support, but Frankie's emotional resources were obviously being eroded as steadily as her husband's health. Fragile as she was, Frankie seemed to think the shell in which she encased herself and her feelings was vital to her survival. But Gaye believed it was important to break through it, to make Frankie understand that she didn't have to go through her crisis alone. In fact, to do what she had failed to do for her mother.

Gaye stopped walking and stood for half a minute, on the point of marching back and making an impassioned plea to Frankie to drop her defenses. But at last she continued along the path to the clinic. She didn't feel she had the words—nor the skill or the strength—to break through that granite resistance. Nor was she sure she had the right. People had to go through their tragedies in their own way.

At least for now it was easier to think so. Easier, too, to believe that there was nothing she could have done long ago but accept the gift her mother had given her, and go.

Every time Gaye saw Frankie over the next few days, the same impulse to reach out to her stirred within, and every time she quelled it in some way. Gaye had only to indicate the slightest sympathy, ask about Will, offer to take him out in his chair for a walk or read to him or come over in the evening to make a meal and spare Frankie the task—anything—and Frankie would either dismiss her with a quick refusal, or pretend she hadn't heard and change the subject.

That was hard enough to bear, but Frankie also limited access to Will. It had started the day after Will's return from the hospital. As soon as Gaye finished work, she'd gone over to the farmhouse to pay a visit. Frankie had answered the door, and told Gaye that Will was resting and too tired to see her. But as she left the house, Gaye noticed lights on in the living room windows, and she could see Will sitting up in his chair.

The following afternoon, at a time when she knew Frankie was away on a farm call, Gaye took a gap between appointments to go to the farmhouse. The door was answered this time by the nurse, a young woman named Janet, who told Gaye she'd been engaged to take care of Will full-time. When Gaye asked to see him, Janet said to return later because Will was napping. That could have been true, but the nurse added that, "Mrs. Bennett's trying to get him on a regular schedule—visitors in the morning and evening, and lots of rest in between."

Gaye interpreted this as restricting her access to Will anytime Frankie wasn't present. Was it only jealousy that accounted for Frankie's need to separate them, a greedy wish to keep for herself whatever time Will had left? Or was she afraid that Gaye might conspire with Will to help him die?

In any case, abiding by the rules, Gaye made her next effort to see Will the following evening after work. Again it was Janet who answered the door, but this time Gaye was admitted and led to the living room, where Will's chair was positioned in front of a glowing log fire. Frankie sat on the swaybacked old sofa, a sewing box beside her, a blouse she was mending in her lap.

Since it was difficult for Will to talk, Gaye's visit with him consisted mainly of keeping up a patter about the patients she had seen, and praising the way what he had taught her was benefiting various cases. Not empty praise, either; her use of reiki had definitely made a difference in the recent recovery of a dachshund that had blown a disk.

Because of the effort required, Will kept his responses short, but it was clear that he appreciated Gaye's visit. He asked only one question relating to clinic matters: "How's . . . Toby's dog?"

As with Toby, her first reflex was to minimize concern. "Okay. I bring him to the clinic every day. He's good company, no trouble. He's over there now waiting for me to bring him home."

"No pain?"

"Controlled."

"Walking?" A key question for a vet. When any animal lay down and gave up moving, it was judged to be a reasonable time to euthanize.

She replied with a quick nod. It made her uncomfortable to talk about Rud with Will. She always felt that he identified with the situation of the animal—and envied the mercy of being helped to die before all of his dignity and sense of purpose had been stolen away. Having Frankie sitting nearby, quietly stitching yet no doubt tuned in to every word, made Gaye acutely self-conscious.

"I ought to be going, Will," she said. "I've got a couple of very full days at the clinic the rest of this week—it's tough to manage without you pitching in—but maybe on the weekend I could take you out for a drive?"

"Great. Count on . . . it."

It wasn't on impulse that she'd made the offer directly to him, and with Frankie present. The difficulty of seeing Will had been a subject in Gaye's nightly phone visits with Toby, and he had suggested the tactic. Will would appreciate the change from being housebound, they agreed, and if he expressed his wish to Gaye with Frankie as a witness, it might be harder for her to veto the outing.

Each time Gaye crossed paths with Frankie at the clinic, the contacts continued to be strained. They kept exchanges restricted to office matters, case notes, prescription recommendations, scheduling, but underneath the words was the threatening hiss of a fuse burning down to the nub. On Friday—before the planned weekend outing—the atmosphere was particularly tense.

Intent on heading off an explosion, Gaye looked for a moment to approach Frankie and speak directly about the issue on both their minds. Toward the end of the afternoon, Frankie was in front of the light panel, looking at X-ray films taken of a brain removed from the carcass of a sheep. A local sheep farmer had found the animal already dead in a field, and wanted to be assured the cause was not scrapie, or bovine spongiform encephalopathy, the same brain-wasting condition called mad-cow disease in cattle.

When Gaye entered the X-ray area, Rud was lying on the floor near where Frankie was standing. The sight offered some encouragement to the prospect of an entente; Frankie had, after all, accepted Rud as a constant presence in the examining room, even seemed at times to like it.

Gaye moved up to the light panel. "How's it look?"

"Clean. I suppose this old ewe just lay down and never got up. Nice way to go."

They stood side by side, staring at the translucent swirl of gray and white. "Frankie, about tomorrow—"

"Yes, I meant to tell you. I don't think Will can go out."

Gaye fought to control herself. "Please . . . wait before you make that the final word. I know you haven't wanted to leave us alone. I know why, too. You think—"

"He needs his rest. He shouldn't—"

Gaye's composure cracked. "A ride in the country, damn it! How can you deny him that? I promise not to . . . conspire with him!"

Frankie acted as if there had been no outburst. She unclipped the X-ray films from the panel and started away. "Some other time, maybe."

Gaye's hand shot out and hooked onto Frankie's arm, yanking her around. "You don't have to be *afraid* of me!" she shouted. Then Frankie was facing her. Gaye throttled her voice down. "I won't . . ." With Frankie's icy blue eyes boring into her, she had to dig for the rest. "If he asks, I won't agree . . ."

At last, deliberately, Frankie pulled her arm from Gaye's grasp. Gaye retracted her hand, showing her palms in a little gesture of apology.

"How do you know?" Frankie asked then in a level voice. "How can you tell me what you will or won't do? How easy do you think it will be to refuse Will if he asks you to help him die? I know how you feel about him, Gaye, and he knows. And doing what we do . . ." Her gaze fell to where Rud lay on the floor. "It's not so much to ask, is it?" She lifted her eyes again to meet Gaye's.

It took Gaye a moment to find her answer. "Trust me, Frankie, please. Just trust me. I want to make things easier for Will any way I can. And you, too. I do . . . care for him very much. But you're his wife, and you've made your feelings clear, and . . . I won't come between you. You have my word."

Frankie looked at her for a very long time without speaking. "I expect there's lots of places he'd like to go," she said at last. "Come early."

Gaye was on the phone that night with Toby for almost two

hours. A good portion of the time was occupied simply by the cozy back-and-forth of lovers on the phone. She sat curled up in her large chair in front of the fire and they exchanged everyday news of their activities, and worried together at what they'd seen on the TV news, and laughed at his descriptions of mishaps in the training process, and they shared their pangs of desire to be together. But there were also personal issues to be discussed. He had talked to Dot, who had revealed her tarot reading to him, after all, arousing his fears for Gaye's safety.

That forced her to make a special appeal for him not to disrupt his training. "Toby, do you really think we should run our lives by your mother's tarot cards? Please! I'm fine. I have locks on the doors, a telephone beside me if I need to call for help, and I've also got Rud."

"There was a time that would have been enough by itself," he said. "But I'm not sure you can rely on him for protection."

"If anything were threatening me, I'm sure he could still come up with a pretty frightening snarl, and hold the threat at bay while I got out the door. But," she added quickly, "I really don't think he'll be pressed into duty. I'm sure I'm safe for now. And you'll be home in another ten days."

He yielded to her, and they picked up another matter—how she should deal with Will. It wasn't unlikely that Will would, as Frankie had guessed, try to enlist her in an assisted suicide. She didn't think she'd only imagined that he'd been laying the groundwork in a couple of previous encounters. The exchange she'd had with the Bennetts' daughter hinted that he might have expressed the wish to her, too. Above all, they shared a profession in which the mercy of euthanasia was accepted and regularly applied—and shared a viewpoint that Frankie apparently did not.

"It's going to be so hard if he does bring it up," Gaye confessed to Toby. "I've given Frankie my word. But in my heart, I'd do anything to help Will. I want to do whatever will make it easiest for him."

"You don't have the right," Toby gently reminded her. "Not by any existing standard—not by law or custom or morality."

"By anything but simple decency," she countered. "To do for him only what I'd do for any animal I truly loved."

"You mustn't let that confuse you, Gaye. This is a man."

"Right. Unlike Rud, he can think for *himself*. And yet I can't give him the peaceful, untortured peace he may beg to have."

"It would be murder, Gaye. You could go to jail."

"It would be mercy. His own daughter said she'd defend me."

They went back and forth like that, a debate of sentiment against strict rules, and, of course, in the end it came down to the fact that Gaye had given her word to Frankie, and it was not her place to do anything but what Frankie wanted.

And one more thing: a veterinarian could play God to the beasts of the field, but not to a man.

It took her a long time to doze off after she got into bed, and even then her sleep was a restless jumble of truncated dreams without beginning or end: standing on a snow-covered summit and looking down on the suddenly close image of a dead sheep hanging in a tree while Hero ran in circles below the tree, barking up at the body.

Her confusion of mind was such that when she heard a dog howling and bolted upright in the dark, she still didn't realize for a second that she had risen from sleep into consciousness. The barking continued, though, and she knew then she was awake. It was Rud, from the other end of the apartment. Her heart, already agitated by the dream, began to beat even faster. Her instant assumption was that he was standing at the glass doors, had been roused by something he'd seen or heard outside. Someone trying to get in! Those doors were the most vulnerable point of entry.

Gaye jumped out of bed and ran into the next room. In the darkness she saw the dog, dimly silhouetted against faint light from outside, standing exactly where she'd guessed. His body rigid, leaning slightly forward as he barked, he was obviously focused on something not far beyond the windows. Gaye crept forward, staying close to a wall so as not to expose herself to view. If Brian were there, the sight of her might inflame him, make her a target.

Closer to the window, the sloping hill down to the river now visible, she looked out and saw nothing, no one. But Rud was still barking, and now he had begun to act in a way that looked even more like he was responding to something close outside. He was

walking back and forth along the windowed wall, as if his movement was provoked by—matched to—someone stalking past on the
other side of the glass. Where there was nothing to be seen.

Gaye moved up to the dog. "What is it, boy? What's bothering
you?"

He ignored her, kept pacing.

Then suddenly, at the exact middle of one of the French doors,
he stopped and his barking ceased. He pressed his nose close up
against the glass and began to make the kind of whining noise that
seemed to indicate a desire to go out, at least to get closer to whatever was there. His agitation was completely baffling.

Then something even more curious occurred. The dog reared
back abruptly, as if something were coming at him, and his neck
arched up and around, as though his eyes were following the path of
something passing over his head, a bird or a butterfly. He didn't bark,
though; he appeared to be snared in the sort of silent amazement a
person might feel when witnessing something phenomenal, unbe-
lievable. A moment later he wheeled around to take up a stance facing in the other direction. And now he did bark, but not very loudly,
short, staccato bursts. This kind of barking wasn't hostile, Gaye
knew; it sounded very much like the language of one dog introducing itself to another, establishing contact. Though it must mean
something else, for there was nothing but empty darkness in front of
Rud.

"What is it, Rud?" She went toward him. But he trotted away
from her and began moving around in a tight circle, sniffing at the
air. Then he started a kind of dance, moving back, hopping up
briefly on his hind legs, prancing around. Then he was rolling over,
his legs pawing at the air, while his head moved side to side, his
mouth occasionally taking little nips at nothing.

The cancer had reached his brain, she realized; he was having
some kind of fit. She moved to grab him, comfort him until it
passed. But the moment she took a step, he stopped and got to his
feet and looked at her, perfectly composed. It gave her the oddest
sense that instead of ending his fit, she had interrupted him at play.

The sort of playful tussling one dog would do with another!

She backed away slowly, and then the dance began again—the circling, wrestling, pawing, nipping.

She stared at Rud playing with the dark emptiness. "Hero?" she murmured. "Oh, God, are you here?" Then her voice broke loudly from her throat, as loudly as if she were calling him in from a field. "Hero?"

Rud was suddenly motionless, on his feet again. It could have been from her call—except that he wasn't looking at her, but still into the dark, his gaze tracking very, very slowly in a path that led to her.

Gaye dropped to her knees. "Hero," she said softly, and held her arms out wide.

What she felt then might have been nothing but an air current, or a place on the skin of her neck where some mechanism like a blush produced a sudden warmth. But it was no less sweet than the times when he would put his muzzle there, and she would hug him and sink her fingers into his fur.

He was there. She believed it. Nearby, Rud had lain down. He believed it, too—could *see* the other dog. Was that because he was dying?

"Stay with me," she whispered. "Please . . ."

Unwilling to move from this spot, she lay down slowly and patted the place beside her. Was this madness? The aftermath of too much stress, the shock of learning about her mother?

But then what was this warmth she felt along her body, this sense of comforting closeness when there was nothing but an empty square of carpet?

Chapter 27

She woke exactly where she had lain down, on her side, one arm crooked outward like a buttress as though it had been thrown across . . . something. Through the windows facing her, she saw the morning light of a fine day. Even on the hard floor, she had slept soundly straight through the night. She'd had no blanket, but curiously she didn't feel at all chilled.

Gaye sat up and looked around, fixing herself in the daytime reality. Memory and dream folded over each other, and she was no longer sure what had actually happened. She remembered *believing* the ghost of her dog had come in the night—but, of course, in dreams you believed whatever was happening. It was even possible, she thought, that she'd sleepwalked to this spot.

She noticed now that Rud was not by the window, where he'd been when she fell asleep last night. She was suddenly gripped by the wild idea that he'd chased after a phantom in his own image, leaped across a barrier into the spirit world. She spun from the window, searching—and saw him at once, asleep in the easy chair, his head hanging over the edge.

She started her morning routine, setting up the coffeemaker so the coffee would already be made by the time she came out of the bathroom. Reminding herself that she planned to pick up Will for his outing no later than noon, she glanced at the kitchen clock to see if she had a few hours to herself—to give Rud a walk, linger over coffee, then clear up some case records.

The clock was showing almost a quarter past eleven! Gaye pushed her hair back and read the time again. Hard to believe. She had slept as if drugged. Maybe it all tied in with imagining things. A weariness of the mind that fudged her powers of perception.

Whatever the explanation, there was nothing to do now but get into high gear if she wanted to be on time for Will.

She drove up to the farmhouse forty minutes later. He was waiting outside the front door in his wheelchair, wrapped in an overcoat and muffler, a plaid tam on his head. Gus Dowd, the sheep farmer whose Great Pyrenees had been Gaye's first patient, stood beside the chair. The dog was there, too. As soon as she saw the large, bearish man Gaye understood that he must have been summoned by Frankie to handle the job of loading Will into the truck. That Frankie herself was absent didn't surprise Gaye; it was one more instance of hiding from the massive inconveniences brought upon her and her husband by the disease.

Gaye got out of the truck and called Rud to follow. With the extra apparatus that had to go along with Will—everything that made it possible for him to remain stationary—there wouldn't be room in front for the dog. He'd have to ride in back.

"Hello, Doctor," Dowd greeted Gaye as she came around the truck.

"Hi, Mr. Dowd. Thanks for helping us out."

"Anything for Will," he said. "And call me Gus. That's short for Augustus—he was an emperor, you know."

As Gaye bent over Will to give him a hug, the farmer's big white dog began barking at Rud. "Let me put him in back," she said. Rud could have easily dealt with any challenge when he'd been in top form, but being hobbled by the disease made him vulnerable. Standing his ground, instead of moving away from a larger dog, could be seen as a challenge that invited a fight.

She pulled Rud gently by his collar to the rear of the truck and dropped the tailgate. Rud made one halfhearted attempt to jump up to the loadbed, another challenge he could have once handled easily. But now it was too high for him. Gaye bent to pick him up, but the farmer stepped in quickly to help. He lifted Rud into the loadbed, secured the tailgate, then moved back to the wheelchair. "How about you now, Dr. Will?" he asked jauntily. "Ready to ride the range?"

"Can't wait."

Moving Will involved more than just lifting him from his chair into the truck. There were tubes and canisters and water bottles and the cumbersome battery pack for his breathing aid and other para-phernalia that had to be disconnected and moved as well. Once that was done, Gus heaved Will up in his arms and placed him in the truck. Then all the accessories that served his needs had to be taken from the hooks and pouches that held them in place on the chair, and tucked in around Will so they were secure. Gaye did this part, and then reconnected everything to the necessary inlets and outlets that had become part of his body. She saw, too, that Will was already wearing a metal brace on his shoulders to keep his head upright, his neck muscles no longer able to respond. All of it made her freshly aware of how quickly he was going downhill.

Yet reduced as he was to being a largely inert object that couldn't even go for a ride in the country without all this undignified and time-consuming fuss, Will still bore it with good humor. "When . . . hooked up," he said to Gaye, "I whistle . . . if go through . . . speed trap."

She rewarded him with a laugh. "No speeding today, Dr. B. We're going to take it nice and easy, and just meander wherever you want to go, see whatever you want."

She wished Dowd could go with them, but after getting Will set-tled into the truck, Dowd explained he had to get back to his farm and asked what time she planned to return. "Tell me when and I'll be here to help."

Gaye finished making Will comfortable. "How much of me can you stand, boss? Shall we make a day of it?"

"Need this," Will agreed. "See much. Maybe . . . last . . ."

Dowd and Gaye exchanged a quick unhappy glance. "None o' that talk, Will," Dowd said. "I'll be ready to toss you in Doc Foster's heap anytime you say. Now you two get goin'. I'll be here at four, and if you get back later that's all right. Geronimo 'n' me will be happy to wait." The big Pyrenees had been pacing beside the truck and looking up at Rud, but at the sound of his name he came over to his master.

Gaye started moving to get behind the wheel. Dowd called to stop her. "Oh, Doc . . . you didn't say anything. . . ." The way he inflected the remark, the farmer sounded disappointed, even hurt.

"Sorry. Thank you, Gus."

"No, not that. About the eyebrows." He gestured to the dog. "See how nice they look? Been snippin' 'em regular. And he doesn't rub at his eyes anymore."

Gaye went back and looked at Geronimo's eyebrows. "Very nice job, Gus," she said. Then she glanced down at the dog's feet. "Tonight you can clip his nails."

For a long while they drove without speaking. Gaye had asked Will when they started out where he wished to go, what he wanted to see, and he answered: "Every . . . thing."

She took a wide circuit, traveling over the roads she knew Will must have taken through all hours of the day and night, over the decades he'd carried out his mission as a vet. They followed the riverside road south, then crossed over into Vermont and came north again through the hills. The weather was cooperating to make Will's excursion as good as it could be—the sky clear, the sun warming the air so the first smell of spring rode the breeze that came through the truck windows. The last snows were gone, the buds on tree branches beginning to burst into leaf, the first wildflowers were spreading along the roadsides. Gaye could see springtime happening in front of her eyes, and whenever she glanced over at Will she knew he saw it, too.

Since talking was an ordeal for him, she gave him silence for as long as he wanted. She was apprehensive, knowing that at some point he was probably going to talk about his dying, and ask for her help. Even so, there was a surprising comfort and ease in being with him, an underlying communion that she was sure he felt, too.

"So lovely," Will said at last. They were going through a pocket valley in Vermont, hills on either side sloping down to meadows, a broad stream meandering through one of them, silver rapids swollen by the spring thaw, sparkling in the sun. "Right place . . . to live."

She took it as his reflection on the way he had chosen to spend his life. Also, an invitation to talk. "Second the opinion," Gaye said. "I'm lucky I came here." Without thinking, her hand reached across the seat to rest on Will's. He turned slightly—as much as he could— and smiled. "Me luckier," he said.

The conversation continued steadily after that. Though Gaye naturally did most of the talking, it was Will who chose the subjects or made his own thoughts known with succinct little two- and three-word phrases and questions. She stopped hearing the pauses. When he said just, "You and Toby?" Gaye knew he wanted to hear about their relationship. She obliged him not only by confessing that she was happily and completely in love, but she went on to share Toby's anecdotes about his training, the things he'd told her about his new dog, Lord Byron, and all she could remember about the relevant poem.

"Marry?" Will asked.

Today she didn't mind at all talking about the obstacles that had to be cleared away first, the divorce, the breach with her father. Though sooner or later it would all be settled, she said. Yes, she couldn't wait to marry Toby, and settle down right here. "The right place to live," she echoed his words.

"Glad," Will said. Then he added, "Sorry not . . . give away."

She drove on a little farther before she understood—stand in for her father at the wedding, he meant. A lump rose in her throat, but Gaye fought against tears. That would be surrendering him to death, looking ahead to when he was gone. "I'd love you to do it," she said. "Maybe . . . maybe it can work out somehow." She glanced over at him.

He smiled back.

Without knowing why it was her next thought, she said, "My dog came to me last night—his ghost, I mean, the one who was killed. This time I'm sure of it." At least she wanted to be; wanted to give Will some sort of hope.

"Tell."

She recounted the experience in full, from the time she fell asleep, until the fevered dream that preceded her waking.

"I believe," he said at the end. Then, "Frankie needs. Tell her."

Gaye gave Will a questioning look.

He answered it. "To let . . . me go."

This was it, she realized, the plea to help him with his dying. And she knew suddenly it was all he would ask. Conscious of both her compassion and his wife's denial, he would not force her to refuse him. Instead he wished only for help in changing Frankie's mind, to sway her if possible with this same vision of a future beyond death.

Released from the apprehension of talking more about his death, she relaxed completely, and the rest of her time with him was joyous. He expressed a desire for ice cream, and she drove to the diner in the Mills and brought two dishes of vanilla out to the truck. He couldn't swallow it, but he could taste, and feel the cold on his tongue.

Then he wanted to pay a visit to Bunky Chatsworth, whom he had known for years, but hadn't visited for a while. She drove to the general store, and Bunky brought one of the rocking chairs outside and set it beside the open door of the truck, and they talked. Bunky struck just the right note of sympathy with the sort of everyday curmudgeonliness he displayed with any other customer. "Sorry to see you this way, Will," he started off. "It's gettin' mud on my rocker, for one thing."

They chatted a little about old times, and the changes that had come to the area, while Gaye let Rud out of the truck's loadbed and took him for a short walk up and down the street. When she came back to the truck, Will was doing the talking while Bunky, gently rocking, patiently sat through all the pauses between the short bursts of words. As Gaye listened, she realized Will was talking about the clinic, what would become of it without him—talking in general as one local businessman to another, she assumed. Then she heard his words adding up to a kind of sales pitch—that it would be a good business for someone with a family, lots of room for kids, and of course, children liked to be around animals. She suspected now that this was the main reason Will had asked to see Bunky. The store was a hub for news and gossip; its proprietor could act as an informal real estate agent, let people know the property was going to be for sale. Gaye felt a pang of loss, not only for herself but on behalf of Will. He'd given his life to this endeavor, and, whatever his wishes, it seemed dubious that the clinic would survive him. From what Frankie had said about veterinary work, she would be willing to sell to any buyer; the land alone had value.

Noticing that Gaye had returned to the truck, Will quickly concluded. "You'll help?" he said to Bunky.

"You bet. Whatever I can do," Bunky said.

She lifted Rud into the back of the truck, Bunky and Will shook hands, and they left. Will admitted to being tired, ready to go home.

"Great day," he said, when they were on the way. "Grateful."

"We'll do it again. Whenever you say."

"No. Too hard."

She let it pass. He wasn't only referring to the physical rigors, she thought, but the emotional toll of saying good-bye again and again to life. From the snatch of conversation with Bunky she'd overheard, Will was already planning for the time when Frankie would be alone.

"I heard you talking about the clinic," she said. "I wouldn't like to see it close, Will. I love working there. I'd like to go on, and use the things you've taught me."

"Sure," he said cryptically.

"I don't know exactly how I'd manage it, but is there a chance I could talk you into some sort of arrangement?" He turned his head as much as he could, a questioning expression on his face. "Sell it to me, I mean. Maybe not all the land—I couldn't afford everything. But the business, the clinic, equipment, goodwill and all that. I could pay for it out of—"

"No, Gaye." There was a finality to it, an emphasis that took extra effort for him.

It took only a moment to adjust; then she accepted it. She didn't even have a down payment. Suddenly the warnings she'd been given about the potential debt incurred in her divorce action, the damage it could do to her freedom, came to mind. Even if she ran the clinic successfully, the money she earned could be leached away from paying for it. It wouldn't be fair to Will's family; this was all he could leave them.

"Can't buy," he added then. "Giving."

His meaning escaped her this time. "What do you mean?"

"My half. Yours."

Now she put it together. What he'd been telling Bunky was that it would be a good business for her, something she could manage even if she and Toby had kids. "Oh, no, Will," she responded. "You can't. It's unbelievably kind. But you can't. I can't let you."

"My choice," he said.

"It wouldn't work," she protested. "You must know that. Frankie and I . . . well, you've seen, we're oil and water."

"Vinegar," he said, still able to make a joke.

But she couldn't laugh. "Whatever. We sure as hell don't mix. If you weren't there, we'd be at each other like cats and dogs."

"Good for vets."

He almost got one from her that time. "Ok, Will. Listen to me. You have to think of Frankie first. And she doesn't even like this work. She told me."

"Not so."

"But being with you was the reason she did it—you must know that. She gave up what she really wanted."

"She says. But loves this. Difficult now. When things all right again, okay."

"It won't be all right without you, Will. She loves you."

"You someday," he said.

Gaye started to protest once more, but he added quickly, "Decided." Then he turned the other way as much as his mobility allowed.

It would be impossible; of that, Gaye had no doubt. But Will's strength and spirit shouldn't be taxed by arguing. When the time came, she could rescind the gift.

They fell into a long silence.

The way back took them through the covered bridge, and as they passed into its shade, bumping slowly over the wood planking that still formed its roadbed, Rud began to bark loudly from his place in the back. The noise echoed along the dark tunnel.

Reminded of the dog, Will said, "Sounds strong."

"He's not moving well, though."

Will knew exactly what that portended. "Like me," he said.

In the darkness of the covered bridge, she wiped the tears that sprang to her eyes before he could see them.

Chapter 28

Over the next week, Gaye looked for the moment to speak to Frankie about Will's wishes. Opportunities were scarce—as Frankie no doubt wanted them to be. Frankie was frequently absent from the clinic, and when she was there Gaye was not only intimidated by the aura of inapproachability the older woman maintained, but held back by her own uncertainty. As quickly as Will was declining, and as terrible as it was to know he was heading into a kind of living hell, it was no easy thing to beg his wife to help him die.

Beyond routine exchanges about clinic business, Gaye still hadn't spoken to Frankie by the time Toby completed training with his new dog at the Seeing Eye Institute and the day came for his return home. She had planned to meet him at the bus in West Greenlea, but a call about a horse with an infected hoof led to a nearly four-hour farm visit. She arranged for a taxi from the Mills to meet Toby and bring him to her place or Dot's, depending on where he wanted to go.

After treating the horse she went straight home. Toby wasn't there, but a message on the answering machine said he was visiting Dot, and looked forward to spending the night with her. She took a long shower to wash off the barn smells, and put on lacy lingerie and a dress bought in Littleton the previous weekend especially to wear for the homecoming. Her work had accustomed her to dressing regularly in jeans and plain denim shirts, and she worried that because Toby couldn't see them she might have become too careless about her clothes. His blindness, she realized, made the experience of *feeling* them all the more important: silk, not denim; lace trimming, not the jeans' metal studs; bare neck, not a collar. She experienced herself differently, too, when dressing this way for him. She had learned that he also liked her to wear perfume, but he was much more sensitive to it than the average man. What a sighted man might think sufficient was too strong for Toby. She dabbed on very little, but in all the places she thought he'd like to find it.

When it came time to leave, Rud didn't follow her to the door but stayed on the sofa, watching her. She went back and coaxed him up. "C'mon, boy, Toby's home." Still he didn't move. She knelt and petted him, while continuing to urge him onto his feet. He just looked at her with moony eyes.

The dog had been slowing down noticeably, and letting her know he needed more painkillers. Still, Gaye had expected him to remain reasonably comfortable and mobile for a few weeks more. A sudden decline wasn't impossible, but she prayed it hadn't come now. Losing him right at this point would intensify the guilt Toby already felt about supplanting Rud with a new dog.

"C'mon, Rud," she pleaded. "You're okay. I know you are. Toby's waiting for you." Then more firmly. "Damn it, it's too soon. . . . I know it is."

He had held her up for almost five minutes, but at last the dog let out an almost human groan of reluctant assent, slid from the couch onto his feet, and walked slowly to the door. Then, curiously, at the truck he pulled himself up onto the passenger seat without needing any urging or assistance. As they headed over to Bartlett Mills, Gaye thought back to the kind of intelligence Rud had always exhibited in his interactions with Toby, and mused on the possibility that what she had witnessed wasn't only a result of his physical problems. Maybe it was his intuition of the humiliation he was about to face—meeting the younger, healthier dog that was taking his place. To give your complete loyalty, and then see that you were no longer needed, had to be a painful thing to face.

For her own part, Gaye was aware that by going to Toby's house she also had to face an awkward situation. She had tried to keep up congenial contact with Dot in Toby's absence, but every time they talked Dot would repeat her gloom-and-doom warnings. It began to wear on Gaye, and for the past week she'd avoided calling. No doubt this evening she'd be warned again; she'd have to be careful to treat Dot's belief in her occult clairvoyance in a way that Toby didn't find disrespectful.

When the truck was in front of the Callan house, Rud balked again. But Toby had heard them arrive, and came out of the house. Alone, able to find his way unguided, he started along the path to the curb, calling out, "Hey, Rud, c'mon, boy! How about a big hello!"

Suddenly Rud flew out of the truck and scampered straight to Toby, who got down on his knees to hug the animal. Gaye watched in astonishment. Considering what she knew of the dog's condition, the surge of dexterity he'd just exhibited was extraordinary. Yet a moment later, when Toby rose and, knowing she must be there on the path, held out his hand to her, she could see Rud revert instantly to the sickly way he'd acted earlier. She went to Toby and they embraced. He told her how good it felt to hold her, and how good she smelled, and kissed her, but he pulled back soon and turned toward Rud. "How is he?"

"This is very hard for him."

Toby nodded, understanding. "That's why he got the first hug."

"I'm not jealous."

He put his arm around her and they went into the house. The new dog was waiting just inside the door—commanded to stay behind. When Rud came in, the two dogs remained facing each other at a distance of a few feet. Neither growled, nor made any threatening move. Lord Byron was no less a beauty than Rud had been in his prime, Gaye thought, slightly smaller, with a tawnier coat, and black "boots"—markings on all four feet—and black over his eyes, like eyebrows. After the dogs had studied each other warily, Byron trotted away to lie down in the living room. Rud remained at Toby's side. It looked as if the new dog had politely yielded, fully aware that his own place was not threatened.

"It's amazing how much they understand," Toby said. He suggested then that they could leave the dogs and go out to dinner, maybe at the inn. He didn't have to work tonight, but it was still the best food in the area by far.

"You think they'll be all right by themselves?"

"They'll have to get used to each other."

Gaye agreed. "Isn't Dot here? I should say hello."

"She went to the movies with a friend."

Maybe, Gaye thought, Dot knew it was a good idea not to pester her anymore. Not only dogs had good intuition.

A convention of Vermont insurance brokers filled the inn this week, and its popular restaurant was fully booked. The manager made room for them, nevertheless, repositioning a serving station so there was room to set up one more table for two.

The food was delicious, complemented by a split of champagne Toby ordered to celebrate being together again, followed by an expensive bottle of California red. Unfortunately, Gaye couldn't relax into a festive mood. Toby had new and amusing anecdotes about training with Lord Byron and some of the other people in his course, but it wasn't long before grimmer subjects came up. It started with Toby mentioning Dot's concern about protecting Gaye from the amorphous perils forewarned by the tarot.

"Don't forget," Gaye said, "she also told me I'm safe when you're around." She reached to take his hand. "And now you're back again."

"Darling, don't think I'm a nut if I pay attention to my mother. She's got a bit of a track record, you know."

"Toby," she argued, "do you really want us to be making decisions based on a deck of cards?"

"It's not just that. From what you've told me about this guy you married, there's certainly good reason to be on your guard."

"I'm being careful—have been from the first. That's how I met your mom, don't forget—because I want to keep secret the fact that I'm living in a different state from my mailing address."

"Can you be sure he won't find out?"

"He's not going to," Gaye broke in. "Only my lawyer knows where I am, and she won't tell. Please, Toby, don't get all worked up over your mom's fortune-telling. What she's getting from those cards, I think, is shaped simply by knowing I was running away. But I'm less afraid now. Really." She reached across the table to take his hand. "Because of you. Remember, your mother said I'm okay as long as we're together."

They picked up their glasses of wine and drank a silent toast to their future with each other. That put to rest the discussion of Dot's omens, but Gaye was soon seeking Toby's consolation in regard to the situation with Will and Frankie. She recounted her excursion with Will and the request he'd made based on her belief that she'd been visited by an animal spirit.

After listening, Toby said, "You didn't actually see a ghost, did you?"

"No. But there was such a strong sense of . . . a presence. And Rud saw it."

"We can't know what Rud saw. His nervous system's been affected by the disease. The movements you describe could have been a kind of seizure."

"I know how one dog acts around another," Gaye insisted.

"Sure. But suppose he was reacting out of reflexes, sense memory."

"So now you think *I'm* nuts. You tell me to believe in tarot cards, but spirits are nonsense."

"You're not being consistent, either. If you believe in one, you should believe in the other."

"Predicting the future is in another ballpark from believing there's an afterlife," she countered. "Native Americans believed they were guided by animal spirits, but they still didn't have women in tepees reading crystal balls."

"Ghost or no ghost," Toby said, "the real question is how to help Will."

"I've got to get through to Frankie," Gaye said urgently. "Help her to see it's his choice."

Toby kept a pointed silence.

"You don't think I should?" she prodded.

"I don't know, Gaye. Isn't it Frankie's choice, too? It's something that can only be settled between the two of them. You can help Will exactly the way you've been doing—by being a good friend. But it's not your place to swing the balance one way or the other."

"Will wants to die, Toby. I love him, and I don't want to see him suffer."

"He doesn't have to. His pain can be eased."

"It's not the pain. It's the indignity, being forced to exist in a way that's not really living."

"Honey, you can't be the judge of when a life is or isn't worthwhile."

She gave him a cool, level stare. "Except," she said, "when it's a dog's life."

He reacted at once. "Look, don't compare—"

"Of course not," she rode over him. "They're two completely different cases. Rud can't tell us what he wants, so we have to decide for him. When he can't move, can't enjoy the world anymore, we'll give him a quick, merciful death. On the other hand, Dr. Will . . . he *knows*, he's one hundred percent aware of the pleasures he's lost, the miseries he's facing, and he can make his wishes perfectly clear. So what do we do for him? Ignore him." She punctuated the diatribe by chugging down the wine left in her glass.

Toby had no comeback. After a pause he said, "I'm so glad to be back here with you. Let's not spoil tonight with an argument." He picked up the wine bottle and poured some more in both their glasses; then he reached for his own as if about to propose another toast.

"I'm afraid it's already spoiled," she said glumly. "There're just too many very sad things happening to make everything all right with a kiss and a glass of wine." She folded her napkin on the table. "I think I'd like to go, Toby. Right now I don't feel right about even *trying* to be happy."

Within five minutes they were in the truck, Gaye driving them back to the Mills. The silence had lasted between them since Toby had called for the bill and the restaurant manager came over to tell them the meal was on the house as a welcome-home present.

They'd had to act all sociable and chatty when he said how nice it was to see them together again.

They had driven a couple of miles when Toby said abruptly, "Pull over."

As soon as she stopped the truck at the side of the road, he put his arms around her. "This isn't anything we should fight over, Gaye," he said. "We may see things differently about Will, or anything else. But however we see it, each of us should do whatever we think is right."

She melted. " 'See things differently,' " she echoed. "That always impresses me, Toby, how easily you talk about seeing. It reminds me there is so much more to it than what comes through the eye."

All she wanted then was to be with him, as close as possible. They'd been on the way to pick up the dogs first, but when she resumed driving, Gaye turned onto a road that would take them back to her place. She wanted to be able to make love for a good long time without anything else to think about, any other needs to consider. The dogs could wait.

It was almost three when she brought Toby back to the Mills. What amazed her about sex with Toby was how right, how untainted by anything prurient or lustful it was compared to what she had experienced with her husband. She felt she could do anything with Toby, even the things she had resisted with Brian, and they would seem right and natural. The difference, she understood at last, was simple: She hadn't loved Brian. What she had mistaken for love was the willingness—no, the eagerness—to please her father by giving herself to a man who had all the right credentials.

At Dot's house an outside light was on, and she had left a handwritten note in the entranceway saying she'd let the dogs out for a while in the backyard, and that they were getting along like old friends. Since Gaye and Toby had been able to spend a good part of the night together, it was agreed he would stay there with the dogs, and she would return to her apartment so she could be at the clinic early and give herself the maximum opportunity for a moment alone with Frankie. The disagreement with Toby over her concern for Will had in fact galvanized her to act on her own convictions.

Before leaving, she went into the house to check on Rud. She'd already supplied Toby with medicines the dog might need, but she was still worried by the signs of weakness he'd displayed last night. Maybe it was a sentimental idea—or maybe she'd swung over to accepting Toby's high regard for Rud's sensitivity—but she thought it was possible that having seen Toby's new dog, Rud would decide it was time to die.

Only a night-light was on in the kitchen, and both dogs were lying on the floor atop two old frayed bath mats that Dot had set down for them. When Toby and Gaye came in, Byron picked up his head immediately, alert and ready to serve. But Rud remained stretched out on one side. Gaye went over and saw that, although he was breathing easily, his eyes were open. She crouched down and stroked him.

Toby moved up beside her. They didn't speak, but the same question was in both their minds.

"Middle of the night," Gaye said, "maybe he knows it's just time to take it easy."

"Maybe he's so pissed off at me for putting him out to pasture, he doesn't want to make the effort."

"Let's see how he is tomorrow," Gaye said.

Toby went with her out to the truck, leaving both dogs in the house. He wouldn't need them to get back inside; he knew exactly the number of steps to take. He felt his way around to the driver's side of the truck, too, so he could open the door for her. "I start again at the inn tomorrow," he said before she climbed in. "If Rud's okay, I'll see you there after you finish work. Or . . . I'll give you a call during the day."

They said good night and kissed. She got behind the wheel, then rolled down the window and leaned out. "Whenever it comes, Toby, it's going to be hard—but only for you and me. Not for him, though, remember that."

He nodded, and when she started the engine he felt his way around to the curb and went up the path to the house. Halfway to the house, aware that the truck was still there, motor running, he faced the truck again and called out, "Don't worry. I'm not going to lose my way."

Gaye revved the engine loudly so he would hear, and drove off.

It might take a little time, but she had to train herself to be blind to his blindness. Because Toby insisted on being treated exactly the same as any other man. A hard thing to remember—because he was so much better.

Chapter 29

Arriving at the clinic at a few minutes after eight, Gaye started the day by looking in on a dog named Joker, a mixed-breed that had been in the kennel since she'd operated on him before the weekend to repair a herniated diaphragm. The animal could have gone home days ago, except Gaye wasn't confident he'd get the kind of follow-up care he needed. In fact, she wasn't sure the dog's injury hadn't been caused by a mistreatment. A suspect sign of indifference from the family that owned the dog was that they'd called only the morning after the operation, not since. People who loved a pet would have called at least every day. Gaye had been deliberating over whether Joker should be returned at all. Yet abuse would have to be proven beyond a doubt to have him removed from a home, and keeping him also involved finding another home—and if one didn't materialize, the possibility of the dog having to be put to sleep.

Observing the healthy appetite with which Joker had wolfed down this morning's food, Gaye decided she could no longer postpone returning the animal to its owners. But whoever came for him, she wouldn't let them get away without probing into the kind of treatment the dog was receiving, and providing counseling if needed—and perhaps a warning.

Returning to the examining room, she was startled to see Frankie just removing her windbreaker. Usually Frankie would have entered through the back door closest to the farmhouse, and would have passed through the kennel first.

"Where are you coming from?" Gaye asked.

"Hospital. Took Will over early."

"Oh, God." Gaye gasped. "What was it?"

"Nothing serious. There's some sort of improved alarm device so if he stops breathing we'll know. He'll be home this evening."

And further equipped, Gaye thought, with something to sustain his life whether it was what he wanted or not. She couldn't wait any longer, she decided, to speak as Will's advocate.

Frankie had gone into the little office that had once been Will's preserve. Through the glass partition, Gaye could see her standing in front of the desk, shaking her head at the mound of old files and veterinary journals and other papers that covered the surface in disarray. Then Frankie sat behind the desk, pulled the clinic checkbook out of a drawer, and began studying it.

Gaye went to the door of the cubicle. "Do you have time to talk?"

Frankie looked up from her survey. "More'n I'd like," she said dryly.

It could be interpreted as a mere confession of private regret for too much time on her hands, Gaye thought, not a hostile jab at her in particular. "Thanks," she said pleasantly, and moved into the office. The one extra chair was occupied by a pile of pharmaceutical handouts and other ancient mail. Gaye picked up the stack and set it on the floor so she could sit. For this conversation, she didn't want to be standing in front of Frankie like a pupil in the principal's office.

"A sit-down, eh," Frankie said. "Gonna take that long, is it?"

"As long as it deserves," Gaye said evenly. "This is something very important."

Frankie stayed ahead of her. "If it's about your dog—I mean, getting some kind of visit from a ghost—you can save your breath. Will told me."

For a moment Gaye was speechless. Perhaps because she'd taken too long getting around to it, Will had preempted the appeal she was going to make. Having the story thrown back at her like this by Frankie made it seem ridiculous. But Gaye tried to salvage the effort. "I suppose you think it's nonsense. But it's not something I made up."

"I don't know what to think. Either way, it makes no difference."

Gaye regarded her sympathetically. "How can you say that? Do you understand why Will wanted you to know? He's longing to be free, Frankie. Free from being a prisoner in a body that can't move or feel anymore. Free from dying by inches, maybe even being 'locked in.' You've watched Will for years practicing a kind of medicine that includes believing every living thing possesses an energy we can't see or measure. Now he wants his spirit to be set free. Is it so impossible that there's more to us than flesh and blood, nerve and bone? If you don't accept that, then you're negating his—"

"Stop!" Frankie screamed out. "I'm not going to murder him."

The sudden outburst stunned Gaye into silence. Frankie, too, looked startled by the ferocity of her declaration. The two women locked eyes for a few seconds, neither knowing how to continue. Then Frankie lowered her gaze to the checkbook ledger in front of her.

To ease what she took for embarrassment, Gaye said at last, "It's mercy, not murder. Something we agree to provide right here." She gestured to the examining room.

"Not much longer," Frankie said, her eyes still down.

"What do you mean?"

"Might as well tell you now," Frankie said. Her eyes snapped up to meet Gaye's. "The clinic has to close."

The news hit almost like a physical blow, making it hard to think. "When?" The word emerged by reflex.

"Pretty much right away."

Gaye shook her head in disbelief. "You can't, Frankie. Not like this."

Frankie picked up the checkbook. "Take a look at what we got in the bank and tell me I can't. For years we've run this place without much more than breaking even. And that was when Will could take in patients. But our business has been dying, too—started even before he did."

"It can be built up again," she appealed.

Frankie shook her head. "Not by me."

"That's what I was brought in for, isn't it?"

"Not by me," Frankie repeated.

Gaye tried a different tack. "This community needs you."

"They can go elsewhere. Enough already have."

Gaye was confounded. How had the attempt to speak on Will's behalf turned so suddenly into this debacle? Was Frankie so infuriated by the approach that she had struck back in this way?

A desperate plea began to spill out of her. "Frankie, whatever your reasons for doing this, you've got to reconsider. For your own sake, not just mine. What are you going to do with yourself if this place closes? Go to Paris to live with your daughter? Be an alien at this stage of your life? This is where you belong, where you can be useful the way you always have been. You and I could be a good team, too; I know we could. Please. Give it a chance. I want to carry on the work here—Will's work and yours. I've already told Will, I want to—"

"Oh, I know what you want," Frankie cut in, "make no mistake. Don't you think I got a call last week from Tom Armbrewster?"

Gaye was baffled. "Tom who?"

"Lawyer down in Hanover who drew up our will? Wanted to know why he was being asked to change it."

It was a moment before Gaye understood the implication. "Wait a second. I had nothing to do with that."

"Maybe not. But Will had his nurse pick up the phone, dial, and hold it for him while he told Tom he's leaving you his share."

"I refused it!" Gaye erupted. "I said I'd buy him out. Told Will I wouldn't take it as a gift."

"Well, that's good, anyway. 'Cause you're not gettin' it. Not when it's a case of—whattaya call it—undue influence. Will's obviously in no state to make a decision like that."

Gaye sat a moment longer, trying to muster an argument against the accusation that she'd connived for Will's gift. What made it particularly brutal was the suggestion that it could be for this benefit that she would urge hastening Will's death.

Yet the sheer enormity of the charge made it seem a burden im-

possible to lift with mere words. Gaye stood up. Looking down at
Frankie behind the desk, she said, "It's so damn sad. Will knows exactly what he wants. And because the most important thing to him
is to die with his dignity intact, to choose not to rot away, you want
to judge him as incompetent, and believe the worst of me." She
went to the door of the office and stopped. "Were you expecting me
to leave today?" she asked.

Frankie hesitated. "Course not. I'm sure you've got patients to
see today, tomorrow. You can wind things up in a reasonable way."

What she'd just been told was that she might stay a few more
days. "I'm concerned mainly about Toby's dog," Gaye said. "His time
seems pretty near, and I think it matters a lot if I'm the one . . ." She
trailed off.

Frankie nodded, and fiddled with papers on the desk to avoid
looking at Gaye. "All right. Meantime, whatever my personal feelings, I've never had a problem with your work. You're a very com-
petent vet. Wherever you apply, you can count on a good
recommendation from me."

"Toby and I are together now. I'll be staying around here."

"If that's the case, you might find it hard to keep practicing,"
Frankie observed. "I know the other local vets. They're fully staffed."

"That's why this would have been . . ." But the will to try again
gave out. She finished a different way. "It's too bad we couldn't have
gotten along, Frankie. I've never wanted a thing from you but your
trust."

As she drifted back to the examining room, Gaye was in a daze.
In effect, she'd been fired. But not because she hadn't done her job
well, only for wanting to do more, becoming too involved with her
boss, letting this place mean too much to her. As for the clinic having to close, she knew it wasn't in good financial shape, but that was
a result of neglect rather than any lack of available business. Veterinary businesses were booming in general. With some investment in
modern equipment, and the application of youthful energy, Gaye
knew she could have turned the place around. The purchase of the
computer alone had increased efficiency. And Frankie, too, would be

an asset, if she could only overcome her depression and enjoy the work again.

If only . . . None of it would happen now.

Looking around at the spare facility, the dingy paint and out-moded equipment, Gaye found it difficult to understand the depth of emotional attachment she'd developed in just half a year. Except that it was infused with Will's spirit; from the first she'd seen that he had a fierce passion to do special work, to heal animals and save them pain. He had inspired her, and his inspiration would stay with her always—more if she could stay close to its source. It was unbe-lievable, Gaye thought, that his wife could have worked at Will's side for her whole professional life without feeling the same inspiration, sharing the same devotion. If Frankie denied it now, went so far as to reject the choices she had made, surely it must be due to the bit-terness of seeing her life fall apart. Of course, it didn't help that nei-ther of the Bennetts' children had endorsed the value of their parents' work by wanting to carry it on.

Which, Gaye understood, was the reason why she had been "adopted" by Will. With Frankie, unfortunately, she hadn't been able to fill that vacuum. For the first time Gaye wondered if she didn't share responsibility for their failure to connect. She'd happily re-garded Will as a father figure, and so the feeling had been recipro-cated. But she'd never opened herself to Frankie in a way that touched a similar emotional chord. After all, how could she? From her own experience, a mother wasn't so accessible, but a figure al-ways distant, uncommunicative, mistrustful.

All at once the rift was illuminated as if a ray of sunlight had emerged from behind a cloud: The failure to connect with Frankie was surely rooted in that past failure, Gaye realized. She'd never been able to win the trust of her own mother, so she hadn't dared make the effort here, with this surrogate. Only today, only out of desper-ation had she finally reached out.

Only when it was too late.

Gaye glanced back toward the office. Would it make a difference if she could share this insight? She could see Frankie busily sorting through the papers on Will's desk, cramming whatever was judged to be useless into an already overflowing wastebasket. Frankie looked hell-bent on clearing things out, getting ready to separate from the clinic and all that it meant. Will might be the only thing she'd hold on to for too long.

The intercom from the reception desk rang. Lori must have arrived to start the day; she always looked at the appointment roster, then let the vets know who and what was expected. Gaye picked up the phone, and Lori went through her schedule; her own was fairly full today with office visits, while Frankie did farm calls. Gaye told Lori in turn to make a call to Joker's owners and tell them they could collect the dog. "But give them an appointment," she instructed. "I'll need half an hour with them."

Lori said there was a gap after lunch for that much time, and Gaye said that would be fine. Lori ended the call with her customary offer: "I'm putting coffee on. You want some?"

More often than not Gaye would stop on the way to buy a cup rather than drink what the receptionist made. This morning, however—as for every other morning until she would have to leave—Gaye was resolved to do what her mentor would have done.

"That would be great," she said. "Milk . . . and a little extra sugar."

As she set the phone down, the impulse was revived to go back to Frankie and try to continue the conversation. But when she turned toward the office, she saw Frankie had gone.

A concern for Rud nagged at her through the morning, aggravated by the way she'd linked her schedule of termination at the clinic to the dog. She wanted to call Toby—needed, in any case, the comfort of hearing his voice—but she knew that his years of playing saloon piano until the wee hours had trained him to sleep late when possible, so she didn't want to disturb him. Anyway, he'd said he would call if she was needed.

It was after eleven o'clock and she had just finished an annual checkup on a hunting spaniel when the intercom rang, and Lori asked if she could take a call from Toby.

"Sure. Put him through." She was sure it was about Rud. As soon as Toby said "Hi," she said. "Do you want me to come?"

"No. I don't think that's necessary."

"So he's okay?"

"He hasn't eaten much, and he's moving with a lot of difficulty, but I did get him up once for a couple of minutes."

"That's all?"

"Enough for a trip outside. Then he lay down again."

That didn't sound good at all.

"What about pain?"

"The usual dosage seems to be taking care of it. Makes him a little groggy, though."

There was a pause. She didn't want to be the one to suggest the procedure, and obviously Toby wasn't ready.

Then he spoke again. "Actually, I wasn't calling about Rud. There's something else I thought you should know about. Someone from the institute contacted me this morning."

He meant the Seeing Eye Institute, she understood, and guessed it might be routine follow-up concerning the new dog. "Byron's okay, I hope."

"Fine. This isn't a vet thing. The call was from one of the administrators. She wanted me to know that there had been a call to the institute yesterday from a man trying to get in touch with the student from Bartlett Mills. He was vague about the reason, said it was official business of some kind. She told him my training period had ended, and I'd gone home."

"Where do I come in?" Gaye asked.

"That's not the end of it. This woman at Seeing Eye thought it was good to let me know—in case it was something important I could figure out—and so I could anticipate hearing from this caller. Because, you see, she'd given him my name, home telephone number, and address. He hasn't called here, though, and I have no idea why anyone would have tried to get me on official business."

"Are you worried about it?"

"Not for me, Gaye—for you. Think a minute: Could your husband know I was there?"

She didn't have to think. The conversation with her father was suddenly in her head—that moment when she'd defended Toby

proudly, explained why Rud was with her. Yes, she remembered saying she was caring for Rud while Toby was at the institute. A fact
her father might easily have passed on to Brian. It might have taken
until yesterday to be mentioned . . . or until Brian decided to act on
the information, use it to follow a trail that led to her. The only address they had for her was the Mills. They might have assumed the
man with whom she'd become involved also lived there.

"Jesus, Toby. This is scary."

"I don't think you have to panic, Gaye. If it was your husband,
he's only taken the first step. So far it's me he's found, not you. He
doesn't know you're living elsewhere."

Gaye wasn't comforted. She was too closely linked to Toby, to
where he lived. She had visions suddenly of Brian following Toby if
he came to visit her, or stalking her directly if she appeared anywhere around the Mills. Or Toby being hounded directly for information.

"It's happening," she said anxiously. "What your mother foretold . . ."

"Hey, don't go off the deep end. Make a call to your lawyer for
a start. Have her check that your husband is at work, where he's supposed to be. Let her know you're worried, and why, and that you'd
like his whereabouts to be checked daily. If she establishes that
Brian's in Philadelphia, you know you're okay. If there's any indication he might be coming up here, we can worry about the next
steps."

The ideas were good, and taking positive action did make her
feel better. "I'll do that right away, Toby. Thanks."

"Let me know what you find out. I want to know you're safe,
funny face. I love you."

Overflowing with her own love and gratitude, she almost slipped
into revealing the other miseries of the day, but held back so she
could check on Brian immediately.

Instead of placing the telephone call to her lawyer, Gaye had an
idea that would yield an answer more quickly. She knew the work
routine Brian maintained: The day started early with rounds of his
postoperative patients; then he went into surgery, preop appoint-

ments left for midafternoon. Brian's heart procedures could last anywhere from one hour to five, and a look at the clock in the examining room showed it wasn't much past eleven. He must be
operating.

Gaye called the hospital to which Brian and her father were both
attached, and asked to be put through to Dr. Leahy. After holding
for a minute, she was connected to a nurse on the OR floor. "Dr.
Leahy is doing a bypass," the nurse informed her.

"When can I speak to him?"

"Could be another hour at least."

Comforting, but while she was at it Gaye went for some insurance. "I won't be able to call back at that time. Are you able to tell
me if he'll be at the hospital tomorrow or the next day?" She knew
operating rooms for heart procedures were often assigned days in
advance.

There was a pause while the nurse checked the OR schedule.
She came back on. "He's operating both days. But if you want to
speak to him, the best way is to leave your name and—"

Gaye set the phone back in its cradle.

Two days of safety, at the least. And maybe nothing to worry
about. Maybe Brian really was going to let things take their course
in a reasonable way. Indeed, perhaps the mysterious man who'd
called the Seeing Eye Institute really had some sort of official business to talk about with Toby, an adjustment to his tax return, a payment for dog training on his health insurance.

She called Toby back and reported what she had learned.

They were both relieved. "I'll be working again tonight," he said.
"Come over and let me serenade you."

"You couldn't keep me away. I'll finish here in time to pick you
up and drive you to the inn." She'd save what had happened with
Frankie for then. Even now, it seemed like much less to cry about.
Being safe, and being with Toby, that was what truly mattered.

Chapter 30

Gaye sat at the same table she had occupied the first time she'd come to hear Toby sing. She always gravitated to this spot; it brought her back to that night, how much she had loved listening to him right from the first. Of course, it thrilled her all the more now, listening to him sing "How Long Has This Been Going On" and knowing all these love lyrics were being sung to her. This Gershwin standard had been sung by Audrey Hepburn in *Funny Face*. Toby often fit it in when Gaye was in the audience.

As the song described an idyll coming to an end, she thought about her own life. The work she loved had been taken from her. In taking the job at Bible Hill she had been willing to travel to a strange new place, but that wasn't an option anymore. If she couldn't find a new position within easy distance of where Toby lived, she would no longer be able to practice. Setting up on her own would have been a possibility—borrowing from a bank—except that the legal action she was facing was probably going to end in sizable court-ordered debts.

Toby segued into some nice piano improvisation. The waitress, Kim, noticing Gaye's glass was empty, took her order for another vodka and tonic, her third.

The waitress hesitated before walking away. "Don't think I can remember you ever ordering anything stronger than ginger ale. Certainly not more than one. You okay, hon?"

True, Gaye had never liked hard liquor—she had seen her

mother drink too much, never to good effect—but tonight she needed something to dull her anxiety. "I've been better," she replied.

"The dog, huh?" Kim nodded toward Rud, who lay where he always had when Toby played, beside the piano bench.

When Gaye had arrived earlier at the Callan house to drive Toby, she had checked on Rud and found he was unable to move, the floor beneath him soiled. She had cleaned him up, and they'd brought him along, leaving the new dog behind. Guided by Gaye, Toby had carried the dog into the bar and set him down in his customary place on a sheet. Having Rud at the inn once more to hear Toby play was not only a way of comforting the dog, but a ritual of letting go.

"Yeah," Gaye said now, "the dog."

Kim gave a commiserating nod. "I'll get your drink."

Toby was singing a repeat of the last verse of the song before ending it. Gaye gazed sadly at Rud. Tomorrow, she thought, the merciful thing was to do it tomorrow. She recalled that night, when the dog was healthy—or at least before she had discovered his affliction—when he had led Toby over to this table, as if insisting he meet her. And she smiled at the memory of his explanation: Rud was choosing her for his doctor. That remark, and the others in which Toby attributed a remarkable level of humanlike thought to the dog's actions, had amused her at the time. It wasn't uncommon for loving owners to attribute such qualities to their pets. But the respect Gaye had since developed for Rud colored her own opinion. What else explained that he was ready to die so soon after Toby had returned with his new guide? He had endured only until he could see that his master would be served, kept safe. Now his work was done.

Toby's song ended to enthusiastic applause from the large audience—the inn had another convention filling its rooms—and he announced a short break. He stood from the piano bench, then turned to where he knew Gaye was sitting. Accustomed to Toby being guided from the piano by the dog, it took her a moment to realize he was waiting for her to come and lead him across the room. Rud had made a futile attempt to rise, rolling half onto his side before he slumped back down.

Gaye went and took Toby's hand as he stepped down from the small platform where he performed. Looking up helplessly, the dog whimpered.

"Back soon, pal," Toby said.

The dog was quiet again.

As Toby sat down at the table, Kim brought Gaye's refill and asked Toby if he'd like something. "Whatever Gaye's having," he said.

"How are you feeling?" Toby asked when the waitress left.

"Merely miserable."

"I should play more upbeat stuff the next set. There's a lot—'Happy Talk,' 'Happy Days Are Here Again,' 'C'mon Get Happy'."

She took his hand and squeezed it appreciatively. But they both knew it would take more than a few bouncy tunes.

"I've been thinking," Toby said. "Why put yourself through doing this for Rud? I can take him to another vet. This guy I used to—"

"No, if he can have someone who loves him right there with him, helping him let go, that's the way it should be. Always."

"I'll be there."

"That's another reason for me to be right alongside."

They looked across the room together at Rud.

"He's happy to be here tonight," Toby said, "I can tell. It was getting too hard for him, having to lie around and watch while Byron took over the job."

"And he likes your singing, too."

The waitress brought his drink. "Sorry about Rud, Toby," she said. He gave her a nod of appreciation and she left. He started to sip from the glass, then shied back. "Whoa! When I asked for the same I expected ginger ale."

"I needed something stronger tonight." She picked up her own drink.

He eyed her with concern. "Is it just Rud, or the trouble with Frankie? Or are you feeling shaky because of that business with your husband?"

On the drive to the inn tonight, she'd told him about being fired, and the way it had come about.

"With all that's happening, my husband's the least of it. In fact, I think enough time has passed that he may have things in better perspective. No doubt he's furious, but he should be content to take it out on me in court."

"So how do you explain that call?"

"I suppose he wants to know where I am," Gaye said. "But it doesn't mean he wants to come and kill me." She suspected, too, that he might have wanted to talk directly to Toby, could have gotten nasty with him. But she didn't want to start Toby worrying that somewhere in the constant darkness around him a vengeful attacker could be lurking. "Anyway, he's staying home, concentrating on saving other people's lives, not interfering with mine." Though she played it down, Gaye was worried nevertheless. Brian was operating for the next two days . . . but what would happen then? She took another big swig of her drink.

Toby could hear her swallowing. He put out his hand, found her arm, and pushed it back down, taking the glass from her lips. "I've got a better idea for calming your nerves. Suppose we move away from here. We'll go wherever you get the next job. There's always a place for me to play the piano."

"Oh, no, Toby, this is your place. And what about your mom?"

"Maybe it's time for her to retire."

"You know it's not." Gaye chuckled. "God bless her, when she says she wants to be carried out of that post office, she really means it." Gaye let go of the glass, and grasped Toby's hand. "Fear of Brian drove me away from one life to another. But I've found the one I want, and I like it exactly the way it is. I'm not going to let him frighten me into running from this life, too." She leaned closer across the small table and they kissed.

To start his next set, Toby told the audience he was going to play a lovely old Jerome Kern song, "The Folks Who Live on the Hill." Slow and sweetly melodic, the ballad contained lyrics that fulfilled exactly what the title suggested, presenting the story of a couple in love who settled in the country and lived happily ever after: "Someday we'll build a home on a hilltop high, you and I./ Shiny and new, a cottage that two can fill." Yes, of course they would stay right here, he was telling her. He would take care of her, and they would be fine. By the time he got to the last verse, she had tears in her eyes. He'd put something special into the song, and even if the audience didn't know it was because of her, they were obviously touched and erupted with a particularly enthusiastic ovation when he was done.

But he cut it short by going quickly into something very snappy, in an entirely different vein, "Forget your troubles/C'mon get happy."

And she did, and she knew he would always keep her that way.

Chapter 31

Toby finished at one o'clock. Gaye drove him home, then continued on to West Greenlea, taking Rud with her. The animal's condition made it hard for Toby to handle him alone, and Toby felt that forcing Rud to lie helpless in the presence of the new dog shamed him, inflicted a needless element of suffering. So for tonight, his last, the two guides would be separated. In the morning Gaye would return for Toby, and they would bring Rud to the clinic together.

In the past couple of weeks the dog had begun losing weight rapidly, so Gaye had no trouble carrying him from the truck. A slight misty drizzle had begun, and knowing the outside wooden stairs down to her apartment were slippery when wet, she didn't use them. Millie had trusted her with a full set of keys since the time the pipe had broken, and she was able to enter her apartment by going through the showroom. She had to put Rud down in the street doorway while she dug the keys out of her pocket. It touched her to see him trying to respond to the simple reflex of going through the open door under his own steam. For a brief moment she prayed a miracle might occur, and he would rise and walk and live—even if for only a few more days. But all he could do was struggle. "That's okay, Rud." She scooped him up. "Let me help."

Downstairs she chose a spot in front of the fireplace where Rud could stretch out, and spread a plastic shower curtain over some soft pillows, since she knew he would have to void while unable to move. Sad as it made her to bed him down for what she knew was the last night of his life, Gaye took some comfort from the task. There had been no such opportunity to perform this essential kindness for Hero, to make sure he had a painless and peaceful death.

After changing into a nightgown and preparing for bed, she didn't want to leave Rud lying there alone. She put a CD of Vivaldi's *Four Seasons* in the player, left it on low volume, and curled up in the easy chair near him. She left one lamp burning in a corner across the room.

With all the intelligence she'd come to attribute to this dog, she wondered if he had any idea his life was ending. In her five years of practicing in Philadelphia, Gaye had euthanized forty-odd dogs, and, as for most vets, it was always the most troubling part of the job. As much as she believed in the necessary mercy of the deed, there was no escape from the impact of being the one whose action brought death. It softened the blow, made it vastly more tolerable, to think that something survived beyond—spirit, energy, soul, whatever it might be called. She thought back to that recent evening when she'd believed the ghost of her own dog had been present, the significance Will had found in the episode. Was it only as an anodyne that she clung to the idea?

"Tell me, Rud," she said aloud, "what did you see that night?"

Expecting no answer, she drifted off to sleep.

The dull thud and creaking of footsteps on the plank flooring overhead brought her back to consciousness. Millie must be in the showroom, Gaye thought drowsily. Then she registered that the music wasn't playing, so it hadn't been mere minutes that she was asleep. Her eyes snapped open, and she sat up sharply, turning to the digital clock on the VCR. The time showed brightly through the gloom, 2:47 A.M. Hardly a time to be taking inventory on the dolls, or doing a mailing. Gaye looked up at the ceiling, straining to pick up the exact location of the creaks, the intervals indicating the speed and direction of movement on the floor above. Not the steady rhythm of someone walking purposefully across the floor. Could it be Millie? Or was it someone creeping around, snooping? It wasn't unknown locally that Millie ran a fairly successful business out of the place. The prospect of finding cash on the premises could have attracted a sneak thief.

Gaye's pulse quickened. Had her preoccupation with carrying the dog caused her to forget to lock up? No—she had a clear memory of putting Rud down a second time especially to do that, and then again to relock the door of the stairway down to the apartment. At least the intruder's explorations would be confined to the showroom. . . .

She hurried now to the kitchen phone. Soon after moving in, she had made a note of the local police contact number and taped it on the back of the receiver.

Her call went unanswered for several rings. Two members of the three-man department were known to Gaye because they owned dogs they'd brought to the clinic, and she remembered that night calls were taken at their homes on a rotating basis. What if no one answered? Should she call Toby? While she hesitated, Gaye was acutely aware of the footsteps creaking overhead.

Before she could decide, the phone was picked up. A man, his sleep obviously interrupted, murmured, "Yah . . . ?"

Gaye thought she recognized the voice: Perry Trumbull, the rookie on the force. "Perry, this is Dr. Foster."

"Mmm, hi, Doc."

"I think Millie's doll showroom is being robbed. I live underneath and someone's moving around up there. If it's not Millie, and the dolls didn't come to life . . ."

At once Gaye could hear background sounds as the bedclothes were pushed back and the policeman jumped to the floor. "I'm on my way, and I'll call the other guys. Could be fifteen minutes, though, before anyone gets there."

They didn't live right in the town, she knew, but on properties in the countryside. "I should be all right. Sounds like just one person up there, and I'm locked in. But hurry."

"Okay. Keep safe. And don't panic." He sounded a little panicky himself.

Gaye put down the phone. The footsteps above were unnerving. An image of Brian as the intruder crossed her mind, except she knew his operating schedule was rigid, and if he'd been able to find her, he wouldn't be spending his time exploring a doll showroom.

Whoever was up there, if she just stayed locked in and waited for the police, she'd be safe. Then her eyes went to the rear wall made up of windows. Suddenly, standing in the lighted living room, she felt too exposed. She went over to the lamp and switched it off.

Rud started to growl. A response to the change, perhaps—or his senses might be reacting to the intruder. The dog's growling got louder, sounded angrier—yes, definitely the threat reflex. Gaye hurried to kneel beside him before he began to bark. "Quiet, boy." She petted him and whispered the command until the growling stopped. If healthy, he could have protected her and she would have encouraged barking. As it was, she preferred not to take any chance that the thief might investigate the sound instead of being scared away.

The creaks of the old wood flooring made it easy to track the intruder's movements. The footsteps told her the intruder had walked to the rear of the showroom . . . into the office, the most likely place to find money. But a moment later the footsteps were overhead again, moving toward the front of the store . . . by a wall. When they stopped, Gaye's heartbeat surged into high gear: The intruder was standing now by the door that opened onto the interior stairway down to her apartment.

At the bottom of the stairway another door led into the apartment. Gaye ran to it and opened it carefully. Leaning into the stairway, she heard a rattle coming from the top—the doorknob being tried. *Don't panic.* She repeated to herself the policeman's prescription. The locked door ought to keep the thief from—

Thief?

Until this moment her mind hadn't been sharp—maybe because the immediate tasks she had to perform were too distracting . . . and because she'd learned that Brian would be operating the next day, and she was eager to cling to self-assurances of safety. But it occurred to her now that the trip by car from Philadelphia was only seven or eight hours. Time enough to finish today's operation, drive here, then turn around and drive back and—if he scheduled it just right—be ready to go to work on another damaged heart before noon.

If it *was* Brian up there . . . *if* he still harbored the kind of rage against her she'd witnessed the night he'd killed Hero . . . if he wanted to kill her . . . then this was how and when he would have come. His surgeries gave him an alibi.

The rattling of the doorknob had stopped. Gaye glanced at the digital clock. 2:51. Only four minutes since she'd awakened? It seemed like an hour had gone by! When would help get here?

Don't panic.

The footsteps moved away from the door. Giving up . . . or looking for something to jimmy it open? Gaye stood tensely in the dark at the bottom of the stairway, straining to hear. The creaking with each step advanced toward the front of the showroom (above her bedroom), and she moved below them. The noises came now from just above the wall of her bedroom situated beneath the street entrance to the showroom. Then they stopped. Not a sound.

The intruder had gone out the door.

She stood motionless for another minute. Listening.

Yes . . . gone.

Her heartbeat began slowing down. It no longer seemed impossible that indeed it had been Millie: Bugged by some loose end of business, kept awake, she could have decided on a quick trip to the office to take care of it . . . been tiptoeing around out of consideration for her downstairs tenant. She'd spent half a minute in her office to take care of it, check an address, find a phone number, whatever it was . . . checked the locks, then gone home.

The ring of the phone exploded into the silence, made her jump as much as if a bomb had gone off. Gaye lunged at the bedroom extension, her adrenaline still pumping. "Hello?"

It was the policeman on his cell phone, telling her he was on the way, and others would follow. "Wanted to be sure you're holding up," he said.

"I'm fine. Whoever it was may have gone." The possibility that it could have been Millie embarrassed her; she didn't mention it.

"Well, sit tight. We're coming anyway."

It crossed her mind to say they could all go back to bed. But she thanked the cop and hung up. Let them come. Whatever her ears told her, she couldn't see who it had been, whether or not they'd broken in, done some damage.

Still quiet. Gaye went back into the living room to check on Rud. He had settled again, but she was wide-awake, her nerves jangled. How long would it take before the terror that Brian had planted in her soul would be gone? She could risk it now, she thought, stop hiding in the darkness. She crossed the room to turn the lamp on again, lifted her hand to the switch—

At the exact moment the light went on, the air was filled with the explosive sound of two dozen panes of glass shattering, flying inward, and sprinkling on the floor. For a second she was disoriented. The coincidence of timing, her hand just touching the lamp as it happened, made her believe the switch had been wired to a detonator. But when she whirled toward the sound, she saw a ten-foot-long branch from a dead tree lying on the floor as if broken off and hurled through the windows by a high wind. The impact had opened a large jagged arch in the wall of windows at the rear of the apartment. She stared at it, trying to figure out exactly what had happened.

Then he appeared at the opening and stepped through it.

Rud half rose on his forelegs, which still remained strong enough to hold his weight, and barked at the man as, walking across the scattered glass, Brian came toward Gaye.

Her nightmare had come true. In a split second she understood. Knowing only Toby's address he'd gone there tonight, kept a watch on the house—and he'd seen her drop him off, then surreptitiously driven behind her, followed her back here. Of course he'd gone first into the showroom—because he'd seen her enter the building through *that* door.

She shrank back as he advanced. A stinging pain stabbed suddenly at the bare sole of one foot—a shard of glass that had flown this far into the apartment. "Get out!" she screamed at him. "Get out of here!" She tried to produce a commanding roar, but the shock and fear stole her breath away, and she could muster no more than a throttled plea.

He kept moving forward. "Relax, Gaye, just relax." He spoke just as he might to a patient he was about to sedate. For him to behave so calmly after performing an act of such violence only enhanced his aura of madness.

She kept backpedaling, steering herself toward the kitchen; she was already scheming to grab a knife for protection. "Stay away from me, Brian," she said.

"Why should I stay away? I'm your husband."

Rud had sunk back onto the ground, but he kept growling and barking at the intruder, knowing he was a threat. Brian gave the dog a contemptuous glance. "Another one. Always a fucking dog. This one looks like a pretty sad specimen. . . ."

"Listen," Gaye warned, dredging up a firmer tone. "I've called the police. They'll be here any minute. Please—just go before there's any trouble."

"Why should there be trouble? I'll tell them I'm here to talk to you. Your husband," he said again.

"Coming in the middle of the night—smashing all the windows?"

"You wouldn't answer the door if I knocked, would you?"

He kept coming on and she backed away at the same pace. Then he glanced past her and saw they were nearing the open kitchen. He must have guessed her intention, because he darted sideways and around her, putting himself in her way. At once Gaye altered her own path, keeping the distance between them. But she could no longer grab for a knife to defend herself. He was nearer the knives now—a set in a block visible atop a kitchen counter.

"Brian, I'm begging you. Just leave me alone." She wanted to speak calmly, avoid exciting him further. But she couldn't keep the whining note from creeping in, hysteria beginning to take over.

"Sit down, Gaye." He gestured to the sofa. "You've been hiding from me for so long, I haven't been able to talk to you. But you need to hear what I—"

"No! I don't need to hear anything. There's nothing to talk about."

"You see, that's the problem. You never gave me a chance." He stopped coming at her.

It struck her now that refusing to listen could be the wrong tactic. If she did what he asked—a simple thing—that might keep him calm until help arrived. She stood her ground, too, and said quietly, "What do you want to tell me?"

"That I love you. I'll never love anyone else. It's only you I want." His eyes raked over her body, barely concealed beneath the filmy nightgown fabric. "Come back to me. You belong with me."

How did she reply? All she wanted to do was scream out how wrong it was to call his obsession love. As she pondered an answer, he made a sudden lunge and managed to get a tenuous grip on her arm with one hand, but she yanked it free and dodged away.

Frustrated, Brian let his temper begin to uncoil. "You're still my wife!" he roared. "I'm not going to let you throw me away." His eyes burned with fury.

The craziness of his desire, his need to possess her regardless of her own feelings, threw Gaye into utter despair. "Why do you want me?" she wailed. "Why can't you leave me alone? I've found a man who knows how to love—who understands it's more than this insane need to own someone, who doesn't want to make me into his . . . slave."

Her cry roused the inbred instinct of the dog to those to whom he gave his loyalty. But he was unable to move, and his barking gave way to a pitiful howl.

"Shut up!" Brian shouted at the animal, and for one awful moment Gaye feared she might witness another bloody assault. But he kept his rage concentrated on her. "You're the one who ran away, wouldn't tell me where you'd gone. Now you say *I* can't love, that *I'm* the one who doesn't know how? Well, I've found you. Your daddy told me you'd rather fuck a blind man, and tracking that poor blind bastard led me straight to you. So now I can show you how wrong you are—how well I know how to love."

He spoke of love, yet what she could hear beneath his threatening tone was hatred. The prospect of being taken again by him, touched by him, was so chilling that it made Gaye feel as if she had actually turned to ice, cold and immovable.

Then Rud barked again, a surprisingly strong, decisive sound. Glancing over at the dog, Gaye saw that a miracle had occurred: Somehow he had managed to rise up onto all fours. He wasn't moving, but with his teeth bared in a vicious snarl, he held a pose that made it appear he was ready to spring.

Brian saw it, too. Unaware of Rud's infirmity, he focused his attention on the dog, afraid that in the next second the animal might leap at him.

Gaye realized that the distraction gave her a chance to escape. She darted away through the door she had left open to the stairway, and bounded up the stairs. No time to throw the switch that lighted the stairs; in the dark she stumbled on a step and stubbed her toe, but she made it quickly to the top. There she had to pause to feel for the bolt.

A sound drew her glance back to the bottom of the stairs. "I'm not going to let you get away again," he shouted up to her. "You're either going to be with me . . . or with nobody." He found the switch for the stairway light and flicked it on. Gaye saw now that he had one hand wrapped around the handle of one of her large kitchen knives. He started mounting the stairs.

Even while she'd been eyeing him, she was fumbling with the bolt. Now that the light was on she found the small knob. Her nervous fingers struggled to turn it for another second. He was only a few steps below her when she threw the door open and ran into the showroom.

Dollhouses and display counters and tables covered with doll furniture were placed all around the floor, forming a kind of obstacle course to the street door. The showroom was dark, but the bulb in the stairway cast enough light through the open door that Gaye could avoid bumping into anything. She headed for the exit. A crowd of dolls looked on as spectators of her race to survive, their glass eyes glittering with the faint ambient light, painted smiles faintly visible.

She was halfway to the door when Brian emerged into the showroom. He chased her by a different route, pushing aside or toppling over anything that stood in the way of the shortest, most direct line to her means of escape. Dolls fell onto the floor, some giving out plaintive cries of "Mama" from their internal mechanism.

He heard it and laughed crazily. "Mama can't help you now," he called out to Gaye.

But she could make it to the door ahead of him, she was sure, and scream for help in the street, and help would come. The police should be here any minute!

Then suddenly, inexplicably, something pulled her up short, held her back. She threw a frightened look over her shoulder and saw a display counter with dolls lined up, the hem of her nightgown stretched toward it. In the midst of this living nightmare, she thought one of the dolls had come to life and grabbed her nightgown. Across the floor Brian had seen her stop, and changed course to move toward her. Gaye grasped the trailing length of nightgown fabric and pulled sharply. It tore away—and she saw the scrap of it left dangling from the sharp corner of the display case on which it had snagged.

She was free to move, but Brian had reached a point between her and the exit door. The only escape route left to her was down the stairs again. She'd have to run across the glass-strewn floor, but if she could handle that, she could get out of the apartment through the broken windows.

Don't panic. Not much good anymore, giving herself that order. She was trembling so badly she could hardly move. Her limbs felt weak, rubbery. She didn't think she was going to survive this, not unless the police came in the next minute . . . or unless he didn't really mean to kill her.

Though he did. No doubt. She knew from the look in his eyes, the way he held the knife. She didn't feel capable of running, but she forced herself to move. All she had to do was maneuver to the stairway door, keep intervening objects between her and Brian. Backing away along an aisle, she stumbled over some of the dolls that had been scattered on the floor when he threw a table out of his path. He advanced toward her.

"You can't really want to do this, Brian," she cried out.

"You're right, darling. I don't really want to hurt you. I want you to come back to me. But you won't, will you? So it's not my choice. And I . . ." He shook his head, confounded by his own impulses. "It's too hard for me to think you'd always be with somebody else—a man who can't even see what it is I love so much. . . ."

"You'll be caught! It'll be the end of your life, too. The police are on their way!"

"If you'd really called they'd have been here by now."

"I swear—"

"Well, then, I'd better hurry and get this over with. I've got to be back in Philly by morning. There are lives to save."

She had backed to where she had a clear path to the lighted doorway of the stairs. He, too, had reached a point where he might be able to block her path if he moved fast enough. But she had to try. Summoning all her will and strength, she launched herself into a dash for the doorway, focused on that frame of yellow light as if it were the frontier of life itself.

She was nearly there, just two steps from a chance, when his clawed hand caught the nightgown at the back of her neck. Still trying to move forward, she felt the filmy fabric rip as he pulled her back, and she tried to tear loose. The gown tore more, baring her upper torso, but she couldn't get free. She waited for the pain of the blade plunging into her back.

But he switched his hand quickly to her arm and pulled her around to face him, at the same time shoving her aside so he was blocking the stairway.

The hand that wasn't locked on her arm held the knife straight out, blade up, at the height of her stomach. As a surgeon, she thought, he'd know just how to cut so it hurt her before she died. Her only consolation was the knowledge that the police might come before he got away.

"I'm sorry," he said. "It could have been so different." His arm moved back, pulling the knife away so the thrust would be longer, go deeper.

On the point of death, she sent a message into the ether. "I love you, Toby," she whispered.

The words had just left her lips when something bumped hard against her legs, knocking her sharply off balance. It caused Brian to lose his grip on her arm, and she stumbled sideways. As she did, she was aware of a dark blur flying across her field of vision, indistinguishable except for the two extended forelegs that slammed into the chest of her murderer and knocked him backward. His own balance lost, he tottered through the door he'd been blocking and onto the landing of the stairway; then his feet dropped back onto the top steps. Trying to regain his balance he windmilled his arms around, but all equilibrium was gone and he went tumbling down the flight of stairs in an uncontrolled backward somersault.

Gaye had no view of the stairway, but she heard the thuds as he went down and landed at the bottom, then a cry of pain, fading to silence. She didn't even bother to look down the stairwell, however; she was scanning the area around her for the dog. "Rud?" she called.

It didn't seem possible that he had managed to get up the stairs and spring with that much power—and without being seen—but love and loyalty could be the fuel for an even greater miracle than the diversion he'd provided before. It must have cost him the last of his strength, though. It wasn't unlikely that he was lying on the floor behind a display. . . .

She ran to the showroom's light switches and threw them on. "Rud?" she called again, hoping to elicit an acknowledging sound as she began to prowl the aisles. "Where are you, boy?"

The sound that came to her was the voice of a man calling: "Doc! Open up!" Then came loud knocking on the plate glass of the street door.

Perry was outside, his police cruiser in the street. She went to the door and opened it. As he stood on the threshold gaping at her, she became aware that the torn nightgown was hanging off her shoulders, her breasts exposed. She gathered the fabric and wrapped her arms around herself.

"Jesus," he said. "Sorry I took so long."

"I'm okay," she said. Though she barely got the words out. "But go down there. . . ." She pointed a trembling hand toward the stairs. "Quickly," she added. "He fell, but he might still be able to get away."

The cop nodded and ran straight to the stairs.

Gaye turned back to the showroom and continued looking for Rud.

The cop called up the stairwell, "This guy's not goin' anywhere. Do you know who he was?"

"I've got to find my dog," she shouted back, his words not registering.

"There's a dog down here, sleeping on the floor."

Couldn't be. She'd seen him leap at Brian, knock him back—but not go after him. Though in fact she could recall seeing nothing more than a blur in the half-light. Gaye ran to the stairs, started down, then halted at the sight of the body at the bottom, the pool of blood around it, lying on its side in an odd position, arms, legs, neck bent at extreme angles. She would have turned around, but her concern for the dog overcame her queasiness and she continued down. As she came closer, she saw the knife embedded in Brian's chest. Shielding her eyes, she stepped over his body into the living room.

Rud was where she had left him, prostrate atop the plastic sheeting and pillows. Bending over him, she saw he was alive. He turned his eyes to meet hers. There seemed to be sadness and regret in his gaze, an apology that he had not done more.

"Did you push him?" the cop asked as he moved out of the stairwell. "Is that how it happened?"

Gaye rose and turned to the policeman. She had the answer now, only it wasn't one the police could accept. The truth would only raise suspicions about her.

"Not a push exactly," she said. "I . . . I struggled with him up at the top . . . and he lost his balance and fell. . . ."

Perry nodded. He pulled a little notepad and pen out of his breast pocket and began writing. Then they heard the other cops arriving, tromping into the showroom and calling out. Perry went into the stairwell again. "Down here!" he shouted up.

Was it Toby who'd told her a ghost was the restless spirit of a being that had died violently? Then Brian's death would finally allow this ghost to have eternal peace.

She gave Rud a hug, and went into the bedroom to put on some clothes.

Chapter 32

They brought Rud to the clinic together a couple of hours earlier than originally planned—a change resulting from the events of the night. In the hours just after three a.m., Gaye had been kept busy dealing with the police and other local officials—the county coroner, state police commandant, district attorney—who kept arriving at her apartment. Before long there were reporters from local papers, and stringers from the national and local TV networks. Even in this generally peaceful backwater, a disgruntled husband stalking and trying to kill a wife who'd deserted him or taken up with another man was not a completely unknown happening, and probably wouldn't have made such a stir. But when the situation involved a celebrated heart surgeon from out of state driving hundreds of miles to carry out a murder plan, and dying violently himself after a heroic struggle in which the wife saved herself, that was a more sensational story. By dawn, when Gaye went to sign her statements at the local police station, a couple of TV satellite trucks were already in the street outside the showroom, and local curiosity seekers were beginning to gather.

Gaye had made the decision not to call Toby immediately. Still operating on adrenaline, she didn't think she needed to rouse him from sleep and upset him with the report of a brush with death she had overcome. She felt sufficiently cared for by the local police. Aware of Gaye's concern for Rud, Perry had made sure the dog was carried to the police station and kept near her.

Later, though, as the shock ebbed and the fuel of nervous energy gave out, she broke down completely. In the middle of telling her story once more for the DA—inventing, of course, when it came to explaining how she had been able to overcome her bigger, stronger assailant and send him off balance down the stairs—she suddenly fell apart, crying so hard she couldn't speak.

"Is there someone we can call?" the DA asked.

They sent a police car for Toby at once, and within a half hour he was there with Lord Byron. Since then, he'd been at her side every second. It was only having him there that propped her up enough to complete the formalities.

From the police station they'd gone back to her apartment, but only to pick up her truck: She didn't know how long it might be before she would want to reenter the apartment—maybe never. From there she and Toby had driven to the diner in West Greenlea; they left the dogs in the truck and went in for breakfast—a respite that was cut short when they were followed in by reporters.

Now, driving a back road to the clinic, they hoped to escape attention for a while. At least, until she had completed Rud's procedure.

Since Toby had joined her, they had communed mainly in silence. He understood that she was completely drained; she needed nothing but to be with him. So they were already halfway to the clinic when he said, "We don't have to do this today."

"Rud can't move anymore, Toby. He used up the last, the very last, of his strength to save me. Why make him spend another day in this condition? He's ready to go. Now it's my turn to help him."

"But after what you've been through—"

"I can handle it. Loving him makes it tough. But also makes it possible." She paused, wondering how to explain the other part of her readiness to help the dog die—the sign she'd been given that a place existed where that banquet Toby dreamed of might someday occur. But the words to tell it convincingly eluded her.

He broke the silence again. "What really happened?"

She glanced at him. Was his hearing so developed he could hear her thinking? "What do you mean?" she said, testing his perception.

"Between telling your story to the cops and the lawyers and the reporters, I must have heard you go through it half a dozen times. And you didn't tell it once in a way that made me believe it."

"What do you find so hard to believe? Brian was chasing me, and we struggled, and he fell down a flight of stairs."

He turned to her, smiling a little "I've never put you on a scale, funny face, but I've had my hands on that lovely body—and I'd say you're not much over . . . what—a hundred and ten pounds?"

She smiled, too. A hundred and six when curiosity last made her step onto the animals' scale at the clinic.

"And while we were with the cops," he went on, "I picked up on the coroner's description of your husband. He was six foot one, well built. I'd guess maybe twice your weight. I don't see you getting the best of him in a struggle or knocking him over. On top of which, I've gotten to know the music of your voice. I hear when the pitch isn't true as easily as if you were singing every note off-key. Like each time you made one of those sworn statements. And that worries me. Because taking a false oath is against the law, especially where a death is involved. I don't want you getting into trouble."

"You think the police didn't believe me?"

"I doubt their ears are as good as mine. But if there's more to the story, Gaye, don't hide it. Not from me, anyway. I want to be able to help you."

She concentrated on steering straight down the road for another few seconds. "There is something else," she admitted finally.

She started to tell him, but it was too hard to drive at the same time she relived the experience, describing the terrifying mayhem that had led up to it. So she stopped the truck by the side of the road. They were next to a broad meadow, part of a sheep farm on the far side of the ridge from Bible Hill. It was a clear, sunny day, the warmth of spring finally in the air, the colors of grass and sky and wildflowers all vivid. Across the meadow a scattering of sheep grazed, half a dozen of them new spring lambs. The bucolic scene around her was a pacifying influence, helping to steady Gaye as she recounted the ordeal of the night, and the phenomena that had saved her life—the diversion Rud had created, and the phantom that emerged from nowhere.

Toby was silent for a while after she finished. Turning to the open window on his side of the truck, he breathed in the smells of nature, his head tilted back as if he were looking up into the heavens. "Mom had it just about right with her cards," he said at last, "except I wasn't the one you had to stay close to."

"It was a piece of you, Toby." She looked back at Rud. "He'll always be a piece of you."

Toby nodded and turned to the small back area where Rud was stretched out, awake but immobile. He reached back and stroked the dog. "Thanks, pal," he murmured. Facing front again, he said firmly, "Let's go. I think Rud's got a friend waiting for him."

Frankie was in the clinic when they got there. She knew everything: A longtime friend who was a sister of one of the older policemen had called. "I wasn't sure you'd be in today," she said. "But if you came, I wanted to be available to help." Gaye had told Lori yesterday that she might do the euthanasia today.

"That's very nice of you, Frankie," Gaye said. Since their last argument their interactions had been stiff, but today Gaye felt no animosity at all. Confronting and defeating Brian's hatred had purified her own emotions, shown her the folly of wasting any part of herself on negative feelings.

They worked together quietly while Toby stood over the examining table where Rud lay, one hand caressing his side. Byron had been left in the truck; Toby felt he would understand enough to be frightened, and Gaye agreed.

It was a simple procedure: a couple of drugs administered intravenously, one as a sedative, the other to stop the heart. The dog submitted without a single yelp of protest, even though the needle that went into the cephalic vein in his leg must have hurt.

One moment he was alive, and then gone.

"It's over," Gaye said to Toby. She'd been monitoring the heartbeat with a stethoscope.

"I know," he said. "I felt him leave."

He and Gaye looked at each other, their eyes brimming. "Maybe you'd like some time alone here," she said.

"Yeah. I would." Softly, he added a line from Kipling's poem:
" 'Why in heaven before we are there,/do we give our hearts to a
dog to tear?' "

As she followed Frankie out, Gaye paused a second and looked
back. Toby had hiked himself up onto the examining table and taken
Rud onto his lap to hold him.

It was still before the clinic's opening time, so Gaye was alone with
Frankie in the reception area. They stood together silently, neither
knowing what to say. Finally Frankie went over and unlocked the front
door. She opened it and looked out, the morning sun full on her face.
"Spring," she said. "Everything coming back." She drifted outside.

Gaye was inclined to follow, get a taste of the breeze.

Side by side, they looked down the hill, across the valley beyond.

"Always one of the best times of year in our business," Frankie
mused aloud when Gaye was beside her. "Makes me wonder."

"Wonder what?"

"Whether to keep this place goin'."

Gaye gave her a puzzled look.

Frankie met it squarely. "I didn't know what you were dealing
with, child," she said. "You never really let on. Made me suspicious,
I guess, the way you turned up, and the little fibs you told right off.
Like about traveling so light, no clothes. Then going off to buy it all
and ship it over here."

"You knew about that?"

"They were puzzling over it down at the P.O. in West Greenlea.
Joe Cray, the postmaster, he asked one day when I was in there why
you'd have a whole trunkful of duds shipped from Littleton 'steada
drivin' over to get it."

Small towns, Gaye thought, *better intelligence than the CIA.* She
shook her head and laughed lightly. It didn't matter now.

"Heard you were driving across the state line to get your mail,
too," Frankie continued. "Hell, I've known Bunky since we could
go skinny-dipping in the river and waste no time lookin' at each
other. All that looked mighty strange, see. Mysterious. Not like
someone who's . . . aboveboard. It was pretty clear you were running away, but, sayin' nothing about it."

"So you thought I'd done something wrong. Why didn't you just ask me?"

"Ask?" Frankie said wryly. "Did you ever give me one damn clue that it would be all right if I did? That you thought I deserved the truth?"

Gaye looked into the older woman's pale blue eyes for a second, then had to look down as she shook her head. She was surprised to feel Frankie's hand cup her chin and lift it up, a sweet gesture. It felt . . . motherly.

"But I've got it clear now," Frankie said. "You were being beaten down by something every bit as cruel and unasked-for as what I've had to face with Will. A sick husband—just a different kind of disease. Makes me think we could belong together, if you're willing to work with me. . . ."

Flabbergasted by the turnaround, Gaye couldn't answer right away.

"You'd get Will's half of this place, of course—like he wanted."

Gaye could only stammer, "Well . . . I'm . . . I don't know what to—"

"Don't have to say anything," Frankie cut her off sternly. "All you have to do is make sure you work your butt off to keep this place goin.' "

Gaye had an impulse to grab her and hug her—yet there remained some ineffable force field around Frankie that still made it impossible. For today, anyway.

Toby came out into the parking lot. "I'm done," he said.

"Lori and I will take care of the rest," Frankie said. "If you want," she added to Gaye, "you can take the week off."

"No, I'd really like to work," Gaye said. "Keep the momentum going."

She needed the day off, though, with Toby. They stopped off at her apartment so Toby could pack a bag for her—Gaye wouldn't go in, even though Millie met them there and said she'd already gotten most of the mess from last night's "ruckus" cleaned up. Gaye moved into the Callan house.

Dot was about to leave for work when they arrived. She welcomed Gaye with the news that she'd done the cards right after breakfast, and the outlook couldn't be better. "Clear sailing ahead far as I can see," Dot said. "Long as you keep Toby close at hand. Though one other thing is a little unclear."

What now? She had a newfound respect for Dot's readings.

"Not sure whether it's two boys and a girl . . . or two girls and a boy. See you later." She was almost out the door when she paused. "Oh, Gaye—I can give you a post office box now. I think you've got a permanent address."

Alone in the house, Gaye and Toby got into bed. She slept for a while and they spent the rest of the day making love.

On a Saturday night three weeks later, Gaye worked with Frankie to get Will into his tuxedo, and then Gus Dowd came over to the house and helped move Will into the van borrowed from the county hospital outfitted to transport wheelchair-bound patients. Earlier, Gaye had gone with Frankie to help her buy a new cocktail dress—and what a stunner Frankie was now, putting aside her jeans and flannel shirts for an evening, her hair freshly done at Curl up and Dye, and her eyes accented by the sapphire earrings Will had given her for their fortieth anniversary.

They drove over to The Inglenook and had a meal brought in from the restaurant while Toby played every one of their favorites, topping it off with "The Way You Look Tonight." Will could no longer speak, but Gaye could see in his eyes that he was taking it all in, and was happy. The whole time Frankie sat beside him holding his hand, and they stayed until after midnight.

When Gaye arrived at the clinic Monday morning, she was shocked to see a hand-lettered sign taped to the front door that said, CLOSED. Underneath, written smaller, it read, EMERGENCIES CALL AT HOUSE.

Gaye ran to the farmhouse. Through a window by the back door she could see Frankie at the kitchen table sitting over a teacup. She entered without knocking.

"I thought we were staying open," Gaye protested at once. "You told me—"

Frankie looked up. "Will went yesterday," she said.

It didn't matter that she'd known it had to come sooner or later.

Didn't matter that she knew it was so much better for him. The tide of sorrow that swept over Gaye made the world go dark for a second, made her feel that she might faint. Before she could sink to her knees, she grabbed a chair at the table. "I'm sorry, Frankie," she said. "I'm so . . ." She couldn't say any more before her throat closed and the crying came on.

Frankie got up, poured another cup of tea, and brought it to the table for Gaye. For once she set the cup down quietly, not with the angry clatter she'd always made in the past.

Gaye's tears subsided and she drank her tea. They sat together quietly for a long time. At last Frankie said, "He was so happy night before last. Hearing those songs. Being with you and Toby. Made him feel good about the future. Can you think of a better way to feel at the end?"

Gaye studied Frankie. "No," she said, "I can't imagine a better way."

"You don't mind, I hope, that I didn't call you right when it happened," Frankie said. "But the way things were, I just thought it was best to handle things alone. Do you understand?"

"I think I do," Gaye said.

There was a silence. Then Frankie said, "There was a time, Gaye, when I didn't feel I could trust a thing you told me. But I came to know I could believe anything you said." She waited until Gaye's gaze met hers. "Anything and everything."

For another moment they looked at each other, all questions asked and answered without a word.

Frankie got up, sighed, and straightened her shirt. "Funeral's tomorrow at the church in town. Carol's already on her way with her family. But I was hoping you'd speak—about his work, y'know. No one could do that as well as you."

Gaye nodded. "I'd be honored."

Frankie carried the teacups to the sink. "Took a call this morning from a farm over the river. I'm goin' out there now."

"You shouldn't. I'll take it."

"No, child. I need to keep busy." Frankie had gone to the counter, where her instrument bag waited.

"I'll go along."

"I can manage," Frankie said in her usual crisp manner, and headed for the door.

"I know." Gaye hesitated, then added, "But maybe . . . just for the company?"

Frankie stopped to look at Gaye. The expression of surprise on her face lasted a moment, then faded. "Just for the company," she said. "I'd like that." She held out a hand for Gaye to take. "I'd like that very much."

Chapter 33

The wedding was at the Blue Hill Inn on a Sunday at the end of September. Not a lot of advance planning had gone into it. They'd assumed they'd get married, of course, but it hadn't been easy to find a time when they could make the arrangements, enjoy their own festivities, and take time off for a honeymoon. The effort that Gaye had put into rebuilding the clinic business throughout the spring and summer was producing results far beyond her expectations. Without any drain on her finances from legal bills or complications, she'd been able to get the bank in West Greenlea to agree to loan her the money to modernize and expand the facility. Summer, of course, was a time when there were so many extra families in the area, along with their pets, that she had anticipated some increase in business. But her reputation—helped, perhaps, by a little notoriety and the curiosity it created—and the word that spread quickly about the modernization, also attracted new clients. So many, in fact, that the placement offices at Cornell and Penn vet schools had been informed that the Bible Hill Animal Clinic was seeking a new associate, and postings had also been put on the Internet veterinary sites. It was, in fact, the hiring of a young single woman from Penn, a recent graduate specializing in large animals, that had finally permitted Gaye to find a time when she and Toby could marry and manage a couple of weeks away.

In recognition of Toby's value to the inn, the owners not only donated all the food and facilities for the wedding and reception, but, under the guise of insisting that Toby show up for work as usual even the night before his wedding, they had surprised him by re-naming the Inglenook Toby's Place—not such a big gesture, they ac-knowledged, since it had been informally known that way already for years. Nevertheless, it was symbolic of assuring him the job was his for as long as he wanted it.

At the ceremony there was no best man, but a best dog: Toby had Byron carry the ring to the altar. Dot and Frankie were the brides-maids.

And Gaye was given away by her father. He had first shown up in West Greenlea on the day after the news stories about Brian's attempt on her life appeared in the Philadelphia newspa-pers. For all his abject apologies, however, Gaye's forgiveness had not been instantaneous; in some sense, she thought, Brian's crime would not have been possible if her father had not allowed him so much tacit support for so long. Did he understand that? Owen Foster said he did, but she needed more than such a quick turn-around.

During the summer he had visited several more times; he'd got-ten to know Toby, and they'd formed a relationship of mutual re-spect. Even though her resistance had begun to melt, it was Toby who finally persuaded Gaye to drop this last barrier to a completely open heart. Having never known his own father, she found it car-ried a special weight when he conveyed his belief that Foster was sincerely sorry, and told Gaye to "give the poor bastard a chance. Isn't it better to have him in your life now than not at all?"

As before, her father had offered the honeymoon as his gift, but this time Gaye didn't take it. She had a different wedding present in mind, she said. And that was how the clinic had gotten its new vet-erinary X-ray machine.

The flight from Boston to their honeymoon destination was scheduled for the evening of the day after the wedding. That morning Gaye went first to the clinic with Byron; Frankie had agreed to live with the dog during the honeymoon, while Gaye and Toby would always be together. Gaye also needed to do some last-minute paperwork relating to repaying the bank loan; since taking it, she had learned she wouldn't need it. The final irony of her husband's dreadfully warped conception of love was that he had never changed his will; the bulk of his sizable estate had been left to Gaye.

The one other bit of business Gaye had at the clinic was to brief Frankie on meeting Rebecca Varney, the chosen associate who was to arrive that afternoon. Gaye had gone down to Philadelphia to interview her and convince her she could be happy in rural New Hampshire, and she had agreed to take the job on a six-month trial basis. But this would be the young woman's first meeting with Frankie.

"Her bus gets in at three," Gaye said. "I want you to promise me two things."

"What?" Frankie said sharply, wary as ever. No contract would be signed before she knew the terms.

"To start with, I don't care what else comes up, you'll be there to meet that bus on time."

Frankie said nothing.

"And second: This is a sweet, sensitive girl, Frankie, only twenty-four, and this is her first job. So you be nice."

"Sorry," Frankie said. "But you know that's too damn much to ask."

Then she smiled and wished Gaye a wonderful honeymoon, and gave her a hug, something she did often these days.

By noon Gaye and Toby were on their way to Boston in the truck she'd bought to replace the old Dodge. Along the New England roadsides, the first hints of autumn color were already tinting the trees. When she mentioned it to Toby, he asked her to pull over and take a good look. She stopped at a good viewpoint and did what came naturally to her now, describing it for him, the forested hillsides, the undulating quilt of green with its first patches of orange and yellow, all clear under the autumn sun and sky.

"Beautiful," he mused. "I remember. It'll only get better, too. The golds and purples and deep reds. But you don't see those until later, until the leaves are ready to fall." He reached across the seat, and Gaye gave him her hand. "That's good to remember, too," he said. "You'd never get to see the most beautiful part if they didn't die."

"Hey, we've got a flight to catch," Gaye said suddenly, starting up the truck.

"Well, then, step on it, funny face," Toby said. "I can't wait to see the Eiffel Tower."

ACKNOWLEDGMENTS

To whatever extent I have adequately represented the thoughts, feelings, and dedication—not to mention the expertise—of a young woman practitioner of veterinary medicine, I am indebted in particular to two remarkable DVMs.

Dr. Anne del Borgo, of the Boothbay Animal Clinic in Boothbay, Maine, not only allowed me to observe her at work but shared the insights and experiences of a talented doctor who belongs to the growing wave of women who have entered her field in the past ten years—thus making her a perfect model for my protagonist. (Even if she looks more like Jennifer Connelly than Audrey Hepburn.)

Dr. Joan Kasoff, who practices veterinary medicine in North Penobscot, Maine, informed me not only about the nuts and bolts of veterinary diagnosis and treatment, and animal anatomy, but educated me as to the role that alternative medicine can play in treating animals as well as humans. If anyone who reads this book thinks there cannot be a veterinarian like the one I've created in these pages who effectively and compassionately uses homeopathy, massage and energy field manipulation (reiki) to alleviate the problems and sufferings of all members of the feathered or furry clan, their doubts can be put to rest by visiting "Dr. Joan's Animal Clinic," in North Penobscot, not far from Blue Hill.

I am grateful also to the Seeing Eye Institute for the education I was given there in the truly wonderful work they have been doing for generations that not only helps to erase the boundaries between the sighted and unsighted, but between man and animal.

And last, but certainly not least, a special personal thank you to Chris Kauders—and Rudy—for their help and inspiration.

—R.J.R.

A Night as Clear as Day

R. J. ROSENBLUM

This Conversation Guide is intended to enrich the
individual reading experience, as well as encourage us
to explore these topics together—because books,
and life, are meant for sharing.

A CONVERSATION WITH
R. J. ROSENBLUM

Q. In A Night as Clear as Day *you write about a woman escaping from an abusive marriage and rediscovering her own strength and balance through her relationship with a very independent blind man. You deal, too, with questions of spirituality and even with the issue of euthanasia. Would it be fair to assume that the combination of these themes with such powerful emotional resonance comes from some direct personal experiences?*

A. I haven't personally faced the problems and dilemmas that confront the characters in this book. But there are very good friends of mine who have, and whose experiences have touched me to the point that I was compelled to try providing some positive inspiration to those who face these quintessential life problems. Perhaps the most direct influence relating to this story came from meeting and developing a friendship with a blind man who owns a Seeing Eye dog; he is a remarkable man—and with his dog, they are a remarkable team. I might say that I admired the dog almost as much as the man, and that had a lot to do with creating a story in which a Seeing Eye dog—as well as an ordinary German shepherd dog—were such important characters.

Q. Of course animals figure naturally in the story because your central character is a veterinarian. How are you able to write so knowledgeably about the work of this woman? Do you have a veterinarian in the family?

A. It's a compliment that you think I might. But my knowledge was acquired merely by doing research. Part of my pleasure in writing a book—and I expect a pleasure for most writers—is having an excuse to go on learning. I took a crash course in veterinary medicine, in effect, by going into animal clinics, watching and working alongside some very talented vets—women similar in age and temperament to Gaye Foster, my central character.

Q. Your previous book, Afterlove, *has a spiritual theme. A Night as Clear as Day includes moments that suggest the spirits of animals are playing a part in what happens—in particular the pets to whom the main characters are close. Do you believe that animals have an afterlife?*

A. Or you might ask, then, do I believe animals have souls? That's such a complicated question—touching on everything from theology to evolution—that I think I should simplify it by saying that I certainly believe some animals, those closer on the evolutionary scale to the human animal, have remarkable abilities—some of which seem to exceed our own. I might point out, too, that some admirable religions, such as Buddhism, believe that reincarnation is a process in which a soul can pass through various stages of existence—and that is why all living things are regarded as sacred. Finally, where there have been reported experiences of seeing ghosts, it is not only human forms that have been seen, but dogs, horses, cats, and other forms of life.

Q. You've raised the topic of ghosts—and there are suggestions of spirits affecting what happens in your story. You wouldn't call it a "ghost story" though, would you?

A. Absolutely not. It's a story about people facing very critical moments in their lives, when having some spiritual conviction may make the difference in being able to endure, and face, life positively. Those convictions are affected by being given hopeful signs—like the answers to prayers. Having that much evidence of the existence of spirits is quite different from seeing a ghost. If it needs to be categorized as any particular kind of story, it's a "love story."

QUESTIONS
FOR DISCUSSION

1. Both of the central characters in this book have a love for and dependency on animals that figures in the story. What is your personal reaction to this element of the story? Do you think that it is a healthy relationship or that it shows some weakness of character?

2. Gaye Foster runs away from an abusive marriage. In doing so she also cuts herself off from contact with her father. Do you think she is right to do this, or that she is reacting too extremely? Why do you think her father finds it so hard to give her the help and support she needs?

3. The physical condition of blindness afflicts the man with whom Gaye falls in love. Can you imagine being involved in such a relationship? Do you think there is a parallel to the moral and emotional "blindness" that afflicts other characters in the book? Which characters fail, and in what ways, to see what they should?

4. Dr. Will Bennett becomes a kind of surrogate father to Gaye. Do you think she is right to involve herself in the way she does with his illness, and to argue with Dr. Bennett's wife, Frankie, about how to deal with Will?

5. The author seems to feel that animals, as well as people, have souls. What is your feeling about this? Do you know of any stories where an animal saved the life of a human?